ONE *WAY *OR *ANOTHER

♦ THE ♦ SISTERS ♦ QUARTET ♦

MARY J. WILLIAMS

© 2018

ABOUT THE AUTHOR

Writing isn't easy. But I love every second. A blank screen isn't the enemy. It is the opportunity to create new friends and take them on amazing adventures and life-changing journeys. I feel blessed to spend my days weaving tales that are unique—because I made them.

Billionaires. Songwriters. Artists. Actors. Directors. Stuntmen. Football players. They fill the pages and become dear friends I hope you will want to revisit again and again.

Thank you for jumping into my books and coming along for the journey.

HOW TO GET IN TOUCH

Please visit me at these sites, sign up for my newsletter or leave a message.

http://www.maryjwilliams.net/

https://www.bookbub.com/authors/mary-j-williams

https://www.facebook.com/maryjwilliamsauthor/?ref=hl

https://twitter.com/maryjwilliams05

https://www.pinterest.com/maryj0675/

https://www.instagram.com/2015romance/

https://www.goodreads.com/author/show/5648619.Mary_J_Willia ms

MORE BOOKS BY MARY J. WILLIAMS

Harper Falls Series

If I Loved You

If Tomorrow Never Comes

If You Only Knew

If I Had You (Christmas in Harper Falls)

Hollywood Legends Series

Dreaming With a Broken Heart

Dreaming With My Eyes Wide Open

Dreaming Again

Dreaming of a White Christmas

(Caleb and Callie's story)

One Pass Away Series

After the Rain

After All These Years

After the Fire

Hart of Rock and Roll

Flowers on the Wall

Flowers and Cages

Flowers are Red

Flowers for Zoe

Flowers in Winter

WITH ONE MORE LOOK AT YOU

One Strike Away

For a Little While

For Another Day

For All We Know

For the First Time

COMING LATER IN 2018
The Sisters Quartet

Two of a Kind

Three Wishes

Four Simple Words

TABLE OF CONTENTS

PROLOGUE

CALDER BENEDICT LOVED late afternoon best.

The time of day when she and her sisters stopped whatever they were doing—wherever they were—to gather in their special room.

Their mother never disturbed them. Sometimes loving, but mostly flighty and self-centered, Billie Benedict was happy to leave her girls to their own devices. One less thing for her to think about. One less worry. Though Billie never dwelt on any problem. She'd long ago graduated—with honors—from the Scarlett O'Hara Tomorrow is Another Day School of Life Lessons.

Except in Billie's case, tomorrow never came. Troubles, like men, were easily forgotten. Disposable. Replaceable.

Calder shook off the thought. She closed her eyes, flicked her long, dark hair over her shoulder, and let the room's magic chase away the sad.

The ever-changing parade of servants knew the little girls' inner sanctum was off limits. Not even to clean. On the rare occasions Calder could cajole or bully her sisters to help keep the room tidy, she would. However, for the most part, she was on her own.

Andi was too distracted, her head filled with dreams of the future. Big dreams. Important dreams. Dreams she was determined to fulfill.

Bryce was always happy to help when Calder asked. Her twin started out with the best of intentions. However, after a few unenthusiastic swipes of her dust cloth, she would curl up on the faded, overstuffed sofa they'd rescued from the storage room across the hall, her nose buried in a book.

Then there was Destry. She wasn't lazy. Or forgetful. Unlike her sisters, her head wasn't crammed with dreams or schemes or books. The youngest Benedict was simply too full of perpetual energy to stay put in one place for long.

Ants in her pants pronounced their great-aunt Annis with an annoyed shake of her head. The old woman never had a good word to say about anybody. Especially the four Benedict girls.

Calder smiled as she straightened the plate of little cakes. The four Benedict girls didn't need Great-Aunt Annis' approval. Or anyone else's. They had each other. And always would.

"Chocolate? Yum! Gimme, gimme."

Destry, her eyes wide with greed, rushed forward. Andi swore that after 'no,' 'gimme' was their little sister's first word. Calder had no doubt.

At nine, Calder was a year older, reed thin, and a good three inches taller. With ease, she held the plate of cakes out of Destry's determined grasp.

"You know you have to wait until Andi and Bryce get here."

Destry wasn't a typical eight-year-old girl. She wasn't a typical anything. When she didn't get her own way, she didn't stamp her foot. Or pout. Or cry. She never yelled or threatened. Instead, she narrowed her lids over her burnished gold eyes, while her brain worked at the speed of light to figure out the best way to get exactly what she wanted. Usually, she succeeded.

"Not today." Calder wasn't as intractable as her sister. However, when the moment called for stubborn, she could hold her own. "You're welcome to a cup of tea."

Calder hid her smile when Destry grimaced. She and Bryce were the tea drinkers. Andi would settle for the brewed beverage, but she preferred the days when their housekeeper, Mrs. Finch, provided a pitcher of freshly squeezed, slightly tart, lemonade.

And Destry? She wanted the sugar. Lots and lots of sugar. The sweeter, the better.

Calder loved when she could make her little sister happy.

"I snuck a Coke from the fridge when Mrs. Finch wasn't looking."

With a whoop of happiness, Destry threw herself into Calder's arms.

"I love you."

"Because of a can of soda?"

"Because you're Calder."

Destry's hug tightened. A moment of emotion from a little girl who more often than not, hid her feelings well.

"Where are Andi and Bryce?" Destry was already across the room, a glass in one hand, the newly opened can in the other. "I'm starving."

Before Calder could speculate over their missing sisters' whereabouts, the door opened.

"I'm pooped." With a heavy sigh, Bryce collapsed onto the old sofa.

"You look like a cyclone hit you," Calder observed.

Though born only minutes apart, she and Bryce were opposites in many ways. From their physical features to their personalities. However, despite their differences—or perhaps because of them—they were as close as any twins could be.

Bryce's red hair stuck out in all kinds of interesting directions, the two long, neat braids she'd worn when she left for school, things of the past. One knee was scraped. Her school uniform— and face—smudged with dirt. Whatever happened didn't prey on her mind. She relaxed as if she didn't have a care in the world. Which was probably true.

"Jerry Welker stole Millie Pearson's hair ribbon. I had to chase the little snot around the school three times before I finally caught him."

"And if I hadn't pulled you off, you'd have left him with more than a bruised ego." Andi, the oldest by a whole year and natural leader of their little, exclusive sisters' club, closed the door behind her. "Here. You dropped your latest gore-fest."

Bryce snatched the book from Andi's hand. She ran her hand over the cover like she would an indulged pet.

"Not gory. Thrilling. The blood is incidental."

Andi shook her head. But her green eyes sparkled, and her smile was indulgent. Almost eleven, she already possessed the kind of glossy looks other girls envied. But she would have gladly traded her high cheekbones and silky blond hair for a few more IQ points. In her book, brains trumped beauty every time.

A wave of satisfaction rushed over Calder, something she always felt whenever their circle was complete. No matter the circumstances, everything was better when the Benedict girls were together.

"Can we eat now?"

"Dig in."

As they filled their plates, they chatted away about nothing in particular. Which was often the way. Just the four of them. Sisters. Able to enjoy each other's company. However, when serious matters arose—which they tended to do now and then—they didn't hesitate to share. Sometimes they argued. Often, they laughed. A few tears might fall.

If one sister had a grievance with another, the solutions were swift and, for the most part, satisfactory to all concerned.

Their problems with the world at large weren't as simple. Outside their room, Calder and her sisters led complicated lives. There were no easy fixes. However, talking always helped. Four sets of shoulders to carry the burden instead of one.

"One more month until summer break." Bryce looked from sister to sister, her gray eyes sad.

The calendar they ritualistically replaced each January hung on the far wall. Bright and cheery, yellow daisies adorned the month of May. Calder had looked ahead to June. Purple pansies. Such a happy flower. Too bad their moods didn't match.

"We'll survive." Andi placed a supportive hand on Bryce's arm. "We always do."

"What if we refused to go?"

Three sets of eyes turned toward Destry. More than any of them, she dreaded summer.

"You know we don't have a choice." Calder wished they did. But the law was the law. "Besides, I thought you were kind of looking forward to Europe."

"Texas." Destry grimaced as if the word left a foul taste on her tongue. "Business, as usual, is more important than a vacation."

"I'm sorry." Calder understood disappointment. They all did. But Destry always seemed to get the biggest slice.

"Doesn't matter." Destry shrugged. "Wherever we go, he always hires a big-jugged babysitter who never wants to do anything but sit around the pool and work on her tan."

Andi took a seat in an overstuffed chair. Big enough for two, she patted the cushion. Without hesitation, Destry joined her, burrowing into her older sister's comforting embrace.

"One good thing. If our family fortune ever disappears, we can sell our story to a tabloid for a truckload of money."

The sisters sighed as one. They weren't any different from other children of divorce. Except in one spectacular way. One mother. Three pregnancies. Four different fathers.

Automatically, Calder and Bryce linked hands as they always did in times of turmoil. They'd shared a womb. But not a father. A rare phenomenon—though not unheard of—their mother was married at the time. Billie's husband didn't question whether the babies were his. Why would he? Until Bryce showed up with a shock of bright red hair. A trait they couldn't attribute to either side of the family.

Already on shaky ground, Calder's father saw his way out. He demanded a DNA test. Imagine everyone's surprise when he turned

7

out to be a father. But only to Calder. Bryce, according to their mother, was the product of a one-night stand with an old high school sweetheart.

Bryce's biological father stepped forward and took responsibility. Though he was happy to claim her as his own, like the rest of their mother's baby daddies, he didn't have a lot to do with his daughter for most of the year.

Until summer. Two and a half months of awkward bonding time. By the end, the men were more than ready to resume their roles as absentee fathers. And the girls were happy to let them.

"We'll survive." Andi repeated her earlier words with an added amount of conviction none of them felt.

Of course, they'd survive, Calder thought. They had each other to come home to. Billie Benedict wasn't the best mother in the world. She loved her daughters to the best of her absentminded ability. However, she'd accomplished two things for which her daughters would always be grateful. She gave them each other. And she'd insisted they carry her family name.

"A toast." Calder stood. She waited as Andi, Bryce, and Destry joined her. Head held high, her gaze moved around the circle. "To the Benedict sisters."

Hands raised, four voices became one.

"To the Benedict sisters."

CHAPTER ONE

"YOU SMELL LIKE a summer garden. All sweet and sultry and made for love."

Calder rolled her eyes. For weeks, Milo Prendergast had tried everything he could think of to get her into bed. Groan-inducing lines he probably culled from an old movie wasn't the key. She knew by now he wouldn't get what he wanted. But he kept trying. And because she was in a dating rut, she let him.

"Today is April 9th."

"So?"

"The season is spring. Not summer."

Milo was a smart man. He graduated near the top of his class at Harvard law school. Calder's sarcasm wasn't lost on him. Especially when she used a big dose to practically hit him over the head.

"I'm aware of the season. You were supposed to take my words metaphorically, not literally." Milo's arm tightened around her waist. "In spite of what you might have heard, romance isn't dead, Calder."

Right. If Milo had an ounce of romance on his mind, Calder's opinion of him might have thawed—a fraction. *If* was the operative word. As they danced around their tiny segment of the crowded floor, she wondered if he realized how ridiculous he sounded.

Through her eyelashes, Calder glanced at Milo's handsome profile. Years of careful breeding had gone into his genetic makeup. The result? A classically sculpted profile that screamed upper class. Unfortunately, his ancestors had been so focused on how they looked, something was lost from generation to generation.

Milo and the entire Prendergast family lacked a very important trait. Anything that resembled a sense of humor.

"Haven't I proved how much I want you?"

Calder shivered with revulsion when Milo's wet breath washed over her ear. Naturally, he chose to interpret her reaction as passion.

"Why don't we get out of here? Get a hotel room and enjoy the rest of the evening in private. Or we could go back to my place."

Like Calder, Milo still lived in the Upper East Side mansion where he grew up. She stayed to be near her sisters. His reasons were more financial than familial. Either way, the idea of sex with his mother just down the hall wasn't the most effective aphrodisiac.

What Milo didn't know but was about to discover, he could have offered Calder the top of a cleared-out Empire State Building, and she still would have turned him down.

Most of the men she knew—Milo included—believed sex and romance equaled the same thing. A few candlelit dinners. An off-hand compliment or two. And boom. He expected her to fall at his feet.

Calder was tired of the game. She wanted more. What, she wasn't sure. But she knew she wouldn't find the answer getting sweaty with Milo Prendergast

"No."

"No to the hotel room? Or my place? I suppose I can borrow Bridge Manfred's apartment for the night. He's out of town a lot." As Milo lowered his voice, he waggled his brows. "Drugs."

Her interest piqued, Calder briefly delayed her need to dump Milo for good.

"Drugs? As in, he takes them? Or he deals them?"

"Both." Milo shot her a toothy smile. "How do you think a man with his lack of education and connections can afford the penthouse in that fancy new mid-town apartment complex?"

Honestly, Calder never thought about Bridge Manfred. *Or* what he lacked. On the few occasions they'd met, he gave her the willies. An edge of danger was one thing. Handsome in a lanky, stringy haired sort of way, unsavoriness practically oozed from the man's pores.

"He's your friend?" Calder couldn't form a picture of Milo and Bridge hanging out.

"Hardly," Milo scoffed. "In exchange for a few *goodies*, Bridge gets invited to parties. We call him our recreational advisor."

Milo seemed to find the moniker hilarious. Calder found the entire situation sad. Sad that people she'd grown up with needed illegal substances to have fun. Even sadder, Bridge Manfred was like an unpopular little boy who could only get friends if he let them play with his bigger and better toys. Or drugs, as the case may be.

"Hey. Your mom's here. And looking hot."

The change of subject was abrupt. But Calder couldn't say Milo's declaration was unexpected.

"Mom is a social animal. If there are people, she will come."

"Hmm. Tight black leather skirt. Low-cut blouse. She knows how to get a man's attention."

Billie was a perpetual flirt. And she considered any male to be fair game. A fact Calder and her sisters learned at an early age. Their mother never willfully attempted to seduce her daughters' potential boyfriends. She simply couldn't help herself. Like breathing in and out.

"Wow. Billie hooked herself a big fish."

Without turning to look, Calder had to smile. A new man? What else was new?

"I've been angling to meet Ingo Hunter for over a year. Maybe your mom will introduce me."

Calder's mouth went dry.

"Did you say Ingo Hunter?" She prayed she'd heard wrong. She craned her neck around. *Well, crap.* No such luck.

"Why don't we invite them to our table for a drink?"

Not in this lifetime. Or any other. Ingo Hunter was a sleazy creep in a five-thousand-dollar suit. Money and a veneer of charm couldn't hide the slime. Of all the men in New York, why did Billie have to date him?

As soon as Calder asked herself the question, she knew the answer. Because after almost fifty years of man eating, wealthy, socially acceptable men were harder and harder to come by.

"Calder? Shall we invite them over?"

"No."

"Okay." For once, Milo was smart enough not to push. "What did you decide? A hotel room? My place? Bridge's?"

"None of the above. I'm done. Tonight. Tomorrow. Forever."

Calder left Milo on the dance floor, the song still playing. She weaved her way through the crowd toward the exit, stopping just long enough to grab her jacket. The trouble with hotspot nightclubs, she decided when she finally inhaled a breath of fresh air—or as fresh as the city provided—too many bodies. Not enough square footage.

"What are you talking about, Calder?" Milo grabbed her arm before she could hail a passing cab. "You're done? Done with what?"

Annoyed when someone else grabbed her ride, Calder tried to tug her arm free. Milo held firm, the grasp of his lily-white hand surprisingly strong.

"I left you alone on a dance floor. Left the building. How much clearer do I need to make myself? We don't suit, Milo. In any way."

"But—"

"I don't like you."

"What the hell does *like* have to do with anything?" Milo's smile became predatory. "I want to fuck you, not be your friend."

Milo had dropped all pretense of charm. Which was fine with Calder. The ugly truth was always better than prettied-up lies.

"I don't want your hands on me. Ever again. Let go." Calder glanced at her arm. And his white-knuckle grip. "Now."

"Why?"

Before Calder could respond with a swift kick to his nuts, his hand fell away. A bouncer from the club held Milo by the front of his tailored shirt. Tall, a black t-shirt hugging his well-muscled torso, and with the bluest eyes she'd ever seen.

The man didn't raise his voice, but the tone—deep and commanding—sent a shiver down Calder's spine.

"When a lady tells you to let her go, you better do as she asks. Understood?"

"Do you know who I am, you Neanderthal?" Milo struggled to get free—to no avail. "I can have your job before you blink."

One side of the man's lips quirked upward.

"You want my job?" he chuckled without humor. "Be my guest. But I warn you, what I do is more often a headache than a pleasure."

"Listen, Jackass—"

The man tightened his hold, turning Milo's insult in to a high-pitched squeak.

"The name's Adam."

"Jesus Christ. Why the hell would I give a fuck what your name is." Despite his precarious situation, Milo's chest puffed out with self-importance. "I could buy and sell you in a heartbeat. *Asshole.*"

"Last time I checked, slavery had been abolished. Though guys like you seem to think the rules don't apply if your bank accounts are fat enough. You think money makes you invincible. Above the law." An expression of disgust on his face, the man pushed Milo away. "Leave. Before I ram your peroxide-whitened teeth down your throat."

Shoulders back, Milo straightened his jacket as he gathered what pride he had left—which wasn't much in Calder's estimation. He raised his chin and held out his hand.

"Calder?"

Stunned by the man's gall, Calder's brain searched for a scathing put-down.

"I don't think so."

Hardly the burn she would have liked. She wished she had her sister's ability to turn a phrase. If Bryce was here, she'd have something pithy, to the point, and memorable to send Milo on his way.

Oh, well. Since Calder doubted anybody planned to record their exchange for posterity, *I don't think so* would have to do.

"You heard the lady. Evening's over. Be on your way."

"Calder." Milo took a step toward her only to find his way blocked by a much bigger, much fitter body. Frustrated, he ground out his words through clenched teeth. "If I leave without you, we're finished. Understand? When you come crawling back, I won't do anything but step over your pathetic body."

"For the love of..." Calder sighed. She had to start dating a better class of men. "I broke up with you, Milo. And for the record, I don't crawl. Ever."

"Bitch."

"Why you…"

Calder would have decked him. Honestly. With blood in her eyes, fist clenched, she would have slipped off her four-inch heels and run him down. Probably for the better, her rescuer grabbed her arm before she could take chase as Milo wisely skittered away like the cockroach he'd turned out to be.

"Not worth the effort." The man dropped her arm, apparently convinced Calder had figured out the same thing for herself.

Adam, Calder recalled. He said his name was Adam. Even in heels, Calder had to raise her gaze to look the man in the eyes. She swallowed. He was kind of pretty for a tough guy. His features fit together in a pattern designed to make a woman's pulse spike by a couple dozen beats.

Silly, since he was a stranger. Yet, Calder wondered if he felt the same attraction.

In her experience, men found her appealing to look at. Dark hair liberally laced with natural auburn highlights. Deep, chocolate-colored eyes. A tall, slim body that since she hit puberty never crossed over into skinny. Tonight, she wore a silky teal-blue dress designed to show off what she considered her best features. Long, toned legs.

Yes, men tended to give her a second glance. But the man in front of her didn't seem the least bit impressed.

"Do you want to call somebody to pick you up? Or should I hail you a cab?"

Mildly disappointed to discover her case of instant attraction didn't flow both ways, Calder slid her arm into the sleeve of her beaded evening jacket. To her surprise, Adam reached out to help.

"Thank you. For everything." Calder smiled. If she expected a response, she was sorely disappointed. His lids narrowed slightly over his intensely blue eyes, but his expression remained neutral. Not even a twitch of his lips.

"Phone call or cab?"

"Cab. But I'm perfectly capable of getting my own."

Without a word, Adam raised a hand. As if by magic, a cab stopped at the curb out of nowhere. Handy trick, Calder thought. And under the circumstances, slightly annoying. He opened the door and motioned for her to enter.

Calder was perplexed. The last thing she expected was for every man she met to drool over her. Heaven knew she'd experienced a case or two of unrequited attraction. Her ego had survived quite nicely. So why did *this* man's lack of interest rankle when others were so easily forgotten?

Once in the cab, Calder turned, ready to thank Adam again.

"About Milo? I want to—"

"You should rethink your taste in men." Adam, one hand on the roof of the car, the other on the door, leaned in until their eyes were level.

Calder's back stiffened, more with surprise than anger.

"You don't know me well enough to judge my taste. Good or bad."

"Is Milo a typical sample size?"

"Well…" Unfortunately, Milo was all *too* typical of the men Calder dated.

"Case closed."

As her back went from stiff to rigid, surprise morphed into anger. Of all the nerve, Calder fumed. Giving her unsolicited advice. Self-important jerk. Though she had to admit—if only to herself—he was right. She needed to rethink her taste in men. Starting with him. Arms crossed, she swiveled her gaze to the back of the cabbie's head.

"Good night. *Adam*," she said in her best *screw you* tone.

"Good night. *Calder*."

He shut the door but not before the unmistakable sound of his deep chuckle filled the cab. Stone faced through most of their encounter, he chose to leave her with a mocking laugh? What the hell? Who did this man think he was?

Sexy only masked so many sins. And in Calder's book, Adam's appeal had all but disappeared in a puff of arrogance.

"Where you headed, lady?"

Calder rattled off her address. And proceeded to fume from Tribeca all the way uptown.

CHAPTER TWO

CALDER STUMBLED OUT of bed—hardly an unusual occurrence. She wasn't a morning person.

Once, in her younger days, she tried to change her sleep patterns. Early to bed, early to rise—and all that nonsense. Her good intentions lasted exactly two weeks. She could have stuck to the routine. And been miserable. Instead, she gave into her true, night owl nature, happy to *stay* up, rather than *get* up, to watch the sunrise.

After she brushed her teeth and washed her face—an absolute must before she could function—Calder slipped on her robe—a match to the blue silk nighty she'd donned before falling into bed. Without a glance in the mirror, she piled her hair into what barely passed for a topknot, and padded from the room.

Funny thing about living in a genuine, bona fide Manhattan mansion since birth. As much as Calder loved the building, cherished the memories, luxuriated in the comfort? Most days, she didn't notice the little details.

Purchased by Calder's great-grandfather, Orville Benedict, in the late nineteenth century, the building sported six floors. The elevator—added after World War II—serviced a library, several offices, eighteen bathrooms, and enough bedrooms for a small army—or at the very least a platoon.

Near the top of a long, winding staircase, Calder stopped as the light from a large stained-glass window bounced off her hand. When she was little, the different colors fascinated her. As an adult, they still did. However, always on the go, she rarely stopped long enough to admire the effect.

The polished Brazilian Cherry floors covered every inch of the mansion. Top to bottom. Except for the tiled bathroom. And stained cement basement where nobody but the maids and handymen spent much time.

At the bottom of the stairs, Calder's bare toes dug into the plush Persian rug. Woven over a century ago, the muted blues and greens fit the size of the foyer as if made specifically.

Mindbogglingly expensive pieces of art, painted by long-dead artists, hung on every tastefully painted wall. Sculptures. Prized pieces, small and large, decorated antique tabletops.

Immaculate and perfectly maintained, at a glance, a casual observer might think they'd entered a museum. However, to Calder and her sisters, the brick and mortar, marble and glass, and everything inside, was simply home.

Then, unbidden, she remembered the man from the night before and the words he spoke to Milo.

You think money makes you invincible. Above the law.

Said with such contempt, Calder wondered if Adam would spew the same words at her if he could see her now. Probably. But, damn it, he didn't know anything about her. How dare he judge? How dare he—?

Calder groaned. She'd convinced herself she'd put her encounter with Adam out of her head. Seemed he and his piercing blue eyes were harder to forget than she could have anticipated.

"Jerk," Calder muttered. Unfortunately, for a house with so many rooms, somebody—and their big ears—always seemed to lurk around the corner.

"If you mean Milo Prendergast, I concur. Wholeheartedly."

Andi, her burnished gold hair fashioned into a perfect French twist, entered the foyer from the direction of the downstairs office. Spiked heels clicked her arrival as her long legs quickly ate up the distance across the room.

From her fall fashion line, the outfit Andi wore was perfect for the working woman who insisted on the latest in haute couture. An immaculately tailored coral-colored pencil skirt, silk blouse, and jacket in a slightly darker contrasting shade showed off the best of her svelte figure.

She could have walked the runway if she had the desire. And wasn't so busy building her fashion empire.

Calder glanced at the grandfather clock which stood guard by the front door for as long as a Benedict had occupied the residence. *Seven fifteen*? She could never understand how her sister looked so put together at such an ungodly hour. Or why she wanted to.

"Milo is history."

"Good. I can't believe he lasted past the first date." Andi nodded decisively as she slid an arm around Calder's waist. "You can do better."

You should rethink your taste in men. Adam's voice piggybacked Andi's. Apparently, the harder she tried to get the man out of her head, the more his words clung on for dear life.

Normally, Calder would have agreed with Andi's assessment. However, thanks to judgmental Adam, her dating history had become a sensitive subject.

"Milo isn't the *worst* the New York singles scene has to offer."

"Hardly a ringing endorsement." Andi chuckled.

"Mmm." Calder wished she had a solid argument. But anything she could add would be so full of holes, the result would resemble a piece of Swiss cheese.

"Billie's up bright and early. Humming. Loudly. The last time she crawled out of bed before noon..." Andi let out a sigh when she realized the implications. "Oh, crap. Mom has a new man in her life."

"And I know who he is." Some people relished the role as bearer of bad news. Calder wasn't one of them. "We need to talk. All of us."

Andi glanced at the clock.

"I don't know if I have time for a full-fledged, private room meeting."

These days, their sixth floor, sisters-only room was empty more often than not. The daily afternoon get-togethers ended as their lives morphed from childhood fancies to adult responsibilities. However, when the situation was serious, they found their way back. A place of comfort and safety. Like a warm, well-used security blanket they could wrap themselves in, if only for an hour or two.

"The kitchen will do. I can have a cup of strong Earl Grey, and you can watch."

Arm still around Calder, Andi laughed as they made their way toward the back of the house.

"Breakfast never tastes good until at least twelve o'clock."

"You mean lunch," Calder teased. She'd lost count of how many times they'd had the same conversation.

"I'll be twenty-nine in June. I've earned the right to eat my strawberry waffles any time I choose. And call the meal anything I like."

"Whatever you say, Grandma. Just don't let Billie hear you talk about your age. She'll go apoplectic."

Andi rolled her eyes. Their mother was forever thirty-five. A lie she told anybody who showed the least bit of interest. *And* those who couldn't have cared less. If Billie had seriously considered the ramifications when she gave birth to four daughters—all of whom would inevitably grow older—she most likely never would have procreated.

"Lucky for us, Billie never thinks beyond today."

As Andi pushed open the kitchen door, raised voices greeted their entrance.

Bryce stood with hands on hips, an annoyed expression on her face. Instead of her usual casual jeans and t-shirt, she was dressed in a chic pair of crushed black-velvet leggings, knee-high burgundy leather boots, and a tunic top which brushed past mid-thigh. She'd sleeked her naturally wavy red hair back into a braid.

"All I wanted to do was fix myself a bowl of oatmeal. What's the problem?"

Her stance equally combative, Ellen Finch, long-time Benedict head housekeeper and cook, stood between Bryce and her prized possession. A six-burner gas stove with more bells and whistles than anybody in the house could comprehend—besides Mrs. Finch.

"When was the last time you cooked?"

"Well—"

"Not just oatmeal." Mrs. Finch crossed her arms over the apron which read *Quiche Me, You Fool.* "When have you prepared anything that required heat? Even a piece of toast."

Bryce knew when she was backed into a corner with no room for escape. But Calder had never seen her twin back down from an argument without at least a token fight.

"If I don't start now, when will I?"

Eyes crinkled at the edges, a look of indulgence in her pale-blue eyes, Mrs. Finch patted Bryce's shoulder.

"Oh, Bryce. Honey." The woman's ample bosom shook with laughter. "You don't want to learn how to cook."

"I might," Bryce declared. Though the stubborn gleam in her gray eyes had dimmed to resignation.

"Relax. I didn't mean to single you out. Andi and Calder are the same. And don't get me started on Destry. That girl doesn't stay in one place long enough to catch her breath, let alone heat up a frying pan." Her expression indulgent and filled with affection, Mrs. Finch shooed Bryce away.

"The fault lies firmly on your shoulders." Calder brushed a kiss over Mrs. Finch's cheek, breathing in the familiar scent of lemon and cinnamon. "If your cooking wasn't so scrumptious, one or more of us might have turned toward the culinary arts."

Mrs. Finch looked pleased. For most of her adult life, she'd taken care of the Benedicts. She'd been there when each sister entered the world. Watched as they took their first steps. Nurtured. Scolded. Comforted. Disciplined. As well as anyone, she knew how the sisters had often been left to navigate the twists and turns of childhood and adolescence without the guiding hand of a loving parent.

Speaking to a friend, Mrs. Finch once called the Benedict girls forces of nature. Good luck to anybody who tried to stand in their way. Calder smiled at the memory as she watched the only true motherly figure they'd ever known. If what Mrs. Finch had said were true, the reason was simple. They'd learned from a master.

"You don't need to worry about the *culinary arts* as long as you have me." Mrs. Finch started to prepare Bryce's oatmeal. "And if any of you would get your act together and find a decent man, I'll do the same for your children. The good Lord willing, your grandchildren as well."

"A good man isn't hard to find." A shadow passed over Andi's features. "Holding on to him is another matter."

Calder and Bryce exchanged worried glances. Andi was their rock. An immovable pillar of strength. She did such a good job of hiding her pain, sometimes they forgot she wasn't invincible. However, even the heart of a superhero could be broken.

"Andi—"

Andi brushed off Calder's concern with a shake of her head.

"Tell us about Billie's newest boyfriend."

The trace of sadness that never quite left Andi's eyes made Calder's heart twist with sympathy. But because she understood, she let her sister change the subject.

"Hardly newsworthy." Bryce took a seat at the counter. Andi joined her while Calder fixed a cup of tea. "Billie wouldn't be Billie if she didn't have six or seven men dangling at her whim."

"She was up awfully early this morning." Mrs. Finch frowned as she stirred the cereal.

"I heard her humming," Andi added.

"Oh, boy." Bryce rubbed her temple in anticipation of a headache to come. "The ink on her divorce papers is barely dry."

"Legally, she's still married to Howard for another three months." Calder carefully sipped the steaming liquid from her favorite cup. "Normally, Billie doesn't hit the humming stage of the relationship until the ghost of her latest ex-husband has a chance to dissipate."

"I liked Howard." Andi sighed.

"We all liked Howard." Calder thought about the gentleman with the backbone of a jellyfish and felt a twinge of pity. "Billie liked him. Until she didn't. Six months after she said I do, and his sweet face was barely recognizable for all her metaphorical footprints."

"Yet, like most of Billie's discarded conquests, Howard is still in love with her. Or is the word obsessed." Bryce shrugged with a

29

world-weary cynicism beyond her years. "Perhaps they're the same things."

"Love is completely different than obsession." To punctuate her point, Mrs. Finch waved a large stainless-steel serving spoon through the air. "A fact I can attest to."

At eighteen, Mrs. Finch had married her high school sweetheart. To her sorrow, two years later, he died in the first Gulf War. She grieved. Mourned. Was certain she would never love again. Until she met Dougal Sheen. A butcher with a very successful Upper East Side shop, he'd courted her with gifts of juicy briskets and perfectly trimmed pork chops. How could she resist? They'd happily kept company for the past ten years.

"You're the exception, Mrs. F. Not the rule," Bryce said.

"No. The exception is a mother with six divorces and fathers who aren't much better." Mrs. Finch never held her tongue where their mix-and-match parental gene pool was concerned. "You can't let their example cloud the way you live."

Calder had heard Mrs. Finch's argument more times than she cared to remember. Truth was, their parents had left them with emotional scars. Happily ever after would be nice, but none of them held out a lot of hope. Andi was a perfect example. Not long ago, she was convinced she'd found *the one*. Turned out, she was wrong.

As for the rest of the Benedict sisters? Calder, Bryce, and Destry hadn't come close to anything that resembled forever after. And, to varying degrees, were doubtful they ever would.

"We're here to discuss our mother's love life. Not ours." With purpose, Calder switched the conversation back to its original track. "Billie's found a new man. Or perhaps he found her. Either way, the news isn't good."

"Come on, Calder. Billie needs a man in her life. So what?" Unconcerned, Bryce continued to concentrate on her breakfast. Until she met Calder's gaze.

Calder and Bryce might not have the same father. Yet, they shared a connection beyond one of mere siblings. A strong, mental bond. Not exactly two bodies, one brain. But sometimes, like now, the description wasn't far off.

Without another word, Bryce set down her spoon. Calder had her full attention.

"I wouldn't have said anything." The decision to burden her sisters with something that might be nothing had weighed on Calder. "We know the signs. The early morning. The humming. Seems Billie's further along in her new relationship than I anticipated."

Andi, impatient at the best of times, checked her watch.

"Enough prologue, Calder. Get to the meat. Who is Billie's newest conquest? And why should we care?"

"Ingo Hunter."

"Yikes." With a grimace, Bryce pushed away her half-eaten bowl of cereal. "So much for my appetite."

"Are you sure? Of course you are." Andi's clear green eyes clouded with worry. "Crap."

"Exactly." Calder wished she was wrong.

"Wait. Back up a second. Did I miss something?" Mrs. Finch looked from sister to sister, her expression puzzled. "What's wrong with Ingo Hunter? Isn't he one of the most successful businessmen in New York?"

"In the world. If you want to believe him." Calder refilled her cup. "Money isn't the problem."

"A man like Ingo Hunter never has enough money." Andi should know. She dealt with fortune-driven egos all the time. "Though Billie's inheritance is safe from Hunter."

Their grandfather, Thomas Benedict, had taken a vast family fortune from his father and built an empire. He'd always planned on siring sons. Little princes to learn at the feet of the king. Three marriages and he couldn't do better than one child. And a girl to boot. To say he wasn't happy would be a massive understatement.

Wilhelmina Carlotta Benedict. Beautiful as a child. A gorgeous woman who would undoubtedly stun until she took her last breath. Her father had drawn up his will long before he knew the extent of his daughter's intelligence. Or the direction of her personality and temperament.

Some might say Thomas Benedict had been psychic. Some sixth sense told him not to trust his legacy to a woman who would turn out to be utterly hopeless in matters of money.

Billie's daughters knew better. Forethought had nothing to do with his decision.

"While *dear* old Granddad was a misogynistic curmudgeon—"

"Asshole's a better word," Bryce interjected.

"Hard to argue with the truth." Calder's smile didn't reach her eyes. "He did us a favor when he made out his will. If Grandfather had left Billie everything instead of her trust fund and a yearly allowance, I don't know where we'd be."

"Out on the street," Andi said. "Years ago."

The street was an exaggeration. Each sister inherited a sizable amount from their grandfather—though they weren't allowed full access until either they married or reached their thirtieth birthday. And except for Destry's father, Billie married men with money. A lot of money. With each divorce, their mother received a hefty settlement.

The women in the Benedict family were financially set for life. However, the house they called home—and the bulk of the fortune—would never legally be theirs. Thanks to good old Gramps, only a male heir could inherit.

"I still don't understand." Mrs. Finch placed the breakfast dishes in the sink. "You've always been philosophical about your mother's need to have a man in her life. Why is this time different? What is wrong with Ingo Hunter?"

"Ingo Hunter is a wolf. The big, bad kind," Calder said. Should they tell Mrs. Finch everything? Or spare her the sordid details? Bryce shrugged. Andi nodded. Decision made. "We've all dealt with him. And the man does *not* like to take no for an answer."

"You mean he tried to...you know?" Mrs. Finch looked shocked. Though she'd passed her fiftieth birthday, she'd led a fairly sheltered life.

"Yes, Mrs. Finch. He propositioned each of us." Calder had to smile. "Separately. But his intent was the same every time."

Mrs. Finch, her face scrunched in disgust, slapped her dishtowel onto the counter.

"You need to tell your mother."

Bryce snorted. "Tell Billie she landed fifth on Hunter's list of Benedict women? I don't think so."

"Count me out," Andi agreed.

"Billie's ego wouldn't appreciate the slap," Calder pointed out. "*If* she believed us."

"Still—" Mrs. Finch's eyes grew round. "Wait. You said Billie came in fifth?"

"Yes."

"Destry, too? Unbelievable."

In Mrs. Finch's eyes, the youngest Benedict would always be the most vulnerable. Her baby girl. In fact, Destry had the toughest skin. And an uppercut that could down a man three times her size.

"Speaking of Destry. Should we let her know what's going on?" As soon as the words were out of her mouth, Bryce held up a hand to stay any comments. "I know. Stupid question. I still remember the last time we kept her in the dark. She's small, but her lungs are mighty. Six years and my ears just stopped ringing."

"I'll call her." Andi chuckled at the memory as she took a bottle of water from the refrigerator. "Obviously, Hunter wants something. Maybe all he's after is some fun. In which case, he found the right woman."

"For Billie's sake, and our own, we have to assume Hunter is after more than her body."

Calder agreed with Bryce. Forewarned was forearmed.

"For now, all we can do is keep our eyes and ears open."

"Billie likes to talk." Bryce rolled her grey eyes. "Especially when *she's* the main topic. One or two not so subtle questions and she'll keep us up to date on *her* end of the new romance."

"In the meantime?" Mrs. Finch asked.

Again, Calder exchanged silent, telling glances with her sisters. What choice did they have?

"We do what we've always done in the wake of Billie's dramas. We live our lives." Calder placed her cup in the dishwasher. Cleanup. Another lesson Mrs. Finch had taught them well. "I'm going to get dressed and enjoy my day off."

Andi gave Mrs. Finch one of her patented comfort hugs.

"Don't worry."

"I'm Irish. And Catholic. Worry is what we do."

What Mrs. Finch did was care for them. Love them. The housekeeper's diligent concern for their wellbeing was one of the reasons *they* loved *her*.

"I'm off to work. I have business meetings all morning."

"Sounds boring," Calder teased. She knew Andi loved every aspect of what she did. A details nerd, what most people found tedious, the oldest Benedict sister thrived on.

"What are your plans?" Calder asked as Bryce slid from her chair.

"My agent needs to see me about something or other. Life or death, from the sound of things. But Antoinette's sense of urgency is one of the things I like about her." With a yawn, Bryce stretched her arms over her head. "She stresses over my career, so I don't have to."

"As I recall, your nerves were pretty raw before the release of your last book."

Bryce dismissed Calder's reminder with a wave of her hand.

"I worry for a few days. If the numbers are good, party time. If not—?"

"The numbers are always spectacular."

"Knock wood. I never take book sales for granted. I'm no longer the new kid with all the buzz. The trick is to remind readers why they liked the last book while we tease them with why they have to get their hands on the new one." Bryce grimaced. "Advertising and the dreaded publicity. Why do I have to pose for a camera when all I want to do is write?"

Bryce had turned her love of reading into a wildly successful career as an author. Her books received rave reviews. More important, they sold. What caught the public's interest from the start was how the beautiful redhead with delicate features and a winning smile could produce such page-turning, blood-curdling works of suspense and horror.

"What's so hard to understand?" Bryce often mused. "A vivid imagination kind of goes with the whole writing territory."

Calder understood. Bryce didn't strive for fame or fortune. Since childhood, her head was filled with words. She felt compelled to fit them together into stories, if only to keep her brain from exploding. Success was great. Heady. Gratifying.

Yet, if Bryce never sold another book, she would get up every day and plant herself in front of her keyboard. The need to write was in her blood.

Dressed in her robe, her hair piled into a messy mass, not a lick of makeup on her face, Calder waved Andi and Bryce on their way. Without the least bit of guilt. Days like today when she could simply lounge around the house were rare. She planned to enjoy every second.

"The fresh strawberries you had delivered the other day? Please tell me you have some left."

"I stashed a bowl in the bottom drawer just for you." Mrs. Finch knew what each of her girls liked and disliked. Calder craved fruit. Varieties of all kinds. The more, the better. Given a choice, she would take a basket of apples over a box of chocolates without hesitation.

"Any thoughts about what you'd like for lunch?"

Eyes closed with pleasure, Calder savored the first bite of juicy berry. Perfectly cold. Just enough sweet mixed with the tart.

"Grilled cheese and whatever soup you have handy."

Calder's tastes were simple, yet specific. Only sharp cheddar would do. Sourdough bread. Lightly buttered and grilled to a deep golden brown. Just the thought brought a smile to her face.

"Easy on my end. I made a big pot of cream of tomato to take to the shelter. Dougal should be here anytime to make the delivery. I'll ladle out a bowl for you before he leaves."

"Dougal is a keeper, Mrs. F." Calder popped another berry into her mouth. "Ever thought about making an honest man of him?"

"We've both been down the aisle before. Good, solid, happy marriages." Mrs. Finch shook her head. "For now, we like things the way they are. He has his home. I have mine. But you never know. When we're old and gray, we might decide to share our waning years as husband and wife."

Between her mother and father, Calder had witnessed almost a dozen weddings. And the flip side? A near dozen divorces. Though she couldn't remember the early ones, the more recent were vivid. She'd lived to tell the tale, but had little faith in the notion of long-term relationships. Genetically, she was cursed. Mrs. Finch and her Dougal gave her a sliver of hope. But try as she might, she didn't hold out much hope for herself.

"You go and enjoy your day off."

"I will. And give Dougal a big kiss for me."

Mrs. Finch's cheeks colored. An honest to goodness blush. Calder took the shortcut toward the back stairs, chuckling as she went. Lord, she loved that woman.

The scent of fresh paint hit Calder when she was halfway to the top landing. The rumble of voices followed. In such a large house, some kind of maintenance was always underway. Mrs.

Finch would announce when and where so no one would be surprised by the presence of workmen—or workwomen.

More often than not, Calder forgot.

Since she was certain the painters wouldn't be here without the housekeeper's approval, Calder didn't pause except to cinch the belt on her robe a bit tighter. Eyes on her task, she turned down the hall. And ran straight into a large, hard, immovable object—of the human variety.

"Excuse me. I wasn't looking where I—" Calder's words—and smile—faded when her gaze met a pair of impossibly blue eyes. Certain he must be an optical illusion conjured from her thoughts, she leaned closer to get a better look. "Adam?"

"Hello, Calder."

CHAPTER THREE

AFRAID HER JAW was somewhere around her knee, Calder snapped her mouth shut. The man was real all right. And the slight lift of his eyebrow was just as annoying as she remembered.

"What are you doing here?"

Silly question. One quick yet thorough glance and Calder could see the paint splatters. On his work boots, worn jeans, and plaid flannel shirt. A few dots flecked backs of his hands. The pale-blue color stood out, sprinkled on random strands of his wavy dark hair.

"I'm here to do a job." Adam motioned towards the half-finished wall.

Calder blamed her spiked heart rate on the surprise she experienced to find Adam in her home. She was honest enough with herself to admit his undeniable masculine appeal contributed to her racing pulse. However, when she recognized the glint in his eyes as condescension, her blood cooled.

Obviously, the arrogance she'd witnessed from him the night before was more of a permanent personality trait than a temporary aberration. *The jerk.* Luckily, Calder had dealt with self-important males her entire life. Cool, calm, with an air of bored disinterest worked best on her father—the most arrogant man she'd ever known.

"Are you a house painter who moonlights as a bouncer? Or the other way around."

"I prefer to think of myself as a jack of all trades." Adam's lips twitched as though amused by a joke he didn't want to share. "However, I'm *not* a bouncer. Never have been."

"But last night—"

"You jumped to a conclusion."

"You could have corrected my error."

Adam shrugged. "I didn't expect to see you again. Why waste my time?"

Calder started to count to ten. *Cool and calm* she reminded herself. But she barely reached five. Something about the man made her forget her good intentions.

Another minute and Calder would start pacing, a sure sign her temper was on the rise.

"I made a mistake. All you had to do was politely correct me. A little thing called common courtesy shouldn't be too much to expect."

"Seems to me you expect a lot." Adam crossed his arms. "I did you a favor when I sent your boyfriend on his way. Then, as any gentleman would, made certain you had a ride home. I didn't owe you an explanation about how I make a living."

"And *I* didn't need your help. Yet, I managed to thank you. Which you threw back in my face. Gentleman, my ass."

Calder muttered the last bit under her breath. Adam heard every word.

"What makes a gentleman in your book? Someone like your boyfriend who doesn't take no for an answer? I guess you can forgive a lot if he wears an expensive suit and knows the proper fork to use."

"Milo Prendergast is not my boyfriend." Which was beside the point. Yet for some reason, Calder felt the need to set the record straight. "As for a gentleman? In my book? He isn't judged by his clothes. Or table manners. But by how he treats other people."

"I treated you just fine."

"A gentleman would have acknowledged my thank you. And he wouldn't have told me I have lousy taste in men."

"Okay. You said thank you. I should have responded in kind. My mother taught me better." When Adam's lips curved upward, Calder had to admit he had a nice smile. Naturally, he ruined the moment. "However, I stand by my opinion. Your taste in men is questionable at best. If your boyfriend is any indication."

"How many times do I have to tell you? He *isn't* my boyfriend!"

Adam's smile widened. "Good to know."

Suddenly, Calder realized the ridiculous turn of the conversation. And the situation. Dressed in a robe and nightgown, her feet bare, she was in the middle of an argument. But somehow, she'd forgotten why. Calder frowned.

"What are we talking about?"

"Hell if I know. Maybe—"

"Hey, Adam," a man called from down the hall. He wore a painter's cap, coveralls, and a disgruntled expression on his weathered face. "Melvin opened one of the new cans. The store sent the wrong color."

"Relax, Asa. We still have some of the old. Load the wrong stuff into my truck. I'll take care of the mix-up and be back before you finish your lunch break."

Should she say goodbye? Or walk away without a backward glance. Awkward for no particular reason, Calder shoved her hands into her robe pockets.

"I'll let you get back to work."

When Adam didn't respond, Calder skirted around him. She was almost out of sight when he called out.

"The suit isn't your boyfriend?"

"Milo?" Who else could he mean? "No. He's not my boyfriend."

Before Calder could ask why he cared—because in spite of herself, she really wanted to know—Adam sent her an enigmatic look and disappeared down the stairs.

"What the hell?"

Calder looked around for someone, anyone, who would commiserate with her exasperation. But the hallway was empty.

"He must be crazy," Calder decided.

Happy with her assessment, she headed to her room, determined to put Adam out of her head. Unfortunately, crazy or not, one thing was for certain. Unlike other men who came and quickly went from Calder's thoughts, Adam would prove harder to forget.

CALDER STARED OUT her office window at the bird perched on the ledge. Pecking away unconcerned, the pigeon raised its head and stared back as if to say, *'what's your problem'*?

"I wish I had an answer."

Out of sorts was the best way she could describe her state of mind. For the last two days, she'd gone about her business with an outward calm she didn't feel. Calder hated when her emotions felt prickly and wouldn't settle. Especially when she knew the reason but couldn't for the life of her think of a doable solution.

"Ad copy for our *Spring Romance Gala* is ready for your approval."

Annabel Brock set her iPad on Calder's desk with a flourish. The best right-hand woman a person could hope for, she was young—but not green. Enthusiastic—but not giddy. And efficient—in every way possible. Polished and professional. Without her, Calder didn't know how she would have managed in the early days, before her charity took root.

Erica's Angels ran like a well-oiled machine. Calder liked to think the reason was the years she'd spent setting up the business model. At first, she and Annabel were a two-woman operation.

Helping children in need was Calder's passion. Though the cause was worthy, she had to fight tooth and nail for every donation.

The Benedict family connections helped. And her sisters pitched in whenever they had the time. Still, New York City was filled with charitable organizations. Fresh out of college with a bright, shiny degree, she wasn't taken seriously. Another rich girl with too much time on her hands.

New. Untried. Calder had to start at the back of the line. Which was fine. She was used to people underestimating her. For as long as she could remember, one of her favorite pastimes was proving doubters wrong

While others laughed behind her back—and some right in her face—Calder calmly and ruthlessly wheedled and schemed and sometimes trampled over anyone who stood in her way. She earned a reputation as a woman who wouldn't take no for an answer. Not where her baby was concerned.

Six years later, *Erica's Angels* was no longer an also-ran. The organization soared right up there beside the cream of New York charities. Calder had conquered one of the toughest cities in the country. Next? The world.

The plans were all in place for global expansion. A slow rollout starting next year as they tested the waters. Failure wasn't an option.

"How will I ever find someone even half as good to take your place?" Calder had informed Annabel of her promotion day before yesterday. The woman hadn't stopped smiling.

"I have a year to train my replacement before I leave for England." Stars in her light-blue eyes, Annabel sighed the name as she ran a hand through her light-brown, shoulder-length hair. "Until I'm satisfied, you won't have to deal with anybody but me."

After extensive research and debate, Calder had decided to base the charity's secondary headquarters in London. Central enough of a location, Annabel could do all her traveling within a few hours.

"I know you're the best person for the job. Europe won't know what hit it. But I'll miss you."

"I know." Annabel placed her hand over Calder's. They weren't just work colleagues. They were friends. "Think of the fun we'll have when you come to visit. Often, I hope."

"Be careful what you hope for. Between checking on *Erica's Angels Europe* and shopping sprees, I might spend more time with you than here at home."

Unconcerned, Annabel laughed. Calder belonged in New York. She thrived on the energy. Loved the people. Adored the theater and art galleries. She enjoyed traveling, but she was always glad to come back.

Home is where the heart is. And for Calder, her heart only beat properly when she was near the ones she loved. Her sisters.

Her focus returned, Calder picked up the *Spring Romance Gala* advertisement which would run online starting in mid-May, a month before the actual event. The print copy had been sent to select newspapers and magazines.

One of the biggest moneymakers of the year, the gala had become a must-attend evening. Everyone who was anybody—and anyone desperate to be somebody—requested tickets months before they were available. Each year, the budget and venue grew to keep up with demand. Still, they had to turn people away.

Personally, Calder hated the hierarchy system where money and social standing equaled power. In a perfect world, she would have distributed invitations on a first-come, first-serve basis. A broadminded approach to raising money.

Unfortunately, facts were facts. While Calder could afford to thumb her nose at New York's elite, *Erica's Angels* couldn't. They needed to fill the *Spring Romance Gala* event with fat bank accounts. Even if the owners often possessed equally fat heads.

"Traditional was a good choice." Annabel leaned over Calder's shoulder. "Who doesn't love red roses?"

Calder wasn't a fan. Then again, she was biased. They were her mother's favorite. A fact every husband, lover, and potential boyfriend played up to the hilt. She couldn't remember a time when vases of roses didn't dot the Benedict mansion. Every floor carried the scent even when flowers weren't around. As if the fragrance had permeated the walls.

In the minority, Calder had agreed an old-school approach would be a nice change of pace. They liked to mix things up. Edgy one year. Avant guard the next. Last year, they went back to the sixties and the *Summer of Love*. While not a favorite of some donors, the younger crowd gushed over the tie-dyed banners and peace signs.

They already had next year's theme. *The Roaring Twenties.* Calder looked forward to flappers, the Charleston, and bathtub gin. For now, she could live with roses.

"The new agency hit a home run." Calder nodded her approval. "The advertisements should bring in some extra donations."

"I was about to make a cookie run. Can I bring you something?"

The bakery on the corner featured a new kind of cookie every day. Annabel allowed herself one as an afternoon treat. Calder usually passed but today she felt in need of a sugar pick-me-up.

"I'll take a *Cherry Delight*." Calder paused, then gave into an impulse she might later regret. "Get a couple dozen."

"Wow." Annabel chuckled. "When you go off the wagon, you go all the way."

"They aren't all for me."

"If you say so."

Alone again, Calder had second thoughts. Her spur of the moment decisions rarely ended well. She liked to think things through. Form a plan. Polish the edges. Impulsive wasn't her style. Ready to tell Annabel to cancel the cookie order, she'd barely started to rise when her phone rang.

Each of her sisters was assigned a different ringtone. Andi or Bryce, she might have ignored the call since she would see them later tonight. But when the strains of *Free Bird* filled the office, she answered immediately.

"Destry. Are you in one piece?"

A family joke with just enough truth and worry to make the question necessary for her peace of mind.

"Hale and hearty. Not a bruise on my delicate frame."

Calder smiled. The last thing anybody who knew her would call Destry was delicate. A person foolish enough to make the mistake soon learned their lesson. Often the hard way.

"Where are you?"

"Duluth."

"As in Minnesota?" Calder didn't try to hide her surprise. She'd expected a more exotic location than mid-western America.

"Mmm." Destry didn't sound pleased. "I'm sure the town is very nice. Except for the snow in April. And the crappy hotel my client booked me into. Oh, did I mention the lousy food?"

"Otherwise, you would recommend Duluth as a vacation destination?"

"Sure. Why not." Destry let out a breezy chuckle. "If you have any friends you'd like to convert into enemies, recommend away."

"I don't think so. In my business, I need all the friends I can get."

"Better you than me."

Destry wasn't known for her winning personality. She didn't smile if she weren't in the mood. She shunned small talk like the plague. And she could count on one hand the number of people whose opinions mattered. Calder was damn proud to be among the chosen few.

"Andi and I have played text-tag for two days. Bryce doesn't answer her phone when she writes—which means she *never* answers. So—"

"I was your last resort?" Calder asked without rancor.

"Actually, I called you first. For once, you didn't answer."

Frowning, Calder checked her messages. Sure enough, Destry *had* tried to contact her.

"You must have called when I was in the bathroom." A place Calder refused to take her phone.

"What's up? I figure something must be hopping or Andi would have left details."

"Billie's dating Ingo Hunter." Calder saw no reason for a long preamble.

"And once more, our dear mother proves she has about as much sense as the average gnat." Destry sighed. "Is she serious about him?"

"Hard to say. I saw them together the night before last. Since then, she pops in for a change of clothes. Usually when none of us are home. But she's glowing, Destry. Like when she's convinced she's found the love of her life."

"The love that will last forever." Well-earned cynicism dripped from Destry's voice. "How many times have we heard that one? Not counting the six husbands?"

"I've lost track." All of them had. "In the past, love or lust, Billie's men were equally enthralled. Ingo Hunter doesn't care about anyone but himself. And the size of his portfolio."

"True. When Hunter tried his line on me, I didn't detect a trace of desire in his beady eyes. Only dollar signs."

"All Billie will see is her own reflection. Until Hunter gets whatever he's after."

For decades, Calder and her sisters had dealt with the aftermath of their mother's relationships. From the heartfelt sobs to the declarations she was through with love for good. They'd learned to weather the storm with the knowledge neither lasted long. Within days, Billie's tears had dried, and she was on to the next man.

"Must be wonderful to have such a short memory." Destry snorted. "You know our lives would be easier if we didn't give a flying leap."

Calder agreed. Their mother was vain. Shallow. Self-centered. The center of her own universe. Yet, she drew people to her like the sun. A beautiful, flitting butterfly. They might feel different if they had to deal with her 24/7. In small increments, Billie was hard to hate. Impossible not to love.

"Somehow Billie's managed to avoid men who wanted nothing but her money." Some were useless. Some dumb as a post. But none tried to take their mother to the cleaners.

"Hunter can't get his hands on the Benedict fortune," Destry pointed out. "So, what does he want?"

"The question of the moment. When we figure out the answer, we'll let you know."

"I can be there tomorrow. Just say the word."

Calder was tempted. But for her own sake, not Billie's.

"I'd rather you were here. Always. But Billie is fine for now. She can't remarry until six months after her divorce is final."

"Good old Granddad. He really believed women can't make rational decisions." Destry let out a noise somewhere between a chuckle and a snort. "In Billie's case, he was right."

"I wonder what he'd say if he were alive to see what his granddaughters have accomplished."

"I doubt our little endeavors would change his mind. His will is very specific. Men rule the roost. Women should be seen, not heard, and always defer to the closest man."

Calder waited a beat before she burst out laughing. Destry joined her. The younger Benedict women were a lot of things. Silent, without strong opinions they weren't. A self-involved mother and mostly absentee fathers meant they didn't have to listen to anybody's idea of how they should behave or who they should become. As a result, they were simply themselves.

"I have to be someplace in twenty minutes." Destry had snapped back into professional mode. "And since felons are notoriously unpredictable, I don't want to be late."

Every instinct in Calder's body screamed to beg Destry to be careful. Years of experience said her youngest sibling would bristle at the warning. No matter how heartfelt. So, she did what she always did. Bit her tongue and said a little prayer.

"Call if you need anything." Since Destry never needed anything, Calder rephrased her request. "Just call. Any time. Day or night. And a visit would be nice. We miss your pretty face around the old homestead."

"Next week. I promise. Love you."

"Love you, too."

Calder set down her phone with a smile. A promise from Destry was as much of a sure thing as life could guarantee.

"Here are the cookies." Annabel breezed into the office, her cheeks rosy from her brisk walk to and from the bakery. "They only had eighteen *Cherry Delights* left. But when I told Marvin they were for you, he threw in a dozen fresh-baked *Chocolate Dreams*. Free of charge. Then asked oh so casually if you were dating anybody at the moment."

Honestly, Calder didn't think of the owner of *Lee's Bakery* in a romantic way. Not because Marvin Lee wasn't attractive. He was. Very. However, the few times they'd met, she was in a hurry, and he was swamped with customers. They hadn't even flirted.

"I didn't think he noticed me."

"Oh, he noticed." Annabel grinned. "He's a great catch, Calder."

"I'm flattered." And she was. Though, Calder wondered if Marvin's interest would dim if he knew the free cookies he'd sent were for another man.

"I know how sensitive you are about your personal life. I informed Marvin that I didn't know what your romantic situation was at the moment."

Before Calder could answer with a mighty thank you, Annabel continued.

"However, if you're the least bit interested, you should move fast. At least half of Marvin's business comes from women who think the buns on his backside are tastier than the ones in his oven."

"Charming." As she reached for her coat, Calder had to laugh. "Thank you for effectively ruining my love of dinner rolls."

Annabel sighed. "Fine. I know when to admit defeat. You could have any man you want with a snap of your fingers."

If Calder wanted a warm-blooded companion who would come when she snapped her fingers, she would get a dog. As for a man? She knew exactly what she wanted. Someone who looked beyond her net worth. Beyond the mansion and her family connections. She'd looked—once or twice. And came up empty.

"Unless an emergency crops up, I'm out of touch until Monday."

Annabel trailed Calder to the elevator.

"One more word on the subject of men?"

"Only one?" Calder said with a sideways look.

"For now." Annabel held the elevator door as Calder stepped inside. "Find yourself a hunky, sexy playmate. Don't worry if he's after your money. Just have some fun."

Intense blue eyes popped into Calder's head. She didn't have any problem pairing them with a ruggedly handsome face and tall, muscled body. She looked at the box of cookies. Bait? Why not.

"I think I remember how to do fun."

"Sure you do." Annabel stepped back, letting the heavy door close. "And Calder? When you find your playmate? Find out if he has a friend for me."

CHAPTER FOUR

SLOWLY, ADAM STONE walked the length of the hallway checking the walls with a critical eye. He wasn't a professional painter. But he knew the difference between shoddy and perfection. When he was in charge, nothing but the latter would do.

"Melvin!"

"Coming!" Melvin Delray, head down, trudged around the corner like a man walking toward his doom. "Just once, I'd like to finish a job without you telling me something's wrong. Your bellow is worse than nails down a chalkboard."

"I only bellow when necessary. Look."

Squinting, Melvin followed the path between Adam's finger and the floor.

"What? I don't see anything."

Arms crossed, Adam didn't repeat himself. He simply waited.

Melvin had known Adam long enough to recognize the look. When he said there was something to see, there was *always* something to see. Almost a foot shorter, Melvin was naturally closer to the floor. Yet he had to crouch to detect the practically infinitesimal splash of paint near the bottom of the baseboard. A minor flaw a man with normal eyesight would have missed.

"Damn, Hawk. I thought the first thing to go was the eyes. If anything, yours keep getting sharper."

Hawk. Adam rarely heard the nickname anymore. A holdover from his Navy days—where he and Melvin met. After a five-year stint, he'd been happy to leave the military behind. Melvin hadn't been as easy to shake. And Adam was eternally grateful.

Friendly acquaintances were easy to come by. True friends were rare. On the fingers of one hand, Adam could count the people he held dear. For all his grousing and complaining, Melvin was loyal as the day was long. A fact he'd proven on more than one occasion.

Adam and Melvin had a lot in common. They grew up poor, their fathers died young without a penny to their names. With few options, both men joined the military right out of high school. Both left the service with ambition for a better life. They'd come a long way in five years. And they weren't done yet.

Adam shook his head as Melvin tried to scrape away the offending streak.

"Needs turpentine."

"I know," Melvin huffed. "Otherwise you'd take care of the problem yourself."

One of the reasons Adam maintained the respect of the men he worked with was his willingness to pitch in whenever necessary. He didn't consider a bit of cleanup beneath him. In the case of the wayward paint, Melvin had access to the proper tool for the job. Adam didn't.

When Melvin returned, Adam took the turpentine-soaked cloth and knelt on the floor. As he concentrated on the offensive paint stain, Melvin leaned over his shoulder to watch.

"Salami for lunch again?" Adam grimaced as the scent of garlic and onions filled his nose

"Tamara knows what I like." His dark eyes filled with contentment, Melvin patted his stomach. Once flat as a board, he had developed an ever-growing paunch. The result of a love of rich food, and a wife happy to indulge him.

"Tamara is a saint if she puts up with your breath."

"My wife is an angel. Loves me no matter what." Melvin grinned. "But just to be sure, I always brush my teeth and chomp a handful of breath mints before I kiss her hello."

"Wise man." Adam wasn't interested in marriage. Yet, he envied Melvin. Tamara was one in a million. "I see the crew is almost done in the library. What's your timetable for the office?"

"Should wrap up by the end of the week."

Finished to his satisfaction, Adam handed back the cloth. "Do you think you can get to the boutique over on Madison Avenue by Monday? The owner's scheduled the grand opening in four weeks."

"Kind of a close call." Melvin stuck the rag in the back pocket of his coveralls. "Why wait until the last minute?"

"Thank your lucky stars. When a client puts off until tomorrow—so to speak—the payout can be sizable."

"I do like a bonus. Especially now that Tamara is determined to buy a house in Brooklyn near her parents. I vote for near where we are. The Bronx provides just the right amount of buffer between the in-laws and us."

"Something wrong with the apartment?" Adam helped the couple move into their current home less than a year ago. After he brokered the lease.

"The place is great," Melvin assured him. "We need more space. Or we will in six months. When the baby gets here."

Adam knew how much Melvin and Tamara wanted to start a family. The road hadn't been easy. She'd miscarried twice.

"Congratulations, man."

"We aren't spreading the word quite yet. Just in case." A cloud crossed over Melvin's face. But he wasn't one to dwell on the dark side of what ifs. With a quick shake of his head, happiness replaced worry. "Tamara's glowing. And in the nesting mood. If you hear of a place on the market—at least four bedrooms and three baths—let me know."

Before Melvin finished asking, Adam already had something in mind. A fixer-upper with great bones and endless potential. Not even listed, if they liked the house and moved quickly, Melvin and Tamara could get the major renovations done well before the newest member of the Delray family arrived.

"I'll text you the number of the agent. I've known Gina McMurray forever. Just mention my name, and she'll handle the rest."

"Amazing." Melvin looked suitably impressed. "No matter the situation, you either solve the problem or know somebody who can."

People had always interested Adam. Even as a child, he listened when they told their stories. Remembered the details without a thought for the future. He couldn't know with each encounter, he laid the groundwork for his future. Eventually, the backlog of information stored safely in his computer-like brain provided him with an unusual and very lucrative business.

"I should get back," Melvin said. "The new guy, Junior Freemont, is a bit of a wildcard. I don't want to leave him unattended until I have a better take on his reliability."

Adam walked with Melvin down the hall toward the library.

"Has he given you trouble?"

"Nothing specific. I get the impression he chafes at any kind of authority. Even when a paycheck is attached. And..."

"Might as well spit the whole mouthful out at once, Mel. And what?"

"Freemont seems overly interested in the ladies who live here." Melvin shrugged. "Don't overreact, Adam. Can't fault a man for noticing. Happily married as I am, I'll be the first to admit the Benedict sisters are easy on the eyes."

Adam felt a wave of unease. Even a hint of misconduct was enough in his book. The crew was warned upfront not to harass anyone in the house. Women. Children. Men. Pets. Do the job. Period. If a member of the crew crossed the line—by even a fraction of an inch—he was out on his ass.

"Freemont can look," Adam conceded. "You let me know if he does anything else."

"You set up the job, Adam. For which I'm grateful. But *Delray Painting* is my baby. *I'm* responsible for my crew's behavior. Unless you don't trust me to keep them in line."

"I trust you." With a sigh, Adam rubbed the back of his neck.

"When I hire somebody new, the rest of my crew knows to keep their eyes peeled."

Melvin was one of the few people who understood why the subject was a sore one. Why Adam's behavior where a woman's safety was concerned often bordered on the unreasonable.

The good thing about a close friend? Explanations weren't necessary.

"Dinner. Our place. Next week." Melvin lightly punched Adam's arm. "You name the day. And bring a date."

"Maybe you should ask Tamara first. With a baby on board, she might not be in the mood to entertain."

"She's the one who told me to invite you." Melvin paused. "You should bring a date."

Certain Melvin wasn't serious, Adam laughed. When his old buddy didn't so much as crack a smile, he sobered. Quickly.

"I always come alone. What's the deal?"

"Tamara has a cousin," Melvin said. Sheepish didn't begin to describe his expression.

"No." Adam groaned. In all the time he'd known Melvin's wife, she'd never attempted to set him up. Not once. "Why now?"

"Baby hormones. Tamara's been afflicted with a weird kind of double vision." Melvin held up a finger. Then added another. "Two by two. Everyone needs a mate because a person alone can't possibly be happy."

"I'm very happy."

"Try and tell her. But I warn you. One wrong word and she'll start to cry."

Adam froze. "What words should I avoid?"

"Hell if I know." Melvin shot him a distressed look. "Sirloin steak? Fettuccine? Paper towels? Pick your poison. Far as I can tell, there's no rhyme or reason to what will set her off. When the waterworks start, I hold her close and ride out the storm."

A pregnant woman who cries for no good reason? Adam couldn't think of a scarier combination. He wasn't the father. He wasn't ready. Wasn't sure he ever would be. As happy as he was for Melvin, he couldn't think of a single reason he would want to change places with his friend.

"About dinner—"

"I didn't mean to scare you off, buddy." Melvin chuckled. "Come to dinner. I can't control Tamara's hormones. But I'll do my best to make certain she doesn't spring a mystery woman on you. Or..."

"Or what?" Adam wasn't sure he wanted to know. But he asked—in spite of himself.

"Do as I suggested. Bring a date."

With a shake of his head, Adam slung the satchel he'd stashed by the pile of paint equipment over his shoulder. Everything he needed for his busy day was packed into the leather case. From his laptop, to a change of clothes, to the sandwich he always threw together before he left his apartment.

When Adam was younger, his mother would make him a sandwich every morning. Without fail. Until the day he joined the

Navy. Once he was on his own without a parent or the military to guide his life, Adam couldn't shake the influence of either. Not entirely.

Each morning, he rose with the sun. And after breakfast, he tossed together a couple pieces of bread with whatever he could scrounge from his refrigerator in between. Today? Ham and cheese.

More often than not, the snack went uneaten. But some habits were hard to break. Especially when they were tinged with sappy sentimentality.

"I'll come to dinner," Adam assured Melvin. "Can I get back to you on the night?"

Melvin nodded. "And?"

"Jesus. You're like a dog with a freaking bone. I *might* bring someone. I'll let you know."

Adam *would* let Melvin know. When he arrived. Alone. He didn't want Tamara to have enough time to spring her cousin—or any other relative—on him.

"Tamara's cousin is a cutie," Melvin said as Adam left the room. "A bit of an overbite. But—"

"No, Melvin. Absolutely not."

Adam shouted the warning over his shoulder, his attention was on Melvin instead of where he was headed. And ran smackdab into Calder Benedict. Again.

To keep them both upright, Adam wrapped one arm around her waist. The other, he used to keep his balance. As a result, her soft body was pinned between him and the wall.

Not that Calder seemed to mind. Eyes like rich, dark chocolate sparkled with humor as her full, red lips curved into a smile.

"We have to stop meeting like this." She laughed.

And Adam, though he couldn't have known, was a goner.

CHAPTER FIVE

CALDER DIDN'T TRY to move away from Adam's impromptu embrace. Why would she when the press of his body against hers felt so good? So right.

"You're very tall."

"Maybe you're short."

Adam's breath was warm against her face. And smelled faintly of peppermint. Not her favorite flavor. However, given the source, she might rethink her opinion.

Oh, boy. If the scent of Adam's breath was enough to give her libido a jumpstart, she could be in serious trouble.

"Five nine in stocking feet." Calder glanced down. "Or, bare feet, as the case may be."

"Six three." Adam flashed her a grin. "You okay?"

When Calder nodded, Adam slowly straightened. Assured she wouldn't topple over, he removed his steadying arm. Fancifully, she told herself she witnessed a flash of reluctance in his blue eyes.

"I've walked these stairs my entire life and never run into anybody. Now, I've barreled into you twice in one week."

"Sorry to break your streak."

"Believe me, I wasn't complaining." Calder wanted to reach out. Draw Adam back. Rather than give in to the impulse, she kept her hands at her sides.

Adam gave her a long, contemplative look, one brow raised, his eyelids half-closed.

"Are you flirting with me?"

"If you must ask, I need to take a refresher course."

In what Calder could only term gentlemanly, and a bit old-fashioned—endearingly so—Adam took her hand, leading her to the top of the stairs.

"When I barely know a woman, I always ask. Saves misunderstandings. On both sides."

"Smart." Calder's smile widened when Adam kept her hand in his. "Just to be clear. My flirt is in full gear."

"Good to know."

Adam moved a step closer. And Calder's senses went into overdrive. She noticed the way he tipped his head just a bit to the side, his gaze intent. For the first time, she noted the silver striations in his wildly blue irises. And her brain went from crystal clear to fuzzy.

"I have cookies." A nonsensical thing to say. But Calder wasn't thinking straight.

"Is cookies a sexual metaphor? As in...?" Adam looked confused. Rightly so. "You'll have to help me out."

"*Cherry Delights* and *Chocolate Dreams*." Calder laughed when she realized how her brief explanation could be misconstrued considering the direction of their conversation. "Both are cookies. I bought them at my favorite bakery. For you and the other painters."

Adam leaned a little closer, his eyes locked with hers. "I'd love a cookie. Even though I'm not a painter."

"Mrs. Finch set them out in the kitchen with iced tea and lemonade. If you want to tell the others, I'll..." Calder paused as Adam's words sank in. "Wait. The other day you had paint in your hair. On your boots. Which makes you—"

"Someone who helps out when a friend is shorthanded."

Now, Calder was confused.

"You don't paint walls for a living?"

"Nope."

"Not a bouncer."

"A fact we established the other day."

"You have on a suit." Between her thumb and forefinger, Calder touched the material of Adam's lapel. Lightweight gray gabardine. Finest quality. And if she didn't miss her guess—which she rarely did—sported a designer label. "A very nice suit."

"My tailor and I thank you."

The twinkle in his eyes made Calder's stomach do a slow roll. Was there anything sexier than a man with a sense of humor? And a hard, well-conditioned body? And a face with an interesting flaw or two—to allay any comparisons to perfection.

"Funny, you like expensive clothing, yet you seemed to have a problem with my date's attire. Called him the suit, if I recall, Mr....?"

"Stone." Adam shook Calder's hand. "Nice to meet you. And I didn't have a problem with what he had on, but his attitude.

Calder couldn't argue. Milo Prendergast *was* a jerk.

"What exactly *is* your occupation, Mr. Stone?"

"What I do is hard to explain."

Damn it. Calder felt a wave of disappointment. She was all too familiar with prevarication. Her father was a master of the art. And though she loved him, she wouldn't bet a nickel on his ability to tell an undoctored version of the truth if his life depended on it.

"Illegal?"

Adam looked surprised. Then annoyed. "Of course not."

"Illicit?"

"What's the difference?"

"Depends on who you ask." Calder's father loved to split hairs. She was more of a black and white person. At least where the law was involved. "Is your profession legally or morally suspect?"

"No."

His gaze steady, Adam's response was firm. Not a twitch or tick to be seen. So, if he were squeaky clean, why didn't he simply answer her question?

"The explanation of what I do is convoluted, not illegal. Or immoral. I promise." Adam literally crossed his heart. "Have dinner with me tonight. I'll satisfy your curiosity. And anything else you want."

"We'll start with my curiosity and see how things go from there. Pick me up at seven. Casual? Dressy?"

"I'll take you any way I can get you."

Holy crap. Calder mentally fanned herself as Adam's blue eyes heated. The man was dangerous. Hopefully, in all the best ways.

"However," he said. "Wear something like the blue number you had on the night we met, and you'll be fine."

Flattered that he remembered, Calder nodded. "Mid-casual chic."

"If you say so." Adam looked amused.

Calder started back the way she came. Down the stairs at her usual jog.

"And don't forget to tell the painters about the cookies," she reminded him.

"What about me? Don't I get one?"

At the bottom of the stairs, Calder turned. Casually leaning against the wall, Adam waited.

"As long as you tell me the truth, you can have anything you want."

"And if I lie?"

"Take a cookie. As for the rest?" Calder made a slow turn so Adam could have a good look at exactly what he would never touch. "Not even a taste."

Adam seemed a bit bemused—exactly her intention—as if he had yet to wrap his head around the consequences of a lie. Never a taste of her? She hoped he found the prospect unacceptable.

"See you later, Adam Stone."

"I DON'T HAVE a thing to wear."

Billie burst into Calder's room, highlighted blond hair in curlers, the ends of her silk robe flapping in her wake. As always, her face was perfectly made up. She never left the safety of her bathroom without several coats of what she liked to call *glamour*.

If the house caught fire, Calder was certain her mother would make the fireman wait while she made herself *presentable*. Billie's version of the holy trinity. Lipstick, mascara, and blush.

Used to such declarations, Calder stood back rather than risk bodily injury. Nobody got between Billie and a closet filled with potential outfits. Not if they wanted to live to tell the tale.

Less than a month ago, Billie had returned from her bi-annual European excursion. As always, she'd done her best to pluck the crème de la crème from every Paris design house.

"You must have something left."

Billie never wore anything twice—much to the delight of New York gossip rags and various thrift stores where she donated her *used* couture.

"Nothing." Billie let out a dramatic sigh. She walked the length of Calder's extensive wardrobe with the critical eye of a seasoned shopper. "I can't leave the house in the same old rags! Ingo and I are dining at *the* new restaurant. The one with a waitlist a mile long. My outfit has to be perfection."

Billie held up a dress Calder had yet to wear. She dismissed the ruby-red satin with a shake of her head and a flick of her wrist.

"Hey," Calder protested. With a frown, she rescued the dress from the floor. "Either respect the clothes or get your butt out of the closet."

As usual, Billie didn't hear anything if the comment came close to a criticism.

"You really should update your wardrobe, Calder. These?" Billie held up a pair of strappy sandals. "So last year."

"I imagine my feet will survive the humiliation."

Calder watched with growing exasperation as her mother continued her search. Desperate to hold onto her youth, Billie dressed young and acted younger. She believed age was a state of mind. And with the help of expensive creams, facial massages, and the best plastic surgeons money could buy, she planned to be young forever.

Genetically blessed, Billie hadn't found a reason to go beyond the Botox and chemical peel stage. Yet. She checked the mirror every morning. And afternoon. And evening. The second her skin betrayed her? A sag here or a wrinkle there? Wear and tear her doctor couldn't fix with an outpatient procedure? She would jump in without hesitation.

"We could pass for sisters," Billie declared.

The comment hadn't come out of the blue. Billie made the same statement to one daughter or another at least once a week. Calder reacted as expected.

"Absolutely." *A much older sister*. But Calder wisely kept the last part to herself.

"Ingo couldn't believe I have four grown daughters. He thought I was twenty-five. When I told him to add ten years, he was shocked. Said he couldn't believe his ears." Billie giggled. "Or his eyes."

So many responses, so little time. Calder bit her tongue. Billie had given her the perfect opening, she didn't want to kill the moment with a snippy remark.

"Ingo Hunter?"

Under her blackened eyelashes, Billie sent Calder one of her patented coy looks. Perfectly designed to set a reasonable person's teeth on edge.

"What about him?"

Calder wished she could shake some sense into her mother's lovely head. Tell her some much-needed home truths. Tempting. But, as experience had taught her, unproductive. Billie closed her ears to what she didn't want to hear. As for the lies men told her? She lapped them up as she purred like a cream-starved pussycat.

To get the information she needed, Calder had to pick her words carefully.

"Do you enjoy his company?"

An innocuous question. Yet, from the way Billie's face lit up, the right one.

"I do." Billie smile beamed. "Ingo is attractive. And attentive. He's interested in my brain, not just my body."

Calder tried not to roll her eyes. Billie wasn't stupid. However, she'd never wanted to expand her mind beyond fashion magazines and the latest gossip. Current events? Politics? The economy? Boring!

"Don't get me wrong. Ingo is a very passionate man." Billie let out a contented sigh. "*Very* passionate. If you know what I mean."

Eww. Calder didn't want to know about her mother's sex life. Ever. The idea of Billie and Ingo Hunter? Together? Her skin crawled.

"He's not your usual type."

"Ingo is exactly my type, silly girl. Handsome beyond words and crazy about me." Billie's eyes sharpened. "I like what you have on."

The shimmery silver dress was brand new. And showed off Calder's long legs to perfection.

Calder had to laugh. Between her daughters and herself, Billie literally had a house filled with designer clothing to pick from. Naturally, the only outfit she wanted was the one already in use. A classic case of the grass was always greener.

"You can't have the dress off my back."

"Fine." Billie's smile turned into a pout. "I'll find something. I still have a few things Ingo hasn't seen."

Billie swirled past Calder. In her wake, she left a trail of expensive perfume—a one-of-a-kind fragrance Andi's father presented his wife on their wedding day. She changed husbands— many times—but she never changed the scent she dabbed on each morning.

Sentimentality over the first man she married? Or the fact the scent bore her name. *Billie*. Calder imagined the truth was a little of both.

"Hey." Calder paused. Deliberately, she called out the name she rarely used. "Mom?"

At the bedroom door, Billie turned, her expression vague. Obviously, the difference hadn't registered.

"Yes?"

Be careful, Calder wanted to tell her. *For once in your life, look before you leap.* Knowing they would fall on deaf ears, she kept her warnings to herself.

"I hope you have a nice evening."

"I always do."

With a dramatic sweep of her hand, Billie disappeared. Calder walked into the bathroom to finish getting ready for her date. As she brightened her lips with a touch of color, she looked herself in the eyes.

"Wish all you want, Billie will never change," Calder told her reflection. "And for all her exasperating ways, you'll never stop loving her."

For the first time, Calder realized what she and her sisters were up against.

Time would tell if they could protect Billie from Ingo Hunter. Lord knew they would do their best.

The question was, could they accomplish the impossible? Could they protect their mother from herself?

CHAPTER SIX

ADAM TRIED TO remember the last time he'd spent so much time thinking about a woman.

High school? The night he'd been one hundred percent certain he would finally get lucky with Mavis Emery? Months of sweaty make-out sessions with nothing to show for his efforts except what felt like a case of terminal blue balls, he spent hours dreaming of how glorious sex would be—if the day ever arrived.

The definition of a blond bombshell, Mavis was every high school boy's wet dream. Teased-out hair. Fire engine red lips. When Adam looked into her eyes, he saw a wealth of womanly knowledge in the pale blue depths. Mavis carried herself with worldly sophistication. Or so his sex-obsessed teenage imagination thought.

Turned out they were a couple inexperienced kids with more hormones than brains. The night Mavis confessed she was still a virgin, Adam didn't know whether to laugh or cry. He knew the basics. He'd counted on *her* to guide him.

Eventually, they fumbled their way through. In retrospect, Adam suspected he enjoyed the experience more than Mavis. She'd smiled as he held her close. Said all the right things to stroke his fragile ego. And because they were young, he believed they were in love.

A month later, Mavis turned her sights on the captain of the football team. His heart fully intact, Adam started dating a cute little brunette. Her name was stored in his memory beside all the other women he'd been with. Sherry Klein.

Names were easy for him. Lasting relationships, not so much.

Adam straightened his tie. He'd fallen into a pattern of one forgettable relationship after another. More like one or two-night stands if he wanted to be brutally honest. Mavis was memorable because she'd been his first.

With very few exceptions, he moved from woman to woman. All he needed—or wanted—were a few laughs. And a lot of sex.

Until one night on his way home from drinks with friends when he encountered a leggy, dark-eyed beauty and her asshole of an escort. Barely a blink in time.

Yet, her face lingered in his mind well after he'd watched her cab drive away.

As he lay awake, Adam told himself she was just a woman. When her image was still with him the next morning, he tried to convince himself she was like all the rest. Female. To be respected. To be enjoyed. To be forgotten.

How was Adam supposed to forget when the next day he literally ran right into her? Or rather, she ran into him. Calder. An unusual name. Like the woman herself.

Not a big believer in fate, Adam couldn't argue that something kept pushing them together. Calder didn't hem or haw when he asked if she were interested in him. Her eyes said yes. Her body said yes. Most important, her words said yes.

As a result, he did what any rational, heterosexual man would do. He asked her out before he gave into the impulse to kiss her. Wrong place. Wrong time.

Adam easily imagined how she would feel in his arms. And he smiled. Soft and warm and willing. Maybe even eager. A match for him. He wanted somewhere private. Not the back stairwell of her family's home where they could be interrupted at any second. Somewhere they could take their time. Explore. Taste. Enjoy.

Leaning close to the bathroom mirror, Adam ran his hand over his freshly shaved jaw. Smooth. As a teenager, he'd lived in jeans and sweatshirts. Yet, no matter what he wore, he always liked to be well groomed.

To Adam's surprise, he'd become quite the clothes horse since he left the Navy. Of course, money helped. For the first time in his life, his bank account was well padded. *Very* well padded. He'd discovered a side of the good life he hadn't expected. Tailored shirts and suits. An assortment of silk neckties. The Italian leather shoes that lined one wall of his closet were a big step up from canvas high-tops—the cheapest his mother could find.

Expensive didn't always equal better. Just because he had the money didn't mean Adam spent with reckless abandon. He saved whenever possible. Invested wisely. However, the first time he slid a pair of hand-crafted dress shoes on his feet, he knew he could never go back to bargain rack specials again.

Adam grabbed his wallet. Checked his image. Again. Same as the last time he looked. And the time before. Pressed suit. Crisp white shirt. Polished shoes. Foolish man.

Chuckling, Adam locked his apartment door. He wasn't a skinny kid, all nerves and uncertainty. He was a man with years of experience under his belt. A man who never doubted his choices. What was the point? Often, he took the right path. On the few occasions he swerved right when he should have gone left, he corrected the error. And moved on. Forward. Always forward.

Nerves and doubts. He couldn't remember the last time he'd experienced either. Yet, Adam wasn't so far removed from the emotions that he couldn't recognize them. What he felt tonight was different.

Anticipation.

Unlike the women Adam usually dated, Calder was a wild card. Not because of her money or social status. He didn't give a flying leap about either. What made her different was... Honestly, he had no idea. But he couldn't wait to find out.

CALDER DIDN'T KNOW what to expect when she accepted Adam's invitation.

She wasn't a party girl. Never had been. Late nights, every night, weren't her scene. Social by nature meant she *did* go out on a regular basis. Sometimes with her sisters. Or with friends. Often with a male escort.

Dinner. Dancing. Movies. Concerts. Calder enjoyed the usual pursuits and gravitated toward people with the same interests. People she'd known for a long time or met through mutual acquaintances.

Adam was different. Calder knew very little about him. Beyond the fact that he wasn't a bouncer. Or a painter. Or that he hadn't hesitated to step in when he thought she needed his help.

He arrived at seven sharp. Which meant he was punctual. Calder knew the time because she glanced at the clock more often than she wanted to admit, willing the minutes to pass.

Perhaps she knew more about him than she thought. While Adam could rock a perfectly tailored suit with the best of them—

comfortable and natural—he looked just as at home in a pair of jeans. And sexy as hell in either option.

The car he drove was expensive. Something low-slung and sporty—Calder wasn't informed enough on the subject to know the make or model. The fact that Adam didn't feel the need to expound on things like horsepower or the astronomical price tag impressed Calder more than he would ever understand.

On top of his growing list of virtues? He smelled amazing. The interior of the car was small. Intimate rather than cramped. If he'd doused himself with cologne, she would have known. Cheap or expensive, Calder was not a fan. Adam's scent was subtle. She breathed deeply. Mild soap and yummy male.

The combination was unexpected. And heady.

"All buckled in?" When Calder nodded, Adam's gaze dropped from her eyes, down her body. "Thank you."

"For?"

"The dress." With a grin, he put the car in gear. "First thing I noticed about you the night we met was your legs."

"These old things?" Calder crossed one leg over the other—in Adam's direction. "I've had them all my life."

Adam laughed. A low growl. He didn't need words to let Calder in on his thoughts. One heated glance as he merged into traffic was all she needed.

"How do you fill your days?" he asked. "Do you have a regular job?"

"Give me an example of an irregular job."

"Off the top of my head, I can't think of any." Adam braked as the traffic light changed from yellow to red. "You have money."

Calder waited while Adam paused to choose his words. The Benedict family fortune landed on the filthy side of rich—a good description, if the stories she'd heard about her ancestors were true. She wasn't particularly proud of her monetary status. Any more than she was ashamed.

Grateful? Definitely. Calder enjoyed her life. She worked. She played. She gave back to those in need through her charity and other worthwhile organizations.

"I have a job, Adam. Not because I need to work. Because I want to."

"Did I sound judgmental?"

"Maybe. A little." Calder liked that he was self-aware enough to ask. Speaking of which. "Did I sound defensive?"

"Maybe." Adam winked. "A little."

"I think I might like you."

"You sound surprised?"

"Like isn't the same as lust." Calder understood the difference. Did Adam?

"I've had sex with women I barely knew." Adam pulled the car to a stop. "Not something I brag about. Simply a fact. I wasn't interested in how they made their living. Or their family. Or their dreams. All I wanted was a yes."

Adam's bald-faced honesty didn't put Calder off. Instead, she found herself drawn to him even more.

"Did you at least get their names?"

"Usually." His eyes carried a roguish twinkle. "I knew a young lady who could hook her leg behind her head. The details don't matter. I—"

"Are you kidding? The details are the best part," Calder declared.

"Another time."

"You think I'll forget to ask. But I won't."

"Then I'll tell you. Another time."

Before Calder could mount an argument, Adam left the car. A few long strides later and he had the passenger door open. He took her hand.

"My point is simple—even if I took a roundabout journey to get there."

"Do tell."

"I like you, Calder. *And* I want you. The two don't always go together. In this case, *our* case, they do. On my side, at least."

Before they crossed the street, Adam tucked her hand into the crook of his arm. A casual gesture. Yet, intimate. Thoughtful without an ounce of premeditation. Not to impress. Natural. Part of who he was as a man and a human being.

"Where are we?" Calder asked.

"My part of town."

Adam led her toward a nondescript brick building. The entrance was lit by a single low-wattage bulb which hung over a simple, unmarked black door.

Since they hadn't crossed a bridge or traveled through a tunnel, Calder knew they were still in Manhattan. Their exact location, she couldn't say. Nothing looked familiar. She hadn't kept track of landmarks or made a note of street signs.

Mentally, Calder kicked herself. If Destry were here, she would be livid. And her youngest sister would be right.

Always be aware of your surroundings. Never let your guard down. Women are vulnerable. Women with money? We have freaking targets on our backs.

Though Destry had better reason than Calder, Andi, or Bryce to be overly cautious, her words of warning applied to them all. The Benedict name meant a life of comfort and privilege. And—unfortunately—a certain amount of danger.

"You aren't kidnapping me. Are you?"

Now was hardly the time to ask. If Adam's motives were nefarious, Calder was already in trouble. She wasn't worried. Not really. Still...

"Seriously?" Adam smiled. However, when he looked into Calder's eyes, her slight concern must have come through. His expression turned thoughtful. "Has someone tried to kidnap you?"

Calder shrugged. She didn't share personal family business with anyone. Especially when the information concerned one of her sisters.

"You're safe with me. Always." Adam's gaze deepened into an intense blue. "I will never hurt you, Calder."

Foolish or not—Destry would fall on the side of foolish—Calder believed him.

"I don't expect you to trust me." Adam touched her cheek—ever so lightly. "Not now. Hopefully you will. When you know me better."

Calder didn't point out the obvious. Trust didn't happen overnight. She and Adam had barely entered phase one of something she refused to define. Relationships weren't her forte. Lovers she could handle—temporarily. Friends. Sure. Though she didn't have many of the male variety. None she would categorize as close.

Maybe Adam would be one of the few. Maybe not. Time would tell. Calder tightened her hand on Adam's arm. Trust—of a sort.

"For now, let's have dinner. I'm hungry." Cars lined the street. However, the building didn't inspire hope of culinary excellence. "Are you sure you have the right place?"

Without a word, Adam gave the door a firm rap. Whimsically, Calder expected a hidden window to open. Shadowed eyes. A whispered password. She had to admit she was a little disappointed when they were allowed to enter with little fanfare.

A large man sporting a goatee shook Adam's hand. His honey-colored skin was set off by a stark white shirt and an equally bright smile.

"Brother."

"Good to see you, Hisham." The handshake became a hug. "You look well."

"I am. As you would know if you came by more often."

"My days and nights aren't always my own."

"Business is good." A statement, not a question. Hisham's gaze moved to Calder. "Since you honored us with such a lovely lady to offset your ugly mug, all is forgiven."

The affection between the two men was hard to miss. Calder sensed a story. Another tale she hoped Adam would share.

"Calder Benedict. Meet Hisham Nader." Adam's introduction was simple. Then, as though he couldn't resist a dig at his friend, he added, "Don't believe a word he says. Hisham tends to exaggerate his charms."

"Why would I exaggerate when the facts support how wonderful I am?" Hisham spread his arms with a *look at me* pose.

Adam chuckled, shaking his head.

"Show us to our table before Calder wises up and asks me to take her somewhere the owner isn't such a fool."

Entertained by their banter, Calder took a moment to look around the restaurant. Square in design, she estimated the room contained close to thirty tables. Each filled to capacity. With so many people seated and enjoying lively conversations over amazing-looking food, she was surprised they didn't have to shout to be heard.

"The acoustics in here are unbelievable." Calder took her seat, her speaking voice at a normal pitch.

"Thanks to Adam, the walls are lined with the same stuff recording studios use." He raised Calder's hand to his lips. "Alas, I must leave you for now. But I will return. In the meantime, welcome to *Journey's End*. Enjoy your meal."

Calder sent Adam an enquiring look. Every clue to his profession was more confusing than the last.

"You soundproof rooms?"

"Not personally."

"I don't mind guessing games, Adam. *If* I have a chance to win." Calder sighed. "What *is* your profession?"

"For want of a better word? I'm a facilitator."

"*Please* tell me facilitator isn't a euphemism for pimp."

Adam let out a noise somewhere between a snort and a wheezing cough. He picked up his glass of water, downing half the contents in one cleansing gulp.

"Good God. The way your brain works."

"Seemed like a fair question." Calder didn't try to hide her smile. "I'll take your reaction as a no."

"*Hell*, no. And then some."

They were interrupted by their waiter. The woman had a job to do. Calder set aside her chagrin—for the moment—and ordered a glass of chardonnay.

"Beer for me, Layla. And an assortment of appetizers."

"Right." Layla batted her eyelashes—a move Calder hadn't seen outside a bad romantic comedy. "I know what you like."

"I've known her since we were kids," Adam explained.

"I didn't ask."

"You were curious."

"I suppose," Calder admitted. "One less Adam Stone mystery to contemplate from an ever-growing list."

"Mystery? Me?" Adam seemed genuinely perplexed. "I'm an open book."

"To the rest of the world? Maybe. To me? Like pulling teeth."

A spark of humor in his eyes, Adam waited while their drinks were delivered.

"I know a lot of people." He took a sip of his beer. "Interesting people. With interesting abilities."

Calder leaned perceptively closer.

"And...?" she urged.

"After I left the Navy, I—"

"Navy?" Now that she had him going, Calder hated to interrupt Adam's flow. But she had to ask. "When? How long?"

"Right out of high school. Five years. Hisham and I met during basic training. His dream was to take over his family's restaurant. After he saw the world."

"How much of the world can you see from a ship?"

"Not a lot," Adam conceded. "We had to wait for shore leave."

"Where you met the young woman and her incredibly flexible leg?"

Adam shrugged.

"I'll tell you about her—"

"Another time?"

"Exactly."

Calder had no one to blame but herself. Normally, she wanted to get from point A to point B in the shortest amount of time. Straight to the point. Not with Adam. She wanted to know everything. All at once. The journey had become jumbled. And a hell of a lot of fun.

"Where were we?" Apparently, Adam was as turned around as she was. And, if his smile was any indication, just as entertained.

"Hm." Calder paused, thinking. "Interesting people with interesting abilities."

"Unlike Hisham, I couldn't see my future. The Navy seemed like as good a place to look as any." Adam gazed at his half-full glass of beer. "In retrospect, not so much."

"Why?"

"The military wasn't a good fit. Don't get me wrong. I learned some things. Grew up quite a bit. Met great people. And some flat-out assholes."

When Calder laughed, Adam joined her.

"No matter where you go, assholes are impossible to avoid," she said.

The arrival of their appetizers came at a natural break in Adam's story. Calder filled her plate with stuffed mushrooms and reminded herself to leave room for the main course.

As she washed down a delicious bite with a cool mouthful of wine, she gently encouraged Adam to continue.

"You were what? Twenty-three when you left the Navy?"

"Around there." He nodded. "Unfortunately, for all my world travels, I came home the same way I left. At loose ends. Until I ran into my old friend Hisham."

Adam went on to explain. Hisham *had* taken over his family's restaurant. And ready to start some renovations. A fresh new look for a new generation. The biggest problem? For as long as he could remember customers complained about the noise. They couldn't talk to the person next to them without shouting.

"I knew a soundproofing specialist."

"One of your interesting friends with an interesting ability?"

"You *did* listen." Adam clinked his glass against Calder's.

"To every word."

Adam didn't comment. However, the look he gave her sent a burst of heat through Calder's veins.

"Hisham was so pleased with my recommendation, he wanted to pay me a finder's fee. I laughed off the idea. Just one friend helping another. I didn't give the incident a second thought. Until Hisham asked me to hook his cousin up with a reliable plumber. The cousin told his brother. The brother mentioned me to his wife. She told her book club."

"And a facilitator was born."

"Better than the living I make? I genuinely enjoy what I do."

Adam's contentment showed in the relaxed set of his shoulders and easy smile.

Delighted by his story and his company, Calder popped another mushroom into her mouth without thinking. Oh, well. If she couldn't finish her entrée, she'd take the leftovers home for the neighbor's cat.

"You're a very handsome man." Calder saw no reason to keep her opinion to herself. The truth was right in front of her. She liked looking. A lot. Why not let Adam know?

"Are you flirting with me again, Ms. Benedict?"

"I never stopped, Mr. Stone."

Candles flickered around them. A nice touch of romantic ambiance. Calder heartily approved. The muted light enveloped them like a cocoon. They could have been anywhere. At that moment as the conversation turned to talk about movies, music, television—the kinds of things people all over the world discussed on a first date—the other diners ceased to exist.

The bill paid, they said good night to Hisham. They had too much to say, too many questions to ask and answer. Rather than a stroll in companionable after-meal silence, they walked and talked through the restaurant. Across the street. To Adam's parked car.

"Kris Kristofferson."

"Really?"

"He's a genius.

"Your favorite songwriter is Kris Kristofferson?"

"*Help Me Make It Through the Night. Me and Bobby McGee. For the Good Times.*" Calder ticked off the song titles with ease. "Listen to *Jody and the Kid.* I dare you not to tear up. I do. Every time."

"I'll download a copy. But I won't cry."

"Too manly?" Calder teased.

"Exactly."

Adam didn't stop by the passenger door. He walked until they were on the sidewalk, safe from traffic. With skill—and her cooperation—he maneuvered her until her back was flush with the car. Adam rested his hands on the roof, effectively trapping Calder between his outstretched arms. Their bodies remained inches apart. Not even their clothing brushed. Yet, the heat of him enveloped her. The whisper of his breath close to her ear sent a shiver of need across her skin.

Calder's fingers curled into a ball. Every instinct screamed to touch him. But if she started, she didn't know if she could stop.

"When I was a teenager, I wanted to own something fast, expensive, and foreign." Adam's lips brushed the sensitive curve of Calder's neck. She gasped with pleasure. "I closed my eyes. Imagined a hot car and a hotter woman draped over the hood."

Teenage fantasies were intense. And lasting. Calder had experienced a few of her own. The sidewalk was dimly lit. The foot traffic non-existent. If Adam wanted to fulfill a dream from his youth, she would gladly play her part.

"What did she have on?"

"Varied. Sometimes a tank top and pair of cutoffs. You know, with the frayed hem? Tight. Short. The kind that showed off her long, long legs."

Adam's kisses remained light as he peeled away the fabric of her jacket to expose more skin. Grateful for the two tons of solid steel at her back, Calder felt her bones melt.

"What did she wear the rest of the time?"

Against her shoulder, Calder felt Adam's lips curve upward.

"Nothing but a tan and a *come and get me* smile."

The sound of voices—not Adam's—broke through the building sexual haze he'd expertly weaved around her.

"Are they close?" Calder cared if someone saw them. Though not enough to lift her eyelids. She'd let Adam check the location of the unwanted intruders.

"Close enough."

Adam straightened. His sigh of regret echoed Calder's sentiments exactly.

"Fun's over."

"For now."

Cautiously, Calder shifted from one foot to the other. Four-inch heels and wobbly legs were a recipe for disaster. When she was certain she wouldn't land on her face, she let Adam help her into the car.

"We could go for a drink. Dancing. Or..." Adam let the car idle as he gazed at her through half-closed lids. "Did I mention my apartment is only a few blocks away?"

Calder felt a wave of genuine disappointment. Many times, a man had asked her back to his place at the end of a date. The last time she said yes? No idea. Over the years, she'd used every excuse in the book to say no. And then some. Tonight, when she had a legitimate reason, all she wanted was to say yes. The irony wasn't lost on her.

"If I didn't have an extra early plane to catch, I might ask you to show me your apartment."

"Business trip?"

Calder nodded. She watched as Adam linked his fingers with hers. She had quickly become a fan of his touch. Just the way his thumb caressed the back of her wrist was enough to make her long for a fogged-in airport.

"When will you be back?"

"Monday."

Adam's gaze rose from their linked hands to meet hers.

"Early enough for us to have dinner?"

"Sounds like a plan. Except *I'll* pick *you* up." Calder knew the perfect place. One of her favorites she was certain Adam would enjoy. "Dinner will be my treat."

"Okay. But I warn you. Just because you buy me a meal doesn't mean I'll put out."

With a wink, Adam glanced at the street before he eased his foot down on the gas. Laughing, Calder buckled her seatbelt. Whether he put out or not—her money was on a big, enthusiastic yes—she knew one thing. Monday couldn't get here soon enough.

CHAPTER SEVEN

OVER AN EARLY breakfast, Calder visited with Bryce and Andi. She appreciated the barely post-dawn company. Though getting up hadn't been a hardship for her sisters. Unlike Calder, both were early risers. Their presence gave her a chance to grouse to something other than an empty room.

"Tell me again why I let you talk me into such an early flight? My first meeting isn't until afternoon."

Andi yawned. As usual, her hair was combed, her robe perfectly pressed, her skin glowing. In other words, better than anybody who'd just rolled out of bed had the right to look.

"The airlines don't care about your schedule. Check-in is always a nightmare. Your plane could be delayed. And what if you have to wait on the tarmac after your flight lands? Trust me, two hours early is always better than a minute late."

Andi was big on schedules and didn't appreciate when hers was disrupted.

"We need to revisit the idea of a private jet," Bryce declared as she set her breakfast on the counter.

Because Mrs. Finch slept in on Mondays, the one morning of the week she allowed herself the luxury, they had to fend for themselves. Coffee only for Andi. A huge bowl of cereal, a homemade sourdough roll smothered in butter, a peeled banana, and a cup of hot cocoa for Bryce.

Calder's appetite fell somewhere between her sisters. Since she'd missed last night's lasagna, she heated up a generous serving with the help of the microwave. Hardly traditional fare, the leftover casserole appealed to her right now. She doubted her stomach would complain about the unconventional hour.

"Our own plane would mean constantly fighting Billie for flying time. She would look on the purchase as her own personal toy. Paris. London. Los Angeles. Sydney. She'd never be home."

The second the words were out of her mouth, Calder realized the *real* advantage of a private jet.

"I vote yes."

Bryce laughed.

"Or, we buy the plane and don't tell darling Mother."

"Either way, we'd have to clear the purchase with Bertram Tresbaum."

By the terms their grandfather's will, only the approved trustee had the power to release funds not already allocated to Thomas Benedict's female heirs. If they were men, they could have burned hundred-dollar bills, and nobody would have the power to stop them.

Dear old granddad fanatically believed women needed constant supervision. In all aspects of their lives, but especially with anything that involved money.

"Mr. Tresbaum is surprisingly liberal minded." Though they had all met the lawyer, Andi dealt with him the most. "He must have kept his opinions on women to himself whenever Grandfather was around."

"Even if we get the money, we can't have a plane ready today," Bryce pointed out. "For now, Calder is stuck with commercial travel."

Calder sighed. She wasn't a huge fan of flying. She'd considered taking the train to Chicago. But she wanted to get there and get back as quickly as possible. Train travel meant an investment of time she didn't have to give. A plane was her only option.

"Tell us about your date with the hunky painter." Bryce peeled her banana, taking a bite. "Or is he a bouncer?"

"Turns out Adam's job is much more intriguing."

As she polished off her lasagna, Calder clued in Bryce and Andi the same way Adam explained to her.

"You have to admire a man who carves out an occupation where none existed," Andi said.

"One where he gets to be his own boss."

Calder smiled at Bryce's comment. Her sister had worked for someone else. Once. When she was a teenager and wanted some *real-world* knowledge to add color to her writing. The experience didn't last long. Or end well. For the sake of the workforce in general, she decided to gain whatever color she needed where she didn't have to take orders.

"Aside from his interesting job, what about Adam Stone the man? Good name by the way." After years of searching high and low for character names—harder than the average reader could imagine—Bryce had developed an ear for the perfect combination of monikers. "Is he second date worthy?"

"We've already made plans."

"Really?" Andi and Bryce exchanged surprised looks. "You usually wait until you've had time to mull over the evening."

Andi and Bryce did the same. They took their time. Evaluated if the man in question was worth a few more hours of their time. Life was short. Why waste another hour or two—hers *and* his—with someone they already knew was a dud? As for their baby sister? Destry didn't date. She had *encounters*—her words. Short. Sometimes sweet. But she would never qualify what she did as a *date*.

"The entire evening with Adam felt like a long, slow seduction. And believe me, I was with him all the way. We teased. Flirted."

Calder described what happened after dinner when she and Adam reached his car.

"You canoodled." Andi sounded impressed. "Color me a trifle envious."

"Me, too." Bryce nodded. "I can't remember the last time I had a good canoodle."

Once more, her sisters proved why she always told them everything. They understood. And knew exactly the right things to say.

"Adam walked me to the door."

"Describe the kiss." Bryce reached for her ever-present notepad. "And don't leave out a single detail."

"We didn't kiss."

Calder had expected Adam to take her into his arms. Anticipated. Wanted. When he brought her hand to his cheek, his lips brushed her palm. The intensity in his deep-blue eyes took her breath away. She swayed toward him. He backed away.

"Adam said he would see me Monday night."

"And…?" Bryce gripped her pencil, though she hadn't written a word.

"He left."

Andi's eyes narrowed suspiciously.

"Power play?"

Calder shook her head. She understood why Andi would ask. Sister looking out for sister.

"All our lives we've witnessed certified masters at relationship machinations. Billie. Our fathers. We've seen almost every trick in the book. Adam's different."

"For your sake, I hope you're right." Bryce squeezed Calder's hand. "In the meantime, enjoy Adam's company. If things get serious—"

"Whoa!" Calder didn't do serious. "I like Adam. He's fun. And sexy. Nothing more."

"In other words, we shouldn't print the wedding invitations?" Bryce teased.

"A weekend on a tropical beach is as much of a commitment as I can handle. No invitations necessary."

"Amen." Bryce raised her hands.

"Unfortunately, one member of the family loves to say *I do*," Andi reminded them. "Billie left a note under my door. She's gone away with Ingo Hunter. Some golf resort in Florida he might invest in. He wants her opinion before he makes a final decision."

Neither Calder nor Bryce commented on how much Billie's opinion was worth on a business deal. What was the point? In truth? Their mother was a smart woman. When she wanted to be.

Instead, she purposefully filled her head with fluff designed to block out what she considered boring day-to-day trivialities. Unless Ingo Hunter wanted advice on the latest in wallpaper, he was out of luck.

"Billie didn't mention anything about a trip when we spoke last night. I tried to draw her out. For once, she seemed almost circumspect."

"Last minute, so the note says." Andi tucked a stray lock of blond hair behind her ear. "She's safe enough. I suppose."

"Hunter's reputation is skeevy. But I haven't heard any rumors he abuses women."

"Rumors can be squashed with enough money and intimidation."

The wonderfully familiar voice came from behind them.

"Destry!"

Calder rushed across the room. She pulled her sister close. Bryce and Andi joined them. For the first time in months, their circle was complete.

"Hey. I didn't come home for the mush."

Destry was a classic grumbler. Yet, she didn't push them away. She held on tight.

"We didn't expect you until next week."

"My calendar suddenly cleared."

As Calder kissed the top of Destry's head, the smell of manure wafted upward. "Did you bed down in a barnyard?"

Destry chuckled, extracting herself from the group hug.

"My business took me into the wilds of Minnesota. Dairy country. Good news? Good conquered evil. I was able to hitch a ride with a farmer all the way to the Albany train station."

Good conquered evil. Destry's go-to description of her actions. She could have added dangerous, plus occasionally life threatening. Calder and Bryce had stopped asking for details. They couldn't talk sense into their sister's head, why listen to tales bound to haunt them? Andi was Destry's confidant. Though Calder wasn't sure how much information was shared.

Destry sniffed at the sleeve of her black hoodie. Her nose wrinkled.

"I need a shower. Long and hot. I will say the passenger seat in Mr. Hinkle's rickety old truck was surprisingly comfortable. Best sleep I've had in weeks."

Considering the way she'd spent the better part of twenty-four hours, Destry looked only slightly worse for wear. Her dark hair hung down her back, the thick, shiny tresses gathered into a messy ponytail—in some magazines the look was considered the height of fashion. Her jeans were torn at the knee, smudged near the cuff with what Calder suspected came from the back end of Mr. Hinkle's cows.

Her sisters often joked that Destry had the energy and determination of an avenging army. All housed in the body of an ethereal fairy. She looked as though a gentle breeze could knock her over. Good luck to the fool who tried. Under the deceptively soft layer of porcelain-colored skin laid muscles of iron.

Determined. Tough. Smart. Destry was also loyal, kindhearted, and sentimental. Traits she carefully kept hidden except when surrounded by the safety of home and her sisters.

No one asked why Destry didn't catch the train to New York. Or hop a flight. Commercial transportation frowned on passengers with weapons. Even when the object in question was fully licensed.

"What did Mr. Hinkle say about your gun?" Calder tossed Destry a bottle of water from the refrigerator.

"Are you kidding? He was thrilled. Extra protection."

"From what? Cow hijackers?"

Andi snickered at the idea.

"Laugh all you want. You'd be surprised what happens on the highways and byways of our fair country. An open road. Late at night. Mr. Hinkle had some stories you wouldn't believe." Destry emptied the bottle without coming up for air. "You should give him a call, Bryce. *Danger on the interstate*. Might make a good book."

"Text me his number. What?" Bryce met Andi's surprised gaze. "I keep a file of potential storylines on my computer. A nice backup in case my personal well of ideas ever runs dry."

"Damn." Calder looked at her phone. "My ride to the airport is two minutes out. Promise you'll be here when I get back on Monday?"

"Can't promise." Destry squeezed Calder tight. "But I'll try my best."

Andi and Bryce took their turn. A round of hugs and a trio of wishes for a safe journey later, Calder was on her way. As she always did when she knew she would be away for more than a few hours, she looked back at her home. *Where the heart is*. Today, the old adage never rang more true.

ADAM HAD A routine he followed most mornings. Five years in the Navy, five years out, he'd forgotten more than he'd learned. Still, certain things were indelibly ingrained.

Attention to detail. Loyalty. And the way his eyes popped open at five a.m. sharp. Late night or early. Rain or shine. Cold as a witch's tit or hot as Hades' balls. He didn't exactly greet the day with a smile—more of a reluctant grunt.

By nature, he would have preferred to sleep an hour or two longer. Adam would be the first to admit an early start had served him well in civilian life.

A five-mile run. Then hit the nearby gym. By the time he'd showered and finished off a hearty breakfast, his mind and body were humming. Whatever task fell his way, he was ready. He checked his messages. Sorted through emails. Returned calls. Most days, he was out the door by eight o'clock.

Adam made his own hours. Answered to no one. He was on the go, non-stop, by choice. If he wanted a day off, he took one. A week's vacation at the drop of a hat? No problem. He'd streamlined his operation to a finely tuned machine. The people he worked with were the best in their fields. Professional. Conscientious. Diligent. Adam made certain he only associated with business owners who believed in doing a job right the first time.

Reputation was everything. Adam had built his business through word of mouth. He didn't advertise. Clients came back to him—recommended him to their friends—because they knew they could rely on him. His office staff consisted of one assistant. Period. If a problem arose—on either side of the job—he was available by phone or text. 24/7.

Monday through Saturday, Adam rarely knew where he would be. He went where he was needed. Different was good. The moment he grew bored with his job was the moment he would find a different way to earn his living.

Sundays were different. Oh, he still rose at an ungodly hour. Worked to keep his muscles strong, his body healthy. His mind clear. What changed was his schedule. Once a week, for a few hours, Adam knew exactly where he would be. At his mother's place on Long Island.

A home-cooked meal was just an excuse. Not that Adam needed one. He loved his mother. Adriana Stone was the best woman he'd ever known. A single mother. Loving. Supportive. With enough steel in her glare and a rock-solid belief in right and wrong to keep a growing son in check. For the most part.

Adam didn't get through his teenage years without a few brushes with trouble. However, two things kept him from crossing the line from rebellious youth to an adult with a criminal record.

First? Just the thought of jail scared the crap out of him. His neighborhood was littered with ex-cons more than happy to share their harrowing experiences. Some of Adam's friends looked on the men as heroes. *He* thought they were fools. The last thing he wanted was to find himself barely pushing thirty, no job, no prospects—except another trip to prison. Certain he'd reached the pinnacle of his potential.

Luckier than most, Adam had a mother who would have cut off her right arm before she let him fall through the cracks.

Adriana Stone was the second, the most important reason Adam graduated high school with nothing more than a slightly smudged reputation. She was why he'd joined the Navy. Why he knew he could make something of himself. If he failed, he knew how disappointed she would be.

Adam could endure a lot without flinching. His shoulders were broad, his jaw like granite. However, the look he imagined in his mother's eyes if she had to visit him, a set of iron bars between them? Just the thought was like a sucker punch to his gut.

The old neighborhood had changed in the last ten years. Gentrification was the term used by politicians. The word fit, Adam supposed. Once filled with barely livable houses, vacant lots, and overrun with crime, the corner of each street sported spiffy new lampposts decorated with hanging baskets overflowing with seasonal greenery. Well-tended lawns graced the fronts of freshly painted buildings.

Adam parked his car in the driveway of his childhood home. He'd spent many a summer afternoon trying to keep the weeds at bay in his mother's meager flowerbeds. The window panes sagged but the glass sparkled. The result of an equal measure of pride and elbow grease.

They kept the place neat and clean. All they could do at the time.

As soon as Adam had some money to his name, he'd offered to find his mother a place in a better neighborhood. A spiffy new house with all the amenities. Adriana Stone wouldn't budge. She moved in as a bride. She was firm in the conviction she wouldn't leave until the day she took her last breath.

Faced with an intractable force of nature, Adam had the place refurbished. Top to bottom. Under Adriana's supervision, he gave her the home of her dreams.

Slowly, the entire neighborhood followed suit. Adam could breathe easier now that his mother could walk to the grocery store and back without fearing some thug might snatch her purse. Or worse.

Worse *had* happened. When he was thousands of miles away, unable to protect her. Or track down the bastards who put Adriana in the hospital. As far as he knew, their heinous crime went unpunished.

The woman who spent her life taking care of him had recovered from her injuries—on the outside. Through counseling and the help of her friends, she was mentally fit. She was a strong woman. And he loved her with all his heart. But he knew the trauma would always be with her.

Shaking off the weight of sadness—and guilt—Adam took a brightly wrapped package from the trunk. He always brought some sort of surprise. Simply because he could.

Today, a silk scarf in the colors of a setting sun. The routine was always the same. Because anticipation was as much a part of the joy as opening the actual gift, she would sit the box aside until after dinner. The smile on her face when she finally looked inside, whatever the contents, made his day.

Some might say Adam Stone was a momma's boy. Proud of the fact—to the bone—he didn't argue.

"Just in time."

Adriana opened the front door before Adam could knock. Smile as bright as a polished penny, she enveloped him in her familiar embrace. Her head barely hit him mid-chest. Though he couldn't remember the man who'd sired him, his mother claimed he'd inherited his height from his father. The many framed photographs she had displayed throughout the house of Brendan Stone confirmed her words.

"You look beautiful."

"I won't argue." Adriana laughed. She patted her hair. "A trip to the beauty parlor, followed by church, does wonders for a woman."

Adam closed the front door. Pausing, he breathed in the scent of home. *Lemon Pledge* and cinnamon. Plus, the subtle undertone of lavender. Her beloved husband's favorite fragrance. Each morning, Adriana applied a dab behind each ear. A lasting tribute to the man—long gone—who still owned her heart.

"Church I understand." Adam followed his mother toward the kitchen. "I thought beauty parlors were closed on Sunday."

"Donna Wilcox fits me in every two weeks. We catch up before services while she fixes my hair. And speaking of church. When was the last time you graced the inside of one?"

Adam let out a sigh. Quietly. So, Adriana couldn't hear. He would never tell her the closest he came to any form of religion was when he worshiped a woman's body. Not the kind of information a sane man shared with his mother.

"Dinner smells fantastic." Adam sniffed the air. "Pot roast?"

"Mm." Adriana let the subject drop. For now. "And mashed potatoes."

"Baby carrots and biscuits?"

"Naturally." Adriana nodded. She tied a crisp white apron around her slender waist, checking the progress of her meal.

Adam took his usual seat at the small wooden table. New and shiny, the kitchen's design was the same as before the remodel. Rather than replace the cabinets and countertops, the contractor refurbished them to their original glory.

No saving the faded Formica—who would want to—gleaming tiles covered the floor. A brand-new sink and appliances—after all, Adriana pointed out, she wasn't a fanatic. She loved to cook. For her son. For her friends. For every charity bake sale. Decorated in warm tones of yellow and cream, the kitchen was her favorite room in the house.

"Speaking of Donna Wilcox. Her daughter just moved back to town." Adriana set a cup of freshly brewed coffee in front of Adam along with a tray of crisp vegetables and homemade caramelized onion dip. "You remember Nancy. Pretty young woman. Light-brown hair. Trim figure."

"Great personality?"

Adriana beamed. She either missed or chose to ignore the sarcasm in Adam's tone.

"You *do* remember her."

With a snap, Adam bit into a liberally coated carrot stick. "Nope. Not even a little." Nor did he plan to remedy the fact.

"I know how you like to stop by *Ike's Bar* on your way back to the city. Why not ask Nancy to join you? Sort of a neighborly welcome back gesture."

"We aren't neighbors. And before you continue, I'm not interested."

"Nancy is…" Adriana's words faded away as she met her son's unwavering gaze. Sheepishly, she shrugged. "I knew you wouldn't agree."

"Yet, you had to try."

Adam wasn't angry. She hadn't tried to fix him up in months. Wouldn't try for several more. Since she never pushed beyond the first foray, he could live with her occasional interference in his personal life.

"I want you to be happy."

"What makes you think I'm not?"

"A man needs a woman." Adriana shrugged. "Nature's law, not mine."

Seemed to be a popular theme. Melvin's wife felt the same.

"Sometimes a man needs a man. Then what does nature have to say?"

Adriana didn't miss a beat. She rarely did.

"If you were gay, I'd set you up with Paul, Donna's son. Who, for your information, *is* gay. And single. And very handsome."

Adam laughed so hard tears spilled from his eyes. The woman was incorrigible. And he loved her to death.

"Maybe in my next lifetime." With a coughing hiccup, Adam wiped at his cheek. "For now, I enjoy the company of women. Plural. Of my own choosing."

"Fine." Adriana handed him a pile of silverware for the dining room table. "Though the more I think, the sorrier I am. Seems like such a waste."

"I'm sure Nancy can find a man on her own."

"You're right. You and Nancy wouldn't have worked. You and Paul on the other hand..."

Adriana's eyes twinkled, her lips twitching as she turned toward the stove. Grinning, Adam set the table. Where mothers were concerned, he hit the freaking jackpot.

CHAPTER EIGHT

CALDER UNDERSTOOD HOW to pour on the charm. Thick as cream and twice as smooth. A handy skill.for a woman who spent most of her time asking fiscally minded companies for handouts. Talent aside, she would have preferred to stay behind the scenes.

The business end of *Erica's Angel's* was where she thrived. Crunching numbers. Working to distribute funds. Watching as her efforts paid dividends for those who asked for a hand up, not a handout.

Honestly, Calder didn't mind the travel and the smiling and the shit she had to shovel. The Benedict name opened doors. Once inside, donors expected to deal with her, not an emissary. Passionate about the cause, her time was a little price to pay.

As she kicked off her shoes, Calder collapsed onto her bed. Her trip had been a huge success. She'd secured sponsorship from two major corporations and had another on the line. A few phone calls, a little weedling, and she was confident she would soon reel them in.

Tired, yet satisfied, Calder wiggled her toes, glad to be home. Adam's face reflected on the insides of her closed lids like the best kind of personal movie. Slowly, a smile lifted the corners of the lips.

She'd had an early breakfast meeting. Her flight to New York had been smooth sailing. Now, she had six hours to relax and get ready for her dinner with the handsome, sexy, interesting Adam Stone.

Calder weighed her options. All tempting. She could take a nap, though she wasn't sleepy. A long bath was a possibility. No. Better to wait. The closer to date time, the better.

Food sounded good. Days since she'd checked, the refrigerator would be filled with a whole new selection of Mrs. Finch's prepared goodies. Only one problem. With a sigh, Calder snuggled deeper onto the mattress. If she wanted food, she would have to move.

"Are you asleep already?"

Lifting one lid, Calder watched as Destry hurled herself onto the bed with a running jump—damn the consequences. The same way she traveled through life.

"Hello to you too." Calder turned to her side, head propped on her hand. "You smell better."

"Mm." Destry mirrored Calder, facing her sister, comfortable and relaxed. "I've taken a shower or two since our last meeting."

Destry wore what Calder considered her *at home* look. Gone was the ubiquitous hoodie, jeans, and black work boots replaced by softer, gentler items. Loose linen pants in pale gray. A silk tank in contrasting pastel pink, and matching oversized shirt. Bare feet. Her dark hair hung down her back in glossy, natural waves most women would have killed to possess.

Calder didn't think twice about the two sides of her complicated sister. She loved Destry—the rough and the soft—without reservation.

"Enjoying your downtime?"

Destry nodded.

"I have a whiff of a job. Nothing set in stone."

"Your favorite kind."

When Destry grinned, her eyes clear of their habitual cynicism, she looked like a kid. Carefree. Happy. Calder grinned back.

"How was your trip?"

Calder kept to the highlights. Short and sweet. Though if she'd wanted, she could have elaborated. One of Destry's greatest talents was listening. She never appeared bored. Or disinterested. Her sister *never* asked a question unless she cared about the answer.

"I'm so glad you're back." Destry sighed. "I needed somebody to talk to."

"Poor little girl." Calder winked. Only her sisters could get away with calling Destry little. Or a girl. "Where is everybody?"

"Bryce is writing. Which is as good as not here. Andi's at her studio working on a fabulous new creation. A wedding dress for some princess somewhere. I think."

Sounded right. Andi was in high demand. Her fashions were worn by movie stars, first ladies, and monarchs. Not to mention her newest off-the-rack line of clothing any woman could afford. If their big sister had her way—and she always did—the entire world would soon be dressed by *AB Designs*.

"Mrs. Finch is shopping. Billie hasn't returned from Florida." Destry's expression grew pensive. "Speaking of Mother Dear and her latest amour. Something you said the other day keeps sneaking into my thoughts."

"Remind me?"

"Hunter's reputation. What exactly do we know outside of gossip and our personal experiences?" Destry shuddered. "Yuk, by the way."

Calder's sentiments exactly.

"Until now, we had no reason to look beyond the surface."

"I wish we could forget the man exists." Destry slowly shook her head. "Billie's less than stellar judgment makes the option of blissful ignorance impossible."

"What's your plan?" Calder asked. Destry always had something good in mind.

"I've done some preliminary research. But to dig beneath Hunter's slimy surface, we need somebody who's a lot more tech savvy."

"You mean tech sneaky."

"Some of my influence has rubbed off." Dramatically, Destry clutched at her heart and sighed. "I'm so proud."

Calder felt a little proud herself.

"Andi and Bryce will agree. I say call whomever you know. The sooner, the better."

"I tried last night. My first choice, Minna Lister, is on vacation and can't be reached until week after next. My other friend, Roscoe, can help, but not until he clears his calendar. At least a week."

"Checking up on the skeevy is a busy business." Calder was impressed and disturbed at the same time.

"No matter what some of these so-called cyber detectives claim, a lot of them have the discretion of an alley cat. Whatever they find, or don't find, we don't want Ingo Hunter to know what we're up to."

"I know a man who might be able to help us."

Destry perked up. "Is he a computer geek?"

"No. He's a facilitator."

"Adam Stone." At Calder's surprised look, Destry smiled. "Andi, Bryce, and I did some catching up while you were gone. Naturally, the subject of your love life turned out to be a lively topic."

"Naturally." Calder rolled her eyes. Sisters. The fantastic, the annoying, and the gossipy. "Well? What was the verdict?"

"Impossible to pass judgment so early in the process. Especially when I haven't met him yet."

The shrugged-off remark would have worked on a stranger. Not Calder.

While experience had taught each of them to be wary of new acquaintances—hell, they had to keep their eyes peeled around most of their relatives—Destry took suspicion to a different level. Often a blessing. Sometimes a curse. As necessary as breathing. Destry *never* took anyone at face value.

"Well?" Calder's stomach slowly twisted into a knot. "What kind of crap did you uncover about Adam?"

Assume the worst. Never get hurt. The unofficial Benedict sister motto. Frustrated with herself for falling into the same old pattern, Calder buried her face in her pillow. She hated the path her thoughts automatically followed. However, letting go of past hurts was hard.

"Adam's a good man." Calder spoke the words with a firm conviction. Mentally, she crossed her fingers.

"You don't want to know what I found?"

Calder *wanted* to believe in Adam. Honestly, she did. However, she wasn't a fool.

"Tell me."

"Smart." Destry gave a nod of approval. "I didn't find anything problematic."

"I didn't think you would." The first knot in Calder's stomach loosened.

Though Destry gave her a knowing smile, she kept any comment to herself.

"I'll reiterate, my cyber skills are minimal. However, Adam Stone— Do you want me to give you his particulars? Middle name? Date of birth? Blood type?"

"You found his blood type during a surface dig?"

"General medical details are easy to access. Adam's health is impressive, by the way. And his teeth? Not a single cavity."

Calder *was* impressed. She ran her tongue over her back molars. Straight, strong, and all her own, she hadn't completely avoided the dentist's drill.

"Forget Adam's blood type. You know what I need to know."

Destry nodded.

"He's clean. But not too clean."

"*Too* clean is bad?" Calder asked. Boring, sure. But she thought a clean record was a good thing.

"Everybody has a bump in their past. A speeding ticket. Overdue bills. Credit card debt." Destry met Calder's gaze. "A police record."

"I was in college."

Youth alone was a valid excuse in Calder's book. The fact she and some fellow students were hauled in when they tried to free live test animals from the science lab—and succeeded—made her police record justifiable. Even righteous.

"Besides, my record was expunged after I spent the summer picking up trash along the highway."

"I never judged."

"Considering the things you've done, I should hope not."

"Big difference? I never got caught." Smug, Destry smiled. "Back to your boyfriend. Adam's bumps consisted of a few foolish indiscretions. Where he grew up, there were plenty of tough crowds he could have run with. For whatever reason, he chose not to."

Calder's insides settled—close to normal.

"Nothing illegal or immoral?"

"Immoral is a judgment call," Destry reminded her. "According to what I found, Adam lightly brushed illegal. He didn't cross the line. What we need to know, what you'll have to decide? Can we trust him?"

Adam and his damn blue eyes had a way of scrambling Calder's wires. Her judgment, usually spot on, was a bit skewed in his favor. Destry's digging helped. Tonight, she would do her best to keep an open mind. In the end, all she could do was go with her instincts.

"I'll ask Adam if he knows a good private investigator."

"Okay." Destry accepted Calder's decision. "But you didn't answer my question. Can we trust him?"

"I guess we'll find out."

JEANS. A PAIR of sturdy boots, good for walking. A coat of some kind to keep out the cold. Gloves—just to be safe. Dirt is a given. So, if your clothes are machine washable, you're golden.

Smiling, Calder tapped out her response to Adam's text. Poor baby didn't know what to wear for their date. Her thumb hovered over send. Then, decided on a last-second addition.

See you at six thirty. Sharp.

Satisfied, she sent the message. Before she could set aside her phone, she received Adam's answer.

I can be ready at six. Sharp.

Either he was anxious to see her. Or… Calder couldn't think of another reason Adam would try to push their date up by a half hour. She was flattered. And frankly, wanted to see him just as much.

Fine, she typed. *Six o'clock. But not a second sooner.*

A few seconds later, her phone chimed.

Six o'clock—to start. How late?

Her smile widened as she considered Adam's question.

I make my own curfew. How late depends entirely on you.

Somehow, Adam shaved several seconds off his last response time. The concise three-word text helped.

Bring a toothbrush.

Determined not to let him have the last word, Calder's fingers flew.

I always do. Been awhile since I've broken the seal on the box.

Calder tossed her phone onto the bed and headed for her bathroom before Adam could answer. She imagined something clever. Maybe a little sexy. But not too suggestive or arrogant. As tempted as she was, she would rather exchange quips in person.

The possibilities when she and Adam were face to face seemed much more interesting. And varied.

Steam poured from the shower stall in billowy puffs. Calder lifted her face to the spray and simply stood, arms to her sides as the pounding pressure washed away the scents of travel in particular and airports in general.

She had decided to give herself a break from family drama and enjoy the evening. Billie. Ingo Hunter. Private investigators. Trust issues. Tomorrow was soon enough to tackle the growing litany of headaches. Tonight, she wanted to have fun. With Adam.

No reason to fuss with her hair or makeup. Casual plans meant casual preparation. However, she refused to skimp on the time she spent on her skin. Moisturizing was an essential. As she smoothed lotion over her body, her thoughts drifted to Adam and his strong, gentle hands.

Masculine—like the rest of him. Long fingers. His palms sported just enough callouses to make them interesting. To spark her imagination. How would they feel against her arms? Her back? Her breasts? Gentle, yet firm. Sure. Knowing.

Calder set aside the bottle, chiding herself. Silly to fantasize about Adam's touch. Why get all worked up when the man himself was only a car ride away?

Ten minutes later, Calder was dressed and ready to go. She checked the contents of her tote bag. Wallet. Phone. Condoms—a modern woman was always prepared.

Almost out the door, she backtracked to the bathroom. What the heck. Just in case, Calder grabbed the bottle of lotion and tossed it into the bag. Right next to her toothbrush.

CHAPTER NINE

SPLAT. FROWNING, ADAM looked up just as a second drop of water landed on his head. Or rather, his face. He should have known better. Something wet landed on his head. He should move away before he tilted his head to check out the source. Common sense 101. A basic tenet Adam failed to follow.

And paid the price.

"Here."

Laughing, Calder handed him a large, square cloth. Red. Soft. Like something a cowboy would wear around his neck in an old Western movie.

"Handkerchief?" he asked as he eyed the unusually large piece of material.

"Technically, the term is bandana—according to my sister. Right now. For you? A towel."

"Thanks."

The overhead lighting was minimal. What at best could be termed the other side of dim. However, as Adam wiped his face, and the back of his head, and his neck, he easily identified more than mere water on the used cloth.

Grime and sweat. Mixed with... Blood? Adam didn't remember hitting his head. Or, perhaps he hit his head, and he didn't remember. Either way, he was more perplexed than concerned. He sniffed at the substance.

"Oil." He nodded. "Thank the Lord."

"You like when viscous matter ends up in your hair?" Calder looked amused.

When Adam would have returned the bandana, she shook her head. Taking a square of blue, she wiped off her own share of dirt and perspiration. "I packed more than one."

"Thanks again." He tucked the cloth into his back pocket. "And I don't give a flying leap about the oil. But if I cut myself, you'd probably insist on a trip to the emergency room."

"Definitely," Calder corrected.

"And I don't want to leave. Not yet."

Calder let out a delighted chuckle. Adam had to put her laughter right near the top of his best sounds ever list.

"Having a good time?"

He nodded. Though Calder had proved during the past hour she didn't need his help—the woman was intrepid—he automatically took her hand, helping her over a large outcropping of rusting pipes.

"We have to come back. Soon."

"Sure. But, you can always come by yourself. I'll give you Reggie's number."

Reggie was a small, wiry-looking man with a shock of orange hair and front teeth made of gold. After a brief introduction, he grunted a greeting. He hadn't said another word since. Their official guide—Calder's words. Or unofficial. Adam wasn't sure how many laws they'd broken. Maybe none. Maybe a dozen. He hadn't asked. Nor did he care.

One thing he knew for certain. Tonight was the best time he'd had in longer than he could remember. And the reason had nothing to do with their location. The reason was Calder.

True, Adam admitted to himself as they walked around the next corner. He was a man who appreciated his own company. Especially after the Navy where he'd spent months at sea crammed into small quarters with hundreds of other sailors.

What his fellow servicemen and women didn't have was Calder's never-ending verve. She raised the concept of companionship to a new level. She was fun. And funny. One didn't always go hand in hand with the other.

Plus? She smelled a hell of a lot better than any sailor he'd ever met.

And talk about full of surprises. If given a month of Sundays, he never would have guessed their date destination.

Calder arrived at his apartment—five minutes early. Beautiful to be sure, the woman who greeted him with a winning smile was not the perfectly put together fashionista he'd come to expect. Her clothing reflected the texts they'd exchanged. Faded jeans—not the designer variety—hugged her long legs. Her boots were scuffed at the toes, worn down at the heels. Obviously, they'd seen serious activity.

"I hope you're ready for an adventure." On the way to her car, Calder shot him an impish grin. "Where we're headed isn't for the faint of heart."

Adam had laughed, certain the endgame couldn't match the buildup.

"Don't worry. I'll catch whatever you throw my way."

Calder zipped through evening traffic with the skill of a race car driver. Her skin, free of the artifice makeup often provided, carried a healthy, natural glow. And her dark eyes sparkled with life.

"My advice? Don't try to field tonight's curveballs."

"What do you suggest instead?"

"Duck."

More and more intrigued, Adam barely winced as Calder changed lanes. She had some mad moves. Emphasis on mad.

Born and raised in the area, Adam had explored most of New York City. Visited every borough. Seen the highs. The lows. The in between. Yet, in all his twenty-nine years, he had *never* trekked beneath the streets.

A ride on the subway didn't count. Calder brought him to an area not meant for the general public. Or, as she'd said, the faint of heart.

Caverns and tunnels and weeping walls. Oh, my. The smell of mildew with an overlay of gasoline. A touch of moldering garbage added to the already dank atmosphere. Adam hadn't hesitated when Calder led him down a dark stairwell. She'd said they were about to embark on an adventure. And she hadn't been joking.

"You've been down here before?"

"A few times." From her tote bag, Calder removed two bottles of water, offering one to Adam. "Bryce set a book in the underground caverns of a fictional city. She wanted to do some hands-on research and dragged me along. Took me about five minutes to morph from reluctant companion to enthralled explorer."

"I understand completely. Wait. Bryce? Your sister is *the* Bryce Benedict?"

"The one and only. Are you a fan?"

"I am."

Adam had learned not to read a Bryce Benedict book before bedtime. Not if he wanted a good night's sleep.

"I'll let her know. Millions of books sold, and Bryce still worries her fanbase is going to dry up."

Adam had the feeling he'd scored some unintentional points in the pro column. He really was a huge fan. But where Calder was concerned, he'd take any leg up he could get.

"If you're game, why don't we have our dinner here?"

An electric sconce brightened the small area. Fairly rock free, the area was small, but would suit their purposes.

Adam watched as Reggie, without explanation, disappeared down the next narrow passageway. Apparently, their reticent guide had other plans for his meal.

"Takeout seems unlikely."

"Most pizza places frown on underground transactions," Calder agreed. With a flourish, Calder whipped a blue and white-checked tablecloth from her bag. "Exactly why I brought all the makings of a picnic. No delivery required."

"Do I tip you?"

Calder laid the cloth on the tunnel floor.

"In your case. I'll accept a kiss."

Her tone was casual as though the weather were the topic at hand.

Adam didn't give her a chance to change her mind. Three long strides and he had her in his arms.

"I plan to take my time," he whispered.

Calder dropped her bag. He dropped his water. Their gazes locked as she wound her arms around his neck.

"I plan to let you."

A man could easily lose track of the women he'd kissed. After so many years, so many sets of lips, the numbers blurred. In a heartbeat, Adam knew he would remember everything about his first taste of Calder. For the rest of his life.

Like silk, he thought. Her lips. And her hair. With a single tug, the dark tresses fell free. He let the metal clip fall from his fingers. Long, fragrant strands cascaded past her shoulders, over his hands, around his forearms.

A spontaneous offshoot of their banter, Adam thought the kiss would be light and uncomplicated. An appetizer, so to speak. To be continued at a more convenient, more romance-conducive location.

When he touched Calder, plans tended to fly out the window. When she returned his kiss with total abandon, Adam forgot everything else. The hell with light and uncomplicated. And to hell with the place. He held in his arms the sexiest, most exciting woman he'd ever met. They could be in a hole in the ground. He'd still want her naked.

Oh, wait. They *were* in a hole in the ground. Point proven.

Adam ran his hand up the length of Calder's thigh to the hem of her jacket. Underneath, he found a sweater which covered a t-shirt. He burrowed, determined to find skin. Nope, another shirt.

137

Layers were practical in a dank, dark cave. Not so much when all he wanted was the feel of her soft, warm flesh.

Just as he lifted the last barrier, Reggie interrupted them. For over an hour the man was like the Sphynx. Now, as Adam was about to reach nirvana, he chose to speak.

"Hey, Calder. You need anything else tonight?"

Adam let out a growl of frustration. *I need something*, he wanted to shout. *You. Anyplace but here*. However, when Calder's laughter vibrated from her chest to his, the tension in his body floated away. She pressed a kiss to his cheek.

"To be continued," Calder whispered. With a promise-filled wink, she picked up her bag.

"Thank you, Reggie." She handed the little man some money. From the way his eyes lit up, Adam assumed the bills weren't singles.

"Tell Bryce I'm only a phone call away. Any time. Day or night."

"Reggie has a bit of a crush on my sister," Calder said when they were alone.

"I figured."

"I try not to take advantage."

Calder kneeled on the tablecloth as she removed a plastic container from her bag. Followed by another and another. Fascinated, Adam watched as the number grew.

"How many people do you expect to feed?"

"Blame Mrs. Finch. I mentioned a picnic. She did the rest."

Ah, the indomitable Mrs. Finch. Adam met her after she called in search of someone to paint the second floor of the Benedict mansion. A friend had recommended him, the housekeeper explained. However, she didn't take anyone's word. Not when her family's home—and her girls—were involved.

Adam went through a thorough—but fair—interview process. Tea and delicate pastries were involved. He had wondered if the refreshments Mrs. Finch served during their first meeting were part of her test.

If he'd showed the least bit of reticence over the less than manly offerings, would she have shown him the door? He would never know. Adam was raised by a woman who loved her afternoon tea—and insisted her son know the finer points. As a result, he didn't blink when faced with the prospect of cucumber sandwiches and tiny iced cakes.

In the end, Adam had the job. And he'd gained a lasting appreciation for Mrs. Finch and her baking skills.

"I hope you like fried chicken and potato salad." Calder filled a paper plate. "Chocolate cake for dessert."

Adam chuckled. Good old Mrs. Finch.

"I can probably force myself to eat a helping or two." Adam's stomach rumbled. "Maybe three or four."

"No problem. Mrs. F. sent plenty."

Calder added a thermos and glasses to the laid-out bounty. Adam looked over Calder's shoulder as she continued to dig. At any moment, Adam expected her to pull a three-piece band from her bottomless bag.

"Where'd you get that thing? From Mary Poppins?"

"I'm an expert packer."

Without missing a beat, Calder handed him a cup of steaming coffee.

"You, Calder Benedict, are many things." Adam took a sip, sighed, and savored. "All of them interesting."

Calder looked pleased. She crossed her legs, taking a generous mouthful of salad.

"Tell me about Adam Stone."

"Nope." Adam had dominated the lion's share of conversation on their first date. "Your turn. You mentioned your sisters. I know there are four of you. Who's the oldest? Are you close?"

"You didn't Google me?" Calder seemed genuinely surprised.

Adam shook his head. The thought hadn't crossed his mind.

"Did you?" he inquired. "Google me?"

"My youngest sister did a bit of digging. Don't worry. I only wanted to know if you were a desperate character. Destry gave you a passing grade."

Adam understood caution. Knowledge was an important building block of trust. Without trust, they could be casual friends. Casual lovers. Anything more? Not in Adam's book. Or, he realized, in Calder's.

Whatever information Calder needed, he was happy to supply. Because the longer he was with her, the clearer his intentions. At least for his foreseeable future. Adam wanted Calder. How much, for how long? He didn't know. But he wanted to find out.

Adam took a bite of crispy chicken and sighed. Fantastic.

"I would love to know your definition of desperate."

"No criminal record. No overt ties to shady characters. No gambling debts." Calder shrugged. "Gambling is a major red flag. Especially for Destry. Your health was discussed. Clean as a whistle, by the way."

"I'm aware."

Before Adam could decide if his medical history was a line Calder's sister shouldn't have crossed, she shared a bit of her own.

"To balance the scales? I can send you a copy of my last physical. Spoiler alert. I'm healthy as the proverbial horse. Would you set this up?"

This turned out to be a compact battery-operated space heater. From annoyed to bemused in less than thirty seconds, he did as Calder asked. Adam flipped on the switch. Surprisingly powerful for something so small, he was impressed.

"Where were we? Oh, right." Calder sipped her coffee. "My sisters. You could say we're close. Very close. Mess with one, the rest of us will make sure you lose your ability to walk straight for a week."

Adam winced as a twinge of male sympathy zinged his balls.

"Andi is the oldest. Mother hen—in a good way. I mentioned Destry, the youngest. She's hard to categorize in twenty words or less. When you meet her, you'll understand."

When not *if*. Off-hand. Perhaps unintentional. Adam didn't care. He took Calder's words to heart.

"And Bryce? Older or younger?"

"Younger. By fifteen minutes. A point I lorded over her more than once in our younger days."

"Twins?" He tried to remember if he'd noticed a photo of Bryce Benedict on her books. For the life of him, he couldn't. "Identical?"

"The truth isn't a secret." Picking at her salad, Calder hesitated. "Bryce and I are twins. Fraternal. We shared a womb. However, we have different fathers."

Adam let the revelation sink in. He understood the basics, but he was hardly an expert. Two eggs fertilized at different moments by two different men. Reality could be stranger than fiction.

"So many questions. I don't know which to ask. Or which are too personal."

"I'll let you know."

From what he'd learned about Calder, Adam had no doubt.

"How did your parents find out?"

"The thing about blood types?" Calder sounded as if she were teaching a class. "Though paternity can't unequivocally be proved, a man *can* be eliminated. Basic biology. Still, if Bryce hadn't been born with a shock of red hair, the secret might have remained buried."

"Ah." Adam didn't need a medical degree to understand how recessive genes worked. "I assume red hair doesn't run on either side of the family? Who was the other man?" Adam groaned. "I didn't mean to make Bryce's life sound like something out of a soap opera."

"You aren't far off. Turned out, our mother had sex with two different men within a week of each fertilization. Her husband— my father. And her ex-high school boyfriend—Bryce's father. I imagine at the time the headlines were pretty salacious."

"And hard to ignore."

Calder nodded. "Luckily, the furor died down before we were old enough to read."

Adam refilled his cup. "More coffee? Unless you have something stronger in your magic bag."

"Wine or beer?"

"Not for me. For you."

"I don't need a drink," Calder assured him. "What seems like a mess to you, is simply my life. Bryce and I are twins. Period. We weren't torn apart by our parents' idiotic behavior. In fact, we're freakishly connected."

"Can you tell when she's hurt? Feel what she feels." Adam had a disconcerting thought. "When we kissed, did Bryce...?"

"Get a vicarious thrill?" Calder's lips twitched. She didn't quite smile, but Adam could tell she wanted to.

"Silly question?"

She patted his hand. "Since you're so darn cute, I'll give you a pass. And, an answer. My sisters and I talk all the time. About everything. Or nothing. Yet, there are times when Bryce and I are the only two in a room, and we don't have to say a thing. We just are."

"I think I understand." Or as close as an only child—happily so—could get. "One thing I need clarified."

"Only one? I'm impressed."

"You told a clean, concise tale, Ms. Benedict." Adam chuckled. "What I want to know is..."

"Go on," she urged.

"Isn't Benedict your mother's maiden name?"

"You noticed. Not everybody does." Calder held out her cup. When he'd refilled her coffee, she continued, "To know Billie Benedict is to never understand her. She's a contradiction on top of a contradiction. For a woman who can't spell feminist, let alone call herself one, she decided to take a stand after her first husband, Andi's father, filed for divorce shortly before she was born."

Thoughtfully, Calder paused. "Or, maybe she did the whole thing out of spite. With Billie, you never know."

Apparently, Calder explained, Andi's father had a wandering eye. A nice way to say he slept around. Women. Men. He wasn't choosy. One year into their marriage, ready to give birth at any second, Billie caught him with the downstairs maid. And outdoor gardener. In the upstairs guest bedroom. The maid and gardener were married at the time.

Talk about a soap opera, Adam thought.

"Billie kicked all three out of her house. She decided then and there to give her child the Benedict name. After she gave birth, I don't know if sentimentality won out. Or the pain medication. Either way, she named her newborn daughter Anderson."

"I don't understand the significance?"

"Billie's husband was Sterling Anderson."

Anderson, aka Andi. And the light dawned.

"If Bryce and I were born to the same father, I don't think Billie would have continued the tradition. However..."

"Calder is your father's last name?

"Give the man a cigar." Instead, Calder served him another piece of chicken. "Edwin Calder. Daddy number two? Dermott

Bryce. By the time the last Benedict sister came along, a short year later, naming her was a no-brainer."

Another light went off in Adam's head. Destry was an uncommon name. He should have made the connection sooner. "Miller Destry. Isn't he in prison?"

"*Was* in prison. Miller's out on parole. For now."

Adam sensed Calder was ready for a break. She deserved one.

"Didn't you mention something about chocolate cake?"

Calder sent him a look of gratitude. In her eyes, he caught a definite twinkle.

"You sure?" She held the dessert just out of Adam's reach. "After everything I told you, I thought you might want to run for the hills."

"I'm always sure about chocolate cake."

Her smile sent a slow burn through Adam's veins. He wasn't going anywhere. Not now. Not tomorrow. Not next week. How could he? Calder Benedict was in his blood.

CHAPTER TEN

"BURR." CALDER SHUDDERED. "Explain why the air feels colder above ground?"

They had just emerged from their underground adventure. Slung over his shoulder, Adam carried Calder's bag. The plastic containers were almost empty—between them, they'd polished off most of the food. Still, the canvas tote weighed a ton.

If Adam had realized, he would have insisted Calder let him carry the bag from the beginning. Not because he thought of her as weak or incapable. Hell, she lugged the damn thing for miles without breaking stride even once.

His mother raised him to at least ask a woman if he could help. Whether Calder would have agreed was another matter. Something told Adam her answer would have been an emphatic no. With a *thank you* added for good measure.

Since they'd started their underground adventure, a slight drizzle had started to fall. Calder was right. There was a definite chill in the evening breeze.

"We had a space heater," he reminded her.

"I suppose." Calder shivered again. "I'm not a big fan of cold."

Adam unzipped his jacket. In the way of an invitation, he opened the ends and met Calder's gaze. He didn't have to ask twice. Without hesitation, she walked into his arms. When he wrapped her in a cocoon of leather and body heat, she snuggled close.

"You, on the other hand, are hot." Her arms snaked around his waist. "On every level."

Calder's sigh held a note of contentment. And just enough of a teasing lilt to bring a grin to Adam's lips. Hot didn't begin to describe the path of his thoughts.

"Do you have someplace to be in the morning?"

"Depends." Calder kissed the line of his jaw. "Do the women you take to bed usually sleep over?"

"No."

"Never?" Calder tipped her head back, a teasing twinkle in her dark eyes. "You have your way, enjoy what they have to offer, then throw them out on the street? Shame."

"I've never kicked a woman out of bed in my life."

For one simple reason. Adam didn't take women home.

Understanding lit Calder's face.

"You always go to their place?"

"Usually."

What could he say? Adam liked his privacy. Yet, in a complete about face, he wanted Calder in bed. *His* bed.

Unquestionably. Truthfully, he wanted her any way he could have her. Damn the implications.

"Or do you rent a hotel room?" Calder teased. "Could get expensive. Depending on the level of your sex drive."

The drizzle had turned into a steady rain. The temperature continued to drop. Didn't matter. The second Adam's lips touched Calder's, they generated heat to spare.

"You don't have to worry about *my* sex drive. How's yours?"

Calder's hand slid down his chest. Wide eyed, her expression innocent, she toyed with the snap on his jeans.

"Whatever you have in mind, I can keep up. In fact, I might even lap you. So to speak."

The city of New York City wasn't keen on graphic displays of public affection. At the moment, they hadn't broken any laws. If Calder moved her hand a little lower, relatively innocent could quickly morph to X-rated.

"Unless you want to explain a charge of public lewdness to your family, we should go. Now."

Calder backed from his embrace. With a crook of her finger, she beckoned him to follow.

"My car is a block away. We can be at your place in twenty minutes. Fifteen if the traffic lights are with us."

Certain he'd never wanted a woman more, Adam used his long legs to eat up the distance between them. Without breaking stride, he took her hand. He didn't worry if she could keep up. If he had to, he'd carry her the rest of the way.

Calder's legs weren't as long, but she was fast. Just as eager, she easily kept pace.

"Did you bring your toothbrush?" Adam asked.

"And a few other goodies."

Parked near a lamppost, Calder's metallic-blue Porsche glistened with rain. The interior lights came on as she unlocked the doors. Adam walked her to the driver's side, opening the door. Gently, Calder touched his cheek.

"Such a gentleman."

"Enjoy the moment. When I get you naked—" A generic ringtone interrupted. "You or me?"

Calder glanced in her pocket.

"You."

"I miss the days before cell phones."

Adam glanced at the screen and frowned.

"Business or pleasure?" Calder asked.

Aurora Charles had nothing to do with Adam's business. Pleasure? Sometimes. Old friends, occasional benefits. They hadn't spoken in weeks. The last time they hooked up? He searched his memory. Months. Probably closer to a year.

"Problem?" Calder seemed concerned when Adam continued to stare at the ringing phone.

"Maybe." He'd soon find out. "Hello?"

"Adam!" Aurora screamed his name. With a wince, Adam moved the phone away from his ear. "How ya doing, lover boy? Need you, baby. Want your big, hard cock. Now."

Shit. Adam glanced at Calder. Head angled to one side as she eavesdropped, her highly amused grin told him she wasn't the least bit perturbed by what she'd heard.

"Sounds like your friend has had a bit too much to drink."

Adam begged to differ. Aurora wasn't drunk. She was blotto. When she went off the rails, she went all the way. Which meant she was almost certainly riding high on more than alcohol.

"Are you on Long Island?" he said into the phone.

"Nope. City. South. Maybe."

Voices and music filled the background. A bar? Probably a club. Aurora liked a crowd when she partied.

"Damn it, Aurora. Give me something. An address, even a partial one."

"Don't ya know?" Slurred, Aurora's voice dropped to an intimate level. "I'll give ya everything. Just ask."

Adam ran a hand over his face. Shit. The rain had become a downpour. The phone in one hand, he took Calder's arm with the other. Thankfully, she didn't resist when he helped her into the car. Before he could shut the door, Calder stopped him.

"Get in," she whispered. Adam nodded.

"Aurora?" Adam jogged to the passenger side. He was soaked, but he had more important things to deal with than some soggy clothing. "If you want me, tell me where to find you."

"*Diggers*. Oops." Aurora snorted. "Tripped. Bye."

Abruptly, the connection ended. Adam didn't bother to call back. He knew Aurora wouldn't answer.

"Damn it! Did she say *Diggers*?" Adam typed the name. "Never heard of the place."

"South? She must have meant Lower Manhattan." Calder started the car. "My guess is she's at *Clam Diggers*."

Before she could shift into drive, Adam placed a staying hand over hers. Aurora could be a handful at the best of times. Hopped up on God knows what? He shuddered to think what he'd find. He didn't want to drag Calder into what could turn out to be a royal-ass mess.

"I'll call a cab."

"This time of night? In the rain? Good luck." Calder wiggled out of her jacket. She tossed the drenched item into the back of the car. As she hit the gas, she used one hand to steer, with the other, she rung the water from her hair. "Even *Uber* or *Lyft* would be an hour's wait. At least."

"We're on a date. I can't ask you to drive me to another woman."

"You didn't ask," Calder pointed out. "As for the other woman? She needs help. End of story. Besides, I know a shortcut."

Adam buckled himself in. He would have preferred not to involve Calder. Except everything she said was true. The rain. The time of night. Especially Aurora. The sooner he found her, the better he would feel.

"Thank you."

"Happy to help." She shot him a sideways glance. "One question? How involved are you and Aurora? Obviously, she's familiar with your *hardness and size.*"

Silently, Adam cursed Aurora and her big mouth.

"We've been intimate."

"Okay." Calder snorted. Then outright laughed. "Look, I ask for one reason. I don't want step on another woman's toes. So to speak. If you're dating, or screwing, or whatever, on a regular basis, I—"

"We aren't. I mean we have. Obviously. Off and on. Had sex, that is. We never dated."

Adam had never attempted to explain to one woman his situation with another. He'd never felt the need. But Calder was different. How and why, he hadn't decided. She'd asked a question. She deserved an answer. Scrambled and scattered as the answer might be.

"I've known Aurora since grade school. We were friends. *Just* friends. After I returned from the Navy, we reconnected. We'd hang out. We'd have sex. Neither on a regular basis. Now?" Adam shrugged. "Tonight's the first time I've heard from her in months."

"Yet, you're the one she called when she needed help."

"She knows I'll come. I don't know what else to say."

"You said enough." Calder smiled. "Aurora's very lucky to have someone she can count on."

"Thanks. Again."

A bit surprised—one hundred percent relieved—Adam relaxed. Calder was quite a woman. A woman he didn't want to lose. She could have balked at his need to help Aurora. She could have argued. Or thrown a fit. Or simply left him to fend for himself.

Instead, she jumped into action. Not to criticize or complain. But to help.

Calder's touch drew him back from his musings.

"You're a good person, Adam Stone."

"So are you, Calder Benedict." Adam squeezed her hand. "So are you."

CALDER HAD AN advantage over the average Manhattanite. First, she'd lived here since birth. Second, to do her job, she needed to know the lay of the land. The best venues for events. The charity-inclined businesses—and those whose owners hid when they saw her coming.

Third—and maybe most important to help Adam find his friend—she'd started dating on the cusp of her fifteenth birthday. Dates which took her to countless restaurants, dance clubs. Taverns. Bars. And, when the mood was right, a few less than reputable dives.

Clam Diggers didn't exactly qualify as the latter. Though the difference was more a matter of semantics than fact.

Traffic had been surprisingly light. In less than thirty minutes, Calder cruised by the bar, eyes peeled for a parking spot. Busy night, cars lined the street as far as the eye could see.

She was about to circle back when a spot opened at the end of the block.

"Good thoughts and a hefty dose of luck." Neatly parked, she turned off the engine. "Okay. What's the plan?"

Calder could tell Adam was worried. Distracted. He'd kept his thoughts to himself during the trip, and she let him.

"I get Aurora. Hopefully with as little fuss and muss as possible."

"Okay. Let's go."

"I'd prefer you wait here."

Of course, he would. And good luck to him. Chuckling to herself, Calder opened the car door.

"Well?" She looked over her shoulder. "Are you coming?"

Calder didn't wait for an answer. The rain turned into a fine mist. More annoying than anything else. The layers of relatively dry clothing kept most of the cool night air at bay as she dashed from the warm car interior, toward the bar.

Adam was right by her side. Just inside the door, he pulled her aside. Music—eighties heavy metal—blasted from strategically placed speakers. The point was to promote dancing and drinking. Not intimate conversations. His lips near her ear, he still had to shout.

"I want to apologize ahead of time for anything Aurora might say or do. She tends to speak before she thinks. Especially when she over-imbibes."

"You're worried about my tender sensibilities?"

When Adam nodded, his blue eyes filled with concern, Calder's insides melted. Honestly, the man was seriously adorable.

"Find Aurora. I promise, nothing she says can hurt my feelings."

Though Adam didn't look convinced, he nodded, his gaze moving around the crowded room. One lone woman with only one set of eyes to find her. And too many continuously moving bodies.

The numbers weren't in Adam's favor.

"Do you have a picture of Aurora?"

"Maybe." Adam held out his phone. Calder watched as the images scrolled by. "There she is."

The photo was a group shot. Four men. Three women. Laughing, their arms around each other. A lake in the background. Since he wasn't in the shot, Calder assumed Adam had acted as photographer.

"A couple summers ago at a friend's cabin."

Adam pointed to a pretty woman with neon bright-red hair. Below average height. Curvy and buxom. *Interesting*. Physically, Aurora was Calder's polar opposite.

"I'll check the bathroom," she told him "Then circle back around. Meet you at the bar."

Adam nodded, albeit reluctantly. "Text me if you find her. Or run into trouble. Or... You know what? Text me every few minutes."

With a jaunty salute, Calder plunged into the crowd. Adorable *and* protective. The first attribute she could take all day and a month of Sundays. The second was fine—in small, appropriately doled-out doses. Adam didn't strike her as a hardnosed male chauvinist. More a cautious pragmatist. He might not like leaving her alone. However, he understood the sooner they found Aurora, the better. Separately, they could accomplish their goal twice as fast.

"Calder? Hey! Calder!"

At the sound of her name, Calder scanned the room. Her frown turned into a look of surprise when she found the source. Furiously waving a hand in the air, Milo Prendergast shoved his way toward her, oblivious to the nasty stares he left in his wake.

"Hey, babe. Good to see you."

Milo's greeting made Calder cringe. *Babe? Really? Ugh.* Even if their last meeting hadn't ended on a sour note, he should have known better. Especially if his goal was to get back on her good side.

"Interesting choice of outfits." Milo looked her up and down, his gaze critical. "And what the hell happened to your hair?"

For some reason, she'd forgotten why she knew about *Clam Diggers*. Now she remembered. Milo had taken her here on their second date. He thought he would impress her with his bad boy behavior. At the time, she'd chuckled to herself. Neither Milo nor the bar could pull off the vibe needed to qualify as *bad*. Wannabes. Both of them.

Milo, the epitome of preppy chic, looked like a refugee from a John Hughes movie. Without the time or inclination to trade fashion quips, she kept the observation to herself.

"I'm looking for someone, Milo. If you'll—"

"Who? Give me a name." Milo made a sweeping gesture. "Kind of my crowd, you know?"

Actually, Calder had no idea. Milo had always been an ass. Tonight, he took the term to another level. But what the heck? No harm in asking.

"Aurora. I don't know her last name."

"About five foot nothing? Humongous breasts?"

Relieved to know Aurora was nearby, Calder let the breasts remark pass.

"Where is she?"

"Table in the back."

Milo nodded toward his right. The best point of reference was a flashing neon beer sign. Calder texted the information to Adam.

"I decided to give them some privacy. Three's a crowd and all that shit."

Only half-listening as Milo rambled on, Calder read Adam's response. *Meet you there.* Frowning, she looked up from her phone.

"Wait? *Who* did you leave alone?"

"Aurora and Bridge. Jeez." Milo rolled his eyes. "I told you. They can't keep their hands off each other."

Calder's ears rang from the never-ending assault to her hearing. Maybe she'd misunderstood.

"Did you say Bridge Manfred? As in the drug dealer?"

"Shh." Milo cautioned. Then proceeded to shout his next sentence. "Bridge likes to keep a low profile on the whole drug business."

"Can't say I blame him."

Milo's news didn't send Calder into a panic. Aurora's business with Bridge Manfred had nothing to do with her. She'd clue Adam in. He could warn his friend. Or not. Otherwise, her job was to drive. And backup him up—if needed.

"Kind of a shame." Calder sighed when a chattering Milo followed in her wake. "I had my eye on Aurora. Sweet little package. Friendly, too. But I'd never try to step on Bridge's toes. He's my guy. *Bros before hos.*"

Calder had heard enough. She swung around, her eyes narrowed. Something was different about Milo beyond his usual clueless self.

"Are you high?"

"Nah." Milo waved off her question. "I did a little blow. No big deal."

Any amount of cocaine was a big deal in Calder's world. At one time, she assumed Milo felt the same way. *Wrong.*

Calder had no words. Stupidity often left her temporarily speechless. She took a deep breath and pushed on. Between the impenetrable crowd, and Milo's ass-hat idiocy, the trip across the bar took longer than anticipated.

Before she could reach her destination, Adam appeared, an unconscious woman in his arms. *Aurora*. The combination of a big, muscular body and grim expression were more effective than a battering ram. The bodies parted like the Red Sea.

"Aurora?" Calder inquired.

Adam nodded. "Let's get out of here."

"Lead on, Moses."

"What did you call me?"

Calder grabbed the back of Adam's jacket and pushed.

"Just go."

"Hey!" Clearly in distress, Milo's voice pitched above the music. "Somebody knocked out Bridge!"

CHAPTER ELEVEN

"CARE TO TELL me what happened back there?"

Calder glanced at Adam, sitting in the passenger seat as though they were out for a quiet evening drive. As though whatever took place inside *Clam Diggers* was an everyday occurrence.

Her gaze shifted to where Aurora lay sprawled, passed out. The backseat was small. She had Adam's jacket wrapped around her and a half smile on her mouth with just enough smugness to set Calder's teeth on edge. She didn't seem to have a care in the world. Or, more likely, she enjoyed the role of the catalyst which caused all hell to break loose.

Calder had never met the woman. And she hated to judge. Aurora was Adam's friend. He'd felt strongly that she needed his help. Which made him one of the good guys. As for Aurora? Innocent—for now. Calder considered the jury still out.

"Well?"

"Bastard was feeding her pills." With a grimace, Adam flexed his right hand. "Who knows what kind of fucked-up shit was in them."

"The bastard is Bridge Manfred. He's a drug dealer."

"A drug—? Shit. How the hell did Aurora hook up with scum like that? Wait?" With the intensity of a laser beam, Adam's gaze landed on Calder. "You know him? How? *Why*?"

Questions? Or accusations? The latter, if his tone was anything to go by. Calder felt her temper rise, then took a deep, calming breath.

Normally, she would tell him to go to hell. *Who* she knew, and *why* she knew them was none of his business. Because his emotions were at a heightened level, she would give him a pass—this time—and explain.

"We met at some party or other. He was introduced as a friend of a friend. Not surprisingly, at the time nobody volunteered how he made a living. I found out later."

"Right. Sorry." All at once, the anger seeped from Adam's voice—and body. Rubbing his eyes, his head fell back as if he no longer had the energy to hold it upright. "All I wanted to do was take Aurora home. Let her sleep off whatever she'd put in her system. Asshole had other ideas."

"So, you hit him?"

Eyes still closed, a slow smile formed on Adam's lips.

"Went down like a sack of wet bricks."

When Calder was thirteen and stuck with her father for most of the summer—the feeling was mutual—he took her to a boxing match at one of the big Vegas hotels.

Front row seats. Surrounded by A-list celebrities. Dressed to the nines. Glitter and glamour as far as the eye could see. Edwin Calder never went anywhere unless he could go first class.

The pageantry of the event had appealed to Calder. The brutality hadn't. After the first gush of blood, she spent the rest of the time with her eyes closed. Before the start of the fifth round, she left and spent the rest of the evening in her room on the phone with one sister or another.

His attention divided between the action in the ring, and his latest girlfriend's sizable cleavage, her father never noticed her absence. The next morning, the girlfriend was gone. As was the twenty grand he'd bet—and as usual—lost.

To this day, Calder didn't care for fights—professional or otherwise. Yet, she would have paid good money to watch Adam clean Bridge Manfred's clock with one mighty blow.

Her gaze left the road for a second, landing on Adam's hand. The knuckles were red and slightly swollen. And by his wince when he flexed his fingers, painful.

"Should I detour to the emergency room?"

Adam shrugged off her concern.

"Just needs some ice."

Calder raised Adam's hand to her lips. Carefully, she placed a soft kiss on each knuckle. Then for good measure, her mouth lingered. His fingers. His palm.

"Better?"

"Forget the ice. Your kisses are magic."

Adam's voice took on a gravelly quality that sent a lovely skittering of electricity across Calder's skin. With one last kiss, she released his hand—onto her thigh.

"The evening isn't going to end the way I'd hoped." Calder checked the dashboard clock. Quarter after one. "Correction. Morning, not evening."

By now, Calder had hoped to be naked, wrapped in Adam's arms. Rounding the corner of orgasm number two.

"No. Much to my discomfort." Adam shifted in his seat. When he saw Calder's mouth curve upward, his eyes narrowed. "Go ahead and laugh. My condition is all on you. Kissing my hand with those unbelievably soft lips. How'd you think I would react?"

"My touch was meant to be strictly medicinal. I have no control over how your body responds."

Adam's hand moved along the length of Calder's thigh. A light, subtle, relatively innocent caress. Yet, diabolical. If he wanted her to suffer with him, he'd achieved his goal. Their thoughts wandered down the same path. A path—for now—that led to nowhere.

"I was afraid you might have changed your mind."

Calder frowned.

"Why?"

"You didn't sign on for a bar fight."

"Does one punch constitute a fight?" Calder teased.

Adam chuckled. A good sound. He'd regained some of his earlier good humor.

"As you said, the evening hasn't ended the way either of us expected."

"Instead of sex with me, you helped a friend." Hardly a difficult choice in Calder's book. "Should I be angry?"

Adam shook his head.

"I've known women who would be."

"You should rethink your taste in women." A twinkle in her eyes, Calder tossed the advice Adam once gave her back in his face.

"I already did," he countered. "The second I laid eyes on you."

Oh, boy. Trouble straight ahead. Calder's pulse jumped. Raced. Was she a fool to believe Adam hadn't just handed her a tried and true line? One he'd used dozens of times? Her instincts said no.

And if, for once, her never-fail gut was wrong? Calder would deal with the fallout when, no, if, the time came. For now, she wanted a chance to get to know Adam better. In *and* out of bed.

"Would you still want to sleep with me if I hadn't been so understanding?"

"Sure." Adam chuckled. "I'm no fool. Then, I'd dump you like a hot potato."

"Harsh," Calder accused.

"Honest," Adam corrected.

"Fair enough." Honesty was right at the top of Calder's wish list. What choice did she have? She put her cards on the table. "I want to see you again, Adam. If you feel the same?"

"Like I said, I'm no fool." Adam glanced out the window as Calder turned onto his street. "Next time, I'll shut off my phone."

"Next time, I'll remind you." She braked in front of the well-lit apartment building. "I have a few fantasies I'd like you to help fulfill."

"Fantasies?" With a groan, Adam cleared his throat. "About me?"

"One or two. Believe me, number three will blow your mind."

Adam hit the release button on his seatbelt, leaning close until Calder couldn't miss the interest in his deep-blue eyes.

"Now I have to know."

For a second, Calder was tempted. Everything about Adam made her want to throw caution to the wind. She might have taken the chance, given into the impulse. Except she remembered just in time they weren't alone.

Calder glanced in the rearview mirror. Thinking back over what was said during the drive uptown, she should have considered Aurora's presence sooner. Just because Adam's friend hadn't moved, didn't mean she wasn't awake. And listening.

Certain Aurora's eyelids twitched, Calder shook her head. *Sorry, honey. The show's over.*

"My fantasies will have to wait," she told him. When he would have protested, she gave him a chaste kiss on the cheek. Then whispered, "I can come back later tonight. Seven o'clock too soon?"

Adam's smile sent her heart racing—and made Calder feel very, very wanted. He squeezed her thigh before he reluctantly exited the car. A second later, the passenger seat fell forward, as he took Aurora's limp body into his arms.

"Need any help?"

"I'm good."

You certainly are, Calder thought with a smile. After he closed the door, she rolled down the window

"Drive safe. The roads can get slick after a late-night downpour. Text as soon as you're home safe and sound. For my peace of mind."

Calder nodded. She pulled away without an ounce of concern as Adam disappeared into the building with another woman.

The reason hit her as she waited at a red light. Between the catacombs and when Adam had coldcocked a drug dealer, something unprecedented had occurred.

For the first time in her life, Calder trusted a man. The feeling was foreign. New. Would need nurturing like a seedling reaching for its first taste of sunlight.

And what do you know? As far as she could tell, hell hadn't frozen over.

CHAPTER TWELVE

DREAMLAND? OR SOMEWHERE between? The images in Calder's brain were in vivid Technicolor. Not the least bit hazy, but as clear and sharp as a bright summer's day. She smiled when she realized she wasn't dreaming. Who needed an altered universe created by her sleeping brain?

Without a doubt. Reality rocked.

Calder stretched her arms over her head. She felt good. No. Better than good. Hopeful. Oddly lighter. As though divested of weight she hadn't been aware she carried. She hadn't crawled into bed until nearly two thirty. Nonetheless, her body and mind were loose and relaxed.

"You look happy."

"Until ten seconds ago, I was."

Calder groaned as the mattress—supposedly designed to be anti-bounce—jiggled like a bowl of Jell-O. She lifted one eyelid. Bryce, fully dressed, smiling—damn her—lay facing her, stretched out on top of the covers. When had her bed become the go-to meeting place for her sisters?

"Come on." Bryce nudged Calder's shoulder. "Don't turn that smile upside down."

In spite of herself, Calder laughed.

"I love you, Bryce. I'd give you a kidney. Bone marrow. The last scrap of bread on my plate. My final dime. Imagine how pained I am, darling twin, to discover you don't feel the same." Calder peered over Bryce's shoulder at the illuminated clock. And groaned. "Just as I suspected. *If* you loved me a smidgen as much, you wouldn't disturb my sleep before the crack of dawn."

"Quarter to eight is hardly the crack of dawn."

"Depends on your point of view."

"My point of view says you better roll your butt out of bed. Pronto." Bryce rolled to her feet. "Sisters' meeting in fifteen minutes."

Sisters' meeting did the trick. Still a bit groggy, but interested, Calder sat up, rubbing the sleep from her eyes.

"Which parent did what? And when can we post bail?"

Bryce let out a snort. Half laugh, half been there, done that. Criminal on rare occasions, mostly self-destructive, at one time or another, each sister had dealt with their fathers' idiocy. As for Billie, she'd yet to find herself behind bars. But, they'd watched their mother's missteps time and time again.

Money could buy a lot of things. Common sense wasn't one of them.

"What is the scariest thing you can imagine?" Bryce asked in lieu of an answer.

A chill raced across Calder's skin. Her sister fashioned stories of psychological horror. Blood, guts, and decapitations? Child's play. Bryce understood the shadow creatures of the mind were a thousand times more terrifying.

When she asked Calder about the scariest thing she could imagine? The answer wouldn't be pretty.

Prepared for the worst, Calder took a deep breath.

"Tell me."

"Ingo Hunter. In our dining room. Dressed in nothing but a robe and slippers."

Horrific indeed. With an image imprinted in her mind no amount of soap would ever wash away, Calder pulled the covers over her head. She jumped a foot when Bryce's voice—low, creepy, and only inches away—added another layer of awful. Words were her job. She knew their effect.

"Billie's with him. Serving him breakfast. Giggling. Like a cross between a Geisha and a demented schoolgirl."

When Calder shuddered, Bryce gave a satisfied laugh.

"Awake now?"

"What do you think?" Calder padded toward her bathroom, grumbling every step of the way.

"My job is done. Fifteen minutes," Bryce called through the closed door.

"I'll be there."

Bryce didn't tell her where. Calder didn't have to ask.

LITTLE CHANGED IN the room that as little girls, they'd appropriated as their own.

The furniture, still old, still worn, was wonderfully familiar. Calder ran her hand over the arm of the faded sofa. She'd lost track of the hours spent curled up on the cushions with her sisters. Laughter and tears. Secrets and sorrows.

The room represented a huge chunk of their childhood. If they were upset when they entered, each felt a little better by the time they left.

Destry wrapped an arm around Calder's waist.

"I used to think magic lived in here."

"What changed your mind?"

"When I realized the four of us make the magic, not the room."

Calder nodded. "The Benedict sisters. Together, nothing can beat us."

"We should have our own superhero movie," Bryce chimed in.

She carried a tray filled with cups, and one of Mrs. Finch's hand-painted china teapots.

"A superhero would have been smart enough to take the elevator," Andi puffed.

Right on Bryce's heels, her tray was laden with a breakfast of sweet rolls, strawberries, and bacon. Mrs. Finch knew them well.

"Why didn't you take the elevator?" Calder took the food, setting the tray on the table.

"My schedule is too tight for a trip to the gym today. I thought six flights of stairs would be a good trade-off."

Never one to wait, Destry pilfered a berry.

"And?" she asked before she took a generous bite.

"I hate exercise. However, my thighs will thank me later."

Except for Destry, they all hated to work out. Yet, for one reason or another, they forced themselves.

Andi liked to eat. If she wanted cheesecake with her lunch, she refused to deny herself. As a result, she had to counterbalance the calories with some kind of vigorous activity. Like today, and the stairs.

Bryce had been blessed with a faster than normal metabolism. Curvy in all the right places, she ate what she wanted, whenever she wanted. Weight gain aside, she prescribed to the belief that a sharp body equaled a sharp mind. If her body turned to mush, and her mind followed, her writing career would be over.

Like Bryce, Calder was lucky. She could eat to her heart's content and never gain an ounce. Which would be fine if she didn't care about muscle tone. Or the fact every woman she'd met on her father's side of the family followed the same pattern. Thin as rails—until they reached a certain age. Practically the day after they turned fifty, they proceeded to gain a corresponding number of pounds.

Calder considered every mile she ran, every squat thrust she suffered through, to be pure preventive medicine.

As for Destry, she was a finely tuned, high-powered machine. Boundless energy from birth, extra pounds never had a chance to fix themselves to her. She excelled at martial arts. However, she liked to mix up her routines and would try everything and anything at least once.

Andi handed Calder a filled cup. She sniffed the contents and frowned.

"The consensus vote was for coffee," Andi informed her "If you want tea, you know where to find the kitchen."

"When did we vote?"

"While you were still asleep." Destry filled her plate, heavy on the bacon. "We all wanted mega-caffeine. Your opinion would have been moot."

Calder didn't bother to point out that tea had just as much caffeine as coffee—with more health benefits. Smart, educated women, they undoubtedly already knew. And couldn't have cared less.

Each picked their favorite place, settling in with food and drink. A bit of reminiscing was, as always, their favorite side dish.

"When we were little, our room was supposed to be a no-swearing zone." Andi's gaze landed on Destry. "The second you learned your first curse word, all bets were off. Mrs. Finch threatened you with a bar of soap—to no avail."

The memory made Destry smile.

"I can say shit in twelve different languages."

"Anyhow," Andi continued before Destry could prove her claim. "Ingo Hunter is worse than any curse word. Thanks to Billie, we need more than soap and water to get rid of him."

The earlier image Bryce had painted of Billie and Ingo Hunter engaged in a warped game of domestic bliss wasn't the way Calder wanted to start her day. Ever. Their home was a sanctuary, and through no fault of their own, scum had oozed under the door.

"Who saw them?"

Destry waved her roll, drawing Calder's attention.

"Burned into my retinas." She took a ferocious bite. "Hunter made himself at home. I couldn't miss his hairy legs. Put on some pants, for Christ's sake."

A detail Calder could have done without. However, one thing was obvious. Ingo Hunter spent the night.

"A trip to Florida? Now, a sleepover? Sounds serious." At least by their mother's past standards.

"Very little sleep. According to Billie."

"Come on!" Calder poked Destry's arm. "Too much sharing."

"If I must live with that disgusting bit of information, so do all of you."

"So much for my appetite." Bryce set aside her plate. "We need to make a move. Have you heard from your friend? The private investigator?"

"Busy." Destry shrugged. "What about Adam Steel? Trustworthy or a bust?"

Three pairs of eyes turned Calder's way. How she felt last night—even a few hours ago—seemed less clear when faced with her sisters' questioning looks.

"I need to get to know him better before I can say for certain." Calder hedged her bets. Which sounded wishy-washy. And, oddly, disloyal to Adam. Annoyed with herself, she decided to follow her instincts. "He's a good man."

"But can we trust him?" Andi prodded.

Calder took a deep breath.

"Yes."

"Good enough for me. Besides, we need the name of a reliable private investigator. Adam doesn't need to know why."

Destry made a smart, logical point.

"I think we should tell him."

To Calder's surprise, the words came from Andi.

"Why?" Bryce asked.

Andi must have sensed the disbelief swirling around the room. After Destry, she was the first to question and argue. *They shouldn't give a virtual stranger ammunition he could use against them.*

"We've decided to hire an investigator," Andi explained. "Information will have to be provided. The more Adam knows about why we need his services, the easier time he'll have finding just the right person."

"And, Calder likes him," Bryce added.

Smiling, Andi nodded. Her gaze met Calder's.

"A definite point in his favor."

"Do we need to take a vote?" Destry asked.

"Before we make a definitive decision, invite Adam to stop by. So we can meet him."

So much for Andi's unqualified support, Calder thought.

"You know Mrs. Finch already put Adam through her afternoon tea test?""

"I didn't." Andi tapped her perfectly manicured scarlet-tinted nail against the rim of her cup. "How'd he do?"

"She hired him," Calder said with pride.

"I'll talk to her." Andi wasn't ready to give Adam a pass quite yet. "Mrs. Finch's opinion is gold."

"Meaning mine is what? Pewter?"

"I didn't mean to imply anything of the kind, Calder."

"Save the patented placating tone for hysterical models and hard-to-handle buyers."

"My tone is patented?" Not the least bit offended—pleased would be a better description—Andi looked from Bryce to Destry for confirmation.

"Should be." Destry's lips twitched. "Damn effective, as I can attest."

"Don't ask me." Bryce held up her hands, the universal sign she declared herself neutral. "Besides, I'm so even-keeled, Andi doesn't need to placate me."

"Oh, come on," Destry scoffed. "Every time you start a book, you rail over your lost inspiration. Who always talks you down?"

"Huh. I guess you're right." Bryce seemed genuinely impressed. "Maybe you *should* apply for a patent."

Calder's sisters were the bedrock of her life. She adored each one of them. However, they tended to drift off subject with only the slightest provocation. To be fair, she could be the worst offender. And, they always found their way back on track. But sometimes? So annoying!

Taking out her phone, she sent a quick text. Warmth spread through the vicinity of her heart when, seconds later, she had her response.

"Adam's free at two o'clock. I assume all of you will be here?"

"Works for me," Bryce declared.

Mouth full, Destry nodded.

"Good." Andi set her cup on the tray. "I'm going to do some sketching in my home office. What are your plans?"

Calder's eye's narrowed on Andi's satisfied expression.

"I've been played."

"Played is such an unsavory expression."

"But accurate."

Andi grinned.

"Eventually, you would have asked Adam to meet us. I simply expedited the process. As you pointed out, we know each other very well."

Calder wasn't upset. More perturbed at herself for falling so easily into Andi's obvious, yet clever, trap.

"You're kind of spectacular." Calder hugged Andi. "Of all my oldest sisters, I love you the most."

Andi's laugh was warm—and equally loving.

"Why the change of heart?" Calder looked into Andi's blue eyes. "Trust a man? Really?"

"I finally hit the saturation point on self-pity."

"After what Noah did to you—"

"What did he do?" With a sigh, Andi's unfocused gaze shifted toward the window as if filled with memories only she could see. "He decided I wasn't the one he wanted to spend his life with. No crime there."

Calder had sworn a silent oath if she ever had the opportunity, she would tear a strip off Noah Brennan's hide. In her opinion, he deserved much worse for the pain he'd caused her beloved sister.

"Is crazy a crime?"

Andi chuckled.

"Should be. However, not in Noah's case. He... I..." Andi let out a frustrated growl. "I'm tired of the same old pattern. Poor Andi. Damn it. I'm not a victim!"

"I never thought you were."

Calder was angry. *For* her sister. *At* the man who'd hurt her. Andi was nobody's victim.

"I've acted like one. Three years." Andi sighed—as if she couldn't believe so much time had passed. "I haven't lived like a nun. But I haven't moved on either."

"Billie doesn't set the best example."

"About Billie. *And* my father. I must stop using them as a relationship barometer. I'm an adult. Time to act like one."

Andi's blue eyes blazed with more passion than Calder had witnessed in a long time.

"Where do we start?" Calder asked. Andi's energy was contagious.

Andi's brows shot up.

"*We?*"

"To some extent, everything you said applies to all of us." Calder nodded to where Bryce and Destry had their heads together, laughing. "Last night, I was positive I could trust Adam. This morning…?"

"Doubt set in?" With understanding and affection, Andi bumped her shoulder against Calder's. "Been there, done that. Want some advice? Though I have no right to give any."

"Shoot." Big sister's advice had never steered her wrong before.

"Take your time. Get to know Adam. Chances are, he's a good man. Some *do* exist."

"If he's not?"

"Heart's mend. Mostly." Andi gave herself a shake. "To prove my point, I finally agreed to go out with Gerry Norton."

"You're kidding?"

On paper, Gerry Norton had all the attributes of a winner. Good looks. Money. A New York City assistant district attorney on the rise, he made no secret about where his ambitions lie. Mayor. Governor. Someday, the White House.

Gerry never missed an opportunity to ask Andi out. Until now, she'd politely, but firmly, turned him down.

"Gerry is intelligent. Interesting."

"Slick." Andi's word, not Calder's. Though she had to agree.

"On the surface, yes," Andi conceded. "I've decided to look a little deeper. I might be surprised."

"Or, you'll end up with greasy hands."

"I'll let you know tomorrow."

Calder gathered up the dishes. Andi was right. They could all do with a new attitude toward men. Less cynicism. More hope. She wanted to believe Adam was exactly what he seemed.

Kind and funny absolutely. Did he have a hidden dark side? Something unsettling she had yet to witness? Time would tell.

Calder hoped Adam Stone didn't turn out to be a liar. Or a cheat. But she could take one thing to the bank. He was handsome, scorching hot, and boy, could he kiss. *Nobody*—not even the most experienced con man—could fake sexy.

CHAPTER THIRTEEN

"YOU HAVE FIVE minutes to get out of my bed."

Rather than bend over, Adam nudged Aurora's near-comatose body with his booted foot. Her response? A long, extremely rude, *fuck you.*

"Fine."

Unceremoniously, Adam threw back the covers. Aurora didn't move. He sure as hell wouldn't douse his mattress with water. Only one solution came to mind.

"Hey! My head!"

As he hefted Aurora over his shoulder fireman style, he felt her wrath. The ungrateful twit yanked on his hair. Hard. Determined, he didn't break stride. Time for some tough love. Both physical and verbal.

"Getting a little hippy, Rora." He patted the offending area. "You might want to reconsider your lifestyle. Alcohol is nothing but empty calories."

"Keep bouncing me around, asshole. I'm about to barf what empty calories are left in my stomach down your back."

Son of a bitch. Adam picked up his pace. In two long strides, he deposited Aurora onto the floor of the shower stall—right on her ass. He turned the water on full blast—nothing but cold. When the icy spray hit her in the face, the resulting screech could have broken window panes from Manhattan to Buffalo.

"If you decide to vomit? Use the garbage can."

Adam set the plastic-lined basket within reach of a still cursing Aurora, walking away without a backward glance. He stripped the sheets from the bed, dumped them in a pile on the floor, and left the room.

Small, compact, but serviceable—like the rest of the apartment—the kitchen didn't get a lot of use. Adam knew how to cook. Could put together a damn fine meal when the mood hit. However, he was a single man in New York City. Drawn by the energy and nightlife, he rarely stayed in to eat.

Breakfast was usually a quick grab. Cold cereal. A piece of fruit. Whatever was handy.

Today would be an exception.

Coffee first. Strong and plentiful. Adam reached for his cast-iron frying pan, a carton of eggs—borderline expiration date, but doable—and some bread for toast.

Experience was a great teacher. As nasty as food sounded the day after, the best cure for a hangover was a basic, rib-sticking, stomach-settling breakfast.

Aurora could—would—balk all she wanted. If Adam had to shove the food down her throat, she would eat every last crumb.

Stupid. Still fuming from the night before and Aurora's foolhardy behavior, Adam slammed the pan onto the stove. What if he hadn't been available? Hadn't answered his phone? A bad situation could have ended much worse.

"Do you have to make so much noise?" Hair wet, rubbing her temples, Aurora shuffled across the room. "Thanks for ruining my dress, by the way. First time I'd worn the thing. And the last. Jesus, Adam. If you had to drown me, couldn't you take my clothes off first?"

The t-shirt he'd set out for her was ten sizes too big and hit just above her knees. Matted-down, bright-red hair, and none too happy, Aurora resembled a hissing wet cat.

Without the least bit of sympathy to her plight, Adam turned back to the stove.

"Aspirin's on the counter. Be sure to drink all the water."

Grumbling under her breath, Aurora followed his instructions. Her reward, a cup of coffee. Filled to the brim.

"Bless you."

As she sipped the steaming brew, Aurora's gaze landed on the sofa. She frowned at the neatly folded blanket and pillow.

"You slept out here?"

"I did." Adam placed a plate filled with scrambled eggs and dry toast on the small dining room table. "Sit. Eat."

Again, Aurora did as Adam told her without argument. A definite first. Her hangover had to be worse than he imagined.

"Why?" Though she frowned at the food, she took a tentative bite. "Big bed, little woman. Plenty of room for both of us. We could have had a nice morning cuddle."

Adam had deposited Aurora in his bed the night before. He removed her shoes—nothing else. Even if she hadn't been the worse for drink and drugs, he wouldn't have joined her. They had always been friends. One day, they crossed the line to occasional lovers. He wanted to keep her friendship if possible. Nothing else. Not anymore.

"Look, Aurora. The last time we had sex was the last time. Period."

"Because of the skinny brunette?" She sneered around a mouthful of eggs. "Your taste is slipping."

The fact that Aurora had been conscious enough to notice Calder shouldn't have surprised him. Her hangover wasn't an act. But the rest? Obviously, she hadn't been as intoxicated as she'd led him to believe.

If Adam knew at the time, his actions wouldn't have changed. A woman in need was his weakness. A fact Aurora knew and exploited without a single qualm—damn her. Adam had to tip his hat. She took her shot and hit a bullseye. But she used up her reserve of goodwill. He was tired of her games. If she ever tried to pull the stunt again, he'd call the police and let them deal with her drunk ass.

"Nice car, though. Girl must have money. Or a rich boyfriend." Thoughtfully, Aurora tapped her fork against her chin. "Not a husband. You don't do married women."

"Calder isn't the point."

"Definitely a rich girl. You wouldn't find anybody with a name like Calder where we grew up."

"Do tell... *Aurora.*"

Annoyed by Aurora's attitude, Adam crossed his arms. She might not have a problem with reverse snobbery. He did.

"Nothing high end about my name. The Charles family doesn't have a pot to piss in. Hasn't for generations. Something tells me your Calder can't say the same. Dressed down, she still reeked of old money."

Adam wasn't about to argue. Would he prefer if the size of their respective bank balances were a little closer to equal? Sure. However, Calder's net worth had nothing to do with why he wanted her. His reasons—his feelings—were as close to righteous as he expected to get. And, none of Aurora's business.

"Finish eating. I'll drive you home before I head to work."

"You're going to haul my sweet ass all the way to Long Island?" Aurora perked up. "You *do* care."

"I always will, Rora. But—"

"Say no more. Have your little fling. Get Ms. Blue Blood out of your system. I'll be here when you're ready for some good old-fashioned, down-to-earth, home cooking."

Aurora patted Adam on the cheek before she walked away. Sad instead of interested by the exaggerated sway of her hips, he could have talked himself blue in the face, she wouldn't listen.

Calder wasn't the issue. Without marking the exact moment, Adam had moved on. Any desire he once felt for Aurora's body was gone.

Adam loaded the dishwasher. Another convenience he rarely used. Plates from a week ago lined the near-empty interior. Rather than wait until he filled the machine—which could be a month from now—he decided to run a wash cycle.

As he hit the start button, his phone chirped. Calder. He hoped like hell she didn't have to cancel their plans. Seven o'clock already seemed like a lifetime away. Another hour? Another day? Freaking torture.

Are you free this afternoon? I need your unique facilitating skills.

Relieved—and stoked—Adam's thumbs flew over the keys.

Two o'clock work for you?

He waited. But not for long.

You know the address. See you then.

Grinning, Adam set the phone aside. Seemed he would see Calder sooner than expected.

AURORA PEEKED AROUND the bedroom door, observing Adam. And his goofy smile.

Had to be that damn, rich girl. Calder.

Aurora hadn't let on, but she recognized the name. How many Calders could exist in the world?

One too many.

The Benedicts were a favorite topic in the gossip rags Aurora poured over while she had her hair colored and trimmed at *Harriet's Hair Salon.*

Calder. Her sisters. Their mother. More than once, Aurora and her friends envied their beauty. Their wealth. Their lifestyle. The bitch already had everything. Could have any man she wanted. Did she have to take Adam?

From the moment they met, Adam belonged to her. Always had. Always would. Her belief was unshakable and bone deep. Didn't matter if he knew or not. One day he would.

Adam Stone was her destiny. The wind-up Barbie doll? An insignificant blip. For now, she'd let him play.

Aurora's gaze hardened. *For now.*

CHAPTER FOURTEEN

AT TWO O'CLOCK sharp, Calder answered the front door. Adam waited, the sun at his back. Dark glasses covered his blue eyes, his perfectly tailored suit a reminder he was there for business, not pleasure.

To prove his visit didn't have to be one without the other, she didn't invite him. Instead, took his hand, guiding him into her home.

"Ms. Benedict."

Formal in tone, Adam inclined his head. He slipped off his glasses, the twinkle underneath unmistakable.

"Different suit." Dark blue with the thinnest of pinstripes. "How many do you own?"

"I lost count." Adam didn't take back his hand. Nor did he step closer. "May I ask a question, Ms. Benedict?"

Calder's lips twitched—just a little—as she did her best not to smile.

"Of course. Mr. Stone."

"Before we talk business?"

"Yes?"

Adam's gaze dropped to her mouth.

"May I kiss you?"

Happy to play along, Calder looked around, as if she gave a damn who might see them.

"If you feel the inclination, I don't mind."

Adam wasn't in a hurry. Slowly, he wrapped an arm around her waist. Calder wore a pair of strappy sandals, the perfect foil for her pale-yellow silk dress. The four-inch heels meant she could practically look him in the eyes without tilting her head.

"I'm inclined to do many, many things to you, Ms. Benedict," Adam whispered near her ear.

The heat of his breath combined with his words sent a shiver of anticipation down Calder's spine. She rubbed her cheek against his. *Smooth.* She sighed, breathing in the slightest scent of citrus.

"Please. Do tell."

"Like your fantasies, my thoughts on the subject are better left for a more private location. Now, about that kiss."

Adam ran his fingers up Calder's arm, over her shoulder, to rest at the nape of her neck. Strong, yet gentle. If she'd tried to move away, he could have stopped her. Easily. However, she didn't move. She didn't protest. Because she knew, one word from her, and he would have let her go. No questions asked.

Another kind of trust, she realized. Content to let Adam make the next move, she waited.

Then, his lips closed over hers.

Calder was never one to melt. Not under pressure. Not in the heat of the mid-July sun. And never in a man's arms. Yet, as Adam deepened the kiss, she would have sworn her insides turned to liquid. She liked the feeling. Quicksilver in her veins. Hot and dangerous and addictive.

"Hello," Adam said when he finally raised his head.

"Hi."

With her finger, Calder touched the corner of Adam's mouth, the edge of his smile. She hated to end what could have been such a lovely beginning. But her sisters waited. Impatient at the best of times, one of them was bound to come looking.

"Time to switch from pleasure to business?"

Adam sounded as reluctant as she felt.

"Afraid so."

Calder couldn't stay in his arms. However, as she backed away, she kept his hand in hers.

"We thought the second-floor library would be the best place to meet."

"*We*? I thought *you* needed me."

Sexual innuendo of a graphic nature popped into Calder's head. Too easy, she decided. Besides, they'd switched gears. Except for holding hands, overt flirting would have to wait.

"I'll explain on the way. We—"

Out of the corner of her eye, she detected a slight movement. Ingo Hunter. She should have known the second her skin began to crawl. How long had he watched from the shadowed doorway? The ever-so-slight smirk on his lips told her he'd seen everything and enjoyed the show. *The bastard.*

She gave Adam's hand a squeeze. He must have sensed her sudden unease. When she tried to pull away, he held tight.

"Calder. Looking lovely, as always."

The man had slept in her home. Eaten breakfast at her dining room table. Now, he strolled the foyer as if he owned the place. Calder's spine stiffened. Over her dead body.

"Ingo. I didn't realize you'd returned."

Calder had a hard time looking past the smarmy glint in the depths of his near-black irises—as though he pictured every woman he met naked. Yet, in all fairness, she had to admit Ingo Hunter could be called a handsome man.

Pushing sixty, his tanned skin carried minimal signs of the advancing years. Perhaps he and Billie shared the same dermatologist. The gray at Hunter's temples seemed a bit too precise to be natural—especially in contrast to the rest of his stark black hair.

This afternoon, he'd dressed his tall frame in casual attire. Tan slacks. A polo shirt which masked, but couldn't quite hide, the slight middle-aged spread around his waist.

"Actually, I never left." As usual, Hunter's smile didn't quite reach his eyes. "Billie kindly let me use your grandfather's office to make some important calls."

Amazing. In two compact sentences, Hunter managed to let Calder know he'd moved in on Thomas Benedict's former terrain. Plus, he slipped in a not-so-subtle, self-aggrandizing comment. Ingo Hunter didn't just make phone calls. Unlike normal people's, his were *important*.

"Aren't you going to introduce me to your friend?"

"Adam Stone." Adam stepped in before Calder could tell Hunter where to stick his introduction.

"Ingo Hunter." The men shook hands. "Have we met before?"

"Not to my knowledge."

"Hm." A speculative glint entered Hunter's gaze. "I must say, I admire the cut of your suit. Designer or off the rack?"

Mentally, Calder rolled her eyes. The equivalent of a dick measuring contest, Hunter's remark was meant to show his superiority. Both socially and financially. If he'd expected Adam to wilt under such an obvious ploy, he was sorely disappointed.

Smooth as silk, with just the right amount of casual disdain, Adam smiled.

"I never feel the need to drop names."

Nice jab, Calder thought.

"However, since you asked. My suit is an Andi Benedict original."

"When did Andi branch out into men's wear?"

Hunter directed his accusatory question to Calder. As if she should have kept him abreast of the situation.

Andi's new line—her first foray away from exclusively women's clothing—would hit the runway in September. Worldwide outlets by next spring. Calder knew her sister made some of her designs available to a select few exclusive customers. She had no idea Adam was one of them. A fact she didn't share with Hunter.

"I'm surprised Billie didn't mention Andi's new venture."

Hunter let Calder's dig slide. Though he hid his annoyance well, enough snuck through, in his eyes, the stiffness of his shoulders, to brighten Calder's afternoon.

"Andi is talented. In many ways. I look forward to personally sampling her *designs*."

The way Hunter suggestively emphasized the word designs made Calder's blood boil.

"We should go," Adam said.

"Yes." Calder managed the one word. Barely. She had a lot she could say. Another time, she promised herself.

"Until later, Calder. Adam." Hunter inclined his head. "Nice meeting you."

"Sleazeball, sleazeball, sleazeball."

Calder muttered the mantra under her breath as Ingo Hunter used his best *Lord of the Manor* saunter to leave the room.

Adam lifted their joined hands. Matter of fact, he pried open Calder's grip, shaking the blood back into his fingers.

"Sorry," Calder apologized. She started up the stairs. "I didn't realize I had such a stranglehold."

"Glad to be of service."

Adam's positive energy helped dispel Ingo Hunter's negative vibe. Calder breathed in the fresh air. When they eliminated the man from their lives once and for all, she would ask Adam for the name of a good fumigator.

"By the way. How *did* you get your hands on one of Andi's suits?" The story Calder handed Ingo Hunter had been completely off the cuff. "Her designs are guarded better than Fort Knox."

"I know people who know people who know your sister. My suit?" Adam paused with a playful pose, and then continued up the stairs. "A sample design she decided to cull from the final lineup. My friend texted me a picture. Half price. How could I resist?"

"Wow." Calder was impressed. "You really are a devoted clothes horse."

Obviously proud of the label, Adam nodded. As they reached the top of the stairs, he tucked her hand into the crook of his arm.

"About Ingo Hunter? I know the name. And I hate to judge after one meeting..."

"Yes?" Calder was interested to hear Adam's first impression.

"The man's a slimy creep."

Laughing, Calder reached to open the library door. If she hadn't been crazy about Adam before, his perfect, concise assessment of Hunter would have done the trick.

"Join the club."

Inside sat Andi, Bryce, and Destry.

"I assume your sisters are the 'we' you mentioned?" Adam whispered out the side of his mouth.

"Sorry I didn't have time to fully explain."

Calder wished she'd mentioned her sisters sooner. The last thing she wanted was for Adam to feel ambushed. Turned out, she had nothing to worry about.

"Ladies." Adam greeted each woman with a handshake and a friendly, charming smile. First Bryce. Then Destry.

"Nice suit," Andi said when her turn came.

"Seems to be the consensus." Adam gave a self-deprecating shrug. "I hate to come off as a brown-noser. I was already dressed and on my way before I remembered the founder of *AB Designs* is Calder's sister. Too late to change."

"No need to apologize." Andi circled, checking Adam out from every angle. "Good color. Good design. Modern but not too out there. I might have to rethink my decision and add the suit back to the collection."

"My vote is yes."

"Come on." Impatient as always, Destry flopped onto a winged-back leather chair. "Enough with the fashion banter. Can we get down to business?"

Used to her sister's moods, Andi calmly leveled Destry with a cool look.

"Fashion *is* my business. A fact you take advantage of on a regular basis."

Destry couldn't argue. Calder knew the brushed-cotton jumpsuit currently worn by her baby sister came from Andi's Madison Avenue boutique.

"We all love clothes," Destry admitted "Your designs in particular."

"Naturally." Andi's nod was regal. A second later, she winked and ruined the haughty effect.

Calder watched Adam as *he* watched the familial by-play. Relaxed. Joking. Comfortable and completely at ease. Few men ever witnessed this side of the Benedict sisters.

Adam seemed completely entranced.

"Whatever you need—short of murder—I'm in." Adam paused, his expression thoughtful. "Though, if you ever need to dispose of Ingo Hunter's body, let me know. Since I have no doubt self-defense will be involved, I'll be happy to help."

Bryce, silent until now, clutched at her heart.

"To quote the late, great David Cassidy? Adam Stone? I think I love you."

Surprise sparked in Adam's eyes, followed by a deep, robust laugh. Nerves Calder hadn't wanted to acknowledge, fell away. Bryce's opinion? Andi's and Destry's? They mattered. A lot. Her sisters were the most important people in her life. True, she was her own person. Able to make decisions. She didn't need anybody to tell her who she could or couldn't get involved with.

However... Her sisters' opinions mattered.

"I like him," Andi said. Direct. To the point.

Calder smiled.

"So do I."

ADAM TOOK A seat next to Calder. Andi, Bryce, and Destry sat across from them. The preliminary interview might be over. Pleasant and friendly, he had no illusions. They looked at him with hyper-critical eyes.

The meeting wasn't simply a job interview. Calder's sisters wanted to see if he was good enough to date one of their own. He'd passed muster. So far.

"We need a private investigator," Calder began. "Emphasis on the private. Thorough, yet someone who can get the information quickly."

"You want to investigate Ingo Hunter?"

Calder exchanged looks with her sisters. A silent, secret message passed between them. One Adam couldn't read. When Calder nodded, he assumed a decision had been made. Sort of a collective thumb's up go-ahead.

"We can't dictate who our mother dates. Or marries—God forbid things go that far with Hunter. However, he's by far the most predatory man she's ever been involved with."

"You don't think they're in love?"

Destry snorted. Bryce rolled her eyes. Andi slowly shook her head.

"Billie falls in love at the drop of a hat. I doubt Hunter is quite as sentimental." Adam could read the concern in Calder's eyes. "Maybe he'll enjoy Billie's company for a while before he moves on. No harm done. Or, he might be after more. We want to know."

Names ran through Adam's brain as he looked for the right fit to the Benedict sisters' needs. The way his mind worked, he easily continued the search *and* asked questions.

"Money, obviously. How much of your mother's fortune could Hunter potentially access?"

"Everything. Billie has her own money. In her own name. We all do. Thanks to our grandfather's gender-specific will, only a male heir can inherit the bulk of the Benedict fortune. We, as lowly women, have trust funds. The money is ours outright when we turn thirty."

"Or we get married," Destry sneered.

Adam didn't blame her. He always tried to keep his emotions out of any job he took on. Not this time. Neutrality had flown out the window the first time he looked into Calder's eyes.

"No offense. But your grandfather's head was filled with antiquated bullshit."

"We agree." Andi nodded. "None of us can touch the bulk of the estate. However, we do have discretionary access beyond our trust funds."

While the notion of a trust fund was as foreign to Adam as Sanskrit, he understood the concept. As for some of the terms? He needed a bit of clarification. He turned back to Calder.

"What exactly constitutes discretionary?"

"The executor of the will has the power to give us money not included in our trust funds. If we want to buy a big-ticket item— something everyone in the family can use—he'll consider the request. Then, decide yes or no."

What kind of big-ticket item? Adam wanted to ask. He really did. He ran the question through his head. Rude. Invasive. A big, fat no.

"Money aside, do you think your mother is in danger? Could Hunter hurt her?"

"We don't know." Calder exchanged another glance with her sisters. "*We* don't trust him. Unfortunately, Billie trusts everyone. Information is power, right? The more we can find out about Hunter, the better prepared we can be."

Sensible didn't always accompany smart. Calder, her sisters, were both. Billie Benedict wasn't as blessed. Obviously, they felt they had to protect the woman from herself as much as from Ingo Hunger.

"Have you tried talking to your mother? Sharing your fears? Cautioning her?"

"Billie is..." Bryce shrugged.

"She's hard to explain, even if you've met her." Calder's smile was filled with affection tempered by exasperation. "Where men are concerned, her memory is short. Her optimism, boundless. Which, after six failed marriages and countless relationships, is extraordinary."

Extraordinary wasn't the word Adam would have used. Delusional, bordering on crazy was more accurate. Seemed smart and sensible skipped a generation in the Benedict family. Though, from what he'd gleaned, Calder's grandfather had his own issues. Different, yet just as disturbing.

"Think you can help us?" Calder inquired.

"Dee Wakefield." Adam should have thought of her immediately. "She's everything you specified. And more."

"How long have you known her?" Bryce asked.

"Where did you meet?" Andi wanted to know.

"Does she carry a gun?" Destry demanded.

Adam didn't hesitate, directing his answers to the proper woman, in order.

"Ten years. The Navy. Yes."

"Make and caliber?"

Destry seemed to think her follow-up question was perfectly reasonable.

"I have no idea." Why the hell would he? "I'm certain Dee will be happy to provide you with whatever you want to know. If you agree, I'll call her and set up an interview."

"As soon as possible." Andi stood. One glance had Bryce and Destry on their feet. "I think we've settled everything. At least for now. Nice meeting you."

Bryce patted Adam's arm on her way out of the room. Destry, her smile as sweet as molasses, stopped in front of him.

"Don't mess with Calder."

"I won't."

"We'll see. Just remember. I know where you live." A glint of steel entered her gaze. "Taking out snakes is my specialty."

Adam didn't move until the library door shut, leaving him alone with Calder. He let out a low, slow whistle.

"Small package. Scary as hell."

"Destry is an original." Calder radiated with pride.

"I'd say the description applies to *all* the Benedict sisters."

"Would you?"

The business portion of their day was definitely over—if the smile on Calder's face was any indication. She moved into his arms, smooth as the silk covering her long, lean body.

Something about the feel of her next to him. All at once, she excited Adam's senses. And calmed his soul. Beautiful. Inside, and out.

Adam nuzzled Calder's neck. A happy sound slipped from her lips, the perfect combination of a sigh and a moan.

"Any chance I can talk you into moving up our date time?"

"Sorry." Calder snuggled closer. "I have a meeting in an hour with a rather tightfisted media mogul. I'm so close to wresting a donation from Alton Stevens, I can't risk giving him the brush off."

A few more hours. A day. A week. Adam knew Calder was worth any wait. He wanted her to feel the same. To think of him with the same anticipation. The same need.

"Are you tempted?" Adam bit the curve of her neck. "Just a little?"

"You have no idea."

Yes. He did.

"Where's your meeting?"

The office building Calder named was downtown. Adam did the math, traffic factored in.

"Just about enough time."

Calder tilted her head, a question in her dark eyes.

"For...?"

Adam dropped his gaze to perfectly positioned lips.

"This."

Kissing Calder. The thrill was new, but he would bet almost anything the touch of her mouth against his would never grow old. He wondered how he'd lived so long without knowing the sensation of her long, supple body molded to his.

"We keep starting something we can't finish," Calder said, half laugh, half gasp.

"Next time? Locked doors. No phones. Just you and me."

Adam swooped in for another kiss. Arms wound tight around his neck, Calder held on as if she'd never let go. Too soon, she reluctantly stepped away.

"Remind me why I have to go?"

"Donation." Adam cleared his throat. "A hefty one, from what I understand."

Calder's thoughts weren't as sharp as usual—much to Adam's delight. She could scramble his brains. Seemed only fair he return the favor.

"Right. I need to change." Calder paused at the door. "First, I'll walk you out."

"I can find my way. Go. Make your tight-wad cough up a few bucks."

"More than a few when I've finished," she called out as she hurried toward the back staircase. "See you at seven. What do you like on your pizza?"

"Everything. But don't bother. I'll make dinner."

"Wait." Two steps up, Calder stopped. "You cook?"

Adam didn't want to prime her expectations.

"I can fry a steak. Bake a potato. Like most people. Nothing fancy."

"Compared to me, you're a four-star chef."

With a grin, Calder blew Adam a kiss and disappeared from view.

Adam was in his car, halfway home before he remembered the stark condition of his refrigerator. Glancing right, he changed lanes, and headed down the street to where he always shopped.

Calder was the most important thing on tonight's menu. However, he didn't want her to catch him in a lie. Not even about something as seemingly insignificant as a steak.

CHAPTER FIFTEEN

WHOEVER SAID THE best sex was spontaneous hadn't spent an afternoon with Adam Stone on her mind.

Calder wiggled in her seat, anxious to get from point A to the point where she could rip the clothes off his mouthwateringly sexy body. Right now, she was stuck behind a delivery truck. No way forward, honking cars to the rear.

She understood their frustration.

The reason Calder owned her sweet little Porsche was that she enjoyed the adventure of New York City traffic. Unlike her sisters who used a regular car service—or in a pinch, public transportation—she preferred to be in control.

Tonight was the perfect example. If she were in the backseat, helpless, with nothing to do but fume? Her patience wouldn't last long.

Behind the wheel, Calder couldn't move any faster. However, all the options were at her disposal. She could honk the horn. Pound her hand on the dashboard. Roll down the window and scream her frustration.

Calder chose none of the above. Instead, she listened to the drivers in front and behind her spew words colorful enough to make a dockworker blush. And laughed. Lordy, she loved New York.

The chaos around Calder calmed her mentally—not physically. The need for Adam had reached a critical level.

Professional—always—Calder breezed through her meeting. She charmed. She cajoled. She wheedled. In the end, the man didn't know what hit him. A savvy businessman, Alton Stevens had greeted her with a smug smile, certain he would win the day.

An hour later, Calder had turned smug into stunned. She left Alton's office with a sweet smile—no need to gloat—and a hefty check in her purse.

Calder carefully packed a change of clothes before she left home. Something casually chic. Something alluring. And easily removed. After the lengthy meeting, she didn't have time to do anything but get in her car and head to Adam's apartment.

Traffic had been on her side, until now. With each block, each mile, she thought about tonight. About Adam.

He made her think. Feel. Want. He sparked a fire inside Calder she'd almost forgotten. Or, if she were honest, hadn't existed until now. She'd channeled her energy toward business. Happily. Sex was usually an afterthought.

Calder would have sworn nothing was missing from her life. She didn't live at the office. She was active socially. If the men she dated weren't terribly exciting, she put the blame on herself. She picked from what was available. Didn't force herself outside the familiar.

Honestly, Calder couldn't have said what she wanted in a man. She hadn't been interested in looking when out of the blue came Adam. Different from any man she'd ever met. Yet, somehow, wonderfully familiar. Dangerous and safe. Edgy and smooth.

Exciting. And exciting. And exciting.

"Come on!" Calder cried out, her eyes narrowed on the offending delivery truck. "Move already."

Grabbing her phone, Calder pulled up Adam's number.

"Calder." He never made her wait long before he answered.

"I'm stuck in traffic."

"Have to love New York."

As if by magic or the power of frustration, the truck pulled away, the cars started moving. And her anticipation skyrocketed.

"Finally." Calder hit the gas. "My ETA is five minutes."

"Perfect timing. I'll put the steaks on. Dinner will be ready when you get here."

"Hold off on the steaks."

"Why?"

Calder didn't want to explain over the phone. She wanted to show Adam what she had in mind.

"Because dinner will have to wait."

Five minutes turned into four. Foot heavy on the gas, Calder held her breath the entire way, praying she wouldn't be pulled over. She probably deserved a speeding ticket—okay, definitely—but she wasn't in the mood for another delay.

No police. No more traffic. Even the parking gods were on her side. Just as she approached Adam's building, a car pulled out. Calder took just enough time to grab her bag from the trunk.

The doorman greeted Calder with a welcoming smile.

"Miss Benedict?"

"Yes."

"Go right up. Mr. Stone is expecting you."

Calder's heels clicked as she crossed the lobby. She looked like any other young woman, home from a day at the office. Her outfit—one of Andi's designs—was a modern take on the power suit. Warmer than white. Not quite cream. The moment she buttoned the jacket, she felt confident. Ready to take on the world and win.

All Calder cared about at the moment, was one man. Taking him on would be a pleasure. If things went as planned, they'd both come out on top. And the bottom. And all positions in between.

The elevator ride was swift. Calder strode down the hall. She barely had time to ring the bell when the door opened. Adam smiled, his expression puzzled.

"You hung up so quickly I didn't have time to ask. Why does dinner have to wait?"

"Anything in danger of burning?" *Besides me?*

Shaking his head, Adam stood aside to let Calder in.

"Lock the door."

Bemused, Adam followed her instructions.

Calder dropped her bag onto the floor. As she slipped off her shoes, she placed her hand on his bare forearm for balance, just below his rolled-up sleeves. The feel of Adam's warm skin, the tickle of soft hair against her palm, the bunching of muscles, was a nice bonus.

Holding his gaze, Calder unbuttoned her jacket.

"Turn off your phone, Adam."

Awareness flared in his deep, blue eyes. No more questions, Adam turned into a man of action. In one compact, breathtaking movement, he swooped Calder off her feet.

"About damn time," he muttered.

"What about—?"

"The hell with the phone. I'll shut the door."

Calder didn't have time to enjoy the novelty of the moment. When his lips covered hers, everything else ceased to matter. She threaded her fingers through his thick hair, slanted her mouth to a different angle. The taste of him was intoxicating.

Calder landed on his bed. Before she could do more than gasp, Adam covered her body with his.

"Too many clothes," she complained.

"Me, or you?"

"Both."

More than willing to help remedy the situation, Calder unzipped Adam's jeans. She fumbled with the button, but determination won out. Past the waistband, under denim and cotton. Just as she reached the curve of his butt, he moved, dislodging her hand.

"Hey," she protested.

"Soon."

Adam left her with an all-too-brief kiss. Quick and efficient, her skirt hit the floor. Then her jacket. The knit tank was next.

"Sexy underwear." He sighed, his gaze hungry. "My dreams didn't lie."

Dreams were good. In Calder's opinion, reality was better. Adam's shirt joined the growing pile of discarded clothing. She itched to touch his lean, muscled torso. Kiss his impossibly flat, rippling stomach.

A teasing glint entered Adam's eyes as if he could read her mind.

"Age before beauty, gorgeous."

On his knees, Adam rested her foot on his chest. He ran a hand up her calf in one slow, prolonged caress. The blue of his gaze intensified as he divided his attention between his progress and Calder's reaction to his agonizingly sensual touch.

Calder licked her lips, clutching at the bed. She entered the apartment ready for a fast, wild ride. Adam had something else in mind. When his hands made her feel so good who was she to complain?

The look in Adam's eyes was reverential. Worshipful. His touch? Pure sin.

"I could spend hours getting to know every inch of your legs. So strong. Do you run?"

"Every day." Calder let out a moan of pleasure when he found the sensitive skin at the back of her knee.

"I can tell."

Adam's lips replaced his fingers.

"So sexy. They go on forever. Then end at the perfect spot."

He left her, just long enough to remove the rest of his clothing. Adam lay beside Calder, his hand on the inside of her thigh, his lips pressed against the exposed curve of her breast. Through the layer of silver lace, he licked her hardened nipple, drawing the bud into his mouth.

She wanted these moments to go on forever. Yet, she needed more.

"Adam."

Calder didn't try to keep the yearning from her voice.

"I know. I know."

No more time for teasing. When Adam moved toward the bedside table, Calder wiggled out of her underwear. She watched as he rolled on a condom, and said a prayer of thanks. He wanted to protect her. Even when her brain was too muddled to protect herself.

Passion filled, yet infinitely gentle, Adam kissed her as he shifted positions. She twined her legs around him, welcoming the fluid thrust of his hips.

Breath rushed from Calder's lungs. Sex had always been fun. A welcome, physical release. She didn't know what she felt with Adam, but they'd traveled beyond fun. More than sex. She flew. Higher than she'd ever imagined. The burst of pleasure so intense, she swore she saw stars.

Adam collapsed onto the bed, chest glistening with sweat. Turning, he lay on his side, his face inches from hers. He touched her lips. Her cheek. He had the look of a man who'd ridden out a wild, exhilarating storm and lived to tell the tale.

"Sex? With you? My new favorite thing."

Smiling, flattered, and in complete accord, Calder smoothed back a lock of hair from his forehead.

"I say we go again. Soon. And often."

"Two in favor. And no dissenting votes." Adam's sigh held the sound of pure contentment. "The motion carries unanimously."

"You're a fool," Calder chuckled.

"And you're spectacular. Are you hungry?"

With more energy than she thought possible—all things considered—Adam jumped to his feet.

"If I plan to keep up my end of our endless sex pact, I need sustenance."

Calder enjoyed the view as Adam shamelessly paraded naked to the closet.

"I didn't say anything about endless."

Knowing she'd draw his attention, Calder stretched her arms over her head, letting the sheet fall to her waist.

"Wishful thinking. I—"

Calder batted her eyes. Hardly innocent, she took a deep breath. His gaze dropped to her breasts. In three long strides, he had her in his arms.

"What about dinner?"

"Later. Much later."

"But—"

Whatever she meant to say, Calder lost her train of thought the second Adam touched his lips to hers.

Adam brushed a kiss on her shoulder. Her neck. Her lips again. He met her gaze, his blue eyes heavy with desire.

"Dinner can wait. I can't."

THEY ATE. EVENTUALLY. Dressed in jeans and a t-shirt, her feet bare, Calder watched—thoroughly impressed—as similarly attired Adam prepared their steaks.

"You really *do* know your way around the kitchen."

"Why are you so surprised? People all over the world cook. Every day."

Calder wondered if her answer would sound pompous. Elitist. Probably. Facts were facts. She had a privileged childhood which continued into adulthood. She wasn't embarrassed. Nor did she like to flaunt the perks wealth afforded her.

When asked directly, Calder didn't shy away from the subject.

"I don't. Cook, that is. Neither do my sisters. Or my mother. Or our fathers."

"Because you don't have to?" Adam placed a filled plate in front of Calder. "Or you don't want to?"

219

"Both."

With a nod, Adam joined her. He filled their glasses with a deep-red burgundy.

"My mother loves to putter around the kitchen. Her words, not mine. Me? Not so much." As he sipped his wine, his gaze met hers over the rim. "Want to know the truth?"

"As often as possible."

"I eat out more often than not. Tonight? All an attempt to impress you." Adam waited as Calder took her first bite. "Well? What's the verdict?"

Calder slowly chewed the juicy, perfectly cooked piece of meat. She'd observed Adam's technique. Salt. Pepper. Butter heated in a sizzling pan. The process looked simple. She knew better. Nothing that tasted so good could ever be termed simple.

"Slam dunk. Too bad we already had sex, or I'd show my appreciation." Calder dug into the tossed green salad. "Mm. The dressing is outrageous."

"One of my mother's specialties," Adam said with pride. "If you think Mrs. Finch would like the recipe, I can text you a copy."

"She would be over the moon. If your mom wouldn't mind, have her call the house. Mrs. F. can talk food for hours."

"I warn you. Mom will grill Mrs. Finch for every piece of information she can get about you. Your childhood. Your intentions toward her baby boy."

Calder laughed so hard she almost spilled wine down her front.

"For the past few hours, I've made my intentions crystal clear. I say we spare Mrs. Finch *and* your mother the details."

"I agree." Adam clinked his glass against hers.

"Are you and your mother close?"

"We are." Adam's smile was warm, with a nostalgic quality as if the memories were only good. "My father died when I was a baby. My grandparents live in California. They still visit every other Christmas. Mom worked hard all her life. Did her best to keep me on the straight and narrow."

"Obviously, she succeeded."

"For the most part."

Calder sensed Adam had tales to tell about his youth. Interesting stories she planned to ask about. One day soon.

"Why the Navy?"

"As opposed to the other branches of the military?" Adam shrugged. "My father served. Before he married my mother. He was a good man. I like to think he would have been a good father. Guess I decided to carry on the Stone tradition. My way of honoring a man I never knew. Silly, I suppose."

"I doubt your mother thinks so."

Surprise sparked in Adam's eyes.

"She never said."

"Perhaps she didn't want you to feel any pressure to follow in his footsteps. Be your own man. Find your own path."

Adam brushed his hand over hers. A brief, seemingly careless gesture. Calder's pulse stuttered. So quickly she thought she might have imagined the sensation.

"I like your reasoning. Why are you so wise on the subject?"

"Wisdom is easy when someone else is involved. If you asked about my father? Our relationship? I have no answers."

"How often do you see him? Sorry. If you don't want to talk about him, I understand."

Edwin Calder wasn't a subject she discussed outside the safe circle of her sisters. Different fathers, different dysfunctions. Same complicated father/daughter dynamics.

Calder shied away from questions she knew were about a desire for juicy details, not any real interest in her. Another one of those pesky trust issues she could never completely leave behind.

Adam had chipped away at Calder's defensive shell. Cracks were showing. But she knew he would never get all the way in unless she decided to let him.

"Edwin Calder isn't the most paternal man in the world." A massive understatement. "My existence is a fact. One he easily ignores most of the time. When he's in New York, which isn't often, we do the whole obligatory get-together. Usually lunch at a very trendy, very public place. My father loves to see and be seen."

Calder stopped when she heard the tone of her voice. Though she'd come to terms with her parental situation long ago, bitterness occasionally seeped to the surface.

"I can only give you one side of the story. I'm certain my father would—" Calder had no idea what her father would say. "He doesn't make excuses for his actions. Fault or virtue? I have no idea."

"I've never understood why some people think an apology equals weakness."

Because, you, Adam Stone, are a real man. Good and strong and, fingers crossed, trustworthy. Calder felt another crack in her shell—near her heart. A hopeful feeling. And damned scary.

"My father doesn't apologize for one simple reason. In his mind, he's never wrong."

"Never?"

"To my knowledge? No." Calder couldn't read Adam's expression beyond disbelief. "Not exactly *Father Knows Best.* I'd understand if you want to see the back of me."

"I'd rather see the front of you. But I'll take what I can get."

Calder appreciated Adam's attempt at a joke. Bad, but she'd heard worse.

"I haven't met your parents," Adam said as he cleared the table.

"Consider yourself blessed."

A plate in each hand, Calder followed him to the kitchen

"I *have* met the rest of your family. Your sisters. Mrs. Finch."

Adam couldn't know, but when he included Mrs. Finch, he earned himself a mess of brownie points.

"You're a formidable group."

"And proud of the distinction."

Adam laughed.

"I admire strong, independent women." He leaned with his hip against the counter. "I was raised by one. She taught me respect has to be earned."

Cleanup was quick. He shut the dishwasher, wiping his hands with a paper towel.

"Sounds like a woman worth knowing." Calder placed her hand next to Adam's. Close, but not touching. "I should thank you for dinner. Properly."

"Properly." Adam mulled over the word. "As in a handwritten note and a bouquet of flowers?"

Calder smiled when he wrapped his arms around her. Exactly where she wanted to be.

"I misspoke. I want to thank you *im*properly."

Adam backed from the kitchen, taking Calder with him.

"Tell me more."

"Stop." Calder picked up her bag. "I have goodies."

"Don't tease." He maneuvered them into the bedroom. "What kind of goodies?"

"Lotion."

"Sounds promising."

With a push, Calder had Adam flat on his back, onto the freshly made bed. He lay, hands behind his head, eyes alert, as she rummaged through the leather tote for treasure.

"A paintbrush?" Adam chuckled when she held up the item for his viewing pleasure.

"Left, unused, after your friends cleaned up." She straddled Adam's legs, pushing up the hem of his shirt to expose his flat stomach. She lightly swiped the bristles over his skin. "Very soft."

Adam let out a sound of pleasure from deep in his throat. When she loosened the waist of his jeans, tugging them past his hips, all kinds of wonderland were exposed. Slowly, she moved the brush lower, lower.

"What do you think?" Calder paused at the most interesting moment.

The glint in Adam's blue eyes told her she would pay for teasing him. Unconcerned, she showed no mercy.

"Well? Yes, or no?"

One light flick across his hard length brought a moan as his hips twitched, reaching for more. Calder sent Adam a knowing smile.

"I guess I have my answer."

"YOU DIDN'T TOSS me out."

"Of the shower?" Adam handed Calder a towel for her hair then continued to personally and thoroughly dry her damp skin.

"Of your bed. You told me you don't sleep with women."

"You aren't any woman. You're Calder. A class all your own."

Somewhere. Under all the perfect, Adam had to have a flaw. Nothing major—fingers crossed. Perhaps he sang off key. Or left his dirty socks on the floor.

What amazed Calder? She wanted to be around long enough to find out—even if his great flaw was a tendency to leave the toilet seat up.

"Besides," Adam continued. "We didn't do a whole lot of sleeping if you recall."

"Sex on the brain. Typical man."

Calder hid her smile. Adam Stone was the least *typical* man she'd ever met.

"I didn't hear any complaints while you were on orgasm number five."

"You need to learn how to count."

"Four?" Frowning, Adam squeezed a healthy dollop of lotion into his palm. He started moisturizing Calder's legs. "I know the number was higher than three."

"Six."

Calder always gave credit where it was due. Adam's lips curved into a slow, self-satisfied smile.

"Sit."

Calder did as he asked. Adam dispensed more lotion, moving from her left foot to her right. He was very thorough. She kissed the top of his head.

"Thank you. Again."

"After your creative use of a paintbrush? *I* owe *you*. Big time." Adam winked. "Where did you ever come up with the idea?"

"Sex blog."

"You read blogs?" Adam sounded skeptical. "About sex?"

She turned onto her stomach so he could finish.

"I read many things. On many, wide, diverse subjects. Keeps my mind fluid."

"Calder?"

"Mm?"

"If you come across anything interesting, sex-wise? I'll be happy to act as your guinea pig. Experimentation keeps the mind *extra*-fluid."

"You don't say."

Adam lightly patted her butt.

"Flip over. I missed your breasts."

"You spent a good five minutes washing each one. How could you miss them already?"

"Not *miss*, smartass. *Missed*. With the lotion."

"Oh." Calder rolled to her back, arms over her head. The perfect position for what Adam proposed. "My mistake."

"Not a single thing about you is a mistake."

"No?"

"Absolutely not."

The lotion forgotten, Adam joined her on the bed. Eager, Calder welcomed him.

228

CHAPTER SIXTEEN

CALDER WAITED WHILE Bryce checked her email. Adam had set up a consultation with the private investigator, Dee Wakefield, for two thirty. After a brief sister confab, they decided to meet at Calder's downtown office rather than at home, just in case Ingo Hunter popped up—as he tended to do these days.

Calder and her sisters didn't want to give Hunter even a hint of what they were up to. If Dee Wakefield found nothing to worry about? They would chalk the investigation up to a case of *better safe than sorry*.

If, as suspected, something nefarious turned up in Hunter's past and/or present? Calder's stomach turned at the prospect. They would deal with Billie, her boyfriend, and the fallout when the time came.

Perched on the edge of a huge mahogany desk, she ran her fingers over the keys of an antique typewriter. A dust catcher, some might say. Inspiration, Bryce countered. And not a speck of dust to be seen.

The entire room was spotless. The opposite of a temperamental artist, Bryce guarded her latest masterpiece with care, not her life. The maids were allowed to clean on a regular schedule. With ample warning. She, laptop in tow, was always careful to be someplace else.

"I don't believe you." Finished, Bryce turned off her iPad.

"Hand to God."

"You and Adam had sex—no cheating—all night long."

"What constitutes cheating?"

Bryce shrugged.

"I don't know. Battery-powered substitutions. Little blue pills, or the generic equivalent. Tag team."

The image of a professional wrestling match popped into Calder's head. In the center of the ring, a bed. One man. One woman. Observing the action, just outside the ropes, several men ready to tap in if the main man's energy flagged.

Weird. And a bit disturbing.

"Should I worry about the kind of men you date?"

Bryce chuckled.

"Consenting adults, Calder."

"Meaning?"

"If I want to have sex with a dozen firefighters. In full gear. And everyone involved thinks the idea is peachy? Nobody else's business."

"You'd tell *me*."

"Because, I know you wouldn't judge," Bryce reminded her.

"*If* you were happy," Calder qualified.

"A dozen firefighters zeroed in on my pleasure? Why wouldn't I be?"

The alone time Bryce spent with her characters, building worlds, scaring the crap out of her readers, wasn't her entire existence. Parties. Ballgames. Drinks with friends. Unless she was deep in a writing frenzy or buried in edits, she rarely turned down an invitation.

Yet, like the rest of the Benedict sisters, Bryce's dating life could be sketchy at best. At the moment, hers was on the downswing.

"I could set you up with—"

"Stop." Bryce ran a hand over her face, her expression horrified. "A setup? Do you honestly think I've sunk so far?"

Calder wondered if her brain had been fried by a night of unbelievable sex. Offer to arrange a date? Impulsive. Crazy. Borderline unforgivable.

"Sorry. Older sister syndrome."

"By fifteen freaking minutes. Always in a rush, you shoved your way to the front of the line."

"I never shove." The idea appalled Calder. "I cajole. Charm. As do you. And Andi."

Grinning, they finished the thought simultaneously.

"*Destry* shoves."

"She's a pip." Bryce sighed. "I refuse to believe I've run through every decent man in New York. You found one. Why shouldn't I?"

Adam exceeded decent. Right now, their relationship was shiny and new. She didn't know if they would move toward something deeper. She wasn't sure she wanted more.

Fun was fantastic. A jumping-off point to something more—or nothing at all. Why shouldn't she want the same for Bryce?

"I had some news," Bryce said.

Calder let the less than smooth conversation transition pass.

"Well? Tell me."

"My agent received an offer to make *The Last Nightmare* into a movie. Not, maybe we will, maybe we won't. If I agree to the terms, a green light all the way."

"How? When? Who?" Calder gave Bryce a firm shake. "And why don't you sound half as excited as I do?"

"I want to write the screenplay. The director/producer/control freak isn't keen on the idea. I'm not a *proven commodity*. Or some such ridiculousness."

"Don't you hold all the power? Tell him—or her—to talk or walk."

"Him. Zach Devlin."

Bryce sneered the name.

Calder was in her sister's corner. Always. Never a question. But holy crap! *Zach Devlin.* Like a good portion of the world's population, she'd seen every one of his movies. And loved every second. Few and far between, he made stories that entertained, *and* were loved by critics.

Devlin had the golden touch. However, fangirl or not, Calder wasn't happy with anybody who tried to keep Bryce from what she wanted.

"Meet with him. Prove him wrong."

"My suggestion exactly. Unfortunately, the man is a recluse. He only comes down off his mountain, or out of his cave— wherever—to grace the world with one of his masterpieces. The rest of the time, he's incommunicado."

Incommunicado? Really?

"Highfalutin word."

"Not mine. Here's the email from his assistant." Bryce handed over her phone. "See?"

Ms. Benedict,

Thank you for reaching out to Mr. Devlin. Unfortunately, he will not be in New York in the foreseeable future. As for your offer to come to him? Impossible, I'm afraid. When at home, Mr. Devlin is incommunicado. No exceptions.

Sincerely,

Ricardo Peña

"Yikes." Calder had read warmer junk mail. "Still, Zach Devlin didn't actually *write* the email."

"Devlin has a reputation as a perfectionist. Unless something's changed, I doubt he'd let even the most trusted assistant send any form of communication without his approval."

"What are you going to do?"

Bryce opened a pretty enamel compact, took a tube of lipstick from the desk drawer, and applied a new coat to her lips. With a snap, she shut the mirror.

"I drew a line in the sand. Either I write the screenplay, or Devlin can look for a different project."

The familiar glint of resolve in Bryce's gray eyes made Calder smile.

"If the fool doesn't give in, his loss."

"My feelings exactly."

"Hey, are you guys ready?" Destry stood by the office door, an impatient look on her face.

"We're coming," Calder assured her.

"Well, hurry up. The ants in Andi's pants are starting to chafe *my* ass."

Bryce, the writer, hoarded colorful phrases like a miser and her gold. She quickly scribbled down Destry's latest gem.

"If something I said ends up in another of your books, I'll need compensation."

"A hug? A kiss?" Bryce gave Destry both.

"Good thing I'm such a pushover." Destry let out an exaggerated sigh.

Smiling, Calder watched the exchange. None of the Benedict sisters were pushovers. Love and respect. For each other. Some might think the emotions made them vulnerable. Calder knew better. They were stronger together. Always. Forever. Nothing could beat them. Not time. Not space. And especially, not Ingo Hunter.

DEE WAKEFIELD TURNED out to be an impressive woman.

Tall, lanky, with a shock of platinum hair styled into a modified mohawk. Dee sported more tattoos than the naked eye could tally. Up her long legs, down her well-toned arms. Colorful and eye-catching, the varied designs were true works of art.

Calder knew her age to be forty-one. She looked ten years younger.

Black Army boots. Black knee-length cargo pants. Black t-shirt. Her black leather jacket rode the back of her chair. Crisp.

Clean. Minimalistic. In other words, like the woman herself, totally badass.

If Calder was a little girl, she would take one look at Dee and think, *I want to be just like her*. She chuckled to herself. Though grown and completely comfortable in her own skin. A tiny part of the adult Calder wished the same thing.

The five women gathered in the lounge area of Calder's private office. The furniture was stylish yet comfortable. Designed to put visitors at ease. After a round of introductions, Andi, Bryce, and Destry chose the plush blue sofa. Dee picked a chair of contrasting brown. Calder sat in its mate.

Coffee all around. And a tray of jam-filled cookies. Untouched. But they were there if anybody felt the impulse.

"Adam didn't give me the particulars. He's as closed mouth as they come." Dee obviously admired the trait, if her smile was any indication. "You need an investigator. He thinks we'd be a good fit."

Calder had studied up on Dee after Adam emailed an extensive file. She'd sent copies to her sisters. For a good part of the morning, Andi checked out the impressive list of references. Glowing was the best way to describe the responses. Each and every one.

After ten years in Navy intelligence, Dee went on to get a degree in psychology. To help pay her way, she worked security for some heavy-hitter companies. Now a private investigator, her reputation was stellar.

Adam provided Dee's professional qualifications. What they needed was a feel for the woman.

"Does the name Ingo Hunter mean anything to you?"

"We've met." Dee's dark eyes narrowed. "If you need information to help him, you have the wrong woman."

"Not a fan?" Andi asked.

"No."

One word. Circumspect, yet spoken with utter contempt. Calder decided then and there, Dee was the woman they needed. She glanced at her sisters, hoping to gauge their reactions. One look told her Bryce felt the same. Andi would have a million and one more questions, but Calder could see the yes in her eyes. Destry, always a wild card, gave a single affirmative nod.

The Benedict sisters had found their private investigator.

"We want dirt on Hunter. As much as possible. If he's clean—"

"Ingo Hunter was born crooked. Then proceeded to rot from the inside out."

Calder expected heat. Instead, Dee's words dripped with ice.

"He hit on you."

Dee raised an eyebrow as she met Destry's understanding gaze.

"More of a full court press. I'm on quite a few no-hire lists because of Hunter. Luckily, there are enough haters to keep me busy."

Sympathetic, Bryce placed a hand on Dee's.

"He doesn't like when a woman says no."

"Or sends a foot to his gut. If my aim hadn't been off, I'd have sent his balls into his fucking throat."

Destry raised a *hell yes* fist into the air.

"I knew we were going to be friends."

Surprise lit Dee's eyes. She looked around, the stiffness melting from her spine.

"You too?" she asked them all.

"None of us landed a punch. Unfortunately." Andi's sigh was filled with regret.

"Please tell me you plan to bring Hunter down. If I weren't a greedy soul at heart, I'd offer my services free of charge."

Calder loved Dee's enthusiasm.

"Hunter's destruction would be a bonus, to be sure. Right now, our goal is to discover the reason he's latched on to our mother."

"Little Red Riding Hood let the wolf in the door. We need to know if his intentions are relatively benign. Or does he plan to devour everyone in sight?"

Calder raised her cup to Bryce.

"Nice metaphor."

"Seemed to fit." Bryce shrugged.

Andi explained the situation. With pinpoint focus, Dee asked questions when necessary. Mostly she listened, taking notes.

"I can get started immediately. Adam told you my rates?"

Calder had done her research. Dee wasn't cheap. Above what the average private investigator asked, but comparable with others equal to her qualifications.

"We're good. If you'll messenger over a contract, I'll—"

"Brought two with me. Copy for you, copy for me. All we need is a notary. And a check from you to retain my services. Naturally."

"Naturally."

"Naturally." Calder appreciated a pragmatic woman. She pressed the intercom button on her desk. "Sara?"

"Yes, Ms. Benedict?"

"Will you see if Liv Briscoe has a free minute? If so, have her come to my office right away."

"You have your own notary?" Dee asked.

Smiling, Calder shook her head.

"Liv has an office a few floors down. She used to manage a bank before the interior design bug caught her. Did my office for me." Calder looked around, happy.

"I didn't know what to think when Adam mentioned the name Benedict."

Calder understood why Dee hesitated. She'd dealt with preconceived notions her entire life.

"You expected to find a bunch of spoiled rich girls?"

"I did." Dee met Calder's amused gaze head on. "You aren't what I expected. Rich. Undoubtedly. But you don't strike me as entitled party girls."

"We have our moments."

"I'm happy to help stick a fork in Ingo Hunter's plans. Not that the money isn't a nice bonus."

Dee's laugh was genuine and full bodied.

"I wouldn't believe you if you said otherwise. One thing." Calder sent Dee a speculative look. "If you didn't think we'd mesh, why the meeting? Why waste your time?"

"Adam is a hard man to say no to. And before you ask, we're friends. Nothing more. He's way too pretty for my taste."

Calder *had* wondered. Dee was a vibrant, attractive woman.

"I wouldn't have blamed him."

Dee looked pleased with the compliment.

"We hit the brother/sister dynamic right away. Which is the real reason I came today."

"What do you mean?"

"Never seen the man so talkative about *any* woman. Calder this, and Calder that." Dee shook her head. "You have a high-class shine I figured would turn Adam off."

Calder didn't know what to say. Obviously, *high-class shine* wasn't meant as a compliment. Yet, the words were delivered in a friendly manner, completely without rancor. She braced herself for a further insult, ready to fire back. Dee saved her the trouble.

"Whatever happens between you and Adam, I think you're the real deal, Calder Benedict. Solid, twenty-four-carat gold."

CHAPTER SEVENTEEN

CALDER SPENT THE rest of the afternoon answering messages, returning phone calls, sorting through a stack of snail-mail technology experts once claimed the advent of computers would eliminate, yet never did. Seemed the more she relied on the internet, the more she found herself surrounded by stacks and stacks, reams and reams, of paper.

Drudgery, in Calder's book, but necessary.

"Done."

The last letter. Calder wrote her signature with an extra flourish. A vital reason *Erica's Angels* succeeded where other charities failed, was attention to details. If she let the trivial things slide, another thing might follow. And another.

Eventually, Calder would spend all her time playing catch up. Donations would vanish. People in need would suffer the consequences. Paperwork was a royal pain, but necessary.

Calder rolled her head from side to side. When she felt—and heard—a definitive pop, she winced. Too much time bent over her desk. And not in a good way.

A smile lit her face as her thoughts turned from business to pleasure. Adam. A game of boss and secretary?

No, she decided. Neither of them was the subservient type. Better some good old-fashioned playtime. After hours. Door locked from the inside. When she purchased the huge oak desk, sex was the last thing on her mind. Now, Calder realized the surface was big enough for all kinds of non-business-related activities.

"Ms. Benedict?"

Pulled from her fantasies by her assistant's voice, Calder's heart jumped from her chest, landing firmly in her throat. She swallowed once, twice, then answered the intercom.

"Yes?"

"Mr. Calder is on line three."

"Thank you. You can leave for the day, Sara. I won't need anything else."

Calder's father never contacted her via cell phone. He couldn't be bothered. Too many numbers. All of which he could have programed into his cell. Wisely, she kept her mouth shut on the subject. Edwin didn't react well when she pointed out the obvious.

"Dad." Edwin couldn't see her. Yet, Calder plastered on a false smile. "How are you?"

"Like a bee in a field of clover. How's my girl? Bright as a penny, I'll wager."

Calder couldn't help but smile. Edwin *was* her father. The only one she'd ever have. And, for all his faults—of which there were many—she really did love the unreliable S.O.B.

"I'm good. Are you in New York?"

"For the next two days. Business. However, I'm free tonight. How does dinner with your old man sound?"

"Great."

"I'll pick you up around seven thirty. It'll give me a chance to say hello to your mother."

"See you then."

Edwin and Billie. The marriage from hell. The divorce made in heaven.

Considering the contentious nature of every breakup, Billie maintained an oddly harmonious relationship with *all* her ex-husbands. Lunch. Dinner. Phone calls. They exchanged birthday cards. Reminisced when the mood hit. And, though nobody confirmed the fact—thank goodness—Calder suspected her mother had an on and off *exes with benefits* arrangement with more than one.

Seemed to work for them, Calder supposed. Billie and Edwin shared a love for the dramatic. Together or apart, they weren't happy unless they found some reason to stir the drama pot.

For her own sanity, Calder long ago learned to maintain as much neutrality as possible through every up and down.

Edwin claimed he was in New York on business. No reason to doubt him. Up to a point. His definition of the word was as fluid as an ocean's tide. Big business. Monkey business. And everything in between.

More than once, Edwin had tried to suck Calder into one of his schemes. When she turned him down—every time—more time than normal would pass between phone calls. No was a word her father didn't care for when delivered by someone other than himself.

Calder locked the outer office door. Edwin believed he could talk anybody into anything. The fact his only child turned out to be the exception chafed like a burr under his proverbial saddle.

Hopefully, tonight was about dinner and nothing else. If not? Calder would have said no to her father's invitation and dealt with his inevitable pout, followed by months of silence.

And her world, either way, would continue to turn.

EDWIN PICKED THE restaurant. Staid in tone and décor. The kind of place where old New York money gathered. Definitely her father's kind of place.

Calder smiled as their waiter delivered their drinks. Wine for her, bourbon on the rocks for Edwin.

"Morocco was sublime. Have you ever been?"

"No."

"I spent two weeks last fall. Trust me, you must go. The food. The people. The breeze at night. Nothing smells like desert air. North Africa will blow your mind." Edwin waved his glass for emphasis. He didn't notice when some of the six hundred dollars a bottle bourbon splashed over the rim. "But only if you go first class all the way. Remind me to give you the name of my travel agent. She's a magician."

Handsome as always. Tall. Fit. With just a touch of a receding hairline and a bit grayer than she remembered sprinkled through his dark-brown hair. Calder inherited her father's build and coloring. Thankfully, his swinging pendulum of emotions hadn't attached itself to her genic code.

Calder knew from the moment she looked into his too-bright eyes, a slight sheen of perspiration on his brow, tonight would be one of *those* nights.

Edwin was on an emotional high. Borderline manic. Everything was beyond wonderful. Nothing could get him down. Until something did.

What sent him flying? What crashed him back to earth? Calder had no idea. She'd been witness to both phases. Neither was a particularly comfortable experience. Given a choice, she would choose the high over the low any day.

The mood modifier prescribed by his doctor would have helped. *If* Edwin bothered to take the pills. When too high or too low, he preferred to self-medicate. Alcohol, his drug of choice.

"Someday I'd love to see Morocco. When I can find the time."

"Jesus, Calder. You're young. Money sure as hell isn't an issue. Now's the time to enjoy life before you get bogged down by a family."

"A family never stopped you."

Calder wished she had swallowed the words. But she could only bite her tongue so long before her mouth filled blood.

Edwin's eyes narrowed over the rim of his glass as he took a long, thoughtful sip.

"I was devoted to your mother. Billie's the one who screwed around. Tried to saddle me with another man's child. If she hadn't betrayed me—"

"You would have found a different reason to leave."

Edwin shrugged. Then laughed. Loud. Boisterous. A sure sign he hadn't reached the peak of his manic episode.

"Can't argue with the truth. Billie and I were oil and water. Except in bed."

"Stop. Please."

"What do kids say today? TMI? Too much information? I was joking." Edwin snorted. "You're just like your mother. No sense of humor."

"A lack of humor isn't the issue. I'm your daughter. I don't want to know what you do behind closed doors." Calder shuddered. "Ever."

"Too bad you can't hide from your mother's love life. Billie and Ingo Hunter? You could have knocked me over with a feather."

"She told you?"

Edwin had arrived early. When Calder came down the stairs, she found her parents. Heads together. Flirting like teenagers.

"I heard a rumbling from mutual friends. Apparently, they've become inseparable. How long have they been together?"

"Not long." *Or too long, depending on the point of view.*

"Billie always was a fast mover." Edwin rubbed his chin, a speculative glint in his eyes. "Serious?"

"Hard to say."

"Darling, Calder. Getting anything out of you is like pulling teeth." He signaled the waiter for another drink. Number three and dinner was yet to arrive. "I only want what's best for your mother. And for you."

The last time Edwin showed interest in Calder's personal life—beyond *his* minor role—was the other side of never. Which suited her, thank you very much. He didn't ask because he didn't care. A minor ache—one she long ago learned to live with.

"Billie is Billie. *I* can take care of myself."

"You have to be careful." Edwin's tone changed from casual to serious. "Fortune hunters are like cockroaches. They prefer the dark of night. And, kill one, a hundred more will pop up to take his place."

"I guess the secret is to find a man who doesn't care about my money."

"No such animal."

Just in time, Calder stopped herself from blurting out Adam's name. She didn't want to give her father any kind of ammunition. *I told you so* was in the top five of his favorite phrases. As much as she wanted to believe she'd found one of the good guys, things were too new. Too fragile. Too… everything.

If Adam was part of her life the next time Edwin swooped through New York, she might mention the relationship. Or not. Lord, why wasn't she blessed with a less complicated father? And mother? If not for her sisters, bless each one, she didn't know what she would do.

The arrival of their meal meant a much-welcome break in the conversation. Calder took a bite and sighed with pleasure. The lobster dipped in drawn butter melted in her mouth.

Edwin sliced into his steak, so rare blood practically squirted across the plate. He speared the meat with his fork.

"Good," he said, undisguised pleasure in his sigh.

Calder nodded. Quickly, she averted her eyes when a dribble of red liquid landed on Edwin's chin. Breathe deep, she reminded herself while her stomach did a slow roll. The line between raw and cooked was razor thin. The chef should have saved himself a step and simply ripped the steak directly from the cow.

If Calder had remembered Edwin's proclivity for the uncooked, she would have guided him toward tonight's special. Beef bourguignon. Safe. Tasty. And bloodless.

"I met an interesting young man when I stopped over in London."

Defenses down, appetite gone, Calder didn't catch the implications, or see the gaping trap her father had set with his seemingly innocuous comment.

"Interesting is good."

Absently, Calder pushed her entrée from one side of her plate to the other. She'd take the food home. Perhaps Mrs. Finch could use the leftovers for her seafood bisque.

"Glad you agree. He lives in New York."

Frowning, Calder gave up. She set aside her fork to focus her attention on her father. She didn't want to agree to something she'd later regret.

"*Who* lives in New York?"

"Tink Winchester. One of *the* Winchesters?"

Calder was familiar with the family. Tink was short for Thomas. One of those ridiculous nicknames only wealthy prep school boys somehow acquired. He and Milo Prendergast ran with the same crowd. Not exactly a ringing endorsement.

"Does Tink have something to do with why you're in New York?"

"Not really." Edwin lost interest in his steak. With one swig, he downed the last drop of bourbon. "Thought you'd be a good match."

"Me? And Tink Winchester?"

Calder winced when she realized her father wanted to play matchmaker. Payback for this morning and her awkward attempt to set Bryce up on a date. Karma, the bitch, had a nasty sense of humor.

"When your name came up, he seemed very interested."

Edwin discussed her with Tink Winchester? *Ick.*

"I've known Tink for years. We've barely exchanged two words."

"Tink—most men, I imagine—find you..." Edwin rubbed his chin, then shrugged. "What the hell. Men don't care for overly-opinionated women, Calder."

"Oh?"

The expected rush of anger made Calder's blood heat. She didn't give a damn what men cared for. She'd heard the criticism before. But never from her father. The unexpected censure hurt. More than she liked to admit.

"Don't make up your mind so quickly. Men like Tink Winchester don't grow on trees."

"No. They just swing from the branches."

Edwin rattled the ice in his glass, visibly annoyed by her attitude, and the absence of alcohol.

"I have no idea what the hell you're talking about."

Edwin understood her meaning. He simply chose to pretend otherwise. Calder was happy to explain.

"Tink Winchester has the manners of a gorilla. With a much lower I.Q."

"Who cares?"

The waiter delivered another drink, which temporarily mollified Edwin. Calder took the opportunity to ask for the check. And a doggy bag.

"Tink has money. When his father dies, he'll have more. Not as much as you, but enough to partially even the playing field."

"Money didn't keep you and Billie together."

Well lubricated, Edwin graciously handed his credit card to the waiter without a glance at the bill.

"Do as I say, not as I do."

"Should I thank you for the sage words of advice?" From his expression, Calder knew she'd hit the nail on the head. Unbelievable. "I'll give Tink a pass. For his sake as well as my own. He should find a nice, docile wife. One without opinions. Or a backbone."

"You know what you are, Calder?"

"Yes." *Strong. Independent.* "Do you?"

"You're a ballbuster."

Calder wanted to laugh. Right in Edwin's face. Tomorrow, she planned to have a t-shirt printed in bright red letters. For herself and each of her sisters.

Ballbuster. And proud of it.

"Excuse me? Mr. Calder? The manager would like a word."

The waiter looked nervous. Slightly sick to his stomach.

"Tell the manager he can come to me."

"I'm sorry, sir. But…"

The waiter glanced at Calder before he bent to whisper in Edwin's ear. Whatever he said changed her father's attitude.

"Seems I'm needed on the phone. Business. Might take a while, so you should head home."

Confused by his abrupt dismissal, Calder gathered her purse and leftover lobster.

"If you're sure."

Obviously distracted, Edwin patted her on the shoulder.

"I'll call you soon."

Edwin followed the waiter to where the manager waited near the back of the restaurant. The men immediately jumped into a heated, but brief, conversation. Her father pulled out his wallet and threw a handful of cash in the manager's face.

Then, his back iron-rod stiff, stormed off. Out the side exit. Calder didn't follow. Instead, she left through the front. As she slid into a cab, she wondered if she'd read the scene correctly. The argument. The money. If she was right, her father's credit card had been declined. A computer glitch? If she didn't know better, she would suspect money problems. But how? Edwin was a wealthy man. Besides, he had enough to pay the dinner bill.

Edwin Calder couldn't be broke. Could he?

The cityscape outside her window went unnoticed as Calder relived the evening in her head. Her father might ask her to invest in a sure thing, but he never talked about his financial status. Good or bad. Like her grandfather, Edwin believed men earned, Calder women shopped.

Calder would never give her father advice. However, she knew plenty of people—brilliant people—who could. With a sigh, she rested her head against the seat, eyes closed. She hoped she'd misinterpreted the situation. Either way, unless he asked, her hands were tied.

Edwin's attitude toward her—toward women in general—was wired into his hard drive. Calder had tried to point out why he was wrong. The examples were numerous. Andi. Bryce. Destry. Wildly successful, every one. He waved her off like an annoying, inconsequential gnat.

Erica's Angels? Her multimillion-dollar non-profit organization? Cute, according to Edwin. Something to occupy her time until she did what all women were born to do. Marry and procreate.

Damn it! Why did Calder let him get to her? Invariably, an evening with her father ended in one of two ways. Suppressed anger, or mild depression. She would go home. Vent to her sisters. Who better to commiserate than other lifetime members of the *Bad Father Club*?

Same beginning. Same middle. Same end. No matter her resolve, she always let Edwin get under her skin. Unconsciously, Calder's hands curled into fists.

"Andi was right. Enough wallowing," Calder muttered under her breath.

Stopped at a traffic light, the cab driver glanced over his shoulder.

"You say something to me?" he asked in a heavy Brooklyn accent.

"No. I—"

Suddenly, Calder realized where they were. The part of the city. The street.

"Change of plans. Take a right, please."

Calder gave the driver the new address. Energized, she picked up her phone.

"I didn't expect to hear from you tonight."

The sound of Adam's voice warmed the chill that had settled into Calder's bones.

"Good surprise, or bad?"

"What do you think?"

"I think I'd like to stop by. If you don't mind." Calder paused. "If you're home."

"How soon can you get here?"

Eager. Welcoming. A smile formed on Calder's lips as the taxi pulled to a stop.

"A minute and a half. Two at the most. Depends on your doorman and the speed of the elevator."

"I can't predict the elevator. However, Harvey has instructions to let you up. Anytime. Day or night. No questions asked."

"I'm on my way."

Calder paid the driver. With a nod, the doorman welcomed her into the building.

"Good evening, Ms. Benedict."

"How are you, Harvey?" Calder sent the young man a friendly smile.

"Well, thank you." Harvey tipped his hat.

As if in sympathy to her frame of mind, the elevator dinged the second Calder pushed the call button. To her surprise, her delight, when the doors opened, Adam waited inside.

When she walked past him, to the far side of the car. No kiss. No hug. Adam leaned against the wall. Arms crossed. Brow raised.

"Hello," she said.

"Hi." He took in her appearance, slow and sweeping. "Nice outfit. Been on a date?"

A logical deduction, Calder supposed. The dove-gray dress, knee-length, capped sleeves. Ultra-chic. Flattering. Fitted, but by no means figure hugging. Her hair, twisted into a bun, rested at the nape of her neck. Simple hoop earrings were her only jewelry.

"Dinner with my father."

"Sounds nice." Adam's gaze narrowed as he looked into her eyes. "Or, maybe not."

"I need to ask you something."

Not sure of her mood, Adam didn't take her hand. Or lay a guiding touch at the base of her back. When the doors opened, he stood back with a motion for her to proceed him. In his apartment, he turned the locks, leaned his hip against the arm of the sofa, and waited.

After Calder set her purse on the coffee table, she slipped out of her red Prada pumps. At the opposite end of the sofa, she mirrored Adam's stance.

"How do you feel about overly opinionated women?"

As he pondered the question, Adam's expression turned from inquisitive to perplexed. "You'll have to clue me in. Define *overly* opinionated. Cause quite frankly? A woman without opinions of her own is boring as hell."

"You answered my question." *Perfectly.*

Calder could have kissed him. And she would. With pleasure. But not yet.

"Do you think I'm a ballbuster?

Adam was quick on the uptake.

"I *think* I hate your father. What kind of man spouts so much bullshit to *any* woman? Let alone his own daughter?"

His voice stayed calm, but his eyes grew stormy. Adam was angry. Angry at her father and *for* her. Calder wasn't prone to tears. Yet, she had to swallow hard to keep her eyes from filling.

"Am I, or aren't I?"

"Of course you're a ballbuster. Men can be pigs. I know from experience."

Calder felt a thousand pounds lighter. In body and soul.

"You? A pig?" A teasing glint entered her eyes. "Unbelievable."

"Mostly in my younger, dumber days. Don't get me wrong. I'm not perfect. Occasionally, I revert to type."

"Care to share an example?"

"Not on your life. I'm no fool." Adam slid from the sofa's arm to a cushion. With a tug he brought Calder down beside him. "Want the truth?"

Calder smiled. She loved when he asked.

"Always."

"My balls and I are strong enough to take a little busting. When warranted." With a gentle touch, he ran a finger across her cheek. "I trust you'll use your powers wisely?"

One of the good guys. The knowledge sang in Calder's mind. Through her blood. Her heart, pounding wildly, listened.

"I have all kinds of powers." She straddled Adam's legs, her skirt riding up her thighs. "Some you've never seen. Interested?"

Adam pushed her dress a little higher until the hem met the edge of her silk underwear.

"As I said, I'm no fool."

Lips a whisper's breath from his ear, Calder bit the lobe. Adam rewarded her with a deep groan.

Before she could blink, he flipped her around until her back was flat on the sofa, his body blanketing hers. Calder barely managed to gasp out the promise she couldn't wait to keep.

"You are about to get *so* lucky."

Slowly, Adam shook his head.

"I already am."

CHAPTER EIGHTEEN

CALDER APPROACHED THE entrance to the solarium with determination. But little enthusiasm.

Since the incident with her father, Calder had wrestled with the proper course of action. Edwin felt he could ask *her* anything, she didn't feel as free.

She was his daughter. His only child. Had been for close to thirty years. Yet, the entire time he'd relegated her to the fringes of his life. Every time Calder believed she didn't care, he proved her wrong.

Try as she might, Calder couldn't turn off her feelings. If her father was in trouble, she wanted to know. Her mother could be a surprising font of information where her ex-husbands were concerned.

The sound of Billie's slightly off-key singing hit her ears. She only sang when she thought no one was around to hear.

What Billie didn't realize was how far her high-pitched vocalizing carried. For a woman who insisted she was a closet singer, she belted every song as if she were at Carnegie Hall. And the sound system was on the fritz.

Disco was her songbook of choice. Today, Billie did her best Donna Summer tribute, shaking her backside as she arranged a large bouquet of stark white roses. *Hot Stuff*, indeed.

"Nice flowers."

Billie gasped.

"Why do you girls insist on sneaking up? Scared the life out of me. If I die a decade early, you and your sisters will be the reason."

A familiar complaint, Calder simply smiled. Billie, quick to forgive, smiled back. She held up the vase of roses and preened.

"Ingo sends me two dozen three times a week. He's so thoughtful."

Though Calder hated the smell, she could appreciate a rose's beauty. Ingo Hunter was another matter. She had a meeting scheduled with Dee Wakefield later today to go over what she'd uncovered. For now, she had another man on her mind.

The solarium was located on the far west side of the mansion. Billie spent more time in the room than anyone else. She claimed the moist heat, necessary to keep the abundant tropical plants healthy, was good for her complexion.

Calder suspected the true reason had more to do with the connection to Lilianna Benedict. Billie's mother died shortly after the addition she'd designed was completed. Just before her daughter's tenth birthday.

Pictures of Calder's maternal grandmother showed a woman of striking beauty. The shape of her eyes. Her bone structure. Even the way she held her head was Billie's perfect match.

"Have you spoken to my father lately?"

"Edwin? Such a dear man."

With a vague smile, Billie pressed her face into the bouquet and inhaled. Calder sighed.

"Has he called?"

"No. Why would he?"

The filled vase in her hands, Billie left the solarium. Calder followed, determined to get a satisfactory answer. Subtle didn't work with her mother. Time to get direct.

"Did Edwin mention money problems the last time you saw him?"

"He told you? I'm so glad." As she walked and talked, Billie placed the roses on each surface she passed. Never satisfied, she picked up the vase and moved to the next table. Then the next. "I told him you'd understand. But you know your father. Proud and stubborn."

Yet, Edwin confided in Billie. Because...? Calder's stomach sank.

"How much money did you give him?"

Billie brushed off Calder's concern with a wave of her perfectly manicured nails.

"What if I did? He doesn't ask often. Only when his other options have dried up."

Edwin's problems weren't something new? The revelation made Calder's head spin. She believed her father was an accomplished, successful businessman. Obviously, she was wrong.

When she realized Billie was almost to the end of the hallway, Calder hurried to catch up.

"How often does Edwin ask for money?"

"Hmm?" Billie set the flowers on an antique table, stepped back to survey the results, a frown of deep concentration on her face.

"Billie! How often?"

"A few times since we divorced."

"A few?" Calder prodded. "As in twice? Three times? What excuse does he give?"

"Honestly, Calder." Billie rolled her eyes over all the fuss. "Six? Maybe. I've lost track. Bad investments. A downturn in the stock market. That actress who took him to the cleaners. Silly man. I could have told him not to marry her. She had thick ankles."

Since ankles, thick or otherwise, had no correlation, Calder ignored the comment.

"If Dad is in trouble—"

"You don't need to worry about Edwin. He's never down for long." Billie bit her lip. "Promise you won't mention our conversation to Ingo. He doesn't understand why I remain friends with my ex-husbands. I see nothing wrong with helping your father. He might not agree. Understand?"

No problem. Calder avoided the man like the plague.

"Don't worry. I won't say anything."

Her mind already on more important matters, Billie turned her head from side to side as she considered the roses.

"What do you think? Should I leave the flowers here, or move them to the downstairs foyer?"

Any more questions would be useless. Billie had ever so briefly drifted into Calder's world. Now, safely in her own happy cocoon, she was back to her old, carefree self.

"I'm certain wherever you choose will be just right."

The big picture about her father's financial woes had come into focus. The specific details were a murky mess. She could do some digging. Rather, she could put Dee Wakefield on the trail.

To what end? Calder started up the back stairway, deep in thought. Even if she wanted to help—outside of money—what could she do?

"YOU CAN'T DO a thing."

Calder sat in Andi's office as her sister sorted through a stack of gauzy material. She'd come for advice. As expected, the verdict was swift and to the point. Yet, for some reason, she felt the need to protest.

"I might be able to help."

"How? Give him money? If Edwin asked, what would you say?"

"No." For good reason.

When Destry was seventeen, she gave her father money. By Benedict standards, not a lot. Yet, a substantial amount. She didn't expect him to pay her back. Unfortunately, after she gave him a taste, he considered her to be easy pickings. He was wrong.

Destry never made the same mistake twice. The experience added another layer to her already cloudy outlook on life. By example, her sisters learned a valuable lesson.

Never give their fathers money.

"Edwin won't change. Advice is a waste of breath. An offer of support will fall on deaf ears."

Andi's father was the same. Destry's was a lost cause. And while Bryce's father was the most easygoing of the lot, he was unpredictable.

Money was only one of the pitfalls the Benedict sisters had to deal with where Billie's ex-husbands were concerned.

"My problem is, I feel guilty."

"You feel guilty because you don't feel guilty."

"I knew you'd understand."

"Who better?" Andi set aside her work to join Calder on the deep-blue velvet loveseat. "Our parents are screwed up. But at least they gave us each other."

Andi put an arm around Calder's waist. Comforting. Loving. Her hug felt like home.

"Should we thank them?" Calder teased.

Andi's laugh filled the room.

"Let's not get carried away."

THE FILE FELT lighter than Calder expected. After a brief but friendly greeting, Dee Wakefield sat the folder on the desk. She took a seat. Stretched out her legs, crossed her ankles, and relaxed.

"Before I say anything, read what I found. I'll add my take after you get a feel for the information. Warning. A week isn't very long. I've only scratched the surface."

"I understand." Calder started reading.

"Are your sisters coming?"

"Just me. I'll fill them in later."

Dee popped a butter cookie into her mouth. "Between the excellent coffee and the butter cookies? You're my favorite client ever."

Calder smiled.

"If I took away the treats?"

"Top five. With a bullet."

The report started with the basics. Ingo Hunter's age. Place of birth. He was an only child. Parents deceased. The money they left him was enough for several very indulgent lifetimes.

Calder checked the amount of the inheritance against Hunter's current estimated net worth. Frowning, she looked up.

"Are these numbers correct?"

"We haven't known each other long, so I won't take offense." Dee topped off her coffee, then retook her seat. "I check every fact. Every number. Every period and comma. Hunter isn't the savvy businessman he wants the world to believe."

Unlike Calder's father, Ingo Hunter wasn't hurting. However, in thirty-five years, he managed to diminish his fortune by a considerable amount.

"I'm no expert, but some things are obvious. Hunter loses a lot of money for his investors. He tends to skate through with a few bumps then, recoups a hefty chunk of cash on the next deal. Then loses. Recoups. The circle bends."

"But never breaks."

"My guess? His tax returns are this side of dodgy. A good accountant and some high-up friends keep him in clover." Dee shrugged. "You'll never know for certain unless you find someone equally as dodgy to do some digging."

Calder could speak for her sisters without hesitation.

"No."

The approval in Dee's eyes was easy to read.

"Be nice if Hunter's actions were an anomaly. Truth is, what I found is standard operating procedure for the filthy rich. No offense."

"None taken."

The books Calder kept defined squeaky clean. Professionally, *and* personally.

"I haven't been able to scratch up a lot about Hunter's after-hours life. Other than the basics. He was married. Only once. One child. Ingo Hunter the third." Dee sneered. "What's the deal with numbers? The second. The fourth? One is more than enough."

"Legacy, I suppose." Considering the history of her name, Calder didn't feel in any position to judge. "Why don't I remember anything about Hunter's son?"

"Fell off the map ten years ago. And when I say fell off, I mean vanished. Without a trace. I'll keep looking. Even if his address is six feet under, he has to be somewhere."

"You think he's dead?"

Thoughtfully, Dee sipped her coffee.

"Nah. The funeral would have made headlines. Hunter wouldn't let grief get in the way of publicity."

Sad, but true. Calder knew many people who felt the same way. Huge weddings. Bigger funerals. Many, many cameras.

"*The Third* attended Carver Academy. Some snooty, and very exclusive, upstate prep school."

Calder was impressed. Unlike many of the places wealthy families chose to educate their children, money couldn't get a child through Carver's gates, only brains. The entrance exam was killer. For some.

"Carver Academy made a hard push for Destry."

"*They* came after *her*? Like a college after a top athlete?" Dee shook her head as if the scenario was beyond her grasp.

"High school academic recruitment is a big deal. The best minds plus the highest test scores equal prestige."

The ideals of learning were a lofty goal. However, only money kept the doors open, the lights on, and the eighteen-hole golf course groomed. Because of their reputation, Carver charged triple what some schools asked. Tuition alone—forget about all the extra fees—was more than most people made in ten years.

"Destry attended Carver Academy? Maybe she met Hunter's son."

"She aced the entrance exam—to prove she could. Then, the little genius told them where they could shove their blue and gold uniform. Destry isn't a fan of rules. Or uniforms."

Calder chuckled at the memory. Thirteen years old and full of piss and vinegar. The only thing that had changed was Destry's age.

"On the surface, Ingo Hunter's information cupboards are pretty bare. Makes me itchy." Absently, Dee scratched her leg. "Figure if I can't find anything, there must be something."

"What's your plan?"

"Dig, baby, dig. So far, nobody's talking. Yet. One disgruntled employee. A spurned ex." Some of Calder's misgivings must have shown in her eyes. "Don't worry. I won't step on too many toes."

"I'd hoped our meeting would give me a definitive answer."

"I *will* find out if Hunter is a threat to your mother."

"But a threat how?"

Dee shrugged.

"Exactly why you hired me. If Hunter wants something besides your mother's scintillating company, I'll find out."

Calder believed in Dee. Trusted her to find what they needed. Information. Hunter's secrets. His agenda.

Absently, Calder tapped the file with her finger. Nothing would help if they found out too late.

CHAPTER NINETEEN

ADAM DOUBLE CHECKED his schedule. Jam packed, he had just enough time for a quick bite to eat before he zipped across the Queensboro Bridge. After a non-stop morning crisscrossing Manhattan, then back again, the one thirty meeting would take the better part of the afternoon.

Some days he spent more time in traffic than interacting with clients.

Not that Adam had any complaints. Business was so good, he was ready to expand his workforce. He should have made the move months ago. Another body, or two—maybe three—made perfect sense.

The problem? Right now, he controlled every aspect of his one-man operation. Adam had to learn the art of delegation.

"You're killing yourself." Melvin tossed Adam a sandwich. "You know a million people. They know a couple million more. Somewhere in the pool of friends and acquaintances must be someone who you trust to take on some of the load."

Adam could name a dozen off the top of his head. Good men and women. Hardworking. Capable. Reliable. All he had to do was make a few calls. Whenever he tried, he suddenly lost his ability to dial.

"I'll get there." *Eventually*.

To save wear and tear on his suit, Adam leaned against the side of his newly hand-tooled car. Melvin, dressed in his usual paint-splattered coveralls, lounged on a pile of cinderblocks. The job—arranged by Adam—was huge. The newly constructed home needed *a lot* of paint.

Melvin and his crew were almost finished inside. Adam took a tour before they settled down to eat. The exterior was up next—as soon as landscaping and general cleanup were completed.

"Tamara has a cousin."

"Ah, Tamara and her endless supply of relatives." Adam bit into the ham and cheddar. Good sandwich.

"You can scoff. I know what you're looking for. Reggie meets all your qualifications. And more. He's super organized. A wiz with computers. He—"

"Tell him to email me his resume."

"Really?" Melvin did a sitting happy dance, arms and legs waving in the air. "I had a long, step-by-step argument ready. You saved me a lot of words, buddy."

"What are friends for?"

"Coffee?" Melvin held up an oversized thermos.

Adam shook his head.

"I'll stick to water."

Adam's timing wasn't coincidental. He could have stopped by the site that morning. Or later in the day. Tamara was a great cook and always packed more than her husband could eat. Melvin was happy to share. Adam was happy to accept.

More than food, he enjoyed the company. They ate in companionable silence. When Melvin pulled out two thick slices of cake, Adam wondered why he didn't join his pal for lunch more often.

"Banana spice with cream cheese frosting." Melvin took a huge bite.

"Delicious." Adam chewed slowly, savoring the tender goodness.

Melvin let out a hefty sigh as he wiped his mouth.

"I guess I'll have to ask."

No need for Adam to respond. Eventually, Melvin would get to the point. He emptied his water, tossed the empty bottle into the trash. And waited.

"Word on the street is you have a new woman in your life."

Ah, gossip. Adam had planned to mention Calder. No reason not to have a little fun first.

"Why are you hanging out on the street? And does Tamara know?"

"You're funny. Hilarious. If you don't want to tell me, just say so."

Adam's lips twitched. He could always rely on Melvin to give him a good laugh.

"I don't want to tell you."

"Fuck you." Melvin jumped to his feet. Before he could storm off, Adam relented.

"Her name is Calder."

"Holy shit, holy shit. Holy. Shit." Eyes wide, Melvin slapped Adam on the back. "Calder *Benedict*? Super rich? Super connected? Super out of your league? *That* Calder?"

"Calder is the most down to earth person you'll ever meet. As for out of my league? You're right. Luckily, she doesn't agree."

Melvin let out a low whistle.

"Did you meet before or after my crew did the job at her place? Shit, man. The woman lives in a freaking castle."

"We met during. As for where she lives? So what?"

Adam wasn't after her money. Still, he wasn't blind to the differences in their lifestyles. The less impressed he acted, the sooner the feeling would become reality. He hoped.

"Over a month and you haven't said a word. No wonder you didn't have time to come to dinner. I was going to suggest you bring your new lady. But Calder Benedict?" Melvin cleared his throat. "Bad idea."

"Why?"

"Tamara and I live in a one-bedroom walkup. The house will be ready to move in next month. Even then? She can afford the Ritz. The closest we ever get is the cracker."

Adam laughed. Good joke. Except Melvin was dead serious.

"Calder doesn't mind a few flights of stairs. And she likes crackers."

"Adam…"

"At least meet her before you pass judgment."

"I'm sure she's great. But—"

"Are we invited, or not?"

"Sure. What the hell?" Melvin threw his hands up in defeat. "Friday work for you?"

With a glance at his watch, Adam realized he better get going, or he'd be late. Behind the wheel, Adam started the car.

"Unless you hear different, we'll be there."

"Tamara will kill me," Melvin muttered.

He had good friends, Adam thought as he drove away. Calder would love them. And, despite Melvin doubts, he knew they would love her.

CHAPTER TWENTY

THE LAST MILE of Calder's daily run was her favorite. Her blood flowed. Sweat streamed from her face. Her muscles were loose. Best of all, the damn thing was almost over.

Exercise was a solitary activity. A necessary evil. Not a social event. Today, with Adam at her side, she decided some chit-chat wasn't a bad thing. Five miles passed without notice. *Almost*. Right off the top of her head, Calder could think of a dozen things she'd rather do. But for the first time, her companion made the pounding of her feet on the pavement as close to fun as she would get.

The eye candy he provided when he bent to tie his shoes didn't hurt either.

Adam talked as they ran without a single huff or puff. When Calder took her usual detour up a long flight of steps, down, back up, and down again, he didn't complain. Instead, a glint of competitiveness entered his blue eyes. He won the unofficial race by three strides.

Calder chalked his victory up to longer legs—not superior speed.

"Any plans for Friday night?"

"Right now, all I want is a hot shower and a foot massage."

The cushion in her shoes seemed less springy than usual. Calder did the math. Age plus number of miles. Time for a new pair.

"I can help with both."

Calder sent Adam a look filled with gratitude—and promise.

"You'll scrub my back?"

"With pleasure. Might hit a few other spots. Just to be thorough."

An anticipatory shiver traveled down her spine. Adam was a wonderful shower mate. He never shirked his duties. And was happy to let her soapy hands explore every inch of his hard, sculpted body to her heart's content.

"And the foot massage?"

Adam grinned.

"*After* we shower."

"Deal. If you do a good job, I'll return the favor."

"I'll do a dandy job," he assured her. "Then? *I* pick the part of my body *you* massage."

Sexy, smart, and adorable. She'd hit the trifecta when she met Adam Stone.

"I don't have any set-in-stone plans."

Adam's smile turned into a puzzled frown.

"For…?"

"Friday night. You asked. I answered." *Eventually*.

"We're invited to dinner. Melvin Delray and his wife, Tamara."

They stopped by Adam's car. He took a couple towels from the trunk, handing one to Calder.

Since he invited himself on her run, he insisted she pick their route. Calder always started in the same place. On the sidewalk outside the mansion. For variety, she'd go right. Or left. Or straight ahead. Whatever her mood.

"Old friends?" Calder asked as she did her post-run cool down stretch.

"Melvin's an old Navy buddy."

"Another one? Did you know anybody before you joined the military?"

"One or two, smartass." Adam snapped his towel in her direction. The end barely grazed her butt. "Melvin is my best friend. Tamara is a sweetheart."

"Okay."

"Really?" Adam used his towel to wipe Calder's cheek. His other hand snaked around her waist. "No argument?"

"Why? I like to meet new people. Friends of my friends are even better."

"We're friends?"

Calder put her towel around Adam's neck. A hand on each end, she had him right where she wanted him.

"Do I have your attention?"

"From the moment we met."

Unlike any man she knew, Adam could deliver an obvious line with utter sincerity in his eyes. And mean every word. He made her heart melt. Little by little. Day by day. If she wasn't careful, the increasingly thin protective layer of ice, so carefully constructed, would soon be nothing but slush.

Calder moved in for a kiss. She could get used to a warm heart.

"Don't distract me. I have a point to make."

"Who kissed who, sweet lips?

"We can be lovers without friendship." Calder continued without acknowledging Adam's question. "However, I don't run with a lover who isn't a friend. Understand?"

"I can follow your logic. And agree." With the pad of his thumb, Adam traced her bottom lip. "You said you always run alone."

"I did. Until today."

"I'm your first?" Adam let out a sound, half groan. Half chuckle. "Sounded different in my head."

Calder laughed with him—and a little at him.

"Another minute and my clothes will permanently adhere to my body."

Calder took his hand. Normally, Adam didn't hesitate to go where she wanted. Suddenly, he became an immovable object.

"Where are we going?"

"To shower. And so forth. Come on."

Adam dug in.

"I thought we'd go to my place."

"Why? *My* place is right across the street."

"Well. Sure. But…"

Adam's glib tongue vanished. Right down his throat, if his cough was any indication.

"My apartment is private."

"So is my room."

Calder tugged. Hard. Reluctantly, Adam unglued his feet. But he wasn't in a hurry. He made the trip more of a journey than a jaunt.

"What if your sisters are home? Or your mother? Or Mrs. Finch?"

"I'll put a do not disturb sign on my door. In fact, I'll—"

The light dawned. Adam's reluctance. IIis sheepish expression. Worry her family might see him. He was embarrassed.

Afraid he might bolt if she stopped their forward progress, Calder urged him up the steps. She keyed in the security code. When the door clicked open, she pushed Adam through.

"Sometimes you are too adorable for words. We're well above the age of consent. As is every woman in my family."

For a second, Calder considered taking the elevator. She opted instead for the stairs. To keep Adam's mind off where they were headed, she told him a story.

Other than deliveries, the servants, or physical disabilities—Bryce once broke her ankle on a skateboarding dare gone wrong—only her mother used the elevator on a regular basis.

"Billie doesn't approve of sweat."

Adam, whether drawn into Calder's tale or resigned to the inevitable, followed without protest.

"Everybody sweats."

"Billie isn't convinced. I told her if she started taking the stairs, within a week, sweat wouldn't be an issue. Her lung capacity would increase. And, her heart would thank her."

"What was her response?"

"Shopping is her exercise. No sweat necessary."

"Huh."

Calder paused on the second landing.

"Huh, what?"

Brow furrowed, Adam scratched his chin.

"I wonder. Is your mother really as colorful as you paint her?"

"You think I exaggerate her quirks?"

"Your perspective could be skewed. Just a little."

She understood Adam's doubts. Billie was a woman like no other. A true original. The only way he would believe the unbelievable was with his own eyes.

The prospect of the inevitable meeting brought mixed emotions. Men fell like flies at Billie Benedict's feet. Calder wanted Adam to be the exception. If Adam was dazzled—

Calder gave herself a mental shake. Billie was Billie. And Adam? A little dazzle she could live with. He was only human. She wouldn't want him any other way.

Taking his hand, Calder started up the next flight of stairs. Such a simple connection. His fingers clasped with hers at once calmed and excited. A paradox. One she thoroughly enjoyed.

"When we were eight," she continued her story. "Bryce and I spent one rainy afternoon exploring the elevator's possibilities."

Expressly forbidden to enter unless accompanied by an adult, they'd been drawn by the unknown. The dangerous. The chance they might get caught only added to the excitement.

Up and down. Up and down. They giggled like looney thieves. Bryce's whispered imagery set the stage. A rocket ship to outer space. A passageway to an exotic underground world.

The novelty soon wore off. Their imaginations were powerful, but could only take them so far. Each time the doors opened, they weren't presented with something new. Instead, found themselves in the same place. Safely tucked away in their Upper East Side mansion.

"The magic was gone. Since then, I've stuck to the stairs. Good for the legs."

Approval filled Adam's gaze.

"Not bad for your butt either."

Because the compliment was sincere and came from the right man, Calder put a little wiggle in her walk.

"Here we are." She made a sweeping gesture. "My room. We came the entire way without a relative in sight."

"What about the return trip?"

"Worrywart."

"Wait."

When Adam stopped at the threshold, Calder sighed. If she didn't know better, she'd think he was an inexperienced virgin. *Boy, oh, boy, did she know better.*

"I left my change of clothes in the car."

"Seriously? I offer you a hot, soapy, sex-filled shower, and you're worried about clean underwear?"

"I'm a fool." Adam swooped Calder into his arms. Inside the bedroom, he slammed the door shut with his foot. "I'd offer to leave. But I haven't graduated to sheer stupidity quite yet."

"I knew my smooth lover was in there somewhere."

A point toward the bathroom was all the extra encouragement he needed. Shoes hit the tiled floor with a thud. Clothes flew in every direction. Adam had Calder's back against the shower wall. Steam rose around them as he sank to his knees.

Eyes closed. Head back. Calder let out a gasping moan of pleasure as she ran her hands over the slick, muscled flesh of Adam's shoulders. One hand at the base of her spine, the other played havoc with her senses. He teased the tender flesh of her inner thighs. Higher. Higher.

Oh. Yes! She thought she knew her body better than anyone. Adam proved her wrong. One touch. One kiss. A gentle swipe of his tongue. He'd become a master of what she liked best. Shafts of pleasure radiated through her body like a shot of electricity.

"Lovely."

"Lovely?" Adam's husky laugh made her blood sing. "Hold on. I'm about to make you forget the meaning of the word."

"Big words for a big—"

Calder's thoughts stuttered, then fell into oblivion. Big…? Man? Dick? Accurate on both counts, any witty quips would have to wait. Adam was right. She forgot the meaning of lovely. Forgot how to talk. Forgot everything outside the here and now.

Forgot everything—but him.

CHAPTER TWENTY-ONE

ADAM BUTTONED HIS gray twill suit jacket. The jacket he'd left in the car. A pair of pants. And Italian leather shoes. Shirt, socks, etc. The change of clothes he always packed for a *just in case* event like today.

Somewhere between the time he fell onto the bed, with Calder, and the time he woke from a pleasure-induced nap, the garment bag and duffel had appeared in a neat pile. Just inside the bedroom door.

"I gave your keys to Hilly."

"Who? And, when?"

"Upstairs maid. When you dozed off."

The concept of a maid, upstairs or otherwise, was odd. Not exactly beyond Adam's comprehension. He read. Watched TV. Went to movies. However, Calder was the first person he knew beyond a business relationship who employed servants.

"I don't know how I feel about someone fetching for me."

While he dressed, Calder had disappeared into her closet. One dress in each hand, she walked out.

"You make her sound like a dog. We pay Hilly a salary—with excellent benefits. I asked her to walk across the street, open a car door, and bring a few items back to the house—activity hardly beyond her purview. Which one?" She held one dress forward, then the other. "Blue or yellow?"

Without a second thought, he nodded toward the yellow. The color made Calder's skin glow. His answer made her beam.

"Great minds." She blew him a kiss before she disappeared back into the closet.

Adam adjusted his tie in the full-length mirror. He'd acquired a certain amount of polish since his punk-assed youth. He rarely gave a thought to whether he fit in or not. A formal dinner? Piece of cake. The world wouldn't end if he used the wrong fork. While he'd rubbed elbows with some of New York City's biggest movers and shakers without the blink of an eye, money and power were Adam's ambition. *Not* his reason for living.

In the reflective glass, Adam took in the details of the room behind him. Details he'd missed while his mind and body were focused on other things. Calder, to be exact.

Simple. Classy. The kind of off-hand elegance that took years to develop. Or, as in the Benedicts' case, was born in their blood.

Fully dressed, Calder left the closet. Blindly, she slipped on a pair of earrings, a small smile on her lips. She'd done something simple to her hair. Flip and a clip—her words. Perfect. Ready to take on the world.

And all Adam wanted to do was throw her back onto the bed and mess her up. Mess both of them up. For the next week or so.

Suddenly, the source of the niggling unease in the pit of his stomach became clear.

"I don't care about your money."

Eyes like warm honey, Calder met his gaze.

"I know."

"No. *Really* listen to me. *Hear* my words, Calder."

Adam took her hand. The physical connection felt important.

"The maid. The house. The antiques. Hell, I didn't grow up around women who casually slipped diamonds on every morning."

Frowning, Calder's hand went to her ear.

"I wear other earrings."

"Diamonds aren't the point." Adam took a breath. Paused to clarify his thoughts. "For a second, I felt out of place."

"You aren't."

"I know. You live in a mansion." Adam shrugged. "Honestly, I like your mansion. And your antiques. And your maids."

Calder's lips twitched. He let out a sigh of relief. In spite of his less than coherent ramblings, she understood.

"Do you like my diamonds? And silk dress. And—"

"I like your lips more."

To prove his point, Adam kissed her. So sweet. And so damn soft. Reluctantly, he pulled away. But not too far.

"I need you to understand. Take away everything. I'd still be here." He cupped her cheek. "Because of you. Always you."

As close to a declaration as he could make—for now—Adam waited. Had he said too much? Not enough?

"Looks like we're heading in the right direction." Calder turned her head. Her lips lingered on his palm. "The *same* direction."

Adam said a little prayer of thanks. The *same* direction. Sounded good to him. No promises. No guarantees. At some point, they might decide to take different paths. Now? Tomorrow? They were exactly where they wanted to be. Together.

OVER HIS PROTESTS, Calder insisted Adam eat something before he left for work. Naturally, Mrs. Finch fixed them a late breakfast. When she asked what he'd like, for the first time in his adult life, Adam worried he might blush.

"An apple is all I need. Really."

"I try never to send one of mine out the door without a full stomach."

Her smile smug, Calder's look dared Adam to argue. How could he? Mrs. Finch called him *one of hers*. With three words, she stamped him with her seal of approval. The casually delivered proclamation left him speechless.

"Fruit and toast for me, please." Calder piped up with her request. She poured Adam a cup of coffee. "Is everybody gone for the day?"

Mrs. Finch nodded.

"Bryce had her usual lumberjack special before she rushed off to parts unknown. Andi was in such a hurry she barely waved hello. Not that she would have eaten if she had the time. Breakfast wise, she's a lost cause."

"And Destry?"

"Pizza."

"We have leftover pizza?" Calder perked up at the idea. Before she could open the refrigerator, Mrs. Finch dashed her hopes.

"We *had* leftover pizza. Your sister sucked up every last pepperoni. Who knows where she ended up after? Somewhere in the city is my nearest guess." Mrs. Finch, filled with eager anticipation, heated up a cast-iron skillet.

"What sounds good, Adam? Pancakes? Eggs and bacon? Do you prefer sausage? Or something vegan. I might have tofu left from Calder's winter health kick. The stuff never expires. She, on the other hand, lasted two weeks before she rejoined the rest of us meat lovers. Scarfed an entire side of beef."

"A bit of an exaggeration." Calder laughed. "Though not by much. And don't worry about Adam. He's one hundred percent carnivore."

"Bacon would be great, Mrs. Finch."

"Eggs?"

"Scrambled."

A happy whistle on her lips, she went to work.

Eyes twinkling, Calder cleared her throat as Adam dug into his breakfast.

"Still wish we'd headed back to your place?"

"The food is fantastic, Mrs. Finch. Thank you." For Calder's ears only, he added, "And thank *you*. Smartass."

"My pleasure."

Under the counter, she squeezed his leg in what some might call a friendly manner. The way her fingers inched up his thigh? Beyond friendship. *Way* beyond. Luckily, Mrs. Finch had her head in the refrigerator, muttering something about what she would make for dinner.

With a shake of his head, Adam removed Calder's hand.

"Behave," Adam warned.

"Always." Calder battered her lashes. "I'm the original good girl."

Adam almost spewed a mouthful of toast over the gleaming marble countertop. Just in time, he tamped down the impulse. Swallowing, he sent Calder a look of disbelief. Had she forgotten their recent shower activities? Followed by the bedroom? And at one point, the floor?

The memories mirrored in Calder's eyes made him wish he could say the hell with work and enjoy a return engagement.

"Good?" he scoffed. "Don't sell yourself short. You're spectacular."

ADAM WALKED CALDER to her office. She wanted to gather some notes for a meeting. The return walk, up the same five flights, was a perfect way to work off part of his bigger than expected breakfast.

When Mrs. Finch insisted he top the bacon and eggs off with a huge, fresh from the oven cinnamon roll. Who was he to argue?

"Anything interesting on your schedule?"

"Depends on how you feel about Greenwich Village. I have a client in the middle of a big renovation. You'd be amazed how often second thoughts set in. He can't see past the chaos. The expense. My job is to remind him how much he'll love the finished product."

Calder looked up from the stack of papers in her hand.

"Seems above and beyond."

"Just another part of the service I provide."

"The contract I signed didn't say anything about above and beyond handholding."

"I'll hold your hand anytime you want."

"Stay back." Calder formed her forefingers into a make-shift cross. "I recognize the glint in your eyes, fella. Neither of us has the time for another round of hide the sausage."

Adam chuckled. And kept his distance.

"Six thirty good for you on Friday?"

"Fine." Calder paused. "I hate to be such a girl."

"But…"

"What should I wear? Are your friends the casually dressy types? Or should I opt for something weekend chic?"

Adam knew Calder wasn't worried about her wardrobe. Give her five minutes notice and she could dress for any occasion with one hand tied behind her back.

"Are you nervous to meet my friends?"

The idea surprised—and charmed—him.

"Maybe. A little. If they hate me, I—"

"Not possible. Just be yourself, Calder. Believe me, they want to like you."

"And I want to like them," Calder assured him. "Still, for my peace of mind…?"

"A casual skirt. Jeans. A nice blouse. Any variation. Melvin and Tamara want to meet you, not your wardrobe. They won't care if you show up in a burlap bag."

"She'll care. Women dress for each other. Melvin might not notice if the heel of my shoe has a scuff, but Tamara will."

"I notice." Adam noticed everything about Calder. "By the way? You, and your heels, are immaculate. Always are."

"You, my friend, are the wonderful exception." Calder gave him a quick kiss. She scuttled away before he could move in for a prolonged embrace. "Now, go. I don't want to be the reason your nervous client has a breakdown."

"He's nervous. Not certifiable." Adam glanced at his wrist. Damn. "I must have dropped my watch in your room."

"You're welcome to look. Or, if you don't mind going without until Friday, I'll have Hilly do a thorough search. I'm sure your watch will turn up."

Hilly the maid? Mentally, Adam threw in the towel. If he wanted Calder, he had to get used to the way she lived. Would always live.

"Sounds like a plan. Hey."

Calder turned her head to the side, a question in her eyes.

"Stay safe."

"I will if you will."

The smile stayed on Adam's face as he walked down the hall. His good mood vanished when he spied Ingo Hunter. Lurking. The man had no business above the second floor where Billie had her bedroom.

"What the hell do you think you're doing up here?"

Guilt flashed across Hunter's face. Quick to recover his composure, his lips moved into a sly, cunning smirk.

"A better question would be, what the hell are *you* doing up here?

Prevarication 101, with a master class in manipulation. The best way out a sticky situation? Answer a question with a question. Though the technique annoyed the hell out of Adam, Hunter couldn't get the best of him. He knew what move to make next. The old accusation cloaked within another question.

"Did you need something in Calder's room?"

Hunter didn't flinch. But his right eye twitched. Ever so slightly. Enough to let Adam know he'd hit the nail on the head.

"Such a large house. My mind was occupied by other matters when I entered the elevator. I must have pushed the wrong floor."

The elevator was all the way at the end of the hall. If he'd made a mistake, Hunter would have realized his error long before he reached Calder's bedroom.

Adam didn't need to point out the obvious. He knew. Hunter knew. Soon, Calder and her sisters would know.

"Mistakes happen. Since I'm on my way out, I'll ride down with you."

A wise man would have cut his losses. Thanked his lucky stars he would live to fight another day. An arrogant man, certain of his superior intellect, didn't think he needed anything as mundane as luck.

Ingo Hunter, from the set of his shoulders to the glint in his eyes, *reeked* of arrogance.

"You didn't answer *my* question, Adam. Why are you here?" Hunter looked around. "Unaccompanied."

Adam didn't respond. Or wilt under the sheer will of Hunter's cold gaze. So, the older man adjusted his strategy to a more personal tract.

"Seems you and I have something in common."

"No. We don't."

"Come on. Just us guys. The Benedict women are a passionate bunch. I can attest to Billie's charms. But I've wondered about the rest of them. You can tell me. What's Calder like in bed?"

Adam saw red. And blue. And green. Colors he pictured on Hunter's swollen face after a thorough beating. With a deep breath, he didn't act on the impulse. As much as he wanted to wipe the smug smirk off the scumbag's face, he remembered where he was.

Some stains were almost impossible to remove. Adam would feel bad if his actions—and Hunter's blood—ruined the beautiful, obviously expensive, Persian rug.

No blood, Adam promised himself. Not today. But he couldn't leave Hunter with the idea the man was allowed to ooze his slime over Calder—or any woman—without some sort of retribution.

Adam's hand closed around the bastard's throat. Surprise replaced the smug expression. Genuine fear seeped into his eyes.

To emphasize the point, Adam slammed Hunter against the wall with just enough force to knock some of the pompous out of the windbag.

"I'm not one of your country club cronies. We'll never be drinking buddies. You know why?" When Hunter didn't answer, Adam tightened his grip. "*Do. You Know. Why?*"

"Why?" Eyes bulging, Hunter gasped the word.

"My friends respect women. *Respect*. In words *and* actions. Women aren't toys placed on Earth for your enjoyment. Money? Muscle? Neither gives you the right to take what isn't freely offered. Understand?"

Bit by bit. Word by word. Adam could feel his control slip. Hunter's face blurred, replaced by one of the anonymous bastards who hurt his mother. The image his imagination pieced together over the years. *Retribution*. His hand shook at the prospect. Tighter. Tighter.

Someone had to pay for her pain and suffering. Finally—

"Adam. Let go. Please."

The voice—familiar, soothing—drifted along the perimeter of the swirling, enveloping, red haze. Subconsciously, he knew what was right. The grip of revenge was seductive. Strong. Almost more than he could resist. *Almost*.

Calder's hand on Adam's wrist broke the spell. Without an ounce of force, or a harsh word. Her touch slowly cooled his blood. Calmed his anger.

Perhaps, saved his soul. With a shove, Adam let go.

Hunter staggered. He rested his hand against the wall. Rubbed his reddened neck, coughing.

"Call the police," he wheezed. "The lunatic attacked me for no reason."

"Adam? Are you with me?" Calder cupped Adam's chin. She didn't give Hunter a second look. "Are you okay?"

"The hell with him. I'm the one he almost killed."

Finally, Calder spared Hunter the briefest glance.

"Dial down the drama." Contempt practically dripped from her tongue. "Adam didn't want to kill you."

"How do you know?"

Good question, Adam thought. Murder's muse had whispered in his ear. Tempted him. More than he wanted to admit. Without Calder, he didn't know if he could have stopped himself in time.

Calder's response surprised him.

"You're breathing. If he wanted you dead, you'd be dead." Calm, matter of fact, Calder met Adam's gaze. "Am I right?"

Adam gave a brisk nod. Calder *was* right. However, the jury was still out on what he'd wanted before she came along and returned his sanity.

"Case closed."

Aghast, Hunter watched as Calder calmly slipped her hand into the crook of Adam's arm.

"Are you out of your fucking mind? If you won't call the cops, I will."

"You want to explain to the police why Adam caught you snooping around my bedroom?" Calder directed her next question to Adam. "When the press gets wind of the story, what will the headlines read? What will the tabloids call him?"

Adam shrugged. And couldn't wait to hear her answer. She tapped her finger to her chin as she pondered the possibilities.

"Ingo Hunter. Jewel thief? Panty pilferer?"

"Panty— Don't be ridiculous. Nobody would believe such a claim." Though Hunter scoffed at the idea, he wisely didn't reach for his phone. "I'll let the incident slide. But if you touch me again, you'll be sorry."

Hunter staggered off toward the elevator with as much dignity as he could muster. Which under the circumstances, wasn't much. The whoosh of the doors signaled he'd left to lick his wounded pride.

"You okay?"

Multiple unanswered questions about what happened and why hung in the air. He'd carried emotional baggage into her home. Almost spilled blood on the floor only feet from the bed where a few hours earlier she'd shared her body with joy and abandon. Yet, Calder's first thoughts were for him. About his welfare.

Adam felt humbled. And sick to his stomach.

"I should go."

"What you should do is come here." With the strength of steel wrapped in velvet, Calder held him close. Her lips brushed his ear. "Breathe."

"I—"

"Just breathe."

Adam's mind protested. He wanted to go. Crawl into a dark place. Brood until the ugly passed. His body had other ideas. Without thought, air filled his lungs. His muscles slowly relaxed.

The fragrance of Calder's hair, the touch of her skin, calmed his chaotic senses.

"You could make a fortune from your brand of magic."

As she smoothed back his hair, a smile formed on Calder's lips.

"I already have a fortune. Besides, I have a feeling my magic would be useless on anyone but you."

Adam had the feeling Calder was wrong. Selfishly, he hoped she never wanted to find out.

Reluctantly, he stepped away. Calder kept hold of his hand.

"Cancel your meeting. We'll drink some tea. Spend the afternoon snuggling on the library sofa."

"A witch *and* a temptress. How am I supposed to say no?"

"You aren't." Calder met his gaze—and sighed. "But you will. Okay. New plan. You go to your massively important meeting."

Calder never gave up so easily.

"What's the catch?"

"I drive. You ride."

"And I tell you what Hunter did to set me off?

"Such a smart man." Calder beamed. She took out her phone.

"I can drive myself." Adam felt the need to state the obvious— if only for the sake of his pride.

"Your nerves aren't in any condition to deal with New York City traffic. I'll grab my purse and we can— Sara? Reschedule my two o'clock with Declan Springfield. I'm off the clock for the rest of the day."

As her long legs ate up the distance to her office, Calder rattled off instructions to her assistant.

"I can drive myself," Adam called out.

Back in a flash, Calder produced a key which she used to lock her bedroom door.

Adam nodded his approval.

"Smart."

"Sad. Here. In my home. I never felt the need to bar anyone from my personal space. Until now. Another reason to hate Ingo Hunter."

Adam wished he had the power to take the shadow of sorrow from Calder's eyes. The only way was to remove Hunter from her life. Permanently. Since he had his emotions under control—for the most part—murder wasn't an option.

If Billie Benedict didn't come to her senses and toss Hunter to the curb, they'd hope Dee Wakefield could dig up enough dirt to end the relationship.

A bonus would be jail time. But Adam understood how the real world worked. Rich, powerful snakes rarely paid their dues behind bars.

"Come on." Calder stopped at the top of the stairs. "Don't want to keep your client waiting."

The smile on Calder's lips didn't fool him. Under the surface, Adam caught a hint of self-satisfaction. Better than sadness any day, Adam couldn't let the moment pass. He had to set her straight on a very important point.

"If I wanted, I could leave without you."

"I know."

Adam took the hand Calder offered. He wanted her to know he appreciated how much she cared. Besides, he liked to touch her. As often as possible.

"I *let* you win." Adam refused to drop the subject until he was certain Calder understood.

"Of course you did. Now and then, *I'll* let *you* win. To prove my point. You can drive."

In spite of himself, Adam chuckled as they left the house and crossed the street. Two strong personalities were bound to clash from time to time. Knowing himself—and Calder—they were destined for some straight-out fights. Followed by some damn fine make-up sessions.

Adam opened the passenger door.

"You're impossible."

Calder slid into the car. Eyes sparkling, she buckled her seatbelt.

"Would you want me any other way?"

"Not in a million years."

CHAPTER TWENTY-TWO

A PERFECT LATE May afternoon. Blue skies and sunshine. Eyes closed, Calder lifted her face to the light and smiled.

The smidgeon of guilt she'd felt after she pushed her company on Adam didn't last long. He might not realize, but he needed her with him. Alone, he would have brooded. Stewed in his proverbial juices.

Calder could have stayed home. Worried about Adam's state of mind. She felt better beside him where she could pull him out of himself. Make him talk.

Talking was always a good idea.

At the first red light they hit, Adam surprised her. He started the discussion without Calder's urging.

"Hunter must have assumed you weren't in the house." Adam slipped on a pair of sunglasses to combat the sun's glare. "Claimed the whole thing was a mistake. Big house. Wrong floor."

"Yadda, yadda, yadda." Calder didn't buy the lame excuse any more than Adam.

The light turned green. Adam stepped on the gas.

"I caught him before he entered your room."

"How can you be certain?"

"Timing was off. Add the disgruntled, *fuck you*, look in his eyes."

Calder hoped Adam was right. If she believed Hunter had pawed through her things, she would need a fumigator. Doable. But inconvenient and time consuming.

Adam laughed, shaking his head.

"Where the hell did you come up with panty pilferer?"

"Beats me. Besides, Hunter's probably more of a sniffer."

"Jesus, Calder. Did you have to put *that* image in my head?"

"I hate to suffer alone."

"Glad I could help." Adam slowed to let a pedestrian cross. "You should contact your sisters. Tell them to follow your lead and lock their doors."

"I texted them before we left the house." Calder frowned as her thoughts grew darker. "I doubt Hunter was after jewelry."

"Or your underwear?"

With just enough zing to drive home her point, Calder jabbed Adam's thigh.

"From now on, panty jokes are officially taboo. Agreed?"

Adam's lips twitched. But he had the good sense to nod.

"Hunter is many things, but he isn't a fool. You want information on him. Whatever his long game, odds are he'd be after the same."

Logical. Except *they* had Dee Wakefield.

"Why do the dirty work himself when he can afford an investigator?"

"Chances are, he has someone on the case. But, whoever he hired doesn't have access to your home."

Calder nodded.

"Thanks to Billie, Hunter can go wherever he wants when we're not around to stop him."

"I'm sorry. But, yes."

With a simple brush of his hand over hers, Adam told her so much. Though Calder couldn't read his eyes through the dark lenses, she knew he was there for her.

"Right now, an unknown person could be sifting through the minutia of my life. Personal and professional. Past and present." Calder rubbed her arms as a chill ran across her skin. "I'm not happy, Adam. Not happy at all. Am I a hypocrite? You know what? Never mind. I don't give a crap."

Adam—dear, sweet, thoughtful Adam—turned the heat to full blast.

"The hell with hypocrisy. We need to get Ingo Hunter out of your life by any method necessary."

"Fair or foul?"

"Exactly." Adam shot her a look before he changed lanes. Finally, he addressed the elephant in the car. "Short of murder."

"If I hadn't come along, you would have pulled yourself back before you did serious damage."

"I'm not so sure."

"*I* am."

Calder hadn't known Adam long. Yet, they'd achieved an intimacy she'd never come close to with men she knew her entire life. Dinners. Lunches. Late-night phone calls. He'd elevated her sex life to heights she hadn't thought possible.

Obviously, Adam had hidden depths. Parts of himself he held close. Rarely—if ever—shared. Didn't everyone? If Calder had her way, she'd have time to explore every side of his personality—good and bad

For now, she would rely on her gut, a little faith, and the absolute belief in two things. Adam Stone would do anything in his power to keep her safe—come hell or high water. Self-defense was one thing. Calder knew he wasn't a murderer.

However, *something* beyond Hunter's unauthorized snooping set Adam off.

"You can tell me anything. I can't guarantee what my reaction will be. But I promise to listen."

Adam parked the car next to a twenty-four-hour laundromat. Hands on the wheel, he stared out the windshield.

"The story isn't mine. Not really." With a sigh, he rubbed the back of his neck. "I need to ask someone before I tell you. Can you wait a little while longer?"

"Of course. When you're ready."

"Thank you."

No, Calder mused, *thank you*. Adam, so thoughtful and caring about another person's feelings accomplished what she hadn't believed possible. As good as he was? He found a way to get even better.

"I KNOW WE need to talk about Ingo Hunter." Bryce scrunched her face as if she tasted something rotten. "First, I need to get girly."

Certain she knew what was about to come, Calder held up her hand.

"Don't. I beg you."

Calder could have held back the tide before she could put the brakes on a determined Bryce. Like a giggly teenager, her sister plopped onto the sofa.

"You had a boy in your room!" Bryce wiggled close. "I need deets."

"Deets? Really? From the woman who complains the world needs to stop with the slang and use proper words?"

"You think you can distract me. But you can't."

Bryce and her infamous one-track mind. Calder rolled her eyes. For once—and only once—she wished her twin was more like their mother.

"Distract you from what?"

Destry, a can of Coke in one hand, a mammoth sandwich in the other, chose the chair near a small end table. She set down her snack, waiting for someone to answer.

"Calder broke the unwritten rule."

Destry snorted.

"Which one?"

"The no sex in our rooms rule?"

"Ah." Incongruously, Destry took a bag of potato chips from the pocket of her silk pants, an apple from the other. "I thought Andi blew the no-sex rule out of the water a long time ago."

"Never in my room," Andi said. She shut the door behind her. Dressed for her own pleasure, she wore jeans and a long-sleeved Columbia University t-shirt. Her blond hair hung loose, and her feet were bare. "The linen closet by the third-floor landing saw some action. And a first-floor guest bathroom."

"Go, Andi!" Destry popped a chip into her mouth. "I assume *he who shall not be named* was your partner in crime?"

"Yes. And, you can say Noah's name. I won't break into a million pieces." Andi had the good grace to shrug. "Not anymore."

"How are things on the Gerry Norton front?"

Calder was genuinely interested. The change of topic, off her love life onto Andi's, was a happy bonus.

"I like him. He's… uncomplicated."

"I.E.? Boring."

The look Andi sent Destry was meant to quell. Little sister wasn't impressed.

"Gerry is a gentleman. I swear, if you say boring one more time, I will kick your ass."

Grinning, Destry held her hands up in defeat. Andi might look like a fashion model, but she had a right hook that could down a linebacker.

"Gerry's a gentleman. Andi got down and dirty in the linen closet, etc. Doesn't change what Calder did with hunky Adam. *In* her bedroom."

Bryce didn't care about *unwritten rules*. None of them did. They weren't kids anymore. They didn't judge each other's choices. However, their home was a special place. If one sister brought home a man, they all knew he wasn't a casual fling.

"Adam isn't boring." To say the least. "He's…"

Sandwich forgotten, Destry leaned closer.

"Yes?"

"He's Adam."

Destry groaned. Bryce sighed. They didn't understand. Until they met someone indescribable, they never would. Andi remained silent, but her blue eyes spoke volumes. *She* knew what Calder meant. Now and then, when a woman was very lucky, she needed only one word to describe a man.

Adam? Andi mouthed his name. Neither Bryce nor Destry noticed the silent question between sisters. Calder swallowed—and nodded. The moment felt huge. As if she hovered a step away from the vast unknown. No parachute. No net. Unsure if she'd take the plunge alone, or if someone—*the* one—waited to fall with her.

"Can we move on to the real reason for our little gathering?" As she passed, Andi patted Calder's shoulder. Taking a seat near Destry, she crossed her legs. "What did Ingo Hunter think he would find in Calder's room? Has he already checked my room? Or Bryce's?"

"Yuck."

Bryce spoke for all of them.

"How can we know?" Destry asked, as puzzled as the rest of them. "I'm gone so much of the time. Anything of value, I have stored in a safe deposit box. The question is, what does *Hunter* consider valuable?"

"Information?" Calder gave the answer she mulled over with Adam. She tossed in the possibility that Hunter had hired his own investigator.

"Makes sense," Destry said. "Any agenda he might have, the more he knows about us, our family history, the better chance he'll get what he wants."

"Billie doesn't know how to keep anything to herself. I know," Bryce laughed. "Hardly a news flash. Just hear me out. Ask her a personal question, she'll talk for hours. However, even our mother might have her limits if someone asked too much, too often."

Calder spent the better part of a sleepless night as she mulled over what they knew. The result? A major case of mush brain. Bryce, Andi, and Destry gave her a sense of rejuvenation. Fresh perspectives. As always, four Benedict sisters were always better than one.

"Hunter can search the house. Our rooms. Find information a professional investigator wouldn't have access to. Smart." Calder hated to use the word, but she might as well be honest. No one here would judge. "I'd do the same if I had access to his home."

"Not a bad idea."

"No, Destry." Andi's tone, the heat in her eyes, brooked no argument. "Breaking and entering is a crime. And dangerous. And stupid."

"I agree."

Andi's gaze narrowed.

"You never give in without an argument. What's the catch?"

"So suspicious." Dramatically, Destry clutched at her chest. "I'm wounded."

"And *I* smell a pile of crap. What's your plan?" Bryce asked.

"She has no plan because she isn't going near any property owned by Ingo Hunter. Right?"

"Only as a last resort. Do you want me to lie?" Destry asked when Andi looked ready to explode.

Calder didn't like the idea any better than Andi. They couldn't stop Destry once she made up her mind. If the time came for drastic measures, she would rather know what their little sister had up her sleeve than be in the dark while she worried.

"Hopefully, if Dee Wakefield does her job, the only resort we'll need will be one where they serve tropical drinks decorated with little umbrellas."

"Sandy beaches? Ocean, clear and blue, as far as the eye can see?" Smiling, Bryce closed her eyes as if she pictured herself there. "How long since the last time the four of us took a vacation together?"

"Years." Andi looked around the room, from sister to sister. "Thanksgiving in Tahiti. Are you with me?"

"Yes, please," Bryce chimed in.

"Couldn't keep me away," Destry nodded. "Calder? One for all, and so on?"

"I'll be there." Calder hesitated. "What if we haven't solved our Ingo Hunter problem by then?"

Three sets of eyes turned toward Andi and waited. With a put-upon sigh, she tossed her hands in the air.

"Fine. You win. If we can't get rid of Hunter by the end of November? We'll sic Destry on the bastard."

A LIGHT KNOCK sounded, drawing Calder's attention. Completely immersed in budget spreadsheets, she frowned at the interruption.

"Come in," she called out.

The door opened—just enough for Destry to stick her head into the office.

"Do you have a minute?"

"Perfect timing. I was ready for a break." Calder pushed away from her desk. "What's up?"

Destry set her backpack on the floor. Black jeans. Leather jacket. She wasn't dressed for a leisurely afternoon at home.

Calder felt the familiar twist in the pit of her stomach.

"Time to say goodbye?"

"Job just came in. ASAP."

"Do you ever get any other kind?"

"Rarely." Destry sent her a half-smile. "In an hour, I'll be on a flight to Santa Fe."

Twenty minutes after she landed, Destry would be up to her neck in her latest adventure. Calder knew the routine, even if she didn't know the details.

"You'll call?"

"Daily." Destry chuckled as she moved in for a hug. "Weekly at the very least."

"You were around longer than usual. I'll miss seeing your face every day—up close and personal."

"Give me a ring. Anytime. My face will be right there on the screen."

"Not the same."

Calder wanted to hold tight, never let go. She knew better. To love Destry was to accept how she lived her life. She had to believe her sister would come back safe and sound or she would never let her out the door.

"Any idea how long you'll be gone?"

"If anything pops on the Ingo Hunter front, I'll be back right away. Otherwise?" Destry shrugged. "Best I can promise, I'll be here for your big charity bash. You know how I hate to miss a great party."

Four weeks until the *Spring Romance Gala*. Destry had been gone longer. Once, she ping-ponged from one end of Europe to the other. Of course, the circumstances were different. She left right after her father went to prison, a haunted look in her eyes. Six months later, she showed up in the middle of the night. Dirty, thin as a rail. Dragging like the tail end of a battered kite. However, whatever she'd been up to had chased away the shadow demons.

Every goodbye—every time—Calder longed to ask Destry not to go. Every time—every goodbye—she bit her tongue. Instead, she pulled her sister in for another hug. And said what she always said.

"Take care."

"Always."

Destry knew the routine. She let Calder hold on as long as she needed. Then, with a wink, she slung her pack over her shoulder and walked out the door.

CHAPTER TWENTY-THREE

ADAM HELD THE door for Calder. She brushed his arm as she passed.

Friday. Date night all over the United States. They hadn't seen each other since he took her home after their trip to Greenwich Village. Other than a confirmation text earlier in the day, they hadn't been in touch.

Space and time. Somehow, Calder instinctively knew Adam needed both. Time to speak with his mother. Space to gather his thoughts.

The conversation wasn't as painful—and only slightly more awkward—than Adam anticipated. Adriana Stone proved once more why she was the greatest woman he would ever know.

Changed by what happened, she hadn't let the attack define her. She didn't live in fear. Or simmer with what she considered fruitless emotions tagged with hate. Instead, she used the experience to help other victims of violence.

When Adam went to his mother, he wasn't sure what he would say. How he would ask if he could tell her story to Calder. He shouldn't have worried.

"Calder. A lovely name. Is she important to you?"

"Yes. Very."

"Well." Adriana took a moment to absorb the news. "I want to meet her. Soon."

"You will. I promise. Mom." Adam took a deep breath. "I need to tell her. But…"

"You wanted to ask me first."

He nodded.

"What a fine young man I raised."

"I'm my mother's son."

"Tell her." Her eyes damp, Adriana nodded. "Your Calder should know."

Adam *would* tell Calder. Later. When they were alone. Now, he wanted them to enjoy the evening. Good food. Good company.

Melvin and Tamara lived in a modest, but well-maintained building. The floors immaculate, the walls graffiti free.

Automatically, Calder started up the stairs without a glance to see if the building possessed an elevator. Adam, right by her side, wondered how much time they'd spent on one staircase or another. He didn't mind. He thought of the walks as their unique brand of bonding.

Besides, the up and down trips gave him the perfect excuse to engage in his second favorite activity. Holding Calder's hand. His first favorite demanded a bit more privacy than a public stairwell.

In a pinch, he could probably persuade her—and enjoy every second of the process.

"When was the last time you visited the Bronx?"

"Do I hear a touch of the snob in your voice?" Calder asked.

"A touch? Probably." Adam returned her smile. "I noticed you didn't answer the question."

"What's the point? When I step out my front door, I don't see Manhattan. I see New York City. The Bronx is part of the whole. Correct?"

"Technically. Some people are more territorial. The borough you occupy matters. So, be honest, rich girl. And, FYI? A Yankee game doesn't count."

Calder had taken Adam's fashion advice. Paired with a dark-brown leather bomber jacket, she wore a crisp white shirt. Her hair hung down her back in one long braid. Under the hem of jeans peeked a pair of high tops. Converse red.

Effortlessly chic. Adam doubted she knew any other way.

"A wedding."

"Okay." Seemed plausible. "Who's wedding?"

"Friends. I do have one or two, you know." Calder had a challenge in her gaze. "And, Navy boy, I didn't have to join the military to acquire mine."

"Not the first time you questioned my pre-enlistment popularity. We need to make a trip to Long Island. You won't take two steps without tripping over my friends."

"You're a good talker. When you show me some action, I'll believe you."

"Action? You want action?"

The fourth-floor landing, with a secluded little nook, was the perfect spot. Adam backed Calder away from potential prying eyes until shadows blanketed them.

"Remember where we are." Calder's laugh turned into a moan as Adam's lips found the side of her neck. "Tamara won't thank us if she has to serve a cold dinner. Or does Melvin do the cooking?"

"Both." Calder tasted like honeyed wine. Sweet and intoxicating. "Don't worry. I'll take the blame."

"Damn straight, you will."

Calder threaded her fingers through Adam's hair, tugged him close, and gave in. The kiss was short but thorough and wanton.

"More."

"Nope," Calder gasped. She slipped from his grasp before he could persuade her to stay and be bad. "You're part devil, Adam Stone."

With the smile of an angel, Adam ushered her down the hall.

"What about the rest of me?"

Lips twitching, Calder took a small mirror from her purse. Adam could have told her how she looked. Absolutely beautiful. After a quick perusal—and a dab of fresh lipstick—she seemed satisfied his impromptu fun hadn't mussed her up.

"Just ring the bell.

Adam barely grazed the button when the door flew open. Melvin didn't greet him as much as drag him into the apartment. Calder followed in the wake.

"Finally! Where the hell have you been?"

"*We're* right on time. Me. *And* my date?"

Melvin's slightly wild-eyed gaze landed on Calder. His anxious expression turned contrite. "Where are my manners? Welcome. Come in. I'm Melvin. You must be Calder. Nice to meet you."

A bemused/amused sparkle in her eyes, Calder shook Melvin's hand.

"Thank you for inviting me."

"Our pleasure. Tamara will be right along. She's checking something in the kitchen. Roast beef. Or chicken. I can't remember. Would you like a drink?"

"White wine would be great."

"Terrific. Adam? You know where to hang Calder's jacket. I'll be right back."

"Is your friend always wound so tight?"

"Hand to God, I don't know what got into him." Adam helped Calder with her jacket. "One time during basic training, a stray bullet missed Melvin's head by three inches—at the most. I freaked. He hardly blinked. In an emergency, the man has ice water in his veins. Usually."

"His wife is pregnant, right? Could something be wrong?"

Adam's stomach dropped. *Tamara.*

"I don't know. She's here. Surely she wouldn't be in the kitchen fiddling with dinner if the baby was in trouble."

"I don't have experience with pregnant women."

"Me, neither."

"Good to know." Calder smiled. "*If* a problem exists. I'm certain Melvin and Tamara will tell you. *If.* I'm sorry I put the idea into your head."

Calder hugged him close. The best medicine in the world. At least in *his* world. Adam kissed her. And she kissed him back. Soothing, with enough of the underlying zing he'd come to expect—to crave.

The kitchen door swung open. Tamara walked out, looking happy and healthy. Melvin, still frazzled, carried a tray of drinks.

"White wine for Calder. Ginger ale for my darling wife. And a beer for me."

"Forget someone?" Adam held up his empty hands.

"You know." Melvin tapped a finger against his chin as if he had a sudden thought. "I bought a selection of fancy beers. Why don't you come take a look? Pick whatever sounds good. Won't take a minute."

"Okay." Adam didn't know what the hell was going on, but he had the feeling he was about to find out. "Calder? The lovely lady with the mother-to-be glow is Tamara."

"Right. Calder, Tamara. Tamara, Calder. Get to know each other. We'll be right back."

Melvin pushed Adam from the room.

"Before I kick your ass, tell me one thing. Are Tamara and the baby okay?"

"Yah." Melvin waved off the question. "You'd be the first to know if they weren't."

"Then, what the hell is wrong with you? I wanted Calder to get to know my friend. Instead, you show the face of a raving fool. Nice first impression."

"I'm sorry. Honestly. I'll apologize. Unless Calder runs screaming from the apartment and never wants to talk to any of us again." Melvin grabbed Adam by the arms. "Man, we have a potential disaster on our hands. With a capital fucking D."

"Tell me!"

"First, calm down."

Melvin gave him a shake. Not the smartest move he ever made. Adam's patience was one thin thread away from a major break.

"Me? *I* should calm down? You're the one on red alert. I don't have a clue what's going on."

"Don't blame Tamara. Her hormones are out of whack. And you know Aurora. If manipulation were an Olympic sport, she'd own more gold than Fort Knox."

"What the hell does Aurora have to do with anything? Unless…"

Please, Adam raised his eyes toward the heavens, not tonight.

"Tamara invited her to dinner. Before you explode, let me explain," Melvin rushed on.

Adam wouldn't explode. He might cry for the first time in his adult life, but shock had sent his temper into a deep freeze.

"I can't wait to hear a viable reason why crazy is about to crash the party."

"Long story short. This morning, Tamara decided to visit her mother. Out on Long Island. They walked to a nearby café for lunch. They started talking, as people do—"

"Short, you said?" Impatient, Adam sighed. "I'd hate to hear the long version."

Melvin stopped pacing long enough to shoot Adam a disgruntled look.

"Pertinent details take *some* time. And if you wouldn't interrupt, I'd—"

"Damn it, Melvin!"

"Right." Air whooshed from Melvin's lungs along with a breathless string of words. "Innocently, Tamara mentioned you. Calder. Dinner. Tonight. A perfectly natural progression of a mother/daughter conversation. No harm done. Except, the café is small, the tables close together."

"Aurora was there."

"Right behind Tamara."

"Coincidences happen." Adam shrugged. "How does an unfortunate case of eavesdropping turn into dinner here? Tonight? Hell, any night?"

"Tamara isn't sure. Her mother left to use the ladies room, Aurora moved in. Before you can say, *the girl has some nerve*, she finagled herself an invitation."

"The hell you say."

Adam took his phone from his pocket. Damn Aurora. She lived to make trouble. Calder could hold her own. Take anything thrown her way with both hands tied behind her back. But, damn it, she deserved what he'd promised. Dinner with friends. Aurora didn't qualify.

"Damn. She won't pick up." A message would be pointless, but at least he could vent. "Stay away, Aurora. I swear, if you show up tonight, we're through. Understand? Completely and finally over."

A waste of breath. She was certain he'd always be there for her. In a week or two, she'd concoct an elaborate way to draw him back into her life. The kind of life or death situation where only he could save her.

Adam had reached the end of the line. He was tired of her neediness. No matter what happened tonight, he was through with her and her drama.

A few clicks of the keypad. *Aurora Charles. Number blocked.*

"She'll be here any second," Melvin warned.

"I know."

All Adam could do was prepare Calder.

"With a date. Tamara doesn't know who."

"Great." Adam sighed. "Just great."

He left the kitchen, Melvin on his heels.

"Sorry I didn't call to warn you. I didn't know until the last minute. And to be honest? Tamara would feel terrible if she realized what she'd done."

And Melvin didn't want to upset his wife. Adam understood.

"You want to leave, I'll figure out something to tell Tamara. I'm sure the upset won't disturb the baby."

"Guilt? Really?"

Melvin had played the pregnant wife card. And won.

"I'm steamed. But not at Tamara. Or you."

"You'll stay?"

"Yes."

Melvin wilted with relief.

Adam knew Calder. He'd ask, but she would see Aurora's manipulations as a challenge. Run? Not likely.

When the chime sounded, Melvin nervously stated the obvious.

"Doorbell," he called out.

Out of time, Adam took Calder's hand.

"Come with me."

Confused, Tamara looked at her husband.

"When did our kitchen become such a fascinating place?"

With an innocent shrug, Melvin went to answer the door.

Adam didn't have time to mince words. The second they were alone, he gave Calder the facts.

"Aurora invited herself to dinner."

Calder, Lord love her, didn't blink.

"Talk about rude," she scoffed. "Poor Tamara's too nice. Give me a little while, I'll embed some mean in her. Not too much. Her delightful touch of innocent sweetness is charming. But sweet doesn't work on a woman like Aurora."

"My first instinct is to believe she's here to cause trouble."

"Instincts are good." Calder frowned. "But why? What would she gain?"

Adam's knew his theory might sound self-centered and egotistical. He'd let Calder judge for herself.

"She wants me."

"Ah. And I'm in the way." Arms crossed, Calder leaned her hip against the counter. "The woman has taste. What do you think she has planned?"

"Aurora doesn't plan. I imagine she hopes she can somehow offend your high-brow sensibilities to the point you'll never want to see me again."

"High-brow sensibilities? Me?" Calder laughed. "I hope you know better."

"I do."

Obviously pleased by his answer, Calder's deep-amber eyes warmed.

"I shouldn't judge Aurora on one meeting. Though I don't know if her semi-conscious in the back of my car qualifies as a meeting, the woman is seriously messed up."

Aurora was his friend. If she was a mess, Adam didn't want to stop and think what the fact said about him.

"Want my advice?" Calder asked.

"Please."

"Hope for the best, expect the worst." Calder sighed. "Works with my father."

Adam could have kissed Calder. In fact, he did. And felt better. *Much* better.

"You're amazing."

"I'm also hungry. At some point, I might cross over to annoyed. Potentially pissed. Depends. Think positive. Aurora might behave herself."

A loud voice, followed quickly by the same voice only louder, reverberated through the kitchen door. Adam groaned. He recognized the sound. And the implications.

"She's drunk."

Adam took the lead. In the living room, Aurora was already in fine form. Her coat half on, half off, she'd plastered herself to Melvin as she tried her best to give him a hello kiss. Any other time the panicked look on his friend's face would have been comical.

Beside him, Calder shook her head.

"So much for positive thinking. I don't see her date. At least we know her plan. Show up alone, shit-faced, so you feel obligated to drive her home."

Tamara looked ready to blow a gasket—Adam didn't blame her. He felt the same. Neither she nor the baby needed any added stress. Melvin—poor Melvin—didn't deserve the aggravation.

Aurora had to go. But not the way she envisioned.

"Call a cab."

Calder nodded.

"You get her out of here, I'll have a ride outside in five minutes."

Adam didn't question Calder's word. If she said five minutes, he could bank on five—or less.

"Thank goodness," Tamara breathed when she caught sight of Adam. "Melvin is at his wit's end."

"I'll take care of her. And, I'm sorry."

Tamara brushed off Adam's apology.

"Don't be ridiculous. I have nobody to blame but myself. Now, go. Please."

Aurora put up a token resistance. A little pushing. A lot of yelling. Her act fell on deaf ears. Adam quickly lost what little patience he had left.

"Move, Aurora. Or I swear, I'll forget you're a woman and kick your ass out the door."

Adam's empty threat didn't concern Aurora. She knew he'd never raise a hand to her. Certain she'd accomplished her goal, she had the nerve to don a Cheshire cat grin as he escorted her from the apartment.

"Guess I messed up. Again."

Not the least bit contrite, Aurora leaned heavily against Adam. When he didn't answer, she tugged on his shirt.

"You're angry. Shouldn't be. Saved you. Boring dinner. Boring friends. Boring rich girl."

Breath like a sour distillery, Aurora seemed intent on blowing as much foul air into Adam's face as humanly possible. He held his breath and thanked the elevator gods for a mercifully quick trip.

Adam considered depositing Aurora on the lobby sofa while they waited for her ride. Tempting, but he quickly dismissed the idea. She was too unpredictable. He couldn't count on her to behave. Rather than take a chance she might say or do something offensive if they ran across someone who lived there, he walked— half-dragged—her from the building.

"Bet ya aren't so rough with your Park Avenue bitch. Think her farts smell like flowers just cause she has money. Well, they don't. Whatever comes out of her tight ass stinks—just like us peasants."

Adam tuned out Aurora's ramblings and leaned her against a lamppost.

"Stay," he commanded.

In response, she sank like a stone. Adam shrugged. Close enough. The ground was dry and relatively clean—and he wasn't in a chivalrous mood. So, he left her where she landed.

"I'm more fun, damn it! And prettier. *She's* a fucking stick figure." Aurora grabbed her breasts. "One time a man paid me fifty bucks for just a look. Bet *Calder* would starve if she had to depend on her skinny-ass body for survival."

Four minutes and counting. Adam looked down the street. Headlights. Please stop here. His prayer was answered.

"You Adam Stone?" Adam nodded. He wanted to kiss the man. "I'm Phil Potts. Ms. Benedict said you had a lady a little worse for wear and in need of a ride." Phil took one look at Aurora and let out a slow whistle. "More like down for the count."

"You'll make sure she gets into her apartment before you leave?"

"All part of the service."

"You aren't coming with me? No!" Aurora locked her arms around the metal post.

Adam took more care than he felt Aurora deserved. A couple of firm, but relatively gentle tugs and he had her off the ground. Another pull, she was free of the lamppost. Phil held open the car door while Adam deposited one hundred and five pounds of deadweight onto the seat.

Before he could get away, Aurora launched herself into his arms.

"Don't go back to her." The crocodile tears had turned genuine. "I love you. I know you feel the same."

The ice in Adam's veins melted enough to carry a twinge of regret to his heart. He'd never loved Aurora. Not the way she meant. However, they'd shared some good times. In the early days after he'd left the Navy, she was a friend when he needed one. A lover when the mood was right.

The good memories in his thoughts, Adam brushed the tears from Aurora's face.

"You deserve someone who puts you first. A man who loves you with all his heart."

"You!" Aurora sobbed.

"No. I never was. Never will be. Your happiness is out there, Aurora. But not with me."

Adam closed the door. Try as she might, Aurora couldn't follow. Bless him, Phil had locked her in. She screamed. Pounded on the window. To no avail.

"Scary. And kinda sad."

"Exactly." Adam reached for his wallet. "She lives on Long Island."

Phil held up his hands.

"All taken care of. Just give me the address."

Adam waited until the car was out of sight before he slowly walked away. Into the building. The elevator. Away from one chapter of his life.

Toward, fingers crossed, the future.

CHAPTER TWENTY-FOUR

AURORA'S LITTLE STUNT didn't put a damper on the evening. If anything, Calder felt a deeper appreciation for the food, the company, and the people around her.

Melvin and Tamara welcomed her with open arms. The pretty petite brunette and her thoroughly smitten husband were a pleasure to behold. The love they expressed in every look, every touch, gave her hope. For herself, and the rest of the world. Their affection for Adam made Calder like them even more.

As the night continued, she felt she could count them as her friends. New. But with potential for something deeper.

Melvin and Adam talked sports while they did the dishes. In the living room, Tamara put her feet up with a happy sigh and a cup of herbal tea.

"We need to go shopping one day soon."

The age-old female bonding ritual. Calder didn't go often. However, when on the hunt, a store became a battlefield. She never invited someone along unless she was certain they could keep up. Until Tamara was back to fighting weight, Calder would make an exception and temper her competitive spirit.

"I don't know." Tamara patted her barely-there baby bump. "Soon, I won't fit into anything smaller than a hefty bag with arm holes. Maybe a tent—not exactly Madison Avenue haute couture."

"My sister designed a maternity line a few years back. I didn't see a single tent come down the catwalk."

"Really?" Tamara's dark eyes grew dreamy. "Anything by Andi Benedict is bound to be gorgeous. But…"

Andi's clothing was out of most people's price range. Calder would have offered to buy Tamara anything she wanted. A gift. But she didn't want to start their relationship by waving her wealth under the new friend's nose. She had to find a compromise Tamara could live with.

"No harm in looking. Right?"

"I suppose." Obviously tempted, Tamara still hesitated.

"You'll need something spectacular for the *Spring Romance Gala*. If we don't find the perfect dress at Andi's boutique, we'll keep looking. However, my bet is on my sister."

"*Spring Romance Gala*? The big charity event? With all the celebrities and society people?"

Tamara's voice rose an octave with each sentence.

"The one and only."

"What you do with *Erica's Angels* is amazing. But Melvin and I aren't going."

"Yes, you are. Every year, my family buys a table. Huge. *Too* big. We always end up inviting people we don't really like just to fill the seats. For once, I'd like to sit next to someone I *want* to talk to."

"I don't know…"

"Save yourself the time and aggravation, Tamara. Say yes," Adam said as he and Melvin joined them. Grinning, he sat next to Calder, sliding an arm around her shoulders. "The woman is relentless when she wants something. I know. As hard as I tried to guard my virtue, Calder wouldn't stop until I gave her what she wanted."

"Poor, Adam." Calder let out a mournful sigh. "A faulty memory *and* delusional. Sad. Very sad."

Tamara and Melvin laughed. Adam grinned. But for Calder's ears only, he whispered, "I remember the important things. Where you like me to touch and kiss you comes to mind."

Calder gave him a sideways glance. The glint of a promise in his deep-blue eyes made her heartrate soar. He planned to prove his memory was perfect. And she couldn't wait.

"YOUR FRIENDS ARE—"

"Are now your friends as well," Adam finished for her.

Calder smiled.

"Yes. Tamara and Melvin are a gift. Thank you." She patted the sofa. When Adam was by her side, she curled her body into his, her arms wrapped around his waist. "What *I* meant to say is, they are wonderful. Easy to be around. Their home is filled with warmth and happiness. Love. Thank you for sharing."

"You're welcome."

Frowning, Calder snuggled closer. You're welcome was a perfectly acceptable response—from someone else. Adam was the least reticent man she'd ever known. He was verbal. Expressive. He had an extensive vocabulary and wasn't afraid to use his words to state on opinion. Or simply talk. Lord, she loved to listen to him talk.

After he dealt with Aurora, Adam had been understandably tense. A beer, a shoulder massage—gladly offered by Calder—and he finally relaxed. The evening was a complete success. At least, she thought so. She'd even talked Tamara into a shopping trip.

"Did I push Tamara too hard?" Adam made a joke at the time. Perhaps he felt she'd crossed a line. "Just a girl's day out. Andi will give her the V.I.P. treatment. A mini-fashion show. Then we'll stop for lunch. I'll make sure she doesn't buy something she can't afford."

"What?" Obviously distracted, Adam shook his head. "She'll have a ball. By the way, if anything catches her eye, ask Andi to give her a huge discount. I'll pay the balance."

Great minds. Calder already planned for Tamara to walk away with several outfits. Items which just happened to be marked down. Way, *way* down.

"If we're copacetic on the fashion front, what's wrong? You've been unusually quiet ever since we left Melvin and Tamara's."

"Just gathering my thoughts."

"Talk to me." Calder touched Adam's face. Kissed his jaw. Met his gaze. "You can, you know. About anything."

"I need you to listen. *Need* you to hear something I've never told another living soul. Never could. Never *wanted* to. Until you."

Calder rested her head against Adam's shoulder. She sensed he'd have an easier time if she simply held him close. And did as he asked—listened. She felt the rise and fall of his chest as he took a deep breath.

"The run-in with Ingo Hunter? The reason for my less-than-composed reaction?"

"You had to ask someone before you explained."

"My mother." Adam cleared his throat. "I knew she'd say yes. Especially when I told her about you. She can't wait to meet you, by the way."

"Anytime."

"Soon. She's a strong, loving, compassionate woman. Better than I deserve. After what she went through, I... I'm grateful. So damn grateful."

Adam's grip tightened on Calder's arm.

"When I was in the Navy. Thousands of miles away. Where I couldn't help her—or protect her. Three men raped my mother."

Calder gasped. She thought she was prepared for anything. She was wrong.

"Until recently, the neighborhood where Mom lives, where I grew up, was pretty rough. Damn rough. People didn't go out after dark. Anybody who did was either a fool or a thug. Graffiti lined every wall—every fence. Not the pretty, artsy kind. Black paint. Gang tags. Foul language. Stuff you try to hide from a kid, but can't because the shit is everywhere."

Adam's head fell back. His eyes held a faraway look.

"Mom was no fool. She always kept her doors locked. Shopped during the day. She was supposed to be safe during the fucking day."

The tension in Adam's body, the pain in his voice, worried Calder.

"You don't have to tell me the rest."

"Yes. I do. Unless you me to stop."

"You can tell me anything. Remember? Will talking to me help?"

Adam nodded.

"Then finish. I'm here." She held his hand to her cheek. "I'm not going anywhere."

Again, Adam breathed deeply.

"Mom was a manicurist. Still is. She likes the human interaction." A fleeting smile passed across Adam's lips. Then, his expression turned grim. "Once a week, she would use her lunch break to shop for groceries. The corner store is halfway between home and work. As always, she picked up what she needed. She took the same route home. Down the same street. No shortcuts through dark alleys. Like I said, Mom is no fool."

Adam ran a hand over his face.

"The bastards grabbed her a block away from her house. They put a bag over her face. Dragged her into an abandoned building. She never told me the details. I never asked. But I have a friend on the police force. He let me read the report."

Why? Calder wanted to scream. *Why put yourself through the pain? The unimaginable horror?* Sometimes the truth *didn't* set you free but weighed on the soul forever.

"Six hours. What they did to her." Adam's blue eyes darkened, filled with suppressed fury. "My C.O. gave me the news. Took three fucking days to get home. Mom was in the hospital. Her face..." Adam's voice broke. "So many cuts and bruises. The swelling made her almost unrecognizable. The medication they pumped into her kept her mostly unconscious for the first week. Thank God. Otherwise, I don't know how she would have survived the pain—physical and mental."

"You sat with her?"

Adam nodded. His anger had turned to ice. The only visible sign of his distress were his clenched fists.

"All I wanted to do was find the scum who hurt her. I wanted to rip them apart. Slowly. Let them suffer before I did the world a favor and put an end to their sorry lives."

"How would your mother have coped with you in prison?"

"Didn't matter. They were never caught. Not by the police, or me. As far as I know, the three of them never suffered a day in their lives."

"I think they have. Or will."

"In the afterlife?" Adam scoffed. "Mom believes only God has the right to judge our sins. I say, what's wrong with some holy justice right here on earth?"

Calder rested her hand on Adam's chest, directly over his heart. The beat was strong. As strong as the woman who raised him.

"I don't know what happens after we die. Hopefully, the men who hurt your mother have the words *send straight to hell and burn* stamped on what little soul they possess. But the here and now? I have to believe those men have paid some kind of price. They could be in prison."

"Or dead."

Adam's fixation on murder wasn't funny. Yet, Calder almost laughed. By nature, he wasn't a violent man. His instincts were to protect at all costs. However, given the right incentive, the man could be downright bloodthirsty.

Given the circumstances, Calder didn't blame him.

"Tell you what. *You* picture them dead. *Me?* I'll imagine them in three separate snake-filled holes—because they deserve to suffer alone—their bodies covered in large, seeping, festering wounds."

"I changed my mind. I want to trade your imagination for mine."

"Happy to share."

Several minutes passed—Calder wasn't in the mood to count. She held Adam as the tension slowly drained from his body. Slowly—thankfully—the icy cool of his skin returned to a normal, healthy warm.

A little later, Adam stood, Calder in his arms. He didn't speak as he carried her to his bedroom, undressed her, then himself, and settled them under the covers. IIis front nestled to her back. Comfort would later give way to passion. For now, they were content to simply be.

Adam nuzzled Calder's neck. And chuckled. Such a lovely sound.

"I had no idea you possessed such a bloody, vicious streak."

Calder smiled when she heard the admiration in Adam's voice.

"When necessary. Only when necessary."

CHAPTER TWENTY-FIVE

ADAM PACED ACROSS the marble floor. Calder never made him wait. The one night he needed everything to run like clockwork, the night his two favorite people in the entire world would meet for the first time, she had a business emergency.

They arrived outside the mansion at the same time. Once inside, Calder told him to wait, gave him a quick kiss, and rushed up the stairs. Ten minutes, she promised.

His mother would understand if they were late. His stomach might not.

Butterflies had invaded his gut—a huge mass of them, fluttering like crazy.

As he checked his watch for the fifth time in as many minutes, Adam debated his options. Wait. Or go to Calder's room and coax her to hurry.

"Tell me why I should trust you with my sister?"

Fixated on the empty stairs, Adam jumped. He turned to find Bryce directly behind him. He eyed her suspiciously, certain she hadn't been there a second ago.

"Where did you come from?"

"You don't know?" Bryce rolled her eyes. "An egg. Some sperm. Fertilization. Basic biology, Adam."

Adam smiled to himself. Even snarky, a Benedict sister could charm honey from a bee.

"In yours and Calder's case, *two* eggs."

"Touché." Bryce smiled. "I kind of like you. But, are you good enough for my sister? The jury's still out."

"Isn't the decision up to Calder?"

Bryce crossed her arms. Suddenly, Adam saw the resemblance. The set of her chin. The unwavering gaze that seemed to say, *you must be kidding*. She and Calder weren't identical, but they *were* twins. Used to getting what they wanted, and heaven help the man who tried to stand in the way.

"Scary, isn't she?"

Adam swallowed an unmanly yelp. Like Bryce, Andi Benedict came up on him unnoticed. Fast and silent. A handy skill if she were a ninja. In a Manhattan mansion? Kind of annoying.

"Her *books* scare the hell out of me."

"Okay. I definitely like you." Bryce nodded. "However, flattery will take you only so far. Calder deserves the best. Are you?"

The question threw him. The best? How the hell should he know? Adam looked from sister to sister. Something told him for all Bryce's bravado, Andi was the killer—figuratively speaking.

Tall, slender, drop-dead gorgeous. And according to Calder, utterly ruthless where her business was concerned. Quite a combination.

Adam didn't need another Benedict sister to fall from the sky to tell him where he stood. He had to win their approval. Calder's opinion held some sway. But Andi and Bryce would make up their own minds.

"I won't hurt her." Simple and sincere seemed like a good place to start. "I respect her. Admire her. She's…"

"Calder." Andi's blue eyes softened. "She's Calder."

"Yes." He couldn't have expressed his feelings better.

With a nod, Andi patted Adam's arm.

"Sometimes one word says everything."

"Are we finished with him?" Bryce sounded disappointed as Andi tugged her across the foyer. "And what the heck? *She's Calder. He's Adam.* I don't understand."

"I hope you will. Someday soon."

Bemused, Adam waited until Bryce and Andi were out of the room before he checked his watch. One minute. Calder had sixty seconds before he—

"Thirty seconds to spare."

"Son of a bitch!" Adam rounded on Calder.

"Did I startle you?" Calder didn't seem the least bit contrite.

"Quiet as freaking cats, every last one of you." Adam helped her on with her coat.

"Bryce and Andi?" Adam gave a sharp nod. "Did they keep you entertained while you waited?"

With a chuckle, Adam opened the front door.

"Good a description as any."

ADRIANA STONE WAS a surprise. Despite Adam's description of a strong, loving, supportive, resilient woman. A single mother who held her family together through thick and thin.

A cross between Betty Crocker and Wonder Woman.

Naturally, Adam saw Adriana through the distorted lens of an adoring son. After everything she'd gone through, he had every right to put his mother on an unrealistic pedestal.

Calder didn't expect to find *quite* the superwoman he describe.

In her mind, she thought she would find a delicate woman, with a quiet, slightly reserved demeanor. Certain she would like Adriana—after all, she was Adam's mother. She hadn't expected to adore her.

The woman was vibrant. The definition of alive. She kept busy with her job and friends. Volunteered at her church. Worked out three times a week. Hardly a saint, she had a wicked sense of humor. Her stories had Calder laughing all through dinner.

Calder quickly understood why Adam was such an amazing man. With Adriana as a role model, how could he miss?

After a wonderful meal, they moved to the living room. Sitting near the cups of after-dinner coffee and plates of strawberry shortcake, was a gold-embossed photo album. Adriana held a second open on her lap.

"From the moment Adam could crawl, he was into everything. Where he found the paint, I'll never know."

Calder smiled at the picture of a little boy with Adam's bright-blue eyes. A defiant expression on his face, he stood in a bathtub, red from head to toe.

Meeting her inquiring gaze, Adam shrugged.

"Beats me. I was three years old. My personal memories run from none to none. For all I know, Mom dumped a bucket of paint over my head for the sake of an *adorable* picture. And the chance to embarrass me almost three decades later."

Adriana's laugh rang out. Her son's teasing censure didn't deter her. She transferred the beautifully bound photo album from her lap to Calder's.

"Keep looking," she said. "I have two more in my bedroom."

"Mom. Calder didn't come here to pour over endless pictures."

"Don't listen to him. Bring on as much as you have."

Calder turned the page. From his perch on the sofa's arm, Adam winced. Tall and gangly, hair past his shoulders, and proudly decked out in a powder-blue tuxedo, teenage Adam posed for the camera, his arm slung around his date and a cocky expression on his face. The little brunette wore a low-cut, thigh-high, neon-pink dress. The white corsage pinned to her chest was huge. Around the size of the average prize-winning watermelon.

"Prom night?"

"The blissful ignorance of youth. Luckily, my sense of fashion has evolved for the better."

"No more blue polyester?" she teased.

"No more polyester, period."

"Your date was a cutie."

For a closer look, Adam slid onto Adriana's vacated seat.

"Valene Brewster. Constantly chewed cinnamon *Trident*. She'd remove the gum just long enough for a kiss. The second my lips left hers, she popped the wad back in."

"Waste not, want not."

"You're having *way* too much fun at my expense."

Calder couldn't argue. Grinning, she turned.

"Just wait for some payback, baby. I'm sure your mother has a treasure trove of *your* humiliating childhood pictures."

"Good luck." Calder dismissed the idea with a careless wave of her hand. "Billie would gladly show you all the pictures you like. With her front and center."

"What about you and your sisters?"

"When we were little, once a year she had our nanny dress us up like dolls. We'd sit on the floor, gaze up at Billie as if dazzled by her beauty. The pictures are somewhere. Maybe Billie's sitting room. The ritual ended as soon as Andi hit puberty. Photographic evidence of another Benedict with breasts? Intolerable."

Calder could laugh now. At the time, they were in a panic. What if Billie sent them away to school to hide the evidence of their—and her—increasing age from the world?

"Unbelievable."

"I know. How much competition could a twelve-year-old girl be?"

If Billie had even once thought ahead, she would have stopped at one girl. Instead, she had four. A fact her mother lamented every time she looked in the mirror. A fact for which Calder gave thanks every day of her life.

"You don't have any front teeth. How old were you here?"

Calder pointed to the picture. When she turned her head, she came face to face with Adam. Eyes filled with sadness, he pulled her close.

"Hey." Confused, she gave his back a consoling pat. "What's wrong?"

Bewilderment—plus a good dose of anger—clouded his eyes.

"You really need me to say?"

"Yes. Please."

"I don't think the way your mother treated you and your sisters is acceptable. Do you?"

Acceptable? No. Calder's normal? Yes. She should have kept the puberty story to herself. Adam was so easy to talk to, the words slipped out before she realized how they must sound to a man whose experience landed on the opposite end of the maternal spectrum from hers.

How could Calder explain Billie the Butterfly to a man who was raised by a twenty-first century June Cleaver?

"Billie is flighty. Selfish. Beyond frustrating. Occasionally infuriating. Yet, for all her faults, I will always love her. You want to know why?"

"You have to?"

Calder smiled, shaking her head.

"She gave me three amazing gifts. Andi. Bryce. And Destry. *They* are my family. *They* make me strong. *They* made me who I am."

Adam kissed her forehead.

"Something tells me each would say the same about you."

Such a good man. Could a heart sigh with happiness? Convinced the answer was yes, Calder gazed into Adam's eyes.

"We Benedict sisters know when we're on to a good thing."

CHAPTER TWENTY-SIX

"STUNNING." CALDER MADE a slow, three-sixty-degree turn. "Absolutely stunning."

After two days of intensive decorating, the *Spring Romance Gala* was set to be their most spectacular—hopefully successful—charity event ever.

"The fresh-cut flower arrangements arrive in the morning." Annabel checked her list. "When the doors open tomorrow night, romance will be in bloom."

"Flowers? Bloom?" Calder groaned. "Bad pun. Awful."

"During the last forty-eight hours, I've *maybe* closed my eyes for six of them. The way my brain feels, *any* pun is a victory."

Calder was in the same boat. The week before their annual gala meant long hours and little sleep—who could rest with a perpetual, increasingly nervous stomach?

They were prepared for any contingency. Yet, they could never avoid the inevitable minor mishap. A tradition, so to speak, Calder would have gladly foregone.

"The way you eviscerated the delivery guy? I *almost* felt sorry for him."

"Who the hell smokes in a public building? Then drops the lit cigarette into a box of tissue paper to hide the evidence? If one of the decorators hadn't seen the smoke?" Calder shuddered. "I don't want to think."

A few lousy decorations didn't matter. People did. The possibility of injuries? Even death? Calder saw red. She reamed the guy out—in front of twenty-plus witnesses.

"He looked about six inches tall when he slunk out of here."

"Mm." Calder didn't feel an ounce of remorse. "Jerk was lucky to leave with his balls intact."

"I agree." Annabel sniffed the air. "The smell of smoke is gone. Thank goodness."

"Quick thinking on your part to have the smoldering box removed as quickly as possible. And amazing ventilation."

"State of the art. According to the hotel manager, the owner spared no expense. Top to bottom."

Located in the heart of midtown Manhattan, *The Stanton Plaza Hotel* opened a year ago to great acclaim. Before the first customer checked in, the waitlist for a reservation was a mile long. The event spaces— a massive ballroom, two smaller banquet halls, plus a myriad of meeting rooms, offices, etc.—were booked years in advance.

Rumors swirled about a media mogul who paid a million dollars to some lucky soul for his or her reservation. Just so his little darling could have her wedding reception in the already famous *White Orchid Ballroom*.

True or false, the story was entertaining. And the publicity generated beyond priceless. All around, a win/win for the hotel.

Erica's Angel's didn't have a million dollars to spare for what Calder considered to be an *out of the realm of possibilities* venue. When the time came to book the location for the gala, she didn't even try. Why waste her time? She settled, quite happily, on a different, perfectly acceptable hotel.

Calder wasn't a big fan of gift horses—didn't turn out well for the Trojans. Naturally, when—a short three months ago—the *White Orchid Ballroom* miraculously became available, she hesitated.

So many questions. How? A last-minute cancelation. Why? For some time, the hotel's owner followed *Erica's Angels*. He admired what they'd accomplished *and* their methods. He wanted to give them a hand up. All she needed to do was say yes.

The pluses outweighed the minuses—by a mile.

With a three-month cushion, they had time to change the invitations and advertising copy. The other hotel would charge a sizable cancelation fee, but the new venue was much larger. Between extra ticket sales and *The Stanton Plaza* cache, they would recoup the money in no time.

Then came the kicker. An offer Calder couldn't refuse. The Plaza event organizer gave them a discount. Huge. Mindboggling. A gift from heaven. Seemed luck, providence, and a civic-minded hotel owner were on their side.

Whatever the reason, Calder jumped. Eyes wide open. From day one until now, she was grateful.

"Still can't get in touch with the owner?"

Annabel shook her head.

"You mean New York's answer to Batman? I've yet to talk to anyone who will admit they know his identity. Confession? I checked the phone directory for a Bruce Wayne."

"You didn't." Calder had her best laugh in days.

"Figured what the heck? Unfortunately, I came up empty on the billionaire Caped Crusader front."

"What did you expect? Batman doesn't advertise his location—or identity."

Annabel slapped her forehead.

"You're right. What was I thinking? We should—"

"Wait." Calder stopped Annabel before the lunacy could go any further. "Do you hear us? The moment we start to debate how we can track down a fictional character, we have officially passed the point of giddy. Home. Go. Now."

"But—"

"I'll write the owner a long, effusive thank you note next week after I come up for air. As for the gala? We've done everything we can for tonight. We can't put the finishing touches on our minor masterpiece until the flowers arrive." Calder opened the ballroom door. "Get some sleep, or you're fired."

"What about you?"

"As soon as I grab my purse from the office the hotel so nicely provided—another thank you to the elusive owner—I'll be on my way."

"Promise?"

"I promise."

Annabel knew her too well. Calder often put in long hours after everyone else had cleared out for the day. Not tonight. She planned to get to bed early. After a little sexy phone time.

Busy with the training of his newly hired assistant—and his usual go-go schedule—Adam's week had been just as crazy as Calder's. They managed one night together. Otherwise, they settled for texts and calls. Adam's face on a screen was better than nothing, but she missed the real thing.

The closest they'd come to an actual date would be tonight. Eight o'clock sharp. He was in Albany on business. She would be in a hot, steamy tub of water. A glass of wine in one hand, her phone in the other.

The hall outside the ballroom bustled with activity, everyone in a hurry to get from point A to point B. The assigned office—the temporary headquarters of *Erica's Angels*—was near the ballroom. However, the trip turned out to be a game of dodge the tourist. Luckily, Calder had good reflexes. She arrived at her destination no worse for wear.

The mid-June weather was warm but mild. Calder only brought a jacket to work out of habit. *Be prepared for any contingency and the world can't bite you in the ass.* Another Benedict sisters' motto which held them in good stead through years of unpredictable parents and revolving step-fathers.

Purse—check. Jacket—check. Her car keys were with the hotel valet. Another plus for the *Stanton Plaza*—underground parking.

Out of habit, Calder glanced at her phone in case she had a message from one of her sisters. Or Adam. Anyone else would have to wait.

Scroll. Scroll. Nothing. Nothing. Calder stopped when an unexpected name popped up. Aurora? Of all the freaking gall. The only way the woman could text her was if she stole the number from Adam's phone.

Calder's common sense warred with an unbidden wave of morbid curiosity. *Can't be good.* And yet... With a sigh of resignation, she tapped the screen.

You can't keep what was never yours—bitch. You lose. Adam's back where he belongs.

The accompanying picture showed Aurora. Her lips—and body—plastered to Adam.

Aurora's motives were as obvious as flashing neon. She wanted Calder to take the scene at face value. *Oh, no! Adam cheated on her!* Let the sobbing, breast-beating, and finger pointing accusations begin.

Neither a fool, nor unfamiliar with the tactics of a desperate woman—Billie was never so obvious, but she had her moments—Calder didn't buy what Aurora tried so hard to sell.

A blatant setup, the photo was merely a moment in time. What mattered was what happened *after* the click of the camera. From his grim expression? The way he gripped Aurora's waist? If Adam hadn't pushed her away almost immediately, Calder wouldn't be surprised—she'd be shocked.

Almost funny. Mostly sad. Aurora's pathetic last-ditch effort didn't deserve any more of her time. Her thumb hovered over the delete button as she gave the picture one last glance.

What the...? Calder's gaze narrowed. In the background, she couldn't be certain. No. She had to be wrong. Please, please, please be wrong.

She swiped the screen to enlarge the image. And her heart sank like a rock.

"LEAVE A MESSAGE. Or not."

Fucking voicemail.

With a growl, Adam dialed again. Same result. Same message. Couldn't mistake Calder's voice. Why the hell didn't she pick up?

"Did our signals get crossed?" he said into the phone. "Nine o'clock. On the dot. Whatever the holdup, let me know you're okay. I miss you."

Adam was up-state. . Calder in New York City. Too far away for him to hop in his car and drive to her place. So, he waited. And paced. A half hour passed. Then, an hour. After ninety minutes and four more unanswered calls later, he passed concerned to full-on worried.

The woman was punctual to a fault. If something held her up at work, she let him know. Always.

For a week, their schedules had been out of sync. A long-distance date seemed the perfect solution. A modern, twenty-first-century couple, a little technology-based romance would have to do until he could hold Calder in his arms again.

"Where are you?"

The hell with waiting. Adam hit speed dial.

"Dear boy. What a nice surprise. How are you?"

Adam let out a sigh. If something were wrong with Calder, Mrs. Finch wouldn't be so chipper.

"Good, Mrs. F. How are you?"

"Undecided about which dress to wear tomorrow night. I want to do our girl proud."

"You could show up in a paper sack. To Calder, you'd look like a million bucks."

"What a sweet, and utterly ridiculous thing to say," Mrs. Finch laughed. "Now, tell me. What can I do for you?"

"Is Calder there?"

"As far as I know. She arrived around seven thirty. Went straight to her room."

Calder was safe. Adam felt better. Yet, he couldn't shake the feeling something was off.

"Did she say anything? Seem upset, or unwell? I tried calling."

"She didn't pick up?"

"No."

Mrs. Finch made a puzzled humming sound.

"Why don't I go check? I'm sure nothing's wrong, but a little peace of mind never hurt. I'll call you back."

"Wait! Would you keep the line open, Mrs. F.? If you don't mind."

"I understand. Believe me. Calder's tired. She always wears herself thin before the gala. The day after, she'll sleep twelve hours straight and be right as rain."

Adam thought the world of Mrs. Finch. However, as she took what seemed like forever to climb the stairs to Calder's room, he wanted to shout to the dear lady, *get on the damn elevator already*.

"Here we are."

Finally. The distinctive sound of knuckles on a door came through the phone.

"Yes?" someone asked. Not Calder. Bryce? Definitely Bryce. "Did you need something, Mrs. F.?"

"Actually, Adam's on the phone. He called when he couldn't reach Calder." Mrs. Finch paused. "Is something wrong?"

"Tell Adam…"

Tell Adam what? Adam's grip on his phone tightened. *And why can't Calder speak for herself*?

"Just a second."

"Mrs. Finch? What's going on?"

"I'm not sure. Bryce went into Calder's bathroom. I hear voices. Oh, here she comes."

"Calder?"

"No. Bryce."

Shit. Adam's blood pressure started to rise. He wasn't in the mood for blind man's tag team Q & A.

"Calder doesn't want to speak to him."

"Well, I want to speak to her. Damn it, Bryce. Bryce!"

"She shut the door," Mrs. Finch informed him "Though I will say, she looked sorry."

"Great. Just great."

"Adam?"

"What!" he shouted. Breathe, man, breathe. In a quieter voice, he asked again. "What, Mrs. Finch?"

"My girls mean everything to me. They're my world. My heart. I will defend and protect them to my last breath. Which begs the question. What the hell did you do?"

Mrs. Finch hung up before Adam had a chance to answer. Just as well. He didn't know what to say. Yesterday, before he left New York, he and Calder were fine. Great. Over the moon spectacular. Less than forty-eight hours later, his world had turned upside down.

Adam threw open his suitcase, tossing in his clothes as fast as possible. He knew one thing. To fix the problem—no other option—they had to be in the same city.

CALDER WANTED TO crawl into bed. Shut out the world. If she could turn off her brain as well, she would have given into the impulse. Too many thoughts zinged from one corner of her mind to the other to allow her any rest.

As an alternative, she lay on top, Bryce by her side, as she stared at the smoky-blue ceiling.

"For the first time in my life, I understand why people take recreational drugs. Must be one or two—or several hundred—designed to turn the world into a soft, hazy void. Something to mellow the harsh for an hour or two."

"Drugs? Seriously?"

"No. But I understand the temptation."

Calder closed her eyes and breathed. She pictured her lungs expand, then retract as the air left her body.

"Stupid relaxation technique. Doesn't work *at all*."

"You have to try for more than five seconds." Bryce turned to her side. "Ready to talk? Or do you want to wallow a bit longer?"

Like her attempt to relax, Calder's first real wallow turned out to be an epic failure. She didn't understand the appeal. Ugly thoughts begat ugly thoughts. Sadness bred more sadness.

And tears? The one thing she knew could help—in small doses—eluded her. Calder's eyes were bone dry.

Besides, from what she understood, a good wallow was best done in solitude. The second Calder walked in the door, Bryce took one look and knew something was wrong. No questions asked, she followed Calder to her room.

Bryce wouldn't have left if Calder asked. And Calder would never ask.

"Ever wonder about our connection?" she pondered absently. "The bond beyond sisters? I know the whole shared-womb thing. How could we be closer—even if we were *identical* twins?"

"If we had the same father?"

Calder almost laughed.

"I wouldn't wish *my* father on you—or anyone else."

Bryce squeezed Calder's hand.

"We're who we are because Billie slept with *my* father while married to *yours*. Screwed up, yes. But I'm the result of her bad decision. If she'd walked the straight and narrow, I wouldn't be here."

For the first time, Calder felt her eyes prickle with the threat of tears. She rarely let herself contemplate the idea of a life without Bryce. The idea was unthinkable.

"I kinda love you, you know?"

"I kinda love you, too." Bryce gave a low chuckle. "Had enough icky, sticky sentimentality?"

"Mm." Not the Benedict sisters' style. They didn't fall into deep holes of depression. They didn't give into bouts of incessant weeping. And, though they loved each other to the ends of the earth and back, they were *not* overly sentimental.

Face life head on, whatever came down the pike. And never hesitate to kick any sign of trouble right in the balls.

Trouble. Calder couldn't run any longer. With a sigh, she reached for her phone.

"Just before I was ready to head home, I received a friendly little text from Aurora Charles."

"No."

"Yes."

Bryce propped herself up on her elbow as she studied the picture. She dismissed the image as quickly as Calder had.

"Pathetic attempt. Only the teenage heroine of a poorly written YA novel would be fooled by such a sloppy plot ploy."

"I agree."

"Because you aren't sixteen," Bryce nodded "Or prone to idiocy."

When Bryce tried to hand back the phone, Calder shook her head.

"Look again. Concentrate on the background."

Bryce frowned. Then, her gray eyes widened. Her mouth opened, then closed as if she wanted to speak, but the words wouldn't come.

Calder collapsed onto her back. She'd hoped Bryce would laugh off what she saw. No such luck.

"An interesting gathering," Bryce said slowly, cautiously.

"Interesting isn't the word I'd use. Sickening was my first response. For a moment, I thought I might lose my lunch."

"Adam. Aurora Charles. Your father. And..."

"Might as well say the name. He isn't going anywhere."

"Ingo Hunter."

Ingo Hunter. The punch to her mid-section wasn't as sharp as the first time, but packed the same intense pain.

Calder had studied the picture. Looked for clues. Where were they? When? The biggest question of all? Why?

"Everyone seems so cozy. Don't you think? Hunter and my father have their heads together, thick as thieves. Dad's actually laughing."

"Weird."

"No kidding."

"I *mean*, Adam and Aurora don't seem to be *with* the others. They're outside what looks to be a separate room."

Bryce pointed to Hunter and Edwin Calder. They sat at a table, the surface sprinkled with half-filled high-ball glasses. Cigars smoldered in glass ashtrays.

"What? You think Adam was there by himself? At a place where my father and Ingo Hunter just happened to be all buddy-

buddy? Along with Aurora. Oh, and don't forget the third man at the table."

"I was going to ask." Squinting, Bryce brought the phone closer to her face. "He looks familiar, but his face is shadowed."

"Bridge Manfred."

"The drug dealer?" Calder asked, then sighed. Seemed everyone did.

"You know him?"

"*Of* him," Bryce qualified. "He seems to pop up at every party, doesn't he?"

Calder nodded.

"Drug supplier to New York's elite." She rubbed her temples. "Two months ago, Adam knocked the man unconscious. Now, they're drinking buddies?"

"Except Adam isn't *with* Bridge Manfred. *Or* Hunter. *Or* your father."

"He's too busy locking lips with Aurora."

"Adam is an unwilling participant. A fact we both agree is strikingly obvious."

"I don't know anymore." Calder's head felt ready to explode. Too many questions. Not enough answers. "Why did I open the text? My first instinct was to hit delete. If I could go back…"

"Until someone perfects time travel, you can't." Bryce tossed the phone to the foot of the bed, screen side down. "What you *can* do is talk to Adam."

"I don't want to."

"Ever?" Bryce dismissed the idea with a shake of her head. "Hardly a practical solution. Adam won't let you disappear from his life without a few questions of his own."

Bryce was right. If she knew Adam, he'd... Calder stopped herself. *Did* she know him?

Had Adam played her?

Calder thought back to the private moments they'd shared. Until him, she never talked about her childhood. Had never let down her protective walls to any other man. And what about Adam? He'd poured his heart out when he told her about his mother. The facts were real, but what about his motive behind them?

"What if everything was a lie?" Calder curled into a ball. "What if, like so many before him, all Adam wants is my money?"

"Your feelings for him are real."

"Maybe I'm more like Billie than I thought. Latent bad judgment is probably a thing. Right?"

"Forget Billie."

"If only I could."

Bryce inched closer.

"Not many things scare me. But love? Just the thought is terrifying. You took a chance. Opened your heart." Her smile gentle, Bryce hugged Calder. "Makes you the bravest woman I know."

"If I were brave, I'd ask Adam to explain."

"You will. When you're ready for the truth."

Always her haven, Calder rested her head on Bryce's shoulder. For once, she couldn't find any comfort.

"I don't know if I *want* the truth."

"Yes. You do."

"Fine. I do."

Calder wished she was half as certain as she sounded. What she dreaded wasn't the truth. If she looked into Adam's deep-blue eyes and, for the first time, saw a lie, she didn't know how she would survive.

CHAPTER TWENTY-SEVEN

A HOT SHOWER and several cups of strong tea bolstered Calder's sleep-deprived body. Makeup covered the circles under her eyes. Shoulders back, she descended the stairs at her usual brisk pace.

Whatever the day brought her way, she thought she was ready. Time would tell if she were right.

Adam had called. Over and over. She didn't listen to the messages he left. She wasn't a coward, Calder assured herself. Today was about the *Spring Romance Gala*. Too many people relied on the money they would raise. She refused to let her personal problems get in the way.

As she reached the foyer, the front door opened. Logically, she knew Adam didn't have the passcode. Still, breath caught in her throat. Until a dark pair of eyes met hers. And, Calder's hope for a great day rose precipitously.

"Destry. You're home."

Laughing, Destry returned Calder's enthusiastic hug.

"I told you I would be. Big bash tonight. Unless I mixed up the date?"

"No." Calder tightened her hold before she finally let go. "Can't I just be glad to see you?"

"I appreciate the warm welcome. Now, you want to tell me what's wrong?"

Of course Destry knew. The old Benedict sister connection at work.

"If I didn't have some place to be, I'd spill my guts all over your scuffed boots."

"Time for a new pair anyway." Concerned, Destry rubbed Calder's arm. "I wondered what was up. When I arrived, I spied a certain pretty boy camped out in his car."

Calder didn't have to ask who her sister meant.

"Adam's outside?"

With a nod, Destry's gaze narrowed.

"What did he do?"

"The jury's still out. Bryce can fill you in on the details."

Calder glanced at the door. She hadn't slept. Her brain and body were on auto-pilot. She wasn't ready to see Adam when she felt at such a disadvantage.

"Slip out the back. You can catch a cab at the end of the block."

"You're a lifesaver."

With a wave, Calder dashed down the hall.

"What I am is an expert at evasive measures," Destry called after her. Alone, she grinned. "Same difference, I suppose."

"THE LARGE WHITE displays go on either side of the bandstand."

Calder wondered why she bothered to provide the florist with a detailed diagram. Though anybody with half a brain should know that five hundred dollars' worth of roses don't belong next to the men's bathroom.

From across the room, Annabel sent her a sympathetic look. If they could rely on others to do a proper job, they wouldn't have to supervise.

"Why don't you take a break?" Annabel's voice came through Calder's headset. "You've been here since the first delivery. I asked the hotel's deli to deliver a corned beef sandwich to the office. Go. Put your feet up for thirty minutes and enjoy."

Calder's stomach rumbled. A reminder she hadn't eaten since lunch—yesterday.

"You're a gem."

"I know."

Before anyone could waylay her, Calder exited the ballroom. Dressed for physical labor, her jeans, t-shirt, and running shoes received a few looks of mild disdain from the ladies-who-lunch crowd. Another time, she would have looked right back with her own brand of contempt. Running near empty, Calder ignored the women. And the impulse. She didn't have the energy to spare.

Right now, all she wanted was a few minutes of quiet, some much needed sustenance—and maybe a quick nap. Ten minutes would be a blessed miracle.

In the office, Calder locked the door. The sandwich, a side of French fries, and a pot of tea sat on the low coffee table. Slipping off her shoes, she flexed her feet, and settled onto the leather sofa with a grateful sigh.

Thick as her fist and slathered in mustard, the thinly sliced corned beef was lean and succulent. Calder couldn't manage the entire sandwich. As she glanced at the remaining half, her thoughts automatically turned to Adam. He could eat the rest. And another to boot.

Calder frowned. Alone, she could admit she missed him. He'd become an important part of her life. Too important, too fast. Instead of jumping feet first, she should have slowly waded in. Taken more time. Used a safer route.

Damn it. Until yesterday, everything felt so right. Nothing seemed rushed, certain she and Adam were exactly where they were supposed to be.

When her phone rang, Calder answered without glancing at the screen. She knew who was on the line.

"Hello, Adam."

"What the hell, Calder? I've been out of mind."

Adam sounded frantic. *Good*. She was miserable, let him suffer a little, too.

"You knew I was all right. You didn't have to worry."

"And yet, I did. All the way on the train. And, in my car, while I waited for you to take your morning run."

"I decided to skip a day."

"No kidding. Took me four hours, but reality finally sank in."

"Are you angry?" He had some nerve.

"Right now, tired. I desperately need to see you. Face to face. I need to know what's going on. Why you've shut me out."

"I'm busy. In case you forgot, the gala's tonight."

"I know. You invited me. Unless you don't want me to come."

"Of course I want you here," Calder said without thinking. She wasn't sorry. "I have to get back to work."

"Promise you'll make time for me. After."

"I promise."

Calder hung up. Tonight, she would know the truth. Tomorrow? She'd do what she always did. Get up and keep going. What she didn't know? Would Adam be by her side?

CHAPTER TWENTY-EIGHT

CALDER SMILED AT the camera. The curve of her lips felt natural, not forced. The reason? She was surrounded by her sisters—the best mood enhancers ever found.

They posed, arms around each other. Andi had designed their dresses to fit their individual personalities. Calder wore form-fitting blue. Bryce a flowing fuchsia. Destry wore a vibrant yellow with a high-neck, the back completely bare. For herself, Andi chose a long sheath in emerald green.

"Beautiful. A work of art," the photographer effused as he took several shots of the women. But between pictures, he only had eyes for Bryce.

"Somebody's smitten," Andi whispered, eyes twinkling.

"He's cute," Destry admitted through her fixed smile. "He has a kind of geeky bohemian vibe. What do you think? You've never dated a photographer."

"Mm." Bryce contemplated the possibility. "I don't know if I would date him. However, with a little encouragement, I could be convinced to check out his dark room."

As she listened to her sisters, Calder's smile widened. Daniel Morrison was a young, up and coming artist. She loved his work and was thrilled to hire him to document the gala with pictures—casual and posed. Another believer in *Erica's Angel's*, Daniel offered to work for only the cost of his materials.

Calder received the services of a top-notch photographer, while he helped a worthy cause. Plus, the exposure would be a huge boost to his career.

"All done, ladies. Thank you. I have a feeling your pictures will be the best I take all evening."

As Daniel lowered his camera, his gaze returned to Bryce.

"Taking photographs must be thirsty work." Bryce winked at Calder before she turned her smile on Daniel. "Why don't we get some champagne and you can tell me all about f-stops."

Dazzled, Daniel held out his arm, and the two disappeared into the crowd.

"Only Bryce could make f-stop sound like a dirty word," Andi chuckled.

"Speaking of champagne, I'm in the mood for some bubbly," Destry declared. "Who wants to join me?"

Calder motioned over one of the roaming waiters. He presented them with three filled glasses.

"To Calder." Andi raised her wine. "Once again, you've surpassed yourself. The gala is an unqualified success."

"To Calder," Destry agreed.

"Thank you." Calder clinked glasses with her sisters. "But I did have a little help."

"Don't be modest. You—" Destry let out a sigh as her gaze landed on something over Calder's shoulder. "Oh, boy."

"What?" Calder looked to her right.

"Nothing we haven't seen before. Brace yourself. Here comes Mommy."

Their mother loved to make an entrance. Why should tonight be any different? Her *look at me* routine was polished, shiny—and annoyingly familiar.

When Calder caught her first glimpse of Billie's gala dress, she took a deep breath and prayed for patience.

She should have been suspicious when Billie didn't provide her usual preview fashion show. Calder had been too occupied with more important things to worry about her mother's wardrobe choices. She simply assumed like all the guests, Billie would follow the guidelines in the invitation.

In keeping with the season and theme of this year's Spring Romance Gala, we request the women wear color. Something bright and festive. The men are asked to eschew the traditional all-black tuxedo for a white dinner jacket.

Be bold. Be creative. And most of all, have fun.

Calder didn't expect everyone to get in the spirit of the evening. However, she'd hoped her own mother would, for once, play along.

"I'm almost positive she can read," Calder muttered. "Yet, my eyes don't lie. A black dress? Is she serious?"

And not just any black dress. Short, sequined, and cut down to her bellybutton, Billie glittered—quite literally. A diamond tiara. Diamond earrings. Diamonds on her fingers. Even the heels of her shoes were bedazzled. Yikes!

"Hard to tell with Billie. However, black *is* a dead-serious color."

Destry's attempt at a joke did the trick. Calder looked inside and found her anti-Billie zone.

"Are you angry? You are. I am sorry, darling."

Billie didn't look nearly as contrite as her tone implied.

Out of the side of her mouth, Destry muttered, "If she were sorry, she wouldn't have dressed like a hooker in mourning."

Andi covered her laugh with a cough. With a warning look at Destry, she sent Billie her best fake smile.

"You look… sparkly."

"Don't I?" Billie did a graceful twirl. "I planned to wear one of your *lovely* designs, Andi. Honestly. Family solidarity, and so forth. Did I offend you?"

"Not at all. In fact, I insist you tell everyone. I wouldn't want to take credit for another designer's work."

Calder chuckled. Andi would be *horrified* if anybody thought Billie's dress came from one of her collections.

"Black really is my color, as Ingo so wisely pointed out. He surprised me with the dress as I was getting ready." Billie let out a girlish giggle. "Isn't he thoughtful?"

"He's something." Exactly what, Calder hadn't decided.

"I left Ingo with a business associate." Billie flirted with the waiter as he handed her a glass. "He should be along any second."

No, thank you. The less Calder had to deal with Billie's boyfriend, the better.

"If you'll excuse me. I've neglected my hosting duties for too long."

The months spent in preparation for tonight meant Calder had little to do. The gala was in full swing. The music, a group of musicians who specialized in the nineteen-forties big band era sound, was the perfect impetus to get couples out on the dance floor.

Trusted staff members were strategically located throughout the ballroom. Their jobs were to ensure the waiters kept the hors d'oeuvre trays filled and the drinks flowing. Security, stationed at all the doors, had two main functions. To make certain no one was admitted without an invitation. And, as discreetly as possible, take care of any guests who might become a bit *too* rowdy.

Calder's job was to greet and charm. The equation was simple. Happy party goers equaled bigger donations.

As she worked the room, smiling, shaking hands, Calder wondered why she hadn't caught sight of Adam. He said he'd be here. Unless he changed his mind. Suddenly, she felt lightheaded. Breathe, she reminded herself. Don't forget to breathe.

The last thing Calder wanted to do was faint in the middle of the crowded ballroom. Before the evening was over, gossip would either have her pregnant or dying. Maybe both.

"Calder!"

Tamara waved. Melvin, in protective daddy mode, kept one arm around his wife while he cleared a path with the other.

"I'm so glad to see you." Calder returned Tamara's hug. "You look stunning."

"An Andi Benedict original, thank you very much," Tamara beamed. "Seriously, Calder. Thank you. A personal fashion show at your sister's shop was a dream come true. When I left, the proud owner of not one but four outfits? I was on cloud nine for days."

When Calder explained the situation to her sister, Andi arranged to give Tamara the V.I.P. treatment. Tamara fell in love with the flowing purple silk gown the second she saw it. Tonight, the color set off the glow of her skin to perfection.

"You look pretty spiffy yourself, Melvin."

"Don't clean up half bad if I do say so myself," Melvin preened. "Adam talked me into a visit to his tailor. Thought I'd hate all the fuss. Truth is, I may never go back to off the rack."

"Speaking of Adam. Have you seen him?" Calder hoped she didn't sound as anxious as she felt.

"Last time I looked, he and his date were at the bar."

Calder's heart sank—all the way to the floor.

"His date?"

"Adriana." Tamara laughed. "You didn't think Adam would bring anyone but his mother?"

"No. Of course not." Calder brushed off the idea with a smile. Surreptitiously, she checked her heart, relieved to find the organ back where it belonged.

Wide eyed, Tamara looked around. "The room, the decorations. Gorgeous. And the people." She lowered her voice to a conspiratorial whisper. "Just for fun? Point out the nearest billionaire."

"Tamara!" Melvin rolled his eyes.

"What's wrong with looking?" Tamara reasoned. "Harmless fun. Like window shopping."

More than happy to indulge Tamara's understandable curiosity, Calder gave a subtle nod to her left.

"By the rose-covered column. The woman in the lavender Scarlett O'Hara dress."

"Oh. Really?" Tamara sounded disappointed. "I guess money can't buy taste."

"For the love of... Time to hit the buffet." Melvin took his wife's hand. "Excuse us, Calder. When Tamara's hungry, her discretion flies out the window."

Smiling, Calder turned. And ran smack-dab into Adam. Like the moment they met on the mansion's back stairway when Adam's shoes were splattered with paint, and she couldn't take her eyes off him.

He'd replaced the boots with glossy black leather, but she still couldn't look away.

"Hello, déjà vu," Adam said, telling her his memories were just as strong.

"Actually, the name is Calder."

Adam's chuckle did nothing to calm her pulse. If anything, the deep, sexy sound sent her blood racing.

"Adam." He took her hand and didn't let go. "Nice to meet you."

"The pleasure's all mine."

As Adam leaned close, Calder caught the glint in his blue eyes. His warm breath caressed her ear.

"I prefer when we're both... pleased."

Calder drew in Adam's clean, masculine scent. She wanted him. So, so much. But could she trust him?

"Adam, I—"

"I need to speak with you. Alone. Now!"

Her father's voice, harsh, demanding, was like a shot of ice water through Calder's veins.

"I didn't realize you were in town."

She said the words to her father while she kept her eyes on Adam. She hoped to read his reaction to Edwin's sudden appearance. All she found were cool eyes and a blank expression.

"Didn't want to miss the party." Edwin's fingers bit into her arm. "Dance with your father."

"You *will* take your hand off her," Adam growled. "Or I *will* break every one of your fingers."

"Jesus. He thinks he's fucking Rambo." Though his voice dripped with contempt, Edwin loosened his grip. "Calder? Dance?"

"Obviously, I didn't inherit my charm from my father." Calder could feel the growing interest from the people around them. "One dance—to keep the peace. And the gossip at bay."

"You don't have to go with him."

"I'll be fine."

"Of course you will. I'm your father, not Jack the Ripper."

Drama. Always drama. Maternal *and* paternal. One day, they were bound to burn out after a life spent in a constant state of red alert. The sooner the better.

"I'll be here when you get back," Adam said. A promise to Calder. A warning for Edwin.

"Asshole," Edwin muttered.

"Adam? Or you?"

Genuinely perplexed, Edwin led her into a waltz.

"Why would I call myself an asshole?"

"I can't imagine, Dad. I can't imagine."

In perfect time to the music, Edwin smoothly glided Calder around the floor. She'd forgotten Edwin's skill as a dancer. Then, she remembered why. He rarely asked. When he did, they never finished. Not once. Tonight, he kept the streak alive.

"We need to talk."

"So talk."

"Not here." Edwin maneuvered them to the edge of the room before he dropped his arms. "Someplace private."

"My party. I can't take off." Calder hated to state the obvious, but subtlety never worked on her father.

"Surely you can spare five minutes."

Edwin had an odd concept of time. Five minutes could easily turn into an hour. Still, Calder had some questions for her father.

She knew if she didn't ask him now, months could pass before she had another chance.

"Come with me."

Out the side ballroom door and around the corner, they were inside her temporary office. Calder flipped on the light.

Frowning, Edwin looked around.

"I thought your headquarters were downtown."

"They are. Have a seat."

Edwin moved to the sofa. Not in the mood for a cozy chat, Calder perched on the side of the desk.

"I can explain."

Interesting start. Calder crossed her arms and waited.

"Your boyfriend swore he wouldn't go running to you. Said he'd keep his mouth shut. For your sake." Edwin leaned back with a sneer of disdain. "Despite his rough manners, I had a feeling he was a goody-goody. Too pretty by half."

Calder didn't understand what Adam's looks had to do with anything. An attractive man was just as likely to be a snake. Her father was a perfect example. She kept the observation to herself. Edwin was about to spill some important information, and she didn't want to say anything to sidetrack him.

"You need to hear my side of the story before you judge."

As hard as she wanted to push, Calder held back the impulse. If Edwin wanted to slip the noose around his own neck, she let him. Once she had the facts, she would decide whether to knock the chair out from under him.

"I'm in the middle of a small financial downturn. Otherwise, I never would have made the proposition. Seemed harmless enough. Nobody could force you to marry the guy. If you agreed, of your own free will, why shouldn't I benefit? Right?"

Calder knew money had to be involved. Edwin. Ingo Hunter. They didn't take a breath that wasn't motivated by financial gain. However, from what her father had said, her hope for Adam was on the rise.

"Naturally, when I asked Adam to meet, I assumed he would be open to a deal."

"Naturally."

"Don't pout." Edwin didn't see—or chose to ignore—the flash of anger in Calder's eyes. "You're a beautiful woman. But a smart man would be crazy not to consider your other assets as well."

"And Adam? Is he a *smart* man?"

Calder held her breath.

"Dumb as a fence post and twice as hardheaded." Disgust written on his face, Edwin flicked a speck of lint from his jacket. "*I don't want Calder's money,*" he said in a sing-song cadence. "Claims he'd sign the toughest prenup known to man. Your love is all he wants. Please. Who does he think he's fooling? More likely, he wants every dime for his greedy self."

Inside, Calder did the happiest of happy dances. Adam. Darling, wonderful, everything she could hope for, Adam. On the outside, calm. Her voice dripped with ice.

"What did you have to offer in your proposed deal?"

Edwin shrugged.

"I promised to grease his path, so to speak. Use my influence to make certain you said yes."

If Calder hadn't given into the impulse to laugh, her head might have exploded from the building pressure.

"What influence?"

"I'm your father."

Edwin seemed to think his explanation made perfect sense. Calder wondered how a man could be so oblivious. They had what a generous person might define as a barely-there relationship. Basically, he was a sperm donor with visitation rights. Rights he more often than not chose to ignore.

Calder didn't understand the way Edwin's mind worked. Honestly, she'd be afraid to find out.

"When did you and Adam meet?"

"A few weeks ago. A friend made me see that the Boy Scout in him wouldn't be able to stay quiet forever. He'd have to come clean. Make himself look good. *I* wanted you to understand my side."

"Why? What side of the story would make a difference? Unless..." Calder sighed. *Money. Always money.* "You want to ask for a loan."

Edwin smiled. Wide and toothy. His attempt at charm, she supposed. What he didn't realize and never would? Calder was immune. Had been for a very long time.

"A loan? Such a cold word. If you choose to present me with a gift—daughter to father—I would gladly accept."

"An under the table gift."

"You get your brains from me." Certain he'd won, Edwin relaxed. "Why give the government any more money than necessary?"

"Why, indeed? Mind if I ask just a few more questions?"

"Ask away."

"Who's the friend you mentioned. The one who tipped you off about Adam?"

"Ah." Edwin shrugged. "No harm, I suppose. She's a little sweetie by the name of Aurora Charles."

Calder didn't think Edwin could say anything to surprise her. But Aurora? And her father? Unbelievable. Except for the photo. The connection wasn't as farfetched when she remembered the people in the background.

"Ingo Hunter and Bridge Manfred. How are they involved?"

"You know about them?" Edwin looked confused. "They were at the cigar club where I asked Adam to meet me. But I didn't think he saw them."

"He didn't." Calder handed over her phone.

Edwin studied the image.

"Why the little minx." He barked out a laugh. "Hunter won't be happy. But since you know so much, I might as well tell you everything. Then we'll talk money?"

"Don't leave anything out, Dad."

"Hunter knew about my financial problems. He suggested I make a deal with Adam. He doesn't like your boyfriend. Has a real grudge against him."

"Ingo Hunter is a pig."

"Yes," Edwin agreed. "Though no worse than most powerful men."

"A ringing endorsement," Calder muttered.

"I don't have to like him to appreciate his style. He hired a photographer. Brought along Aurora, whom he met through Manfred—Hunter's cocaine connection."

"Better and better." Calder was tired of her father's long-winded narration. She thought she had enough information to fill in the blanks. "Hunter wanted revenge. Aurora kissed Adam when he wasn't looking. Photos were taken. The one with you, Hunter, and Manfred wasn't supposed to see the light of day."

"Aurora really is a handful. And *friendly* handful. Hunter wanted to use the photos after you and Adam were married. A little something to liven up your one-year anniversary."

"To ruin my marriage? And you knew?"

He didn't even have the good grace to look ashamed.

"I figured the pictures would be a good test to see if you had a strong relationship."

"Nice justification."

Edwin had never been a good father. However, until now, he'd never given Calder reason to hate him. And the worst part? She couldn't dredge up enough residual love to care.

"We're done. For good."

"Wait!" Edwin jumped to his feet as Calder snatched back her phone. "What about my money?"

Calder paused at the door and said the one thing she knew would shock Edwin to his core.

"Get a job."

CHAPTER TWENTY-NINE

CALDER STEPPED OUT of the office. The world around her hadn't changed. But she had. Something had shifted inside of her. Irrevocably.

"Calder?"

Adam. Two feet away. Tall. Handsome. Good. So damn good. And all hers.

How did he know she needed him? Right now. More than ever.

Without a word, she walked into his waiting arms. Calder held on for her life. No. She held on *to* her life. To Adam.

"I'm sorry."

"Shh." He kissed her forehead. "How do you feel?"

"Tired. Sad." Calder let the emotions sink in. "Free."

"Sounds about right."

"I have to tell you. God. I don't know where to start."

For once in her life, Calder didn't want to be strong. She wanted to lean on Adam and let him take the weight of the world on his shoulders. Just for a little while.

"I heard." Adam pulled her closer. "Everything."

"How?"

"A word of advice? If you want privacy, make sure you shut the door."

The office door? Adam listened in? The picture? The father? Ingo Hunter? He heard the whole sordid story?

"You know?"

"Yes. When I saw you leave the ballroom with your father, I followed. I had a few qualms about eavesdropping. Considering what I heard, I'm glad I told my conscience to go to hell."

"Every detail?"

"Every last one," Adam assured her.

"Thank God."

Calder didn't know if she had the energy to trudge through the muck again. Not tonight. One thing she had to do.. Apologize, and hope Adam would forgive her.

Adam beat her to the punch.

"I'm sorry."

"You?" Calder couldn't have heard right. "Why are you sorry?"

A passerby knocked into Adam, a reminder of where they were. For tonight, access to the hall outside the ballroom had been cordoned off to anyone not a guest at the gala. Most of the party-goers used the other doors—faster access to the bathrooms. Still, people spilled out from time to time. Enough to make the area less than conducive for an intimate conversation.

Adam took Calder's hand.

"Where are we going? The ballroom's back the other way."

"I have a room."

"Here? In the hotel?"

The elevator opened the second Adam pushed the button.

"I thought Mom might want a place to rest if the dancing and socializing became too much." He laughed. "I left her boogying with the energy of a teenager. I don't think we have to worry about any interruptions."

The ride was just long enough for Calder to admire the way Adam's white jacket fit his lean body. He always dressed well. Tonight, he looked like a living, breathing, dream come true.

"You read your invitation."

As he ran a hand down the perfectly tailored lapel, Adam grinned.

"Didn't everyone?"

"You'd be surprised."

The first thing Calder saw as she walked off the elevator was a bank of windows and an uninterrupted view of Manhattan at night. Like every other part of *The Stanton Plaza*, the penthouse was impressive.

"The view can wait." Adam said, pulling her close. "I can't."

Only a few days had passed since Calder had felt Adam's lips on hers. Yet her body responded as if starved for a year. She couldn't get enough of him. Couldn't wait to touch and be touched.

"Do we have time?" he asked.

"One second."

Breathing hard, Calder fumbled with her phone.

"Annabel?"

"Hey. Where are you?"

"I was waylaid." Adam's hand slid under Calder's skirt and up her thigh. With extreme effort, she bit back a moan. "Any problems?"

"Smooth as clockwork. Take your time. And tell Adam hello."

Busted. Without an ounce of shame, Calder slowly lowered the hidden zipper at the side of her dress. The silk slid to the floor, a gentle pool of blue at her feet. Naked except for a wisp of lace that passed for undies, she stepped out of her stiletto-heeled sandals.

"I've missed you."

"Let me remind you how I like to say hello."

Adam lifted her into his arms. He slid open the balcony door. A warm rush of almost summer air caressed Calder's face as he lay her on the cushioned lounge chair.

The look in Adam's smoldering blue eyes took her breath away. Anticipation made her skin heat.

"Touch me. Please."

"I will. Again and again." He kissed the swell of her breast. The slope of her shoulder. "I'm yours, Calder. Only yours."

Calder knew. Without a single doubt. In her heart. To her very soul. Adam belonged to her.

"So beautiful," Adam breathed. "Are you mine, Calder? Only mine?"

"From the moment we met. Then. Now. Forever." She made the promise without hesitation.

Adam stood. He removed his jacket. His tie. Unbuttoned his shirt. As he revealed inch after inch of muscled, mouthwatering skin, Calder stretched her arms over her head and enjoyed the show.

"I don't want to have sex with you ever again."

"Really?" Calder asked when Adam's pants hit the floor. Her gaze lowered to the proof of his lie. "Did your body get the memo?"

Knowing Adam, she expected him to smile. To make a light, teasing remark. Instead, he covered her body with his. Slowly, reverently, he brushed his lips across her cheek.

"Every time I touch. Kiss your lips. Share my body. I want you to know—here." Adam placed his hand over Calder's heart. "I *kiss* you with love. I *touch* you with love. Willingly, *joyfully*, I share my body with love. Always."

Calder felt her heart might burst from her chest. Adam had to feel the pounding beat. Tears she couldn't contain—didn't want to stop—filled her eyes.

"I love you, Adam Stone." Calder laughed. Happy. She was happier than she imagined possible. "I want to make love with you. Tonight. Tomorrow. For the rest of our lives."

"Want the truth?"

"Always," she nodded.

"I love you, Calder Benedict." Adam nuzzled her neck. "Are you serious about making love—over and over and over?"

"Oh, yes," Calder moaned.

"Then you have no choice. Before you can ask for such a long-term commitment? You'll have to make an honest man of me."

If ever Calder expected a tidal wave of panic to engulf her, now was the moment. She'd always assumed she would never marry. Why would she? All her life, she'd dreaded the word and everything the institution represented. Yet…

Adam. *He* set the standard for everything a good man should be. How could she *not* want to spend the rest of her life with him? Hold him. Love him. Comfort him. Share the highs and the inevitable lows.

Calder waited for the fear and the million reasons why she should run. And waited. And waited.

"Should I get down on one knee?" she teased.

Adam grinned. Lord, the man was gorgeous. Inside and out.

"Maybe another time. Right now, I want to make love to my fiancée."

Calder wrapped her arms around Adam's neck. Her future. Her heart.

"And she wants to make love to you."

"SORRY I DOUBTED you."

Frowning, Adam paused in the middle of fashioning a perfect bow tie.

"You mean the picture?"

Calder nodded. Sitting on the bed, she buckled her shoe.

"Aurora's machinations were easy to dismiss. My father? Ingo Hunter? Every explanation I could think of for the three of you in the same place made me physically ill."

"I haven't seen the photo. Will you show me?"

"Here." Calder handed Adam the phone. "When you're through, hit delete. I want to forget the damn thing ever existed."

"Jesus." Adam looked, shaking his head. "A real clusterfuck."

"Good word. And accurate."

Calder shuddered when she thought how different tonight might have been. If she'd let her worst fears get the better of her, she wouldn't have Adam. Her future without him? Sad and bleak.

"Can you forgive me?"

"For what?" Adam sat next to her. "Take another look."

"I'd rather not."

"One more, then we'll hit delete together."

"Okay." Calder glanced at the offending picture.

"Forget Aurora."

"If I could, I would."

"I have, so you can." Adam enlarged the photo until Edwin Calder and Ingo Hunter dominated the shot. "Two men who have given you nothing but grief. Men you know for a fact are usually up to no good. Any doubts you had about me were completely justifiable."

"But—"

"If the situations were reversed, *I'd* doubt *you*."

"Really?" Calder didn't know how she felt about Adam's revelation. "Why?"

"History. As great and amazing as our time together has been, our backstory is brief. You've known your father much longer. Experience tells you to doubt anything and everyone who associates with him. Add Hunter to the mix?" Adam shrugged. "You doubted me. But you didn't let them win, Calder."

"No. They didn't win. They never will."

"Not if we stick together."

"Delete."

"First—"

"Oh, come on." Calder wanted the picture gone. Now.

"*I* need to apologize. I didn't tell you I'd met with your father because I didn't want to hurt you."

"I understand." And she did. Completely. "But for future reference? You can't protect me from every bruise and bump. I wouldn't want you to."

"Your father's more than a bump." Eyes filled with worry, Adam ran a hand over her hair. "I wish I could take away the pain he caused you."

"You could beat him up."

"I could." Adam smiled. "I would. *If* I thought you really wanted me to."

"I don't." Calder loved how quick he was to understand. "I can't have him in my life any longer. Honestly, I'll miss the idea of a real father—something he never was. I won't miss Edwin Calder."

"I love you."

"My father will never love anyone but himself. So, he'll never know how it feels to be loved. He thinks money is the key to happiness. He's wrong." Calder's heart lightened. "I have you. And my sisters. My friends. *I* am a very rich woman."

"Ready to head back to the party?"

Calder took Adam's hand.

"With you by my side? I'm ready for everything."

CALDER SPENT THE rest of the evening eating, laughing, and dancing. Surrounded by the people she cared about. Who cared about her.

Wisely, Edwin was nowhere to be seen. Calder knew he'd be back. She would deal with him when the time came. For now, he was out of her life, and she was relieved to see him go.

"We are superwomen." Annabel clinked her glass to Calder's. "The gala was a huge success."

A success, and over. The doors had closed behind the last guest. The caterers and hotel staff had started to clear away the plates and clutter. Calder watched, grateful she wasn't expected to pitch in.

"If you don't need anything else, I'm going home."

"Thank you for holding down the fort tonight." Calder hugged Annabel tight. "I was a bit distracted."

"A story I expect to hear in great detail." Annabel slipped on her jacket. "I assume the handsome Adam Stone will play a major role in your narrative."

Calder nodded. Near the exit, Adam spoke with one of the waiters. He'd escorted his mother to the penthouse suite. Tired after her night of revelry, she hadn't felt like making the long ride back to Long Island.

Lucky Calder. She had him for the rest of the night—in her bed and in her arms.

"You look all too pleased with yourself."

Ingo Hunter. Until now, Calder had been blessed not to have her evening marred by his company. The crowd was gone. The lights were lowered. Time for the vermin to scurry out of the woodwork.

"I'm glad to see you."

"Really?" Ingo looked surprised. "Are your eyes finally open to my undeniable charisma?"

Calder let the ridiculous, stomach-turning, comment pass. Adam, ever vigilant, started across the room, ready to dispose of the trash. She shook her head, a silent message to let her take care of business first. Reluctantly, he heeded her wishes. Taking a seat within striking distance, he kept his eyes trained on Hunter.

"I want to say something to you. Hear me and understand."

"I always listen when a beautiful woman talks."

"Don't." Calder sighed. "You think you're charming. You're wrong."

"Your mother doesn't agree."

"Billie is… I can't do anything about her. I can only take care of myself. Let me be clear. Never try to fuck with my life again. The pictures you have? The ones with Adam and Aurora? They're worthless. Always were. Always will be."

"I don't know what you're talking about."

The flicker of anger in Hunter's eyes told a different story. He could deny his involvement all he wanted. She knew the truth.

"You lost. I won." Actually, Calder hit the jackpot. "I don't know what you want. What you have planned doesn't matter. My sisters and I will take you down. Every time."

"Ah, yes. The invincible Benedict girls." Hunter's laugh held an unpleasant edge. "You think you're smart. All the angles covered. You may have won a battle. But the war is mine."

Calder's hand balled into a fist. If Hunter hadn't turned and walked away, she would have knocked the smug off his face.

"You okay?"

"I will be. Hold me."

"With pleasure."

Adam's arms did the trick. Calm settled over Calder. She wouldn't let Ingo Hunter mar her happiness.

"What are your thoughts on a long, hot bath?"

"Will I have company?"

Calder nodded.

"Then, I say yes. The longer, the better. What do you say?"

"I love you. And, let's go home."

EPILOGUE

THE NEXT MORNING breakfast was a lively affair considering the hour everyone got to bed. And the fact Calder woke her sisters early so she could fill them in on last night's events. They agreed her father's actions were inexcusable. As for Ingo Hunter?

"What the hell?" Destry speared a blueberry with extra gusto. "Can he sink any lower?"

"I wish the answer was no," Calder sighed.

"He's a petty slime ball." Bryce smiled when Mrs. Finch set an *everything but the kitchen* sink omelet in front of her.

"The only important thing is, you prevailed," Andi said as she cut into her waffle. "Let's focus on the happy. We get to plan a wedding. I need at least a month to make your dress. You need to decide on a design. The color? Lace? Satin? Not to mention the fittings."

Calder was getting married. The notion hadn't sunk in completely. Still, happy summed up her feelings very nicely. *When* the event would occur was the last thing on her mind.

"We aren't close to picking a date."

"No ring on your finger?" Destry's eyes widened in mock horror. "Bad planning on Adam's part."

"I don't know if I want an engagement ring."

"What?" Mrs. Finch handed Calder a bowl of fresh fruit. "A ring is such a nice tradition. I still cherish mine."

The symbolism bothered Calder. She belonged to Adam. Body and soul. But she wasn't his property.

"I didn't say absolutely not." Calder shrugged. "Maybe *I'll* buy a ring for *Adam*."

"I don't think so." Adam walked into the kitchen shaking his head.

"A pretty diamond for my pretty fiancé?"

"You're funny." He snatched a strawberry. And a kiss. "The subject is non-negotiable. The stone from my mother's ring in the setting of your choice."

As soon as Adam mentioned his mother, Calder's resistance melted.

"Some traditions are worth keeping."

"I agree. Which reminds me." Adam put an arm around Mrs. Finch's shoulders. "Ladies. I know the bond you have. How much you mean to each other. I couldn't marry Calder if I didn't have your blessing. What do you say? May I have your sister's hand in marriage?"

"You really want to make me bawl, don't you?" Calder sniffled.

"Hold off," he whispered. "If they say no, I'll join you."

"We discussed the possibility," Andi said.

"You did?" Surprised, Calder looked at Bryce.

"Just in case, we thought we should be prepared."

"And?" Calder and Adam asked in unison.

"Calder wouldn't have said yes unless she knew you're the one," Destry pointed out. "And I like you."

"Destry's right," Bryce nodded. "I like you, too. And, I trust Calder's judgment."

"We're unanimous." Andi smiled. "Welcome to the family."

"If you start crying now, Mrs. Finch, you won't have any tears left on the day of the wedding," Destry pointed out.

Mrs. Finch wiped her eyes with the end of her apron before she hugged Adam.

"Weddings are for laughter, not tears. Today better be the last time I cry over you and my Calder. Until I hold your first baby in my arms. Then all bets are off."

"Hold up on the babies, Mrs. F."

"I'm not worried." Around her tears, Mrs. Finch looked almost smug. "Someday you'll be ready."

Calder met Adam's blue gaze. When he smiled, she smile back—and had her answer. Someday.

"I have to go. Mom called. She loved her night at the hotel. Ate her room service-delivered breakfast in the lap of luxury. Now, she's ready to go home."

Adam gave Calder another kiss.

"Meet you for some afternoon playtime?" he whispered.

"My room. Two o'clock?"

With a wink, Adam left.

Destry let out an exaggerated sigh.

"I suppose we'll have to get used to all the touching and whispering and so forth."

"Especially the so forth," Calder assured her. "Think you can survive the shock?"

"You're happy?"

"More than I ever thought possible."

"Then bring on the mush," Destry winked.

A moment later, Billie burst into the room in a cloud of perfume and a swirling red negligee. Her face fully made up. Hair artfully arranged. The same as every other morning. Except something was different. Instead of a rather languid, *I can't function until noon*, demeanor, she practically vibrated with excitement.

"Oh, good. You're all here. I have news." Billie paused for dramatic effect. "I'm pregnant. And I just know I'm going to have a boy this time."

Hurricane Billie twirled out of the room. In her wake, silence and devastation.

A baby. Potentially a boy who would inherit the entire Benedict fortune. Including the house. Their home.

The shock Calder felt was mirrored on the faces of her sisters. Now she knew what Ingo Hunter meant when he said he would win the war. If Billie gave birth to his child—his son—he would gain control of everything.

Calder's head fell into her hands.

"Well, crap. Now, what do we do?"

COMING IN APRIL

TWO OF A KIND

BRYCE'S STORY

BOOK TWO OF THE SISTERS QUARTET

**TURN THE PAGE FOR A LOOK AT MORE**

**BOOKS BY**

**MARY J. WILLIAMS**

IF I LOVED YOU

(HARPER FALLS BOOK ONE)

PROLOGUE

IT WAS SOMETHING out of a fairy tale.

Thousands of flickering lights dazzled her senses, almost as much as the tall, wickedly handsome man who so expertly danced her onto the shadowed balcony. The music that filtered from the nearby ballroom only added to the already magical atmosphere.

Women dreamed their whole lives of a moment like this — a prelude to a happily-ever-after ending. Ever so briefly, she let herself drift into that fantasy as if she was one of those women. For a moment, she let herself pretend that her childhood had been filled with the kind of whimsicality that allowed those fantasies to carry over into adulthood.

But no, she wasn't a romantic, hopeless or otherwise. She didn't want a prince to sweep her into his arms and carry her away on his faithful steed. She was more than capable of rescuing herself. She preferred it that way.

The stars were in the sky, not in her eyes.

"I'm glad you asked me to dance," her partner whispered, pulling her closer.

Suddenly, she was nervous. The champagne she downed earlier had completely worn off. No more floating on a cloud of false courage. If she was going to do this, she was going to have to do it on her own.

"Jack," she said. Damn, it was hard to sound seductive when your voice squeaked. "Jack." That was better, lower, and slightly husky. She'd read somewhere that guys liked husky voices.

"Rose."

"Yes?"

"Nothing, I just thought we were saying each other's names." He put his lips next to her ear. "I like the way you say mine."

"Jack." Good Lord, she had to stop repeating his name. "I need a favor, Jack. A big one." Or should she say, she hoped he *had* a big one. Rose groaned to herself. At least she hadn't said that aloud.

"I'll help if I can."

"You're the only one who *can* help." She took another deep breath. "I need you to take me home and screw my brains out."

AFTER THE RAIN

(ONE PASS AWAY BOOK ONE)

PROLOGUE

LOGAN. LOGAN. LOGAN.

Logan Price closed his eyes, taking it all in.

"Hear that, kid?" Starting quarterback Gaige Benson slapped him on the back. "Two games under your belt and you're a star. Now let's go out there and add super to the front of it."

The announcer for the team set them in motion down the tunnel with his familiar introduction.

"And now, let's hear it for your division champion *SEATTLE KNIGHTS*."

The roar of the crowd. There was nothing like it. A packed stadium. Fans chanting his name. Few people would ever experience what it was like to take the field in a professional football game.

Logan Price had been working for this his entire life. He could still remember in exact detail the first game he ever saw. Too small to climb onto the stool in his father's bar by himself, his old man had lifted him onto the seat.

Stay and be quiet.

Not an easy order to follow for an active, inquisitive little boy. One look at the game and for once, Logan had no problem following his father's command. The old TV transported him to a foreign world filled with bright lights and shiny helmeted warriors. Logan didn't know what he was watching. He did know he wanted to be one of those men.

A Sunday afternoon in rural Oklahoma. *Lefty's Pub* was filled with after-church drinkers who figured they had done their duty to God and family. The rest of the day was their time. A beer. Or two. Or six. Cronies who understood a man's need to unwind before the start of another workweek.

And football.

If the Friday night high school game was their true religion, the Sunday afternoon games were a close second. As Oklahoma boys, they hated anything Texas. The men of Denville gathered every week to root for whichever team was playing the Dallas Cowboys.

No matter how the games ended. Whether the crowd was happy or disgruntled. It meant more drinking. Hours later, husbands, boyfriends, and sons would stumble out, pile into beat-up trucks, and weave their way home to frustrated wives, girlfriends, and mothers.

As he grew older, Logan's view changed. He moved from the stool to behind the bar. And he promised himself one thing. He would never become one of those men. He wouldn't spend the week at a job he hated. His home wouldn't be a semi-wide trailer filled with hand-me-down furniture and a wife to whom he couldn't face going home.

His Sundays were going to be spent playing football, not watching it.

"Ready to take down this vaunted Arizona defense?" Gaige yelled at him, butting helmets.

Vaunted. Good word, Logan thought. His QB liked to use what his granny called highfalutin talk. Must have been that Ivy League education. He knew that Gaige Benson didn't grow up with a silver spoon in his mouth. He came from the mean streets of Brooklyn. He had the scars to prove it.

Like Logan, Gaige had vowed to get out of the life into which he was born. In the process, he polished himself up like a new penny. He took advantage of his full-ride scholarship to Yale. He didn't spend all his time on the football field. Fancy vocabulary. Fancy clothes. Fancy women. They were all part of the package Gaige purposefully fashioned for himself.

Seventeen years after clawing his way out of the tenement that he grew up in, very little of that borough-rat remained. Until game time. No one was tougher than Gaige Benson. Three-time league

MVP. Considered one of the best ever to play the game. No one stood in his way when he was playing the game. He had the scars to prove it.

"Gather round."

Knights head coach Harry Coleman gathered the team close. He had to yell over the crowd, but he had the voice to do it. Booming was putting it mildly. The first time Logan heard it, he stood right beside the man. The ringing in his ears didn't go away for three days.

"Divisional game. If I have to say any more than that, you shouldn't be out here. Go kick some ass."

The defense took the field to start the game. Arizona had a rookie quarterback drafted in the second round from a small college in the Midwest. The only reason he was out there was because the regular starter suffered a concussion in last week's game and the regular backup had food poisoning. Thrown into action at the last minute, Logan swore he could see the guy's hands shaking before he took the first snap. When the ball went sailing between his legs, Logan shook his head.

The moment was too big for some people. For Logan, it wasn't big enough. He aimed for the biggest stage of all. The Super Bowl. It wasn't a matter of *if* he would get there, but when.

"Three and out." Gaige grinned, pulling on his helmet. "Come on, kid. Let's go show them how it's done."

Logan ran onto the field. *Kid.* He shook his head, grinning. From the first day of training camp, Gaige had hung that moniker on him. Ironic since he was almost twenty-five, a good two years older than most of the other rookies. However, he supposed when someone had been in the league as long as Gaige, all the new guys seemed like kids.

"We're starting on the ground," Gaige instructed them in the huddle. "Sweep out left. Basic. Got it?"

Lining up as he had a thousand other times, Logan checked the defense. He knew he was fast. One of the fastest in the game. What set him apart was his anticipation. He had the uncanny ability to read the guy covering him. He knew when to fake left or when to fake right. Stutter step or flat out, in your face, catch me if you can.

His speed got him out of Denville, Oklahoma. His brains and determination got him to the NFL.

The sounds of the game were as familiar to Logan as the back of his own hand. The call from scrimmage. Each quarterback had his own unique cadence. Gaige was a master of mixing his up. Study him all you want. Good luck figuring it out. His teammates knew. A signal just before they broke the huddle.

Pay attention, you were golden. Slack off even once? Gaige could ream a guy out with the best of them. And he had no problem doing it in the middle of the game.

419

An entire YouTube channel had been devoted to Gaige and his rants. They were as legendary as the man himself. With a ball in his hand, he was cool as ice. The rest of the time, watch out.

No one would ever accuse Logan of lacking focus. Today was no exception. They were driving down the field. First and ten from the Arizona twenty-yard line. He already had three carries of thirty-five yards. It was going to be a good day.

"Ready to take it in?" Gaige asked.

"Always."

"Then show them what you've got."

A quick snap later, Gaige handed the ball to Logan. The offensive line created a seam. Not a big one. Just big enough. Using the push of his powerful legs, Logan surged through. One more step. They wouldn't catch him. No one could.

Like everything connected with the game, Logan heard the snap of the bone with total clarity. The agony that surged through his body was so intense he almost passed out. In the next few minutes, he was going to wish he had.

"Get back." Logan heard Gaige through the haze of pain. "Goddamn it. Move the hell off."

The three-hundred-and-fifty-pound linebacker didn't get off by standing. He rolled. Crushing Logan's broken leg as he went. He would never know if the move had been deliberate. Now, it was the last thing on his mind. He only cared about two things. How bad was the injury and when would he be able to play again.

"Hold on, kid." Gaige took his hand. "They're bringing the stretcher."

The team doctor checked his eyes. Logan knew he was asked some questions. What they were and how he answered, he would never remember. By the time they carted him off the field, Logan knew the break was bad.

"Gaige." Logan reached for him.

"I'm here, kid."

"Is it over?"

"The game?" Gaige walked with him, his head bent toward Logan. "No. But I promise we're going to win the bastard."

They loaded him onto the open cart. They had him secured and the vehicle rolled away before Logan had his answer. He wasn't wondering about the game. It was his career.

To no one in particular, he whispered the question again.

"Is it over?"

WITH ONE MORE LOOK AT YOU

CHAPTER ONE

"GET UP. WE'RE leaving."

Sophie kept her eyes closed, pretending she was actually asleep. In truth, it was too hot. The air in the tiny motel room was thick with humidity, stale cigarettes, and mildew. Sweat drenched her body, soaking through the scratchy sheet. She could barely breathe, let alone hope for a decent night's sleep. However, when her mother kicked the bed for the second time, Sophie didn't stir.

"If your ass isn't in the car by the time I've loaded our suitcases, I won't wait," Joy Lipton threw their meager possessions into a bag. "You can stay in this shithole of a town and fend for yourself."

When Sophie was younger, that used to sound like a threat. More and more, calling her mother's bluff sounded like a fine idea. Maybe this time, Joy would do both of them a favor and actually leave.

For all intents and purposes, Sophie took care of herself. With what little money Joy provided, she bought groceries. Every time they checked into a motel, she would ask the manager if he had any odd jobs that needed to be done. Cheap labor—paid under the table. That kind of work wasn't hard to find, and it provided Sophie with a little extra spending cash.

Sophie learned fast to keep her stash hidden. Joy had no problem stealing from her daughter. And no shame when caught red-handed. *It was little enough payment for all she had sacrificed—both personally and financially.* Sophie had rolled her eyes at the outrageous claim. That little gesture had earned her a slap across the face. Sophie didn't know which of them had been more surprised. For all her failings as a mother, Joy didn't hit. Verbal abuse was her specialty.

The slap was never repeated. Sophie didn't dwell on the incident. There was no point. She was fifteen years old and looked at her life with a pragmatic attitude. For now, she was legally bound to a woman who ninety percent of the time treated her as though she were invisible. The other ten—filled with rants and crying fits—Sophie had learned to tune out. If Joy had a reason for keeping her daughter around, she wasn't sharing.

"What did I say?" Sophie's only pair of jeans landed on her head. "Move. Now!"

The little voice tempting Sophie to tell Joy to go to hell wasn't a match for the sliver of fear. Bravery was easy—in her head. In reality? The unknown was scarier than following her mother to another town. Sophie was a voracious reader. Since they moved so much, attending school was hit and miss. Books, magazines, newspapers. They had taught her most of what she knew—and provided her with a vivid imagination.

The stories—both fact and fiction—led Sophie to an indisputable conclusion. The world wasn't kind to fifteen-year-old girls on their own. No matter how smart she thought she was. Or how much savvy she possessed. Without some kind of protection—even the barely there sort her mother provided—things almost never turned out well.

Picturing herself in tattered clothes, freezing to death—quite a feat considering the mid-July heatwave—Sophie climbed out of bed. Chances were slim that she would perish as some kind of modern-day *Little Match Girl*. The perverts and/or murderers would probably get her first.

"Finally." Joy shut the last suitcase. "Take a pee and get dressed. We're out of here in under five."

Grabbing a pair of clean underwear and a t-shirt, Sophie took her jeans and shuffled to the bathroom. "What's the hurry?"

As if Sophie didn't know. They typically high-tailed it in the middle of the night for one of two reasons. Either Joy had pissed off her latest *boyfriend*—and Sophie used the term lightly—or they couldn't pay the bill. More times than she could count, it was both.

"There is only one reason that matters." Joy tossed her long, chemically enhanced red hair over her shoulder. "I'm your mother."

Sophie was glad she had her back to her mother. The expression on her face—major eye roll—might have earned her another slap. Joy trotted out the '*I'm your mother*' crap from time to time as if it actually meant something. The days of Sophie wanting Joy's love and approval were long gone. The spark of hope wasn't completely dead. However, she would need more than the occasional smile and a pat on the head for it to bloom into a full-fledged flame.

There was so much about her mother that Sophie didn't understand. One second, she seemed like the dimmest bulb in the box. The next, her mind was sharp as a tack. It changed depending on the situation—and Joy's level of interest. Men were the highest priority. Other women, not so much. Sophie did know one thing. Her mother wanted to be the center of attention. The best way to get information was to act as if she didn't care.

"Whatever," Sophie said with a shrug.

Perfectly mimicking Joy's hair flip, Sophie nonchalantly closed the bathroom door. She barely had the cap off the toothpaste when like clockwork, she heard Joy's raised voice.

"I've finally landed *the* big fish."

Bigger than the plywood salesman in Topeka? Or the guy in Scottsdale who made a living selling bathroom fixtures? Sophie spat into the sink. They had been nice enough—that was her impression from the short amount of time she spent in their company. She could say the same about most of the guys Joy hooked up with. Every man was *the one*—until he wasn't.

These once-in-a-lifetime relationships rarely lasted six months. Once, Joy actually managed to last a year before going off the rails. Sometimes things ended with a whimper. Mostly with a bang. But either way, end they did. Inevitably as the sun came up in the east.

Sophie used the toilet. Washed her hands and face. Combed her shoulder-length dark hair. All the while, Joy waxed on and on about her latest and greatest conquest. Her mother was like a battery-operated bunny. Once she started, she went on and on and on.

"We met at *The Tremont*."

The first thing Joy would do when they hit a new town was scope out every bar. The dives were for fun, the classier ones for business. Hotel watering holes were the best. Sophie had never been inside, but she knew *The Tremont* was the most expensive place in the area.

Technically, Joy wasn't a prostitute. Yes. Sex was involved. And money. But almost never on the first date. The random hand job. Oral when priming the pump became absolutely necessary.

The fact that Sophie knew all of this was disturbing on so many levels. That it no longer bothered her was just plain sad.

"His name is Newt. Newton Branson, to be exact. The edges are a little rough, but he is class all the way. Expensive champagne. Top-shelf whiskey. Do you know that he didn't even blink when I ordered the lobster?"

In Joy's world, not grousing over the dinner bill was a certified stamp of approval. Though she never ate more than a bite or two of her meal—a girl had to watch her figure—she liked when it cost as much as possible.

Joy Lipton was beautiful. Head to toe, she had the kind of looks that attracted attention. Male attention. The only thing average about her was her height. High cheekbones. Full lips. Wide eyes the color of dark chocolate. Sophie had seen her draw a man with nothing but a smile. Curvy and buxom, if she wasn't vigilant, her body tended to run toward fat. Petrified of gaining a single pound, Joy lived on little more than coffee and cigarettes. Add alcohol when somebody else was paying.

Personality wise, Sophie and Joy were miles apart. Physically, the difference was even greater. Other than their cheekbones and the color of their eyes, any resemblance between mother and daughter was harder to find than Waldo.

Sophie was a stick. That wasn't an insult, it was a fact. Tall— at fifteen she already topped Joy by a good four inches—and skinny without a trace of her mother's curves. Though she wasn't terribly worried that her breasts were non-existent. And her hips? Well, she didn't have hips. Or a waist for that matter. Her body was pretty much a straight line from top to bottom. As long as she remained healthy and able to stand on her own two feet, Sophie didn't care about the rest.

Leaving the bathroom, Sophie retrieved the paper bag she had saved from last night's takeout. When Joy saw what Sophie was doing, she stopped her glowing commentary of Newt Branson's stellar qualities long enough to shake her head.

"Forget that crap."

Without a pause, Sophie filled the bag with various toiletries strewn around the bathroom. The almost-empty toothpaste. The bottle of shampoo she had purchased the day before. The counter was filled with potions, and lotions Joy didn't think she wanted. In a day or two, she would change her tune. From experience, Sophie knew if anything was left behind, the fault would fall on her shoulders.

Ignoring the look of disgust, Sophie added the bag to the two suitcases sitting at the foot of the bed she and her mother shared.

"If you've found Mr. Wonderful, why the sudden need to leave?"

"Newt is headed back to his ranch in... I don't remember." Joy made a dismissive movement with her hand. "Somewhere west. He wants us to go with him."

"Us?"

By Sophie's calculations, the romance of the century wasn't much more than a weekend old. Joy never confessed that she had a daughter until much further into the relationship and only when it was absolutely unavoidable.

"Naturally. We're a team."

That wasn't how Sophie would have put it. A team conjured images of them working together toward a single goal. If Joy had an endgame in mind to their perpetual trek from one end of the country to the other, she certainly hadn't shared what it was. Sophie wasn't a player in the game. She was a reluctant observer. At best, an afterthought. At worst? Who knew? Though they had scraped rock bottom a time or two, Sophie had the feeling they had yet to hit it. If that day ever came, she had no doubt it would be every woman for herself.

"Quiet," Joy warned. Picking up a suitcase, she cracked open the hotel room door. Peering right, then left, she motioned for Sophie to follow.

Great. Sophie sighed. They were skipping out on their bill. It wasn't the first time. Joy always looked for crap-hole establishments—with male managers—that were willing to take cash under the table. Flirting and a couple of bucks usually got them a room. Joy's ample cleavage allowed them to stay past the first night. After that, it was down to how much shit the manager was willing to swallow. The promise of sex went further with some men than others.

"Just a second."

Ignoring Joy's hissed warning to get in the car, Sophie sprinted back to the room. With a sigh, she dug thirty-four dollars out of her pocket, tossing it onto the bedside table. The manager was a nice guy. Stupid. But a lot of men fell into that category when it came to her mother. The money didn't begin to cover what they owed. Sophie found it a way to assuage her conscience. Her way of convincing herself that she was better than the woman who gave birth to her.

The second Sophie was in the car, Joy hit the gas. As always, their room was the last unit and the greatest distance from the office. It made getting away so much easier. No fuss. No muss. At least for Joy. She dropped her bombs from a distance. By the time the impact was felt, she was long gone.

"Where are we going?"

"Newt has invited us to stay with him for a little while."

This was a new twist, Sophie thought. Since it was the second time her mother had said they were both going, it might actually be true. Occasionally, Joy went away with her current man for a long weekend. But *stay for a little while*? Sophie included? That didn't happen often. And if history were any judge, it wouldn't end well. The last time wasn't that long ago. Almost a year to be exact. After a few days filled with either heated arguments or pouting silence, they ended up stranded in Poughkeepsie. The gentleman friend stole their car *and* their clothing. The only reason he hadn't gotten away with their money was that Sophie followed her instincts hiding what little they had where neither adult could find it.

With a sigh, Sophie looked out the window. How could Joy learn from her mistakes when she never admitted to making any? According to her mother, the disasters were never her fault. So she kept repeating them. Over and over again.

"You said that Newt lives *out west*?"

"That's right."

"How far? We'll be lucky to make it to the county limits in this rusty bucket of bolts," Sophie warned.

Their current transportation had been little better than when Joy acquired it last month from a used car salesman one town over. Wisely, Sophie had refrained from pointing out that if a beat-up old Ford Escort was the best she could do, Joy had been grossly exaggerating her talents.

431

"We aren't driving. Newt is. He has a brand-new Escalade. That's a Cadillac. Top of the line." Joy practically vibrated with excitement.

"How do you know?" Sophie wasn't averse to a little luxury. She had never ridden in a new car of any make or model. However, Joy tended to exaggerate. A lot.

"He let me drive it. There is no mistaking that smell. Fresh from the factory."

For now, Sophie would take Joy's word for it.

"Any chance you can tell me where we are going. Other than west?" They were in California. There wasn't much *west* left. Unless Newt could magically drive them to Hawaii.

"I don't know, Sophie." Joy's tone was impatient. "You'll find out when we get there."

"Or I could simply ask Newt."

"No." Joy shot Sophie a warning look. "Don't start asking Newt a bunch of questions. Be polite. And keep your thoughts to yourself. Understand?"

"What's the problem with asking where he's taking us?"

"Once you start, you don't know when to quit. The last thing I need is for him to get annoyed and dump us a hundred miles from nowhere. "

Sophie frowned. "Didn't he think it strange that you wanted to meet him in the middle of the night?"

"Newt likes to get an early start. His son's birthday is tomorrow. Talking him into leaving *extra* early wasn't a problem."

"But—?"

"Newt is taking us to his home. That's all you need to know."

Sophie's heart leapt to her throat. *Home*. Just the word was enough to set her pulse racing. So many meanings. A million interpretations. For Sophie, the concept seemed like a dream. A place where she belonged.

There would be no more limping from town to town. Someplace permanent where Sophie could attend school on a regular basis instead of a week here or a month there. A chance to make friends who lasted beyond a tentative hello and no goodbye at all.

Home. Sophie didn't know what it looked like, but she knew what it represented. She held onto the dream—the only one she allowed herself—while her mother pulled her from town to town. The longer hopes and dreams remained unfulfilled, the heavier they became. Sophie's slight shoulders were strong, but there was a limit to everything.

She kept her dreams buried for a reason. It hurt to get her hopes up only to have them broken into a million pieces. Newt. His ranch. His *home*. Sophie couldn't let herself think of it as real. Not with Joy calling the shots. Her mother had the attention span of a gnat. Always looking past what she had. Certain something bigger and better was just around the corner.

Calling herself the biggest kind of fool, Sophie gave herself a shake. She was getting ahead of herself. Chances were high that something would happen to prevent them from leaving town—let alone reaching this so-called ranch.

Joy slowed the car, coming to a stop next to a deserted row of parking meters. Without a word of explanation, she exited the vehicle.

"I know what you're thinking." Joy kicked the temperamental trunk. Once. Twice. Third time's the charm.

"I doubt that." Sophie removed her suitcase and the paper bag.

"You think that I'm afraid to let Newt see the kind of car I drive."

"Close enough," Sophie muttered as they started their walk. Actually, for once, Joy was spot on.

"Trust me, missy. You are not as deep and mysterious as you want to believe." Joy wobbled down the uneven sidewalk in a tight skirt and five-inch heels. "One day you'll understand why I do the things I do."

That seemed unlikely. Sophie was happy in her sneakers and old jeans. No matter her age, Sophie couldn't see herself in her mother's shoes. Figuratively *or* literally.

"I'll let you in on a little secret. Men want perfection. Newt likes the idea of helping a woman who is slightly down on her luck. But I can't actually *look* like I need his money."

"It's better to trudge down the street in the middle of the night than roll up in a crappy car?"

"Yes." Joy set down her suitcase, giving herself a moment to catch her breath. "Besides, he won't see me trudging. When he comes down to the lobby, I'll be waiting. Fresh as a daisy."

"The sweat rolling down your face isn't very daisy-like," Sophie pointed out.

"That's what bathrooms and a change of clothes are for." Determined, Joy picked up the suitcase and her pace. "I've never let a man see me when I'm not at my best."

"What about in the morning?" Sophie had seen Joy when her eyes were rimmed with mascara, and her hair was standing on end. Before noon, Joy tended to look like a frightened raccoon.

"I make certain to wake long before he does. I sponge myself off—a shower would spoil the illusion. Brush my teeth. Put on new makeup. Fix my hair. Then I sneak back to bed before he knows I was gone."

"It sounds exhausting." And ridiculous. Sophie knew that her mother's boyfriends were less than rocket scientists. But only a fool would believe that Joy woke up looking like she stepped off a magazine cover.

"It's necessary."

Joy sounded so sure of herself. So superior. So worldly. So idiotic it was all Sophie could do not to burst out laughing. Perhaps if this were the nineteen-fifties and *Leave It to Beaver* ruled the television airways. Or maybe—just maybe—if Sophie had lived a sheltered life without the benefit of books and the internet. If all of that were true, she might buy the line her mother tried to sell.

By association, Sophie was forced to ride a rollercoaster of secondhand disappointment and frustration. The pity was all on her side. Not for herself. She could picture the day when all of this was a distant memory. On her own. Away from her mother's drama. Sophie pitied her mother because no matter what, Joy would never change.

This was the life Joy wanted. The sad part was that whether she ever admitted it or not, she fought a losing battle. Like the Wizard of Oz, her mother was so afraid that somebody would get a look behind the curtain, she had never learned to enjoy the here and now.

"Finally," Joy said as the hotel came into view.

Their walk was probably the most exercise her mother had in years. The heat didn't help. Though well after midnight, the temperature was still in the high seventies. Breathing heavily, Joy took a handkerchief from her purse, wiping her profusely sweating face.

"Are the rooms as nice as the lobby?" Sophie knew she was gaping, but this was the first time she had seen the inside of a place that didn't rent by the hour. Everything was so clean. And the air conditioning was a slice of pure heaven.

"For Christ's sake, Sophie, close your mouth. You're acting like an unsophisticated yokel."

"Because that's what I am." Sophie wasn't embarrassed. She took a seat in one of the plush velvet chairs and sighed. This was so much better than her imagination—and her imagination was spectacular. However, picturing herself in a place like this had nothing on actually being here.

"I'm going to freshen up." Joy took her makeup bag from the suitcase before setting it next to Sophie. "Don't move. Don't talk to anybody unless they work here. And then, what do you say?"

"I'm waiting for my father." Sophie knew the drill. Adults gave well-behaved children some leeway. Especially when the child claimed a parent was in the vicinity.

Though tall, Sophie looked her age. Maybe a little younger. When she spoke, the story was different. Her mental maturity far outdistanced her body. However, she was smart enough to tone down her intellect when necessary. If somebody wanted an innocent tween, that's what she gave them.

Today, Joy wanted invisible, so that was the illusion Sophie presented. Still but observant, she sat patiently, doing nothing to draw attention. Her feet didn't swing, her hands lay unmoving in her lap. But Sophie's mind was anything but quiet. She took it all in. Every sight. Every sound. It didn't matter that this was a small hotel. Or that the patrons weren't even close to celebrity status. All around her was a different world than the one she normally inhabited.

To pass the time—and amuse nobody but herself—Sophie made up stories. For example, the couple at the reception desk. Young. Attractive. Obviously in love. Newly married, they were running away from disapproving parents. She had a job waiting for her in San Francisco. He was a hopeful author. She would work while he completed his half-finished book. When it hit the bestseller list, she would go back to college. Perhaps they would start a family. The future was limitless as long as they were together.

Then on the opposite end of the happiness spectrum, the man waiting near the entrance looked uncomfortable. The man speaking earnestly to him was his lover. Married, they met on the down-low whenever possible. The smaller, animated speaker stated his argument for the umpteenth time. They should confess everything to their families. Didn't they deserve to be with each other—the person they loved? From the first man's reaction, it didn't seem that he agreed. Sophie didn't try to feel sorry for the men. Her sympathy lay with the deceived wives—not the cheaters.

Enjoying the game, Sophie looked for another target for her harmless musings. Dismissing several possibilities, her gaze came to rest on a tall, lean man who seemed to be looking for somebody. Handsome. Not too young. Not too old. Sophie wasn't very good at guessing ages. For her story, she settled on forty-five. Maybe a little younger. His dark-blond hair was worn short, and he was clean shaven. In his hand, he held a cowboy hat. That was interesting.

His boots were in the same vein. Blue jeans that looked like they were straight from the store. A crisp white shirt, tucked in, fastened with silver snaps. Neat as a pin, and a little nervous if the way his fingers clutched the brim of his Stetson was any indication. He had a kind face. Sophie hoped whoever kept him waiting was worthy of that kindness.

"Well? What do you think?"

Not exactly a miracle, but Joy had worked wonders on herself. In Sophie's opinion, the makeup was too heavy, and the dress was still too short, but Joy's long hair hung loosely around her shoulders softening her look considerably.

Knowing her part in this play, Sophie said her lines without a stumble or stutter.

"You look beautiful. Not a day over twenty-five."

Thirty-five was more like it. But Sophie wasn't supposed to mention her mother's real age. *Ever.* One of Joy's hard-fast rules.

Happy, Joy scanned the room. Slowly, her smile widened, and her body took on a sultry pose.

"There's Newt."

Sophie turned. She should have guessed. The cowboy with the kind face waved his hat. As he made his way toward them, her emotions were mixed. For her sake, she wanted Newt to be a good man. For his sake, she hoped his skin was thicker than it looked.

"One more thing," Joy whispered to Sophie out of the side of her mouth. "I'm your sister. Don't forget."

Sophie watched as Newt swung a laughing Joy into his arms. *Sisters*. Not the first time they had perpetrated that particular deception. Maybe it was his sweet smile or the warmth in his deep blue eyes. Something about Newt made Sophie want to tell him the truth. Damn Joy and the consequences.

"Is this your little sister?"

"That's right." Perhaps sensing Sophie's hesitation, Joy sent her a warning look.

"Hello, Sophie." Newt took her hand in his. "Are you ready to go home?"

That one word sent all others from Sophie's brain. She swallowed hard.

"Home?" she asked hopefully. When Newt nodded, his kind eyes crinkling at the sides, the hope in Sophie's heart canceled out her twinge of conscience. Taking a deep breath, she smiled. "Yes, sir. I am."